Jimmy

Other books by Robert Whitlow

Jimmy

ROBERT
WHITLOW

THOMAS NELSON
Since 1798

Published in Nashville, Tennessee, by Thomas Nelson, Inc.

WestBow Press books may be purchased in bulk for educational, business, fund-raising, or sales promotional use. For information, please e-mail SpecialMarkets@ThomasNelson.com.

Scripture quotations are from the King James Version of the Bible.

Publisher's Note: This novel is a work of fiction. Names, characters, places, and incidents are either products of the author's imagination or used fictitiously. All characters are fictional, and any similarity to people living or dead is purely coincidental.

Library of Congress Cataloging-in-Publication Data

Whitlow, Robert, 1954–
    Jimmy / Robert Whitlow.
       p. cm.
    ISBN 1-5955-4063-6 (hc)
    ISBN 1-5955-4159-4 (tp)
       1. Children with mental disabilities—Fiction. 2. Georgia—Fiction. I. Title.
    PS3573.H49837J56 2005
    813'.6—dc22   2005012847

Printed in the United States of America

06 07 08 09 10 RRD 5 4 3 2 1

*To those who love children with special needs. Heaven
knows your sacrifice and holds your reward.*

*"Whatever you did for one of the least of these brothers of
mine, you did for me."*

—Matthew 25:40 NIV

— One —

The defense calls James Lee Mitchell III to the witness stand."

Hearing his name, Jimmy looked up in surprise. For once, it sounded like Daddy was proud of him. Mama leaned close to his ear.

"Go ahead. All you have to do is tell what you heard, just like we practiced this morning at the kitchen table. Your daddy is counting on you."

"But Mama—"

"Mr. Mitchell, are you intending to call your son as a witness in this case?" the judge asked.

Mr. Laney jumped to his feet. His freckled, round face flushed bright red, and his voice rose in protest.

"Your Honor, I discussed this with Mr. Mitchell as soon as I received his list of potential witnesses. This is highly improper. His son is mentally limited and not able to provide competent testimony. Parading him in front of the jury is inflammatory, prejudicial, and inherently unreliable!"

Tall, with light brown hair and dark, piercing eyes, Daddy responded smoothly.

"Judge Robinson, I believe the district attorney misstates the legal standard for competency to testify in the state of Georgia. It is whether a witness understands the nature of a judicial oath. Age and intelligence are not the final arbiters of the capacity to offer probative testimony. That determination rests with the Court, and I'm prepared to lay the foundation necessary for this witness to testify. The fact that he's my son is irrelevant."

Mr. Robinson removed the pen clenched between his teeth and peered over the edge of the bench at Jimmy. The young boy stared back through thick glasses held in place by large ears. Jimmy shared the same hair color as his father, but his eyes, like those of his birth mother, were pale blue. Average in height for a sixth grader at Piney Grove Elementary School, Jimmy ran his finger inside the collar of his shirt and pulled at the tie around his neck.

"How old is he?" the judge asked.

"Twelve, but he'll be thirteen in a few weeks," Daddy replied.

"His chronological age is not an indicator of his mental capacity," Mr. Laney responded quickly. "We're not dealing with a normal—"

"Gentlemen," the judge interrupted. "We'll take up the competency determination outside the presence of the jury. Bailiff, escort the jurors to the jury room."

Jimmy watched as the people sitting in chairs on the other side of his daddy left the courtroom. One black-haired woman wearing a cobalt-blue dress looked at him and smiled.

Pointing in her direction, he whispered to Mama, "Does that lady in the blue dress know me?"

"That's Mrs. Murdock. She's a teacher at the high school."

"I hope I'm in her class when I go to high school. She looks nice. What does she teach?"

"She teaches English."

"Oh," Jimmy said, disappointed. "I already know English."

As soon as the last person left and the bailiff closed the door, Mr. Robinson spoke.

"Mr. Mitchell, proceed with your evidence as to the competency of this young man to testify."

Jimmy watched Daddy pick up a legal pad and turn to a new page.

"Admittedly, Your Honor, Jimmy is mentally limited. However, that doesn't automatically eliminate his capability to offer testimony with probative value in this case."

"What kind of testimony?" Mr. Laney asked. "The defendant is charged with felony possession and intent to distribute over two pounds of cocaine. To bring in an impressionable child who can be manipulated in an effort to distract the jury—"

"Don't jump ahead, Mr. Laney," the judge interrupted. "That goes to the weight assigned to his testimony, not the competency issue. We're going to take everything in proper order, and you'll have ample opportunity to raise your objections."

Mr. Laney, his face still red, sat. Jimmy poked his mama's arm.

"Is Mr. Laney mad at Daddy?"

"Not really. They'll still play golf on Saturday, but he doesn't want you to tell what you heard."

"Why not?"

"He's doing his job."

That didn't make sense, but Jimmy could tell that Mama didn't want to talk. He looked at the man sitting at the table beside Daddy. His name was Jake Garner, and Daddy was his lawyer. Garner had long black hair and a very realistic drawing of a blue-and-red snake on his arm. The tail began at the man's elbow and coiled around his arm before disappearing under his shirt. Jimmy stared at the drawing and wished Jake would roll up his sleeve so he could see the snake's head. Jimmy wasn't afraid of snakes; he'd seen several while walking in the woods with Grandpa. He knew not to pet them or pick them up.

"Mama," he said in a whisper. "Will that drawing of a snake on Jake's arm wash off in the shower?"

"No," she answered. "It's a tattoo. It's permanent."

Jimmy thought a moment. "Could I get a tattoo of Buster on my arm?"

"No. Hush."

Mama turned toward Daddy. Jimmy scooted back against the wooden bench and sat on his hands. He'd never talked to Jake Garner and didn't know about cocaine. But he knew what he'd heard Sheriff Brinson say to Detective Milligan.

Daddy kept talking. "Before asking Jimmy any questions, I thought it would be beneficial to offer expert-opinion testimony from a psychologist who has evaluated him. I'd prefer that both the jury and the Court hear this testimony."

The judge shook his head. "That's not necessary, Mr. Mitchell. Whether this young man is competent to testify is for me to decide. Proceed."

Daddy stepped back. "Perhaps you'll reconsider after you hear what the psychologist has to say. The defense calls Dr. Susan Paris to the stand."

Jimmy hadn't seen the psychologist with blond hair and bright red fingernails slip into the courtroom. He turned around and saw her sitting beside Sheriff Brinson.

When Jimmy first met Dr. Paris, he was shy around her, but after she fixed vanilla wafers with peanut butter on them, they'd gotten along fine. She gave him a test at the beginning of each school year. Jimmy's friend Max told him that tests should be given at the end of the school year to find out what a student learned, not in September to find out what had been forgotten over the summer. But Jimmy didn't argue with Dr. Paris. Eating perfectly prepared vanilla wafers with peanut butter was a small price to pay for having to fill in little circles with a number-two pencil.

Dr. Paris walked to the witness stand. When she passed Jimmy, he glanced down at her hands. Her fingernails were so red they looked wet. She took the witness stand and raised her hand. She looked calm and pretty.

"I do," she said after the judge asked her a question with God's name at the end of it.

The psychologist reached into her purse, and Jimmy entertained a hopeful thought that she'd brought some vanilla wafers into the courtroom. But all she did was take out a tissue.

"Please state your name," Daddy said.

"Dr. Susan Elaine Paris."

"What is your profession?"

"I work part-time as a school psychologist for the Cattaloochie County Board of Education and maintain a private practice focused on children and adolescents here in Piney Grove."

"Please outline your educational and professional qualifications."

"I received a BS in psychology from the University of Virginia, and I earned a master's and doctorate in clinical psychology from Vanderbilt University."

"Are you licensed to practice child and adolescent psychology in the state of Georgia?"

"Yes."

"How long have you been licensed?"

"Five years."

Daddy paused. "Your Honor, we tender Dr. Paris as an expert in the field of child psychology."

"No objection," Mr. Laney said.

"Proceed," the judge said.

"Dr. Paris, have you had the opportunity to evaluate my son, Jimmy Mitchell?"

"Yes, as part of my regular duties for the school system, I give Jimmy a battery of tests each fall to determine his status and help formulate an educational plan for the teachers working with him. I also have access to the evaluations conducted by Dr. Kittle, my predecessor."

Jimmy had forgotten Dr. Kittle's name. She had white hair and didn't paint her fingernails at all. Jimmy leaned close to Mama.

"What happened to Dr. Kittle?" he whispered.

"She retired and moved to the beach."

Jimmy liked the beach but not the ocean. Even small waves terrified him.

"Can you summarize Jimmy's general mental status?" Daddy asked.

"Yes. He has below-average general intellectual functioning with deficits in adaptive capability. Age-appropriate IQ testing has consistently revealed a verbal, performance, and full-scale IQ in the 68 to 70 range. An IQ score less than 59 indicates a severe deficit. Over 70 is dull-normal. Thus, Jimmy is in between mental retardation and the dull-normal category."

Jimmy squirmed in his seat. He didn't understand everything the psychologist was saying, but he recognized the word *retardation*. Mean people used that word when they talked about him.

"Where is he placed within the school system?" Daddy asked.

"Jimmy does not have any abnormal behavioral problems and, pursuant to the school board's inclusion policy, is integrated into a regular classroom. His teachers utilize nonstandard testing to monitor his progress, and I review the results on a monthly basis."

"What can you tell the Court about Jimmy's current level of intellectual functioning?"

"Once Jimmy grasps a concept, he is capable of retaining it. However, he faces a formidable challenge in appropriately applying what he's learned. The educational process can be frustrating to him, but he maintains a good attitude and has shown adequate progress."

Mr. Laney stood. "Your Honor, this is a criminal trial, not a parent-teacher conference."

"Move along, Mr. Mitchell," the judge said.

"Yes, sir."

"Why did Daddy say 'yes, sir'?" Jimmy whispered to Mama. "Mr. Robinson doesn't look as old as Grandpa."

"But he's the judge."

Daddy looked down at the legal pad in his right hand. "Dr. Paris, given the results of your testing, and based upon your three years of professional interaction with Jimmy, do you have an opinion whether he has the capacity to know the importance of telling the truth?"

"Yes, I do."

"What is your opinion?"

"I believe it is a concept he understands. One of the primary points I emphasize in testing a student is the need to answer every question truthfully. Some psychological tests incorporate inquiries that reveal whether a child is being consistent in his or her responses. Jimmy is uniformly forthright and honest, even if the truth casts him in a negative light. He does not exhibit an inclination to manipulate his answers and try to fool the test."

"What is she saying about me?" Jimmy asked.

Mama patted him on the leg. "That you're a good boy who tries to do his best and tells the truth."

"Will Jimmy understand the language of a judicial oath?" Daddy asked.

"If it is explained to him in the right way. He believes in God and will tell the truth because he believes it is a sin to lie. In fact, I think he understands what it means to be a false witness. We discussed the concept recently when he told me that his mother was teaching him the Ten Commandments."

"Will I have to say them?" Jimmy asked Mama, touching the ends of his fingers. "I can do it with you in my room, but I'd be afraid in front of all these people."

"Not today."

Daddy stepped closer to Dr. Paris. "What can you tell Judge Robinson about Jimmy's memory?"

Dr. Paris sat up straighter and looked up at the judge. "When he works hard, Jimmy can memorize rote information. The Ten Commandments are an example. However, there is another side to his memory that is, at times, remarkable. He will occasionally remind me of a phrase or sentence I said months or even years ago. I've discussed this unusual ability with members of the school staff, and others have noticed the same capability."

"Objection," Mr. Laney said. "The opinions of other teachers would be hearsay."
Daddy responded, "She's been qualified as an expert and can rely on statistical data to support her opinion."

"I don't hear her claiming to have collected statistical data, but I'll allow her to state her opinion and give it the weight I deem appropriate," the judge said.

Daddy spoke. "If Jimmy told you the substance of a conversation he'd overheard, would you believe him?"

"Generally, yes."

"That's all from Dr. Paris."

"Mr. Laney, you may cross-examine the witness," the judge said.

A few stubborn strands of reddish hair clung to the top of Mr. Laney's head. His face no longer appeared flushed.

"Dr. Paris, are you aware that Jimmy is in the courtroom?"

"Of course. I saw him on the front bench with his mother."

"Does his presence have any effect on your testimony?"

"No. He doesn't understand the terminology I'm using. He knows he's a special boy."

Jimmy sat up so he could pay attention. He'd lived almost thirteen years with the word *special* hanging around his neck. Teachers told him that being special was good, and even though he knew he could get in trouble for disagreeing with his teachers, Jimmy thought they were wrong. He'd been special all his life, and it had created a lot of problems for him, especially at school. Being special meant being different from other children, and differences brought persecution and loneliness.

However, when Mama told Jimmy he was special, the word took on another meaning. Coming from her mouth, the word wrapped around him like a hug. Mama couldn't have children of her own, so Jimmy was the one and only object of her love. She chose him when she married Daddy, and from that day forward, Jimmy enjoyed unique status in his family as a very special boy.

Mr. Laney spoke. "Dr. Paris, are you claiming that Jimmy Mitchell has a photographic memory for everything spoken in his presence?"

"Photographic memory relates to visual images. Jimmy's ability is auditory."

The side of Mr. Laney's neck flashed red all the way to the top of his left ear.

"Dr. Paris, if you want to engage in a semantic—"

"But I know what you mean," Dr. Paris continued calmly. "Jimmy can't recall everything he hears. In fact, his memory of conversations appears somewhat random. All I can say is that he sometimes has a parrotlike ability to repeat what he's heard, including words he can't define."

"Does he understand the significance of what he's repeating?"

"Only if it falls within his level of current cognitive functioning. His world is expanding, but at a much slower rate than for a typical child."

"Does he remember the information verbatim?"

"I can't answer that because I've never had the opportunity to quantify it in a reliable way, but in my experience the substance of what he remembers is accurate."

Mr. Laney turned toward the judge.

"Your Honor, the defense is trying to tout this boy as a human court reporter. This is exactly the type of prejudicial activity I warned the Court about before the jury left the courtroom. You have a handicapped young man who will play on the jurors' sympathies when they need to be focusing on the hard evidence in the case."

"Are you finished with your questions?" the judge asked.

"Uh, no sir."

"Then save your argument for later."

Mr. Laney refocused his attention on Dr. Paris.

"Am I correct in stating that not all of his teachers have noticed Jimmy's remarkable memory?"

"That's true."

"And there's been no attempt to document this purported ability in a scientific way?"

"No, it's just an observation."

Mr. Laney walked to the table where he'd left his papers.

"Dr. Paris, besides a low IQ and random memory, what other mental or psychological abnormalities have you identified in Jimmy?"

"Objection, Your Honor," Daddy said. "Only matters relevant to Jimmy's ability to tell the truth and accurately relate information are before the Court."

"Mr. Laney has Dr. Paris on cross-examination, and given the unusual nature of the competency issue, I'll give the State wider latitude than normal. Overruled."

"Go ahead and answer," Mr. Laney said.

Dr. Paris put the tissue back in her purse without having used it.

"He has a persistent, irrational fear of water. Jimmy won't swim in a pool or go out in a boat. He will take a shower but won't get into a bathtub full of water."

"How do you know about this fear of water?"

"He's mentioned it generally, and his mother verified it with specific examples."

"Why does he have this fear of water?"

Dr. Paris glanced at Mama. "His mother believes it may be related to an early childhood trauma, but I've never discussed it with Jimmy. It has no impact on his academic program, so I haven't pursued the origin of his phobia."

"What kind of trauma?"

Daddy rose to his feet. "Objection to continuing this line of questioning as irrelevant."

"I agree," the judge replied. "Sustained."

"Any other abnormalities?"

Dr. Paris shifted in her chair and looked at Jimmy before answering. He smiled at her. She was good at talking in front of other people.

"He has infrequent hallucinations and delusions."

Mama reached over and squeezed Jimmy's hand. He looked up at her.

Mr. Laney let Dr. Paris's words linger in the courtroom. After a few moments, he threw his arms wide open and spoke in a loud voice.

"Dr. Paris, let's hear everything you know about Jimmy's hallucinations and delusions."

Dr. Paris pressed her lips together and tapped one of her red fingernails against the wooden railing that surrounded the witness chair.

"Jimmy sees people who aren't there. He calls them Watchers."

— Two —

Mr. Laney waited. When Dr. Paris didn't continue, he lowered his voice and asked, "Watchers? Please tell the court about these Watchers."

Dr. Paris looked up at the judge. "Jimmy shared this with me in confidence. Am I required to relate this information?"

"Yes."

Dr. Paris looked at Jimmy.

"Jimmy, I'm going to tell what you told me about the Watchers. Is that okay with you?"

Jimmy didn't move. He wasn't about to say anything. Mama looked at Daddy, who shook his head with a frown.

"Go ahead, Dr. Paris," the judge said.

Dr. Paris turned toward the judge. "Your Honor, I need to give you some background information. Jimmy is a pleasant boy, but he will only engage in extensive conversation when he believes he is in a safe environment. In the classroom, he rarely speaks and doesn't socialize with other students except for a few classmates who have known him a long time."

Jimmy leaned close to Mama. "I've known Max since we were little babies."

Dr. Paris continued. "He observes but doesn't interact. I'm sure he's suffered a degree of persecution from his peers, and instead of acting out in anger or rebellion, Jimmy has chosen a path of limited isolation. Faced with conflict or pressure, he withdraws to wait out the storm. In the classroom, he will sit quietly unless specifically asked a question. Even in a one-on-one setting, it's a challenge to convince him to open up and share private information. During my first year at the school, I never gained his trust, and our interaction remained superficial.

However, toward the middle of the second year, he began to reveal the delightful young man he truly is. Recently, we've reached a new level of trust, and he told me about the people he calls Watchers. It came up during a testing session. I noticed him looking up from his workbook and staring at a spot near the doorway of the room. When I asked him about the reason for his distraction, he told me a Watcher had come into the room."

Jimmy remembered the day of the test. The Watcher roamed the halls of Piney Grove Elementary just like Mrs. Bacon, the school principal. He didn't tell Jimmy any answers on the test; he just wanted to see what Jimmy was doing.

"Did he describe this person?" Laney asked.

"Just as a man he sees from time to time at the school. In a few seconds, Jimmy returned to his work and finished the test. When he gave me his paper, I asked him to tell me more about the man he saw. He didn't offer any additional information except that he was a 'school Watcher.' I asked him why he called him a Watcher, and Jimmy said, 'Because he watches.'"

"What did you conclude from this incident?"

"Initially, I categorized it as an encounter with an imaginary friend. Children often create fantasy figures who inhabit their world. It's a way for a child to work through issues and experiences without facing real consequences, and there's nothing psychologically significant about it. This phenomenon occasionally occurs in children with limited intellectual capacity like Jimmy, and it fits his personality type. The Watcher would enter his private world in a nonthreatening way and help him process external stress and pressure. The day following the test, I asked Jimmy more questions, and he told me that he sees Watchers in different settings: at home, on the street, at friends' houses, at church, even in Hankins's Pharmacy. At that point, I realized this was clinically significant enough to bring up with his mother. She confirmed my observations and provided additional details. Jimmy is convinced these people are real, even though he's the only one who can see them."

"Mama," Jimmy whispered, "are you going to tell?"

"No, honey."

"Does he communicate with these Watchers?"

"Telepathically. He claims that sometimes he can hear their thoughts in his head, which makes it a more complex type of delusion than a strictly visual image."

"Do they know his thoughts?"

"He believes they do."

Mr. Laney held his hands in the air with his palms facing upward. "So, we have a young man who lives in a fantasy world inhabited by imaginary people who tell him things the rest of us can't hear and who know what he's thinking even if he is completely silent."

"At times, although I believe he maintains appropriate interaction with his actual surroundings."

"But how can he pay attention to all these competing voices and separate the real from the false?"

"Overall, he seems sufficiently in touch with reality to function in a manner consistent with his mental deficits. None of his teachers report inordinate distractibility or similar problems."

"Would he believe that the information telepathically communicated to him by these Watchers is the truth?"

"He never gave me any examples, so I can't give an opinion."

"But he believes they're real?"

"Yes."

Mr. Laney looked down at the paper in his hand. "Any other abnormalities?"

Dr. Paris shook her head. "Not to my knowledge."

"That's all," Mr. Laney said.

The judge looked at Daddy. "Any redirect of this witness?"

Jimmy wondered if Daddy was mad at him for telling Dr. Paris about the Watchers. Daddy directed his attention toward Dr. Paris.

"Dr. Paris, do you believe Jimmy knows the difference between his interaction with the imaginary world and what takes place in this one?"

"I'd better stick to my comment that he relates to people and reacts to normal stimuli in a manner consistent with his IQ results. There is always the possibility that a person with pervasive hallucinations and delusions will eventually cross into the fantasy realm and stay there. I can say with confidence that this has not happened with Jimmy. If it had, he would exhibit radically different behavior on a regular basis."

"Do you have an opinion whether Jimmy's delusions would prevent him from hearing and relating information from the real world in a truthful way?"

"I think he could remember events or conversations and tell you the truth about them."

"No further questions."

Daddy sat, and Jimmy took a deep breath. Daddy didn't sound mad, but sometimes it was hard to tell.

"Anything else, Mr. Laney?" the judge asked.

"No, sir. I think we've heard enough."

Dr. Paris left the witness stand.

"Mr. Mitchell?" the judge asked.

"Your Honor, I'd like to give you an opportunity to talk to Jimmy."

"I think that's in order. Proceed."

Daddy came over to Jimmy.

"Come sit in the special, uh, I mean witness chair."

Jimmy looked at Mama, who nodded her head. "Go ahead."

Jimmy stood but didn't move. He glanced around the big room. Mr. Laney, Mr. Robinson, Dr. Paris, Sheriff Brinson, and Jake Garner were all staring at him. He wished he had a cap to wear, but Mama said it wasn't polite to wear caps indoors.

"Why is everyone looking at me?" he whispered to Mama. "I don't like being here."

Mama turned to Daddy and spoke in a low voice. "Lee, are you sure about this?"

"Ellen, a man's freedom is at stake."

Daddy grabbed Jimmy's right hand and led him to the witness stand. Jimmy knew not to resist.

"Sit in the chair," Daddy commanded.

Jimmy swallowed. The wooden chair rocked slightly. When he leaned back, it shifted so suddenly that he thought it might tip over.

"Uh-oh!" he cried out.

"Be still," Daddy said. "The chair will hold you. It's attached to the floor."

Jimmy peered beneath the seat. Sure enough, the chair rested on a single leg that disappeared into the floor. He rocked back and forth more gently and adjusted his body in the seat. It was nicer than the bench where he'd been sitting with Mama, but he still wanted to be with her.

Daddy walked over to the table where Jake Garner sat and began gathering some papers. Jimmy scanned the courtroom. The large, high-ceilinged room had rows of benches. It reminded him of church. He never said anything out loud in church since the time he asked Mama why the woman who sat in front of them every Sunday never put any money in the offering plate. Mama put her hand over his mouth so tightly that he had trouble breathing.

"How do you like it up there?" Daddy asked in a softer voice.

"It's okay," he said, "but I don't want to talk with everybody looking at me."

Daddy patted him on the arm. "People are supposed to talk when they sit in the witness chair. That's why Dr. Paris answered our questions."

Jimmy looked at Mama. She nodded her head. Daddy stepped back toward the table where Jake sat.

"Jimmy, do you know Judge Robinson?"

Of course Jimmy knew Mr. Robinson. They attended the same church, and after the Sunday morning service, Jimmy often saw him talking to Daddy beneath the large trees near the main entrance to the sanctuary.

"Yes, sir," he answered. "But I didn't know until this morning that his first name was Judge."

The witnesses and observers remaining in the courtroom laughed, so Jimmy did too. He had to admit it was a funny name. No one at his school was named Judge.

"If Judge Robinson asks you to promise to tell the truth, the whole truth, and nothing but the truth, will you do it?" Daddy asked.

This question was hard. Jimmy kept his mouth shut. Daddy spoke again with a slight edge in his voice.

"Answer the question."

Jimmy leaned forward in the chair. He knew that being polite was always a good response when he felt confused.

"Yes, sir."

Dr. Paris went over to Daddy and whispered in his ear. Daddy listened for a few seconds. Dr. Paris returned to her seat.

"Jimmy, how old are you?" Daddy asked.

Jimmy relaxed. "Twelve."

"When is your birthday?"

"My birthday is June 5."

"When is my birthday?"

"July 14."

"When is your mama's birthday?"

"My mama's birthday is the day before Christmas. That makes her the best present in the whole world."

Jimmy smiled at Mama. She came to live in their house the summer after Jimmy turned five. She returned his smile in a way that meant she wanted to give him a hug.

Mr. Laney stood.

"Judge, I've been lenient in not objecting, but we're not planning birthday parties today. I can't see the relevance of this line of questioning."

Daddy turned toward the judge. "I'm illustrating Jimmy's ability to truthfully relate concrete pieces of information. He's been correct on all the dates he's mentioned thus far."

"Very well. Move on," Mr. Robinson said.

"Jimmy, what is a lie?" Daddy asked.

"A lie is a sin. People who tell lies will be thrown into a lake of fire."

The previous Sunday, Jimmy had listened in fear as Brother Fitzgerald, the preacher at their church, thundered from the pulpit that people who tell lies will be thrown into a lake of fire. Jimmy didn't like regular water and most certainly didn't want to be thrown into a lake of fire.

"Do you think it's bad to tell a lie?"

Mr. Robinson interrupted. "I think he's made that point more clearly than any witness who's ever appeared in this courtroom."

"Yes, Your Honor." Daddy smiled at Jimmy. "Can you tell us an example of a lie so we can be sure you understand what it means?"

Jimmy adjusted his glasses. "What's an example?"

Daddy kept calm. "How about the fishing story you told me this morning while we were eating breakfast."

Jimmy looked puzzled. "You already know it."

"But Judge Robinson hasn't heard it. He wants you to tell what happened."

Jimmy looked up at the judge. Mr. Laney spoke. "Your Honor, Mr. Mitchell is turning this trial into a mockery and circus—"

"Quiet," the judge responded. "I want to hear the fishing story. Go ahead, Jimmy."

Jimmy took a deep breath. "A man fishing at Webb's Pond the other day told me and Grandpa a lie."

"What did he lie about?" Daddy asked.

"He came up to talk to Grandpa and said he'd caught a big bass that he was going to put on his wall. While he talked to Grandpa, I took the lid off his bucket and saw there was only one fish in it, and it wasn't that big. I caught one the same size a couple of weeks ago, and we threw it back. When I asked the man about the fish in his bucket, he got as red in the face as Mr. Laney did a few minutes ago."

The courtroom laughed again.

"What was the truth about the fish?" Daddy asked.

"That it was a little one. Grandpa said he should have thrown it back into the pond so it could grow bigger."

"If I ask you some questions, will you tell me the truth?"

"Yes, sir."

"You won't tell us a fish is big if it's little?"

"No, sir."

"If Mr. Laney asks you questions, will you tell the truth?"

"Yes, sir."

"Will you tell us a lie?"

"No, sir. That would be wrong."

Daddy picked up a black book and held it up for Jimmy to see.

"What is this book?" he asked.

It was black and had gold lettering on the front. Only one book in Jimmy's world bore those markings.

"It's a Holy Bible."

"Does the Bible tell us things about God?"

That was an easy question.

"Yes. And Jesus too. He is God's Son."

"Does God want you to tell the truth?"

"Yes, sir."

Daddy turned toward Mr. Laney. "You may ask."

Mr. Laney walked up close to the witness stand. He didn't look mad or angry.

"Jimmy, what is an oath?" he asked in a soft voice.

"I don't know."

"What does it mean to swear to tell the truth?"

Jimmy felt his face get red. He'd heard a boy at school say some strange, new words during recess. When he asked Mama about it, she warned him not to use swear words.

"I don't want to say."

"Why not?"

"Because my Mama says there are better words to use."

Daddy stood. "He thinks you're talking about cursing."

Mr. Laney nodded. "Do you know that the word *swear* has a meaning other than saying a bad word?"

"No, sir."

"Do you know why you're here in the courtroom today?"

"Because Mama kept me home from school and brought me."

"Has your father told you what he wants you to say?"

"Yes, sir."

"Objection," Daddy said. "This is outside the scope of the court's inquiry into the witness's competency to understand the nature of the oath."

"Sustained," the judge said.

"Are you going to tell the truth or what your father wants you to say?"

"Same objection," Daddy said.

"Overruled."

"Answer the question," Mr. Laney said.

Jimmy didn't say anything.

"Do you remember the question?" Mr. Laney asked.

Jimmy shook his head. "No, sir."

Mr. Laney glanced at his watch and looked up at Mr. Robinson.

"I asked him a question fifteen seconds ago, and he can't remember it. How reliable can he be about more remote events?"

"A good point, Mr. Laney," the judge replied. "But it goes to credibility, not competency. I've let both you and Mr. Mitchell stray off course on this memory matter, but I remind you that it is not the primary issue in determining whether this young man is competent to testify."

Laney turned toward Jimmy. "I'll ask you again since you can't remember. Are you going to tell the truth or what your father wants you to say?"

"Both," Jimmy answered.

Mr. Laney stepped back. "Why do you say both?"

"Because the truth is what my Daddy wants me to say."

"That's enough, Mr. Laney," the judge said. "I'm going to rule he can testify."

"But what about these imaginary people?" Mr. Laney asked. "I want to question him about his ability to distinguish between reality and fantasy."

"That, too, I will allow on cross, but I don't want to keep the jury waiting any longer. I think Jimmy sufficiently understands the requirement that he tell the truth as best he can." The judge turned toward the bailiff. "Bring the jury back into the courtroom."

Jimmy stood.

"Please, stay where you are, son," the judge said. "We're not finished yet."

"But I'd like to sit with my mama."

"Not yet."

"I'd like to call Dr. Paris to provide background information for the jury," Daddy added.

"That's not necessary," the judge answered. "Proceed with the boy's testimony."

Jimmy looked at Mama. She motioned for him to sit, then put her hands together. That meant she was praying for him.

The people on the jury returned to the courtroom. Mrs. Murdock gave him another big smile. It made him wish again that he could be in her classroom in high school. He guessed she'd be the kind of teacher who found out what students liked to do and made it part of the lessons. The best teachers knew how to do that.

— Three —

"Jimmy, put your left hand on the Bible and raise your right hand," Daddy said.

Jimmy put one hand on the Holy Bible and raised the other one. He heard a chuckle from the direction of the special seats.

"The other hand," Daddy said.

Figuring out right and left was hard, especially when looking at something. Jimmy switched hands, putting his left hand on the Holy Bible and raising his right hand high in the air like a student who knew the answer to a question in school. Another round of twitters came from the people in the special chairs.

"What's funny?" he asked.

"Lower your right hand so that it's even with your ear."

Jimmy carefully lowered his right hand and touched the top of his ear in a sideways salute. Daddy spoke.

"Jimmy, do you promise God and everyone in the courtroom that you will tell the truth?"

"Yes, sir."

"Is that sufficient language for the oath?" Daddy asked the judge.

"Yes, proceed."

"Jimmy, what is your name?"

It was Jimmy's turn to laugh out loud. His voice echoed in the large courtroom. At times Daddy could be impatient with him, but his silly question helped Jimmy get over being embarrassed.

Daddy smiled. "Please, tell the members of the jury your full name."

Jimmy sat up straight and looked at Mrs. Murdock. "James Lee Mitchell III."

"But everyone calls you Jimmy, right?"

"Yes, sir. It's a lot shorter and easier to spell."

"Jimmy, do you know Jake Garner, the man sitting at that table?"

Jimmy looked at Jake. From the witness chair, he couldn't see the colors of the snake on his arm as clearly. Jake looked at Jimmy but didn't smile.

"Yes, sir."

"Have you ever talked to him?"

"No, sir."

"Do you know why he's here in the courtroom?"

"Someone invited him to come."

There was more laughter.

Mr. Robinson spoke. "We've had enough levity. We're here on serious business."

Jimmy could tell that Mr. Robinson, like Daddy, was used to getting his way.

"Jimmy, do you know Sheriff Brinson?" Daddy asked.

"Yes, sir."

"Is he in the courtroom today?"

"Yes, sir."

"Where is he sitting?"

Jimmy pointed to the bench behind Mr. Laney and waved at Sheriff Brinson. The sheriff gave a slight smile but didn't wave back.

"Where do you usually see Sheriff Brinson?"

"Where they keep the police cars. Sometimes on Saturdays I help clean the cars, and after I finish, I'll sit in a car and turn on the blue lights and listen to the policemen talk on the radio."

"Do you turn on the siren?"

"No, sir." Jimmy looked at Sheriff Brinson and remembered that he had to tell the truth. "Uh, there was one time I turned on the siren by accident, but I told Sheriff Brinson I was sorry and wouldn't do it again. He told me it was okay."

"Is Sheriff Brinson always there on Saturday?"

"No, sir."

"Are you friends with any of the deputies?"

"Deputy Askew. Mama calls him to find out if he's going to be there before she takes me to help clean the cars."

"Is Deputy Askew the one who supervises, uh, takes care of you when you're there helping clean the cars?"

"Yes, sir. He drives the number-twelve car."

"Do you ever talk on the radio?"

"No, sir. Deputy Askew won't let me. It's not like a telephone. It is only for the policemen to use."

"Do you ever listen to the people talking on the radio while you're sitting in the car?"

"Yes, sir, if it's turned on."

"Have you ever heard Sheriff Brinson's voice on the radio?"

"Yes, sir."

"How did you know it was Sheriff Brinson?"

"Because I know what his voice sounds like."

Daddy stepped closer. "Have you ever heard Sheriff Brinson talk about Jake Garner on the radio?"

"No, sir."

Daddy's eyes narrowed, and Jimmy knew he was in trouble. "Didn't you hear Sheriff Brinson tell someone on the radio something about Jake Garner?"

"Objection, leading," Laney said.

"I'll allow it for this question only," Mr. Robinson said. "But be sure you let the witness testify."

Daddy repeated the question. Jimmy rocked back and forth in the chair.

"Yes, sir," he answered nervously. "But Sheriff Brinson just called him Garner."

"That's fine."

Jimmy could see Daddy relax, and it made him feel better.

"Who was Sheriff Brinson talking to?" Daddy asked.

"Car number five."

"Who drives car number five?"

"Detective Milligan. I've helped clean his car too."

"What did Sheriff Brinson say about Garner?"

"That he wasn't interested in arresting Lenny but to pick up Garner."

"Are those the words he used?"

"Yes, sir."

"Could you hear what Detective Milligan said?"

"Yes, sir."

"What did he say?"

"Meet me at the jail."

"What happened after that?"

"I kept cleaning Deputy Askew's car. I sat on the ground spraying stuff on the tires that makes them shiny. I heard two cars drive into the parking lot. I looked around the back of the car and saw Sheriff Brinson and Detective Milligan get out of their cars. I looked underneath Deputy Askew's car and could see their feet."

"Did they see you?"

"Objection," Laney said. "Speculation."

"Sustained."

"Did they say anything to you?" Daddy asked.

"No, I was sitting by the tire, and they didn't see me."

"Judge," Mr. Laney began. "He shouldn't be able—"

The judge turned toward the jury. "The jury will disregard the witness's opinion about what any other individuals may or may not have seen."

"Where was Deputy Askew?" Daddy asked.

"He'd gone inside the jail to get us something to drink. We get thirsty washing cars on a hot day."

"What did Sheriff Brinson say to Detective Milligan?"

Jimmy remembered the day at the jail. He could smell the spray he squirted on the tires to make them shiny. He could feel the rough pavement on the back of his legs. He could hear the two men talking.

"Sheriff Brinson said Garner was selling drugs and that the drugs they'd found at Lenny's house couldn't belong to Lenny because"—Jimmy paused—"he was an undercover GBI agent."

"Do you know what that means?"

"No, sir."

"But you're sure that's what Sheriff Brinson told Detective Milligan?"

"Objection, leading," Mr. Laney interjected.

"Sustained."

Jimmy looked at Sheriff Brinson. He'd stopped smiling and had a very serious look on his face.

"What happened next?" Daddy asked.

"Detective Milligan told Sheriff Brinson that he didn't know Lenny was an undercover GBI agent."

"What did Sheriff Brinson say?"

"He told Detective Milligan to turn in an inventory saying that the drugs belonged to Garner so they would have a good case against him."

"What is an inventory?"

"I don't know, but I can still hear the word in my head."

"What happened next?"

Jimmy wrinkled his nose, "Detective Milligan said he couldn't do that because it might ruin his career."

"Do you know what that means?"

"No, sir."

"What happened next?"

"Sheriff Brinson said he didn't care where they found the drugs, because he was going to say that they belonged to Garner and sign the inventory himself."

"What did Detective Milligan say about that idea?"

"He asked him not to do it, because it wasn't the right way to bust somebody."

"Are you sure he used the word *bust*?"

"Yes, sir."

"What did Sheriff Brinson say?"

"That he didn't care what he had to do so long as he sent Garner to prison. Then I saw a cigarette fall on the ground, and someone stepped on it."

The courtroom was completely quiet. Daddy spoke in a soft voice. Jimmy glanced again at Sheriff Brinson, who was staring at the floor.

"Anything else?"

"Sheriff Brinson asked Detective Milligan to keep his mouth shut about Garner. Detective Milligan said he wouldn't tell anyone first, but if the truth came out, he wouldn't lie about what really happened."

"What did Sheriff Brinson do then?"

"He said he would take that chance to protect the people of Cattaloochie County from illegal drugs."

"Do you know what he meant by *illegal drugs*?"

"I asked Mama, and she told me drugs are pills, and illegal drugs are bad pills. I would never take a pill from anyone I don't know."

"What happened next?"

"They walked toward the jail. I watched their feet and could hear their voices but don't know what they talked about. Deputy Askew brought me something to drink, and after I finished cleaning the tires, he let me sit in the car and turn on the blue lights. I told him I wasn't tired and would help clean another car—"

"That's enough," Daddy said. "Are you sure everything you've told us is the truth?"

"Yes, sir. Did it sound like I made it up?"

Daddy looked at Mr. Laney.

"You may ask," Daddy said.

On nights when Daddy worked late, Jimmy and Mama ate supper together at the kitchen table. That happened a lot. There were three chairs around the table: Mama close to the refrigerator, Daddy across from her in front of a big window where the morning sunlight could shine on his newspaper, and Jimmy at the end toward the sunroom. One morning Jimmy sat in Daddy's chair as a joke and opened the sports section as if reading it, but Daddy didn't laugh and told him to move.

The large formal dining room next to the kitchen could seat twelve people around the big oval table. They ate in the dining room only a few times a year. When that happened, Jimmy sat in a chair next to Mama and could watch himself eat in the reflection from a long mirror surrounded by a thick gold frame that hung on the opposite wall. The mirror reminded Jimmy to keep his mouth closed while chewing his food, which was extra important when company came over for dinner. During mealtimes in the kitchen, Jimmy sometimes forgot to keep his mouth closed, but Mama always reminded him.

Jimmy knew their house was old, but he wasn't sure about its exact age. When he asked, Daddy shrugged and told him it was built before Grandpa was born. A broad porch with a gray floor stretched across the front and wrapped all the way around one side. When Jimmy and his friend Max were little, they liked to race their Big Wheels on the porch like they were on a drag strip.

The two-story house was painted white and topped with a gently sloping red roof. The house had lots of windows. Jimmy hadn't counted them, but he'd helped wash the ones on the first floor. He stood on a stepladder to clean the lower windows while Grandpa, who wasn't afraid of heights, climbed a big ladder to clean the others. Grandpa told him a family with four girls lived in the house before Daddy bought it. It was hard for Jimmy to imagine girls sleeping in his bedroom and eating in the kitchen.

Several big oak and maple trees shaded the front yard. When the leaves fell to the ground in the fall, Jimmy helped Grandpa and Daddy rake them into piles almost as high as Jimmy's head. Then Jimmy would hide beneath the leaves and let his dog, Buster, try to find him. Buster had no trouble running right to him. Grandpa told Jimmy that Buster knew his master so well that he could smell him a long way off and hear him breathing underneath the leaves even if Jimmy lay completely still.

The evening after Jimmy testified, Mama prepared one of his favorite meals for supper—mashed potatoes, creamed corn, and meat loaf with a chewy red crust. When she fixed his plate, she scraped some of the red crust from the pan onto his piece. Mama didn't bake meat loaf in the oven; she cooked it on top of the stove. Jimmy had never tasted the other kind, but he knew Mama's was the best in the whole world.

"Will Daddy eat supper with the people who sat together in the courtroom?" he asked.

"No, they don't let the lawyers spend time with the jury outside of the courtroom."

"Then how do they get to know each other?"

"They don't. The jury's job is to listen to people like you who answer the lawyer's questions. That's called *testimony*. After the jurors hear all the testimony, they will decide what is going to happen to Jake Garner. The lawyers can't talk to the jurors except when everyone is together in the courtroom."

"Is Jake Garner a bad man?"

Mama pressed her lips together for a second before answering. "He's your daddy's client."

"Would it be nice to invite him over for supper?"

"No, I don't think that would be a good idea."

Mama bowed her head.

"Let's pray," she said.

Jimmy closed his eyes. Mama always said the blessing before a meal except when company came. Then Daddy prayed in a voice that sounded different from his normal talk. Jimmy usually said a quiet blessing before eating his lunch at school unless he was too hungry and forgot.

"What's going to happen to Jake?" he asked when Mama finished the prayer.

"That depends on the verdict."

"What's a verdict?"

The front door opened. Jimmy heard Daddy drop his briefcase on the floor in the dining room. Mama didn't say anything. She had an anxious look on her face. Jimmy took a big bite of meat loaf. It was delicious, the perfect mix of sauce, onions, bread crumbs, and meat. Daddy came into the room.

"Case dismissed!" he said, clapping his hands together. He sounded happy. "I called two alibi witnesses and then put Garner on the stand. He did better than I expected. Steve Laney risked a mistrial on cross-examination by trying to introduce unrelated criminal charges as similar acts. I don't know what he was thinking."

Jimmy swallowed. "Did he show everyone the snake on his arm? I never could see its head."

"No, he put on his jacket before he testified," Daddy replied, smiling broadly at Mama. "But the real coup de grâce fell when I called Sheriff Brinson. After Jimmy's testimony, Laney knew it was coming, and during a break he sent Brinson over to the jail to get him out of the courtroom. When I asked for the sheriff to come forward and be sworn, Laney told the judge that Brinson had left the courthouse to take care of important law enforcement business. I didn't say a word. I simply put the service copy of the subpoena on the bench in front of the judge and waited for the storm to break. Robinson clamped down so hard on that pen he chews that I thought it might crack in two. He ordered one of the bailiffs to find the sheriff and escort him back to the courtroom, voluntarily or involuntarily."

Mama shook her head. "It's still kind of sad, bringing down the sheriff. Maybe you shouldn't be so happy about it."

"What?" Daddy snorted. "My only pleasure is in exposing a lie."

"Well, it still makes me feel"—Mama paused—"uneasy."

Daddy loosened his tie and smiled slightly. "The chance to ambush the prosecution like that only comes along a few times in a lawyer's career, and there was no way I would let it pass. Anyway, it would have been unethical for me to ignore the sheriff's conduct. I have to represent my client to the best of my ability, even if in a court-appointed case."

Jimmy thought Daddy would get a plate of food and sit down, but he seemed more interested in talking than eating. Jimmy cut off a small bite and dipped it in the mashed potatoes until it appeared covered in warm snow.

"We went into chambers, and Laney informed Judge Robinson that Brinson was going to take the Fifth and refuse to answer questions about the search and seizure."

"Why would he do that?"

"Because falsifying evidence in a criminal trial can be a felony. Brinson could go to jail."

"Will that happen?" Mama asked in surprise.

"I doubt it, but there may be an investigation, most likely by the FBI and the U.S. Attorney's office. If they interview Milligan and he confirms Jimmy's testimony, Brinson will have to resign, and it could lead to an inquiry that uncovers all kinds of corruption."

Mama looked at Jimmy. "And to think, a conversation in the parking lot—"

Daddy kept talking. "Without Brinson's testimony, Laney had nothing. Next week I'll dictate a federal civil rights action on behalf of Garner against the sheriff's department. Before this is over, Jake Garner will be able to get as many snake tattoos as he wants, and I'll make more than enough to compensate me for my time today. I've always liked Brinson, but he got carried away with his theory that Garner was a big-time drug dealer."

"Is he a drug dealer?" Mama asked.

"That's not my job to figure out."

"I realize the sheriff may not have followed proper procedures, but to let a man like that go free—"

"Is the price we pay for the Bill of Rights," Daddy responded. "The rules have to protect everyone if they're going to protect anyone."

"But isn't it important to find out the truth about Garner too?"

"Garner looks like a hoodlum, but he dropped out of college a semester short of graduation. He's probably a drug user, but I doubt he's a dealer. Either way, it's not right to trample the truth in order to get a conviction. Sheriff Brinson thought he was above the law and needed to find out that he's not."

"I think Sheriff Brinson is nice," Jimmy said. "He could have got mad at me when I turned on the siren, but he didn't."

"Which is another reason why this worries me," Mama said. "They've been so good to Jimmy at the sheriff's department. Now, I feel like we're being ungrateful for their kindness."

Daddy shrugged. "It's necessary to put self-interest aside when representing a client. It's the price I pay to be a lawyer."

Mama set a plate of food in front of Daddy, who took a quick bite of meat loaf.

"Did you see Sheriff Brinson after the case was dismissed?" Mama asked.

"We passed each other in the hall on my way out of the courthouse. He wouldn't look me in the eye. I'm sure he's mad and embarrassed. Maybe afraid too."

"Doesn't the sheriff have a wife and two daughters?"

"Yes, but his girls are grown and married. If he leaves Cattaloochie County, he'll land on his feet somewhere else. If he takes to heart what happened today, he'll be a better man in the end."

"And what about Jake Garner? How is he going to get better?"

Jimmy looked up from his plate at the tone of Mama's voice. Daddy didn't immediately answer.

"You have a point," Daddy said, wiping the corner of his mouth with a napkin. "He has a second chance to make something of his life. I'll tell him not to blow it."

JIMMY ENJOYED HIS FOOD TO THE LAST BITE. DADDY CLEANED his plate too, but his favorite meal consisted of fried catfish, hush puppies, and slaw. Jimmy took his plate to the kitchen sink, where he carefully held it underneath the faucet and turned on the water. He could hear Buster barking outside.

Covered with white, brown, and black fur, Buster, a three-year-old Border collie mix, filled the space in Jimmy's heart reserved for a four-legged friend. Jimmy had never been afraid of Buster. Other dogs, like the big black dog that lived near the school and showed its teeth when Jimmy walked by, were scary, but not Buster. He liked to lick Jimmy's face and never tried to bite him.

A chain-link fence enclosed the backyard. Daddy said it kept Buster from running away, but the fence was built before Buster came to live with them, and Jimmy knew it wasn't necessary. One evening Jimmy forgot to put Buster up for the night. When Daddy went downstairs in the morning to get the paper, he found Buster sleeping on the front porch. Buster didn't need a fence to tell him where he belonged.

The backyard contained one enormous oak tree and several smaller trees. Squirrels lived in the big tree, and when they ran onto a limb, Buster would bark at them. Jimmy knew the dog wanted the squirrels to come down and play, but they wouldn't. If a squirrel wanted to leave the yard, it jumped from limb to limb until it reached the fence and hopped to the ground by the sidewalk. Jimmy had watched many squirrels do this, and none of them ever fell.

Buster could run fast. He became a blur when he chased his red rubber ball. Uncle Bart told Jimmy he should name the dog Bandit. Jimmy wasn't sure what that meant, but when he saw the puppy, he thought of the name Buster. Jimmy knew Buster liked his name because he came running every time Jimmy called him.

Buster lived outside except on nights when he had a bath. In the summertime, Jimmy and Mama sometimes cleaned the dog by rubbing him with a soapy brush and washing off the soap with the water hose. On bath nights, Buster got to sleep in Jimmy's room. He would hop onto the bed and lie next to Jimmy's feet. Buster went to sleep as fast as he ran. Jimmy could tell Buster was asleep, not just because his eyes were closed, but because of the way his side went up and down.

"Jimmy, I'm proud of you," Daddy said.

Still thinking about Buster, Jimmy didn't hear him.

"What?" he asked.

"You were a good boy in the courtroom today. You did a great thing for Jake Garner. I know you didn't want to talk in front of those people, but I'm glad you did." Daddy reached over and rubbed his head the same way Jimmy rubbed Buster's head. "Thanks for helping me."

"I felt funny inside when I had to talk," Jimmy said.

"That's called having butterflies in your stomach," Mama said.

Jimmy rubbed his stomach and smiled. "I hope they like meat loaf."

"And lemon meringue pie," Mama added.

It was Jimmy's favorite dessert. After he ate a bite of pie, Jimmy asked Daddy a question that had worried him since he left the courthouse.

"Why did Mr. Laney's face get so red when he talked to me?"

"That happens to him when he gets upset," Daddy answered. "You had butterflies in your stomach. Steve Laney had bumblebees in his gut."

"Was he mad at me?"

"Not really. He was just doing his job."

"He acted mad."

"He felt the pressure of the situation and didn't know how to handle you as a witness. After you talked, he knew he was going to lose the case."

"Will he be nice to me the next time I see him?"

"Yes."

Jimmy swallowed a bite of pie and thought about Mr. Laney's red cheeks. "Does Mr. Laney get upset when he plays golf?"

Daddy smiled. "Yes, then we both get red in the face."

While they ate their pie, Daddy talked about what went on at his office while he was helping Jake Garner.

"It's hard to cover both places at once," he said. "I wish I could find an aggressive young lawyer to come in with me. The phone calls back up, and one of these days I'm going to miss a good case because no one is around to take down the initial information. A hardworking associate could make a good living in a couple of years."

"We can pray for the right person to come along," Mama said.

"I could help," Jimmy offered. "Grandpa says I'm a hard worker. I helped him clean up the messy area in his backyard and didn't stop working to get a drink of water until he did."

Daddy stopped his fork halfway between his plate and his mouth. "You want to work at my office?"

"Yes, sir."

Daddy looked at Mama. "Did you talk to him about this?"

"No, but it might be good for Jimmy to get out of the house and go downtown for a few hours a week. You could find something for him to do, and it would give you more time together."

Daddy turned toward Jimmy. "I thought you didn't like to come to my office."

Mama said, "Lee, be fair. You didn't want your clients to see Jimmy and ask questions. The specialist in Atlanta told us to look for signs of independent thinking and encourage it. Most boys have a curiosity about what their fathers do at work."

Daddy put the food in his mouth and chewed slowly. After he swallowed, he said, "We'll talk about it later."

They ate in silence. Jimmy enjoyed the sweetness and tartness in the lemon pie. He balanced the last bite on the end of his fork.

"Mama, what day is it?"

"Friday."

"So tomorrow is Saturday, right?"

"Yes."

"Can you call Deputy Askew in the morning and ask if I can help wash the police cars?"

– Four –

The town of Piney Grove nestled in the low-slung hills west of Atlanta within tobacco-spitting distance of the Alabama state line. Lee Mitchell and many of those living on the Georgia side of the border looked down their noses at their Alabama neighbors. He claimed that travelers crossing the state line into the central time zone should set their watches back one hundred years. Jimmy wasn't sure what he meant.

Regional prejudices aside, the daily routines of people living in Piney Grove more closely resembled those of their Alabama neighbors than the lifestyle of Atlanta suburbanites. The rural landscape on both sides of the border was pocked with run-down houses inhabited by slow-talking residents. Piney Grove had an Alabama counterpart twenty-five miles to the west.

Boys in Cattaloochie County grew up scratching chigger bites after picking wild blackberries and assumed the most common type of jelly on earth came from dusky muscadines. People knew their neighbors, and if a local family bought a new car or pickup, they couldn't expect to keep it a secret. Compared to the slow pace and simplicity of life in Piney Grove, Atlanta occupied another universe.

The heart of Piney Grove was much the same as when Jimmy's father walked its tree-lined streets as a twelve-year-old boy. But change pressed in from the Atlanta side of the county, and in recent years a few national chain stores had opened their doors. Lee Mitchell complained that Atlanta would eventually swallow Piney Grove. That, too, puzzled Jimmy.

Six months out of the year, the sun beat down on any exposed red clay and baked it brickyard tough. Jimmy didn't mind the heat. He didn't know there were places where cool mountain breezes blew or refreshing afternoon showers fell. He and Buster played outside even if the summer sun made the air above the brown grass shimmer with heat.

Just like his paternal grandfather and father, Jimmy attended the Piney Grove Elementary School. Jimmy couldn't imagine Grandpa young enough to go to elementary school, but he'd shown Jimmy pictures to prove it. In one photograph Grandpa was dressed in old-fashioned clothes, standing next to the flagpole in front of the red brick building. The only difference in the school between then and now was the size of the trees along the sidewalk.

SATURDAY MORNING DAWNED SO BRIGHT AND CLEAR THAT Jimmy had to squint his eyes against the sun shining through the window at the end of his bedroom. The sun only woke him up on Saturday or Sunday. During the week, Mama made sure he was up in time to eat a good breakfast and get ready for school.

The first thing Jimmy did every morning was put on his glasses. He kept them in a little basket that Grandma helped him make from the straw of an old broom. Jimmy lost his glasses a lot, so Mama kept an extra pair at the house and another in her pocketbook. She bought five or six pairs of glasses every time she took him to the eye doctor. People who knew Jimmy returned his lost glasses if they found them, but sometimes they stayed lost. There was a pair of glasses at the bottom of Webb's Pond and another pair in the woods somewhere between Max's house and the field with the black cows in it.

Jimmy had a bathroom next to his room. Mama and Daddy slept at the other end of the hall in a bedroom that was as large as the living room beneath it. There were two other upstairs bedrooms, but nobody stayed in them unless relatives from out of town came for a visit. One of the guest bedrooms had a big bed with a white canopy on top. The other had two small beds, each the same size as the one in Jimmy's room. Sometimes Jimmy would take a nap in one of the beds like his.

On one wall of Jimmy's room were shelves for his caps. Jimmy loved caps. When he wore a cap and pulled it down over his forehead, he looked like any other boy with glasses. Without a cap, people who didn't know him sometimes stared at him for a second or two.

Jimmy didn't know how many caps he had. Every time he tried to count them, he missed one that was in the closet, underneath his bed, downstairs in the den, or stuck inside another one. He didn't wear all his caps—the ones signed by baseball and football players were only to look at and show people who visited his room. His favorite caps to wear were a white-and-red one from the University of Georgia, and a green-and-yellow one from the John Deere Company. Daddy went to the University of Georgia, and Grandpa cut his grass with a lawn mower made by the John Deere Company. When Jimmy and Grandpa went fishing, they often wore matching John Deere caps.

On Saturdays, Jimmy could pick out his own clothes. He pulled open the drawers of his chest and selected a blue T-shirt with a big fish on it, brown shorts, white socks, and tennis shoes. However, his most important choice would be the cap of the day. After picking up several and looking at them closely, he selected a blue one from Delta Airlines. Jimmy had never flown on an airplane and didn't know if he'd be scared or not.

Going downstairs, he found Mama drinking coffee in the glass sunroom beside the kitchen. Unless they had guests, Mama let him wear a cap in the house if he wanted to. A Holy Bible lay open in her lap. On a little table beside her rested a notebook. She told Jimmy once that she wrote down her thoughts and prayers in it. Jimmy had looked at the pages before and saw his name in it a lot. Mama had pretty handwriting.

"Good morning, Mama," he said, walking over to her.

She put her left arm around him, took off his cap with her right hand, and kissed the top of his head.

"Good morning, sunshine," she answered. "Why don't you eat a bowl of cereal?"

Mama made a hot breakfast for Jimmy and Daddy on Monday through Friday but not on Saturday. Jimmy put cereal in a bowl and poured the milk without spilling a drop. He took it to the sunroom and sat at a little table to eat.

"Have you called Deputy Askew?" he asked. "It's a good day to wash cars."

Mama closed her Holy Bible.

"Daddy and I talked about that last night and decided you shouldn't go to the sheriff's office and wash cars for a while."

Jimmy put down his spoon.

"Why?"

Before Mama answered, Jimmy heard Daddy come into the kitchen.

"Lee!" Mama called out. "Jimmy wants to know why he can't go to the sheriff's office and wash cars."

Daddy entered the sunroom with a cup of coffee in his hand. He hadn't shaved, and his face was covered with dark stubble. He frowned. Jimmy worried. Pleasing adults was hard. He tried to do what was right but made mistakes a lot.

"I'm sorry," he said. "Whatever I—"

"No, no," Daddy said. "You didn't do anything wrong. But I don't think Sheriff Brinson wants you to come to the jail."

"Why not?"

"Because of court yesterday."

Confused, Jimmy looked at Mama, who didn't say anything.

Daddy continued, "Sheriff Brinson wasn't happy when you told about his conversation with Detective Milligan."

"But I told the truth," he protested.

"And that was the right thing to do."

"Then why is Sheriff Brinson mad?"

"Because what you said will get him into trouble."

Jimmy shook his head. "No. You said it was a mistake that Jake was in trouble, and I had to help."

"Yes, and you did the right thing."

Jimmy's lower lip began to tremble. Saying he was sorry might not make things right. "Then why can't I help wash cars? I like to do it! And Deputy Askew promised me a policeman's cap!"

Mama came over and put her arm around him. "Sometimes adults punish children wrongly. Sheriff Brinson may blame you for something he did, and until he stops being sheriff, you can't help wash the police cars."

"But he doesn't wash the cars. I help Deputy Askew."

Mama looked at Daddy.

"Your mama is right," Daddy added. "We discussed it last night after you went to bed."

"I shouldn't have told what I heard!" Jimmy said. "Every time I talk I get into trouble. If I promise to do more jobs for you and Mama, can I—"

"No arguing. You can't go," Daddy cut in.

Jimmy started to say something but stopped. Daddy might get mad.

Head down, he slowly stirred his cereal. Daddy started reading the Atlanta paper. Jimmy got an idea.

"Would you do something with me?" he asked Daddy. "We could wash your car and Mama's car. I could show you what I've learned about washing cars."

Daddy closed the paper and looked at his watch. "Uh, no. I'm playing golf this morning with Steve Laney, and I'll have to pay his greens fee after what I did to him yesterday. Why don't you go see your grandpa? The two of you always have a great time."

Mama walked toward the kitchen.

"I'll call him in a few minutes," she said.

JIMMY WENT UPSTAIRS TO HIS ROOM AND PLOPPED DOWN ON the bed. Sticking out from under the bed was the walking stick Grandpa made for him when Jimmy was six years old. Jimmy nudged it with his toe. He heard the front door slam and looked out the window. Daddy opened the trunk of his car and put his golf clubs inside. Jimmy loved to go to the golf course and ride in the cart, but Daddy didn't invite him except when he was playing with Uncle Bart. That didn't happen very much, because Uncle Bart worked on Saturdays and Mama wouldn't let Daddy play golf on Sunday.

Mama called up the stairs. "Grandpa and Grandma say that it's okay for you to come over!"

Jimmy clapped his hands together and went downstairs. Mama had her purse and car keys in her hand.

"Let's go. I need to run some errands this morning."

"You don't need to take me," Jimmy replied. "Buster and I can walk. I know the way."

Mama stopped and stared. Jimmy had walked to his grandparents' home many times but always accompanied by an adult.

"Are you sure?"

"Yes, ma'am."

Mama looked at her watch. "Okay, I'll call and let them know you're leaving the house. Don't forget to stop and look both ways before crossing the street."

"Yes, ma'am."

Mama gave him a quick hug. When she let him go, Jimmy ran to the screened door at the side entrance to the house. The door slammed behind him as he hopped down the steps to get Buster from the backyard. Buster burst through the gate and ran in a tight circle before coming to a stop. Jimmy bent over and scratched the dog's chin. Buster wiggled in delight. Jimmy heard Mama's car going down the driveway.

"We're going to Grandpa's house," Jimmy said. "All by ourselves."

Jimmy and Buster walked across the yard toward the sidewalk and turned right. On the street behind them, Mama pulled to the curb and watched.

Jimmy usually made the trip to Grandpa's house with his left hand safe in Mama's cool grip and Buster tugging on the leash in his right hand. Today both walked free.

Jimmy knew the way by heart, but the thought that he could leave the house alone, walk carefully along the sidewalk, stop at the stop signs, look both ways, cross only if there were no cars, and turn onto Grandpa's street turned the journey into an adventure. Someday he would own a bicycle. Every other boy he knew had been riding a bicycle for years, but Jimmy still waited. Maybe his thirteenth birthday would be the big day.

They came to the first four-way stop. There were cars at all corners of the intersection. Jimmy waited. Mama coasted to a halt beneath the shade of a large tree about two hundred feet behind him. A woman rolled down her car window.

"You can cross!" she yelled. "Pedestrians have the right of way."

"I'm not a pedestrian," Jimmy answered. "My name is Jimmy Mitchell."

The woman rolled up her window and proceeded across the intersection. Jimmy waited. Mama had taught him to be patient, because it could take awhile for all the cars to move forward. Buster sat and began to pant. Even though it wasn't summer yet, the day held the promise of stifling heat. When the way finally cleared, Jimmy and Buster crossed to the other side.

Jimmy's grandparents lived on Ridgeview Drive in a much smaller house than the large home owned by Daddy and Mama.

"Which house is it?" Jimmy asked Buster.

The dog, trotting in front, glanced behind to see why Jimmy had slowed. Jimmy caught up. It was no use trying to fool Buster. The dog went on until they came to the seventh house on the left. Then he ran across the front yard and jumped onto a narrow stoop.

Flower beds stretched across the front of the house. The dark dirt of the beds was different from the red clay that peeked through in bare spots beneath two medium-sized trees. Grandma said the soil came from a river bottom. Sometimes Grandma brought cut flowers to Jimmy's house.

Buster ran up to the front door and barked. About the time Jimmy joined him, the door cracked open, and Buster rushed inside for the treat Grandma always gave him before letting him play in the backyard. The squirrels at Grandpa's house spent more time on the ground than the ones behind Jimmy's house and scampered into the trees a split second before the dog arrived.

Grandpa held the door open for Jimmy. When he was a young man, Grandpa had brown hair like his son and grandson, but in the past few years his hair had turned completely white. Not quite as tall as Daddy, Grandpa had wide shoulders, a barrel chest, and hands that still remembered the strength developed during forty years as a lineman and foreman with the Georgia Power Company.

Grandpa stepped onto the stoop and gave Jimmy a big hug. Grandpa's hugs were more than a hello.

"Where's your mama?" Grandpa asked, looking over Jimmy's shoulder.

"She let Buster and me come by ourselves."

At the end of Ridgeview Drive, Mama drove away toward her first stop in town.

"Did you have any problems?" Grandpa asked.

"No, sir."

Grandpa let Jimmy go, but the boy remained close.

"Can I listen?" Jimmy asked.

Ever since Grandpa's heart attack, Jimmy always took time to listen to the old man's heart. Daddy told Jimmy that Grandpa's heart stopped beating at the hospital, and the doctors had to make it start again.

Grandpa stood still, and Jimmy pressed his left ear against Grandpa's chest.

"How does it sound?" Grandpa asked.

"Thump, thump, thump," Jimmy replied.

"That's good. If it ever quits, let me know."

They passed through a small living room. Grandma rarely allowed anyone to sit on the cream-colored couch and matching side chair. Jimmy had watched her dust the furniture and clean the room. She always put everything back in the same place: the big picture book of scenes from the Georgia coast rested in the center of the coffee table, the clear glass balls with decorations inside went in a corner bookcase, the two pieces of cloth that Grandma's mother had woven on a loom covered matching end tables, and the cross-stitch sampler of the alphabet Grandma made when she was a little girl stood on a small stand atop a small desk.

"Are you thirsty?" Grandpa asked. "It's a long, hot walk from your house."

Jimmy felt his forehead. He'd not thought it hot outside, but there were tiny drops of sweat on his brow.

"Yes, sir."

"What would you like?"

Jimmy grinned. "How much is a glass of water?"

"How much do you have?"

Jimmy turned out his pockets. They were empty.

Grandpa frowned. "If you don't have any money for water, I guess you'll have to drink lemonade."

Jimmy followed Grandpa into the kitchen at the rear of the house. Grandma stood at the sink. Through a window beside the kitchen table, Jimmy could see Buster chase a squirrel that zigzagged up the side of a tree and out of reach.

"Good morning, Grandma," he said.

Grandma dried her hands on a dish towel and gave Jimmy a hug. Her hugs were a simple hello.

"Jimmy walked over by himself," Grandpa announced.

"Does your mama know you're here?" Grandma asked in surprise.

"She called earlier this morning and talked to me," Grandpa replied. "You were outside in the garden."

Grandma always wore a dress. She had fancy ones for church; soft, loose ones for inside the house; and older ones for working in her small vegetable garden or flower beds. A little taller and a lot heavier than Jimmy's mama, Grandma spent all her time around her house and the neatly kept yard. On Saturday mornings, she always went to the beauty shop to have her gray hair fixed for church. She poured a glass of lemonade for Jimmy and looked at the clock on the kitchen wall.

"Time for me to go to the beauty shop," she said. "There are fresh-picked tomatoes for you to take home, Jimmy. Will you be here when I get back?"

"Unless we decide to go to California," Grandpa answered.

"Where is that?" Jimmy asked.

"It's where they grow the lemons your grandma used to make that lemonade."

"Let's go," Jimmy said. "I don't have to be home until supper time."

"We couldn't make it," Grandpa said. "California is way past Alabama. I'll get the map and show you."

After Grandma left, Grandpa unrolled a large plastic map of the United States and spread it out on the kitchen table. They'd looked at the map many times. Jimmy liked the different colors. Grandpa said each color was a different state.

"Where do we live?" he asked Jimmy.

Jimmy pointed to a blue rectangle. "But the color is wrong," he said. "Our ground is red."

"Yep," Grandpa replied. "If you'd colored this map, you would have gotten it right. Where is Piney Grove?"

Jimmy peered through his glasses. He knew where to look. He'd put his finger on Piney Grove so many times there was a smudge on the plastic. The name of the town was in the smallest print on the map.

"Here," he said.

Jimmy understood that the dots and lines were cities and roads, but he thought a good map should show houses, cars, and people. Anyone could make a dot or a draw a line, but the buildings along Hathaway Street would be hard.

"Find California," Grandpa said. "It's the name of a state, just like Georgia, so it won't be in little print."

"How do you spell it?"

Grandpa wrote the name on a slip of paper and left the room. Jimmy stared at the map and began moving his finger across the lower states as he looked for the right word. Mississippi, Louisiana, Texas, New Mexico, Arizona. The first time he reached the Pacific Ocean he stopped near San Diego. Returning to the East Coast, he moved up and touched North Carolina, Tennessee, Arkansas, Texas, Colorado, and Utah. He reached the Pacific again when he saw the word—California. Colored light green, California was a lot bigger than Georgia.

"I found it!" he called out.

Grandpa returned with a cup of coffee in his hand. He looked over Jimmy's shoulder.

"That was quick. You're getting better and better at finding things on the map. Do you know how long it would take to drive in a car from Piney Grove to California?"

"No, sir."

"Three days."

Jimmy's eyes grew big. "Have you ever been there?"

"No, but I understand it's beautiful. I guess I'll never get to see it."

Buster scratched at the back door.

"He wants us to come outside and play," Jimmy said.

Grandpa folded up the map, then they went into the big backyard, which ended at a high, thick hedge. Two gray birdbaths sat across from each other on a wooden deck that Jimmy had helped stain. Grandpa set birdhouses all over—some high, some low—for all the different birds that visited the yard. In the summertime, Grandma made peach pies from fruit she picked herself off the two trees.

But the most interesting item in the backyard was a solitary black utility pole.

Forty-five feet tall, the naked black post rose from the ground like a great tree with no branches. No telephone wires or power lines ran to or from it. No security light hung from its top. No basketball goal was nailed to it.

It was a gift. It was a climbing pole.

When Grandpa retired from the Georgia Power Company, the local office wanted to give him a gift. Everyone knew Grandpa loved to fish, so someone said they should buy him a new motor for the little boat he used to take out on the lakes. However, when the engineer in charge of the office asked Grandma what her husband would like as a reminder of his days as a power-company employee, she surprised them all.

"Are you sure?" the engineer asked.

"Yes." She nodded. "A pole in our backyard."

"Nobody thinks a power pole is a decorative addition to their residence," the engineer said. "Everyone wants underground power."

"Not Jim. He thinks they're beautiful. Without those poles, he wouldn't have had a job."

"But are you okay with a power pole in your yard?"

Grandma smiled. "It won't be in the front yard. Put it toward the rear of the lot."

So, shortly after Grandpa left his house for his final day at work, a three-man crew showed up. In a few hours, the men dug a hole, dropped in the pole, tied an enormous red bow around it, and stuck a flare on top. After taking Grandpa to lunch, his fellow workers drove their yellow trucks in a line all the way up Ridgeview Drive and stopped in front of Grandpa's home. Tying a blindfold across Grandpa's eyes, they led him into the backyard. Then they lit the flare and removed the blindfold. Grandpa looked up and laughed.

"How did you know I really wanted one?" he asked Grandma.

"Forty-one years of marriage," she replied without a change of expression.

Grandpa and Jimmy stepped into the yard. Buster abandoned a squirrel and raced up to them.

"You're getting bigger, aren't you?" Grandpa asked Jimmy, patting him on the back.

"Yes, sir."

"Are you ready?" Grandpa asked.

"For what?"

− *Five* −

At the rear of the yard next to the hedge, Grandpa had built a neat wooden shed for his garden tools and John Deere mower. On the inside wall of the shed, he kept his pole-climbing gear. Beneath his climbing hooks, he placed a worn pair of the high-top black boots linemen wore. Since his heart attack, he'd not been up the pole.

When Jimmy was younger, Grandpa gave him rides to the top of the pole. Leaning against the old man's chest with a safety harness wrapped around his waist and legs, Jimmy would rest his hands on the safety belt as Grandpa moved up the surface of the pole. Linemen dig their climbing hooks into the surface of the pole, and Daddy said that in his prime Grandpa could scurry up the pole as nimbly as a monkey after a bunch of bananas. Even in retirement, Grandpa could carry Jimmy to the top of the pole for a panoramic view of Piney Grove in a couple of minutes. As he climbed, Grandpa would slide the safety belt up while leaning back to keep everything snug. The climbing hooks made a crunching sound as they penetrated the black creosote into the pine wood beneath.

"Climbing a pole is like ballet," Grandpa said. "It takes special muscles that you don't use for anything else."

Jimmy wasn't sure about ballet, but he could sense the strength in Grandpa's thighs.

"I've been on poles when it was raining so hard you couldn't see ten feet in any direction, and I've felt the wind try to rip me off the pole and throw me into a dark cloud. Twice, lightning struck within fifty feet of me. Once, a tree fell and hit the pole where I was working, and I found myself wrapped up in the branches."

When Grandpa told stories, Jimmy could see pictures in his head of what had happened.

"I'm glad for bucket trucks," Grandpa said. "But the younger workers never learned to climb like the old hands."

Jimmy never tired of the view from the top of the pole. Over the roof of Grandpa's house, he could see his entire world. To the north lay the steeples of the town's two main churches: the skinny spire of the First Methodist Church and the thicker steeple of the First Baptist Church. The Presbyterians in Piney Grove worshiped in a smaller building without a steeple. Near the Methodist church, Jimmy could see the clock tower for the courthouse.

To the south, three storage silos for the Cattaloochie County Farmers' Co-op reached toward the heavens. Max told Jimmy the silos held rockets ready to blast off into space, but Grandpa said they were filled with corn and soybeans. Beyond the silos lay an open space for the two baseball fields where the Little League teams played. Jimmy liked to throw and catch a ball but didn't play on a team.

To the west, Jimmy saw housetops that peeked above dark green leaves in summer and pale green pine needles all year round. In the far distance, the trees gave way to a broad pasture that rose up a gently sloping hill.

To the east, the smokestack of an abandoned textile mill rose like a sinister red tower. A faint ring of black soot still clung to the bricks at the top of the giant chimney. A row of glass windows just below the roofline of the factory were visible from the top of the pole. Jimmy knew some of the windows were broken, shattered by boys who climbed the high chain-link fence and threw rocks.

Directly below, Jimmy could look down and see the clothes Mrs. Johnson hung on the line to dry and watch Mr. Nevin, a red kerchief around his neck and a broad-brimmed straw hat on his head, hoe his vegetable garden.

Once, when he was nine years old, Jimmy leaned against Grandpa's chest, looked to the north, and saw a Watcher suspended motionless in the air not far from the courthouse clock tower. The Watcher turned and silently nodded at Jimmy. Jimmy started to tell Grandpa, but with a thought the Watcher stopped him.

"Do you want to go down?" Grandpa had asked.

"No, sir," Jimmy replied quietly. "I want to stay a little bit longer."

The Watcher scanned the town, and Jimmy felt something warm, tender, sad, and happy all rolled into one inside his chest. The mix of feelings caused him to want to cry and laugh at the same time. Wondering what it all meant, he kept looking. Grandpa didn't intrude.

Then Jimmy understood. The Watcher cared deeply about the people of Piney Grove—no matter what they looked like or where they lived. Each person was part of a bigger whole: plain, pretty, rich, poor, black, and white. Jimmy took in the whole scene and listened to another kind of heartbeat—the pulse of a small, out-of-the-way town between Atlanta and Birmingham. The Watcher seemed to share the feelings of the people on the ground beneath him. He knew what was happening in Piney Grove. And he cared.

Jimmy glanced toward the red smokestack, and when he looked back, the Watcher was gone. Sometimes when he lay in his bed at night, Jimmy stared at the ceiling and wondered if the Watcher continued to hover overhead.

GRANDPA OPENED THE DOOR OF THE SHED. IT WAS DARK INSIDE.

"Wait here," Grandpa said.

Jimmy heard Buster bark at the discovery of an interesting scent. In a minute, Grandpa emerged and handed Jimmy a smaller version of the old man's work boots.

"Try these on," he said. "I was going to give them to you on your birthday, but today is a better day."

They sat down beside one another on the single step in front of the shed, and Jimmy turned the boots over in his hands. He ran his fingers over the holes for laces at the bottom and the hooks toward the top.

"Thanks, Grandpa," he said.

"Slide your foot in and pull the lower laces tight," Grandpa said. "Then bring them back and forth in front of your leg under those little hooks."

Jimmy nodded. "I've seen you do it."

It took several tries before Jimmy correctly wove the laces through the proper guides. He pulled them tight.

"Do you want me to tie the knot?" Grandpa asked.

"Yes, sir."

Jimmy watched Grandpa's wrinkled fingers make a bow. Jimmy stood up and shifted his feet from side to side.

"How do they feel?" Grandpa asked.

"Different from my other shoes."

"Walk over to the pole and back."

Jimmy walked to the pole. Buster ran up and sniffed the new boots. Jimmy returned and sat down. He rubbed the end of the toe.

"It's hard."

"There is steel in the toe to protect your foot in case something heavy falls on it."

Jimmy nodded, not sure when he might meet such danger.

"Should I wear them when we go fishing?" he asked.

Grandpa stood up.

"No," he replied. "These are pole-climbing boots."

Grandpa came back with his climbing hooks in his hand.

"Would you like to learn how to climb the pole?" he asked.

Jimmy stared at the hooks and then glanced up at Grandpa's face to see if he was joking. Grandpa's face was serious.

"I can't do that," Jimmy answered. "I liked it when you used to give me rides to the top. It was better than anything at the fair."

Grandpa touched his chest. "I promised your grandma that I wouldn't climb anymore, and you're too big to fit in the harness. But that doesn't mean I can't teach you to do it yourself."

"But I don't know how."

"Do you ever climb the tree in your backyard?" Grandpa asked.

Grandpa had nailed two boards to a big tree so Jimmy could climb the thick trunk and reach the lowest limb. From there it was possible to go about eight feet higher and sit on the forked limb that Mama set as Jimmy's limit.

"Yes, sir."

"Are you scared when you're in the tree?"

"No, sir. I'm like you. I'm not afraid of being up high above the ground."

Grandpa nodded. "And you're getting stronger all the time. Before you know it, you'll be stronger than I am."

Jimmy laughed.

"Do you think I'm kidding?"

"Yes, sir."

"Wait and see. I believe you can learn to climb the pole."

Jimmy wasn't sure. He looked across the yard at the pole that now looked more like a black toothpick than the backbone of a sturdy tree.

"No," he began. But then an idea came to him. "If I learn how to climb the pole, could I work for the Georgia Power Company when I grow up?"

It was Grandpa's turn to pause. "I can't promise you a job, but you would be able to do something most other boys can't do. Can any of your friends climb a pole?"

"No, sir."

"And just think about how much you'd enjoy being high in the air with a breeze blowing in your face."

"Could I see the top of the church?"

"Yes, but you don't have to go higher than you want. You can take it easy at your own pace. We'll practice when you come over to visit me."

"Will you be with me?"

"Always."

Jimmy pressed his lips together in determination. "Okay."

Grandpa sat down beside him. "Very good. First, I'll show you how to attach the climbing hooks to your boots."

AN HOUR LATER, GRANDPA SOAKED HIS FEET IN A HOT BASIN of Epsom salts. Even though Jimmy didn't get more than six inches from the ground, the training session left the old man worn out. He let out a long sigh.

"Your grandma will be back in a minute. Let's keep your pole-climbing practice to ourselves," he said.

"What do you mean?"

"Don't tell anyone what we're doing. That way it can be a surprise to everyone when you make it to the top."

Jimmy was sitting on a low stool in the kitchen. Grandpa's white feet were bumpy and covered with blue veins.

"Can I ask Mama what she thinks?" Jimmy asked.

"No, we'll surprise her too. You can pretend it's like a Christmas present."

Jimmy hesitated. "I tell Mama everything. She always knows what I'm going to give her for Christmas, and she tells me what to get Daddy."

Grandpa wiggled his toes. "I know it's hard for you to keep quiet, but give me a chance to mention it to her first. Can you keep a secret until then?"

"Yes, sir," Jimmy replied slowly.

Grandma, fresh from her appointment at the beauty parlor, walked into the kitchen. Every gray hair was in place, and her head shone like silver.

"All tired out?" she asked Grandpa. "What did you boys do?"

"A little of this and that," the old man replied quickly. "And it takes less of this and not much of that to wear me out."

JIMMY AND BUSTER CROSSED THE INTERSECTION TWO BLOCKS from home. The setting sun cast long shadows across the sidewalk. Jimmy was tired too. But it was a good tired—the kind of fatigue that felt satisfying. He reached the last stop sign before his street. When he looked to his left, he saw a police car. The officer rolled down his window.

It was Deputy Askew.

He took off his hat, revealing a square head and short dark hair cut like a soldier's. He removed his sunglasses. Jimmy grew serious. He knew what he needed to do.

"I'm sorry I didn't help you clean your car this morning," he began. "Mama and Daddy didn't think I should come today because Sheriff Brinson is mad at me for talking in court. I should have kept my mouth shut."

"Get in the car," the deputy said. "Buster too."

His head hanging down, Jimmy walked around the car and opened the passenger door. Buster jumped in and curled up on the floorboard.

On the seat beside Deputy Askew lay a folded copy of the Saturday edition of the *Piney Grove Press*, the local newspaper printed on Wednesday and Saturday afternoons. The deputy pointed at the paper.

"Have you seen today's paper?" he asked.

"No, sir. I don't read the paper. I've been with my grandpa."

"There is an article on the front page about your testimony at the Garner trial."

Jimmy swallowed hard. "Are you mad at me too?"

"No, of course not," the deputy said. "I just wanted to talk to you. I had no idea you could remember everything you hear."

"I don't remember everything," Jimmy responded. "If I could do that I would be in the smart class at school."

"Well, I think you're smart in a lot of ways," Deputy Askew replied. "And if anyone says differently, tell them to come to me. But I'm curious about your testimony. Can you repeat what you said in court?"

"Will I get in more trouble?"

"No."

"Do you promise?" Jimmy's palms were slick.

Deputy Askew turned in his seat. "I promise."

Jimmy looked into the deputy's eyes.

"Okay. What part? I had to talk a lot."

"The conversation between the sheriff and Detective Milligan about Jake Garner."

Jimmy looked straight ahead out the window and repeated the words he heard in the jailhouse parking lot. When he finished, he looked over at Deputy Askew. The officer's eyes were wide open.

"That beats all," he said. "I could almost hear the sheriff's voice."

"Me too," Jimmy replied.

Deputy Askew refolded the paper and placed in on the seat.

"Are there other conversations you remember?"

"Yes, sir."

"Does it happen a lot?"

"Sometimes."

"Can you tell me another example?"

"Of what?"

"A conversation you remember."

Jimmy reached down and patted Buster on the head. "Uncle Bart promised Aunt Jill that he would take her to Panama City. That one got me into trouble too."

"Why?"

"Because I repeated the promise. He made it when we were eating dinner at their house before Christmas. He told her that if she got him a piece of apple pie with ice cream on it, he'd take her to Panama City."

"Did he admit it after you reminded him of the conversation?"

"What do you mean?"

"Did he say you were right?"

"Yes, sir. And Mama told me yesterday that Uncle Bart, Aunt Jill, and my cousin Walt are going to Panama City for a week as soon as school is out for the summer."

Deputy Askew chuckled. "Do you remember what we talked about last week when I took you to get an ice cream at the Stop-n-Go?"

"No, sir, but I ate a banana Popsicle, and you ate an ice-cream bar. I told you 'thank you' because you paid for it."

"That's right. We talked about fishing for carp at Webb's Pond. You wouldn't tell me the bait mixture your grandpa uses when he's fishing in tournaments."

Buster put his front paws on the seat and looked up at Jimmy. "I don't remember about the bait because he uses different kinds. When can I come back to the jail and help wash cars?"

Deputy Askew shook his head. "I'm sorry, Jimmy, but your parents are right. It's better for you to wait until we find out what's going to happen with Sheriff Brinson."

Jimmy's sadness felt worse than it had that morning. "See, I wish I'd kept my mouth shut and not gone to court."

"No, you needed to tell what you heard. Not enough people come forward and tell the truth."

"But what about washing the cars?"

"I promise to let you know as soon as it's okay to come back. You do a great job on my car. You don't think I want to lose that, do you?"

"I guess not."

"Good. I'll give you and Buster a ride home."

When they pulled into the Mitchell driveway, Jimmy opened the door, and Buster jumped out of the car.

"Thanks for the ride," Jimmy said.

"You bet." The deputy paused. "Here, turn on the siren for a second."

Jimmy's eyes opened wide. "Are you sure?"

"Yes. It's my way of showing you that I'm not mad at you."

Jimmy flicked the switch, and the car wailed. It sounded strange so close to his house.

"I'll call you as soon as it's okay to come back," the deputy added.

Jimmy got out of the car and leaned over. "And I promise to do a better job on the inside of your car."

Jimmy shut the door, and the deputy backed out of the driveway. Jimmy waved.

"JIMMY LEE MITCHELL! GET UP HERE THIS SECOND!"

Jimmy turned and saw Mama standing on the front porch with her hands on her hips and a frown on her face. He ran toward the porch. Buster joined him and jumped up the steps beside him.

"Why on earth did someone from the sheriff's department bring you home and turn on the siren? I didn't know what had happened to you. I knew I shouldn't have let you walk over to your grandparents' house by yourself."

Mama paused for a breath.

"It was Deputy Askew," Jimmy began.

"I would have thought your grandpa would bring you home in his truck."

"He was soaking his feet in water."

"That's what towels are for. Where did the deputy find you?"

Jimmy hesitated, then took Mama by the hand. She initially pulled away but then allowed him to guide her down the steps.

"What are you doing now?" she asked in frustration.

"I'm going to show you."

Jimmy held on to her hand until they reached the sidewalk, then he pointed down the street to the stop sign in the distance.

"I was at that stop sign. I looked both ways before crossing the street, and Deputy Askew drove up and told me to get in the car. You told me to obey policemen."

"Were you lost?"

"No, ma'am, and Buster wasn't either."

"But the siren."

"He let me turn it on to show that he's not mad at me." Jimmy paused. "Why are you mad at me?"

Mama sighed and shook her head. "I was worried, and then I heard the siren."

"I don't understand."

Mama hugged him. "It's my mistake. Come into the house and have a snack."

DADDY SAID THAT SUNDAY MORNING WAS THE QUIETEST TIME of the week in Piney Grove. No buzz of lawn mower engines announced the new day. Grass could be cut on six days, but on the seventh it grew without fear of a whirling blade. Neither the thud of hammers nor the buzz of electric saws awakened those who wanted to sleep late, because household chores not finished by Saturday night were postponed until another day. Traffic, even on the main streets, remained sparse until shortly before the time for Sunday school to start.

The Mitchell household had a Sunday routine different from any other day of the week. Daddy rose early and drank two cups of coffee while he read the Sunday edition of the *Atlanta Journal Constitution*. He never finished the paper before church but read enough not to be caught off guard by any discussion that cropped up between Sunday school and the morning worship service.

Mama didn't go to the beauty parlor every Saturday like Grandma, but she spent extra time getting ready. Jimmy rarely saw her until Daddy called upstairs in a loud voice that it was time to go. Even on the hottest days, Mama always looked fresh and cool in the colorful dresses she wore on Sundays. Like most women in Piney Grove, she didn't leave the house on Sunday morning without making sure that she looked her best for everyone in church, and God too.

The Mitchell family attended the First Baptist Church of Piney Grove. Daddy said Baptists were the only denomination mentioned in the Holy Bible and proved it by reading about a cousin of Jesus named John the Baptist. Jimmy couldn't understand why everyone wasn't a Baptist. He didn't think badly of other Christians, but it puzzled him why anyone would go to a different kind of church.

Grandpa didn't go to church, but Grandma had taken Daddy to First Baptist since he was born. Mama was also a Baptist whose father had been a minister in Georgia.

Jimmy slept later than usual on Sundays. When he got out of bed, he kept his pajamas on until after breakfast. He didn't want to risk spilling orange juice or cereal on his church clothes. While eating, he sat with Daddy and looked at the pictures in the paper. Jimmy could read many of the words on the page but didn't always understand the meaning of the articles. And when Daddy was reading, Jimmy knew better than to ask questions.

Mama laid out Jimmy's Sunday clothes before she went to bed on Saturday night. Every male twelve years and older who attended First Baptist wore a coat and tie. Little boys could get by with nice shorts in the summertime, but the men and teenage boys wore a suit jacket even when the temperature and humidity topped ninety. Fortunately, the deacons at the church made sure there was plenty of cool air blowing through the vents.

Jimmy held his comb underneath the faucet in the bathroom sink and then carefully combed his hair. He worked hard to persuade a few stubborn strands of his cowlick to lie down and behave. Next, he carefully buttoned his shirt, matching each button with the correct hole. Many times he hurried and realized too late that he had an extra button when he reached his collar and had to start all over.

After slipping on his pants and shoes, he stood in front of a long mirror in his bedroom and added a tie. Jimmy didn't know how to tie a necktie, but he had two clip-ons: one covered with squiggly creatures that Mama told him were paisleys, and the other decorated with multiple images of the scowling bulldog who was the mascot for the University of Georgia. Jimmy liked the bulldog tie better, but Mama usually told him to wear the paisley one.

Ready for inspection, Jimmy came downstairs. Daddy, dressed in a dark gray suit with a white shirt and striped tie, was sitting in the foyer and reading the business section. Daddy had a long row of suits in his closet, but they all looked alike and weren't nearly as interesting as Jimmy's hats.

"How do I look?" Jimmy asked, standing straight.

Daddy looked him up and down. "Fine, except you forgot to put on a belt."

Jimmy felt the empty loops and ran back upstairs to find the thin black belt he wore on Sundays. It wasn't on its hook in his closet. He stepped out of the closet and looked around his room. Mama had taught him to ask a simple question when something was lost.

"Where are you hiding?" he spoke into the empty room.

He looked underneath his bed and on the shelves where he kept the different-colored rocks he collected. There was no sign of the belt.

"Where would I put a belt?" he asked next.

He pressed his lips together to help him think. He glanced back in his closet and saw a pair of pants with a dark tail hanging down. He took out the pants and found his belt in the loops of a pair of pants he'd worn to a special assembly at school. In triumph, he pulled it out. He met Mama in the hallway as he left his room. She was wearing a dress with a lot of green and yellow in it. Her shoes made her taller than usual.

"You look like sunshine in the woods this morning," he said brightly.

She smiled and kissed the top of his head. "And you are a very handsome young man with his cowlick under control."

They walked downstairs together. Daddy stood.

"I found my belt," Jimmy announced.

"Good," Daddy said, opening the front door for Mama.

"Where are we eating dinner today?" Jimmy asked.

"With Uncle Bart and Aunt Jill," Daddy said.

Jimmy slowed his steps, and the smile left his face. "Will Walt be there?"

"Of course," Mama answered as she walked down the steps.

– Six –

The First Baptist Church boasted a large red brick sanctuary and high portico held aloft by four massive white columns. The church didn't have to advertise its presence in Piney Grove. Anyone passing through town would see it. Next to the sanctuary was a long, two-story educational building.

The church buildings occupied a whole block on the south side of Hathaway Street. Parking lots stretched all the way to a narrow alley. Basketball goals stood at the end of each parking lot. Because the church buildings were used only a few hours a week, the parking lots served as community basketball courts. Bright lights came on every evening at dusk and burned until midnight so that the youth of Piney Grove could play basketball. Vandalism in the parking lots wasn't a problem—the sheriff's office and jail were on the next block and provided twenty-four-hour security at taxpayer expense.

Daddy parked in the lot behind the educational building. His usual place was taken, and he had to move farther away.

"Why is it so crowded?" he asked.

"A missionary from Papua New Guinea is the guest speaker in the couples' class," Mama replied. "She's a Bible translator."

"I bet she'll have a few worm-and-grub stories." Daddy grunted as he pulled into a parking space.

"What kind of stories?" Jimmy asked.

"She's been living in a very poor country," Mama answered.

"Even worse than Alabama," Daddy added.

Mama ignored him. "Missionaries are men and women who go to other countries to tell the people about Jesus."

55

"What does that have to do with worms?" Jimmy asked.

"Some of the people in other countries eat worms and grubs," Daddy said. "They don't see anything wrong with it because they've grown up eating them."

"Walt tried to make me eat an earthworm," Jimmy replied. "But I told him it was for fishing, not eating."

Daddy opened the car door. "Good boy. If Walt ever offers you an earthworm or anything else strange to eat, tell me about it."

Still thinking about worms, Jimmy followed his parents into the educational building.

The inside of the building was as familiar to Jimmy as the hallways of the elementary school. He'd begun in the nursery, progressed to the crawler area, navigated through the toddler zone, and graduated into the prekindergarten and kindergarten classes. As the biggest church in town, First Baptist had a class for each grade level. The same children who went to school with Jimmy Monday through Friday joined him for Bible class on Sunday.

The sixth-grade class was located on the second floor. When Jimmy graduated to the seventh grade, he would stay on the main floor in a room by the nursery. Daddy and Mama's class met in the fellowship hall. Jimmy climbed the steps to the second floor. Inside his classroom, he saw his friend Max staring out the window at the parking lot. No one else had arrived.

Tall and sturdy with blond hair and clear blue eyes, Max Cochran was smart and good at sports. The two boys first played together because the babysitter who took care of Jimmy after his other mama left town was a friend of Max's mom. Max had been Jimmy's best friend for as long as Jimmy could remember.

Max always saved a seat for Jimmy at lunchtime and picked Jimmy to be on his team at recess. He played at Jimmy's house a lot and sometimes invited Jimmy to spend the night at his home. Like Grandpa, Max always treated Jimmy as a normal member of the human race. Recently, Mama had prayed with Jimmy that the boys' friendship would never stop.

Max turned around and looked at Jimmy through a perfectly formed black eye. Jimmy's mouth dropped open.

"What happened?" he asked.

"I was playing first base yesterday, and Mitch threw the ball to me between innings when I wasn't looking. It knocked me to the ground."

Jimmy peered closer. "Does it still hurt?"

"Yeah, but not as bad as it did."

Other students began to arrive, and Jimmy listened as Max told the story several more times. More information came out, including the fact that his father made him hold a piece of raw steak against the eye for over an hour.

"And then he cooked the steak on the grill, and I ate it," Max added. "Eating the steak made the swelling go down."

"That's ridiculous," responded Denise McMillan, the daughter of a local doctor.

"You didn't see it before and after," Max said.

Mr. Morton, the Sunday school teacher, entered the room with a red, sweaty face. A chubby, balding man who worked for a local auto dealer as a credit manager, he wiped the perspiration from his forehead. Mr. Morton knew a fair amount about the Bible and a lot about old cars.

"Air conditioner went out on the car," he said.

Before Mr. Morton became their teacher, none of the students had ever heard of the Studebaker Motor Company. Mr. Morton quickly corrected their ignorance and one sunny autumn day took them on a brief field trip down to the church parking lot in order to provide an up close look at a 1964 Lark convertible the teacher had beautifully restored. He then spent the rest of the class period showing pictures taken during the restoration process and explained that his work transforming the broken-down car was like the work God wanted to do in their lives too.

"Do the air conditioners in Studebakers break a lot?" one of the students asked.

"It's not my Studebaker," he replied. "It's my wife's new Ford."

Mr. Morton saw Max's eye, and the baseball story, without reference to eating the steak, was repeated one last time. Mr. Morton placed his large black Bible on the flimsy wooden stand.

"Besides Max's eye, do we have any prayer requests?"

There were always lots. Jimmy tried to listen closely to what the students mentioned so he could tell Mama about the requests. He raised his hand.

"What is it, Jimmy?" Mr. Morton asked.

"Do we have any prayer answers?" he asked.

Several children laughed, but Mr. Morton didn't.

"That's a good question. Who can remember a prayer request from last week and tell us about an answer?"

There was silence for several seconds. Jimmy waited and then raised his hand again.

"I do," he said.

"What is it?" Mr. Morton asked.

"My grandpa didn't have another heart attack."

Praying for Grandpa's heart was one of Jimmy's regular requests. Mama told him each day of Grandpa's life was a gift from God.

"That's an answer," Mr. Morton replied.

The teacher waited a few more seconds and then opened the lesson book.

"I have one," Denise said hesitantly.

Tears rushed into the young girl's eyes. She reached into her purse for a tissue. Everyone in the class grew still.

"I'm sorry," she stammered. "But you know that my older brother left home a year ago, and we haven't heard from him in ten months. Last night he called and talked to my parents. He's coming home this week."

Jimmy had heard Mama talk about Denise's brother, Sam, who developed a serious drug problem during his senior year in high school and ran away from home. The public humiliation in the family of a physician sent shock waves through the small town.

Denise sniffled. "He's been in a drug-treatment center for four weeks after he got saved at a church in New Orleans. My dad is leaving tomorrow to pick him up."

One of Denise's friends came over and put her arm around Denise's shoulders. Jimmy wasn't sure why Denise was crying. Mama had told him there were good tears and sad tears, but he had trouble knowing the difference. Denise looked up at Mr. Morton and continued.

"Last night my dad read the story about the prodigal son, and our whole family prayed for Sam."

Mr. Morton opened his Bible. "Let's read that passage right now."

It was a different Sunday school class. After the children listened to the story, they mentioned the names of family members who needed to come home to Jesus. Mr. Morton wrote the names on a board at the front of the room.

When the flow of names stopped, Mr. Morton spoke.

"I'd like to tell you how I came to believe in Jesus."

The children grew quiet. Jimmy had heard many adults give testimonies, especially at Sunday night meetings before someone was baptized. Sometimes he didn't understand the sins described by them, but Mama wouldn't explain.

"I grew up in Florida," Mr. Morton began. "My father died when I was twelve years old. My mother and I didn't go to church, but a man who worked with her invited me to go deep-sea fishing in the Gulf of Mexico with him, his two sons, and three of their friends. We caught a bunch of fish. None of them were very big, but we didn't care as long as we had something on the line to reel in."

"How far out did you go?" Max asked.

"About ten miles. We weren't trying to land any game fish, just something for boys to catch."

The thought of being in a boat ten miles from shore made Jimmy's stomach uneasy. He wanted to hear the story but wished it had happened on land.

Mr. Morton continued. "When we took a break from fishing, he asked us all to sit down in the back of the boat while he told how Jesus had changed his life. His story was so much like mine—no father in the house, feeling different from other boys, not enough money to buy the things a child wanted—that I felt like I was looking in the mirror. But then he said everything changed when he asked Jesus to forgive his sins and take control of his life. The anger left, the bitterness went away, and he felt love on the inside. I'd never realized all that was wrong with me until he mentioned his own feelings. When he asked if anyone wanted to pray and ask Jesus to come into his heart, I raised my hand."

Mr. Morton opened his Bible and read a story about fishing. Jimmy knew Jesus' disciples liked to go fishing. He'd seen the pictures in Bible storybooks. The disciples used nets instead of hooks, which seemed like an impossible way to catch fish. It was hard enough to convince a big carp to latch on to a hook carefully prepared with Grandpa's secret mix, much less sneak up on a bunch of fish with a big black net. Fishermen in Piney Grove lied about the fish they caught all the time, but Jimmy knew the fishing stories in the Holy Bible had to be true; otherwise they wouldn't be included in the book. Mr. Morton finished and closed his Bible.

"That day the man who took me fishing caught more than fish; he caught me."

Denise raised her hand. "Is that why you're teaching our class?"

Mr. Morton smiled. "I can't think of a better reason."

The bell signaling the end of the Sunday school hour chimed.

"One other thing before we have our closing prayer," Mr. Morton said. "Does anybody want to guess the kind of car the man who prayed with me drove?"

"A Studebaker!" several students cried out.

After Sunday school, Jimmy walked downstairs and peeked into the fellowship hall. He couldn't see Mama or Daddy. The missionary, a small, thin woman with short gray hair, stood at the front of the room praying. Jimmy stepped back against the wall, and in a few seconds the people from the class poured into the hallway. Everyone who attended the First Baptist Church knew Jimmy. Several smiled and spoke to him as they passed by. Others patted him on the head. Mama and Daddy came out toward the back of the crowd. Jimmy held out his hand to Mama, who took it in hers. He still liked to hold Mama's hand, especially when a lot of people were around. Mama's hand always felt cool and inviting.

"How was your class?" she asked.

"Good. Did you know Denise's brother is coming home?" he asked.

"Yes, her mother told me," Mama said.

"She started crying when she talked about it. Were those good tears?"

"Yes. Her brother's life has totally turned around."

They continued down the hallway. Jimmy glanced up at Daddy.

"Did the woman talk about eating worms?"

"It was worse than I'd expected," Daddy answered in a serious voice. "She described these squirmy green critters that came wrapped up in a banana leaf. They had a little bit of fuzz on them, and I bet they tickled her throat when—"

"Enough, Lee," Mama interrupted.

They went outside. The prickly heat of the day was just beginning to simmer around the edges. The sidewalk was filled with families in their Sunday best. Low-cut bushes kept everyone in line as they flowed toward the broad steps leading to the sanctuary. Children weren't allowed to run around between Sunday school and church, so each family formed its own cluster. Jimmy looked for Grandma's gray head but didn't see her. Grandpa only came to church at Christmas and Easter.

The sanctuary of the First Baptist Church was one of the cleanest places in Jimmy's world. The white walls didn't have a smudge or a crack, and the deep burgundy carpet softly gave way beneath his feet. The air itself smelled extra clean. The church didn't have stained-glass windows. Tall, narrow windows made of creamy-colored glass rose toward the high ceiling. Four massive chandeliers hung from the ceiling. Rows of white pews with the top and side railings stained a light brown marched toward the raised platform, where the pulpit waited for the preacher. Behind the pulpit was a broad choir loft. Mama used to sing in the choir, but after the new choir director arrived, she'd started sitting with Jimmy and Daddy. Jimmy liked having her close to him.

The baptismal pool above the choir loft hid behind a sliding wall. Hope Springs, the other big Baptist church in town, had trees, bushes, and a river painted on the wall behind its baptismal pool. Jimmy's family had visited the church for weddings and funerals, and Jimmy liked the picture, but Daddy rejected his suggestion that their church should paint a similar scene.

The Mitchell family always sat slightly more than halfway toward the front on the left side of the sanctuary. The pews weren't numbered, but Jimmy didn't have to count the rows to know their spot. When it felt right, he turned into the pew. He always sat between Mama and Daddy. Grandma sat next to Daddy. The Roberts family sat in the other half of their pew. Their two children, twin girls, went to college in Atlanta, but no one filled in the gaps in case the daughters came home for a visit.

The pews were padded. Jimmy liked to run his finger around the edge of the fabric buttons that dotted the burgundy pads. Once, he found a loose button that popped off when he barely touched it. Jimmy tried to replace it by pressing down hard, but Mama saw what happened and told one of the deacons about it. The next week the button was sewn back on the cushion. Jimmy felt better when everything in God's house was perfect.

Brother Fitzgerald always stepped into the pulpit to begin preaching at exactly 11:30 a.m.

Daddy leaned over and whispered to Mama, "How does he always hit it right on the dot? He's more reliable than an atomic clock."

Jimmy enjoyed the preaching. It wasn't the message as much as the messenger that kept him focused. Brother Fitzgerald's face and voice revealed what he wanted to say even more clearly than his words. He could twist his face in pain or smile so big that Jimmy could see his teeth. The preacher might speak in a whisper one second and then shout so loud that Jimmy jumped in his seat. Jimmy didn't always understand the words, but the preacher's feelings came through loud and clear. Today he was preaching about a man named John, who, like the missionary lady, ate bugs.

"Is that John the first Baptist?" Jimmy asked Daddy.

"Yes, the original article."

Jimmy sat up to pay closer attention. Brother Fitzgerald reached the climax of his message with loud cries for repentance.

"And if you don't repent, you will all perish!" he thundered, and then he stopped to let the words find their mark.

"He's not really mad," Jimmy whispered to Daddy. "He's having fun."

"I know. Be quiet."

The sermon lasted until 12:10 p.m. and was followed by the altar call. Several people went forward to the front of the church. Some cried; others seemed happy. The choir continued to sing as Brother Fitzgerald called for more people to come forward. Daddy flipped through his Bible and checked his watch.

Jimmy's mind left the sanctuary and wandered past Mr. Morton's fishing story to images of fuzzy green worms eaten by white-haired missionaries and crunchy locusts dipped in wild honey.

— Seven —

After the final *amen*, the sanctuary immediately echoed with a hundred conversations. Even folks in a hurry allowed a few minutes to tell their neighbors hello. Anything less would have been rude.

Daddy left the pew and went outside, where he usually spent time with his friends under one of the large trees. Jimmy felt more comfortable beside Mama. Standing in a group of men and not knowing what to say made him nervous. He waited patiently while Mama worked out a schedule to provide meals to a family with a sick mother in the hospital. He followed her down the aisle into the bright sunshine.

"Go get your daddy," she said. "We need to get the food out of the oven and take it to Uncle Bart's house as soon as possible. The Methodists have been out at least twenty minutes. Your aunt Jill will be miles ahead of me in getting dinner ready."

"Yes, ma'am."

Jimmy found Daddy talking to Mr. Robinson and two other lawyers who attended the church. Jimmy's hope that he could pull on Daddy's sleeve unnoticed proved hollow.

"Here comes the witness now!" Mr. Robinson exclaimed.

Without his black robe, the judge looked like an ordinary person. "What did you think about my courtroom?" he asked.

Jimmy thought for a moment and tried to give an answer that would make Daddy proud of him. "Uh, it had pews and made me think about the church."

One of the lawyers slapped the judge on the back and raised his eyes toward the sky. "If only more people viewed the halls of justice with the same reverence they do the sanctuary of the Almighty."

"The boy is right," Mr. Robinson shot back. "And I'll expect you to start showing proper reverence or find yourself in contempt. I may not be able to send you to a place of eternal punishment, but I can make you regret your stay on earth. What else did you notice about court?" the judge asked Jimmy.

"Uh, I think it would be nice if you had a red coat."

"What does he mean?" Mr. Robinson asked Daddy.

Jimmy wanted to shrink into the ground.

"He means a red robe. It would give the court a little variety."

"That could be fixed easily enough," the other lawyer replied. "The judge could join the choir and use the same robe on Sunday and the rest of the week."

Mr. Robinson shook his head. "A good idea, but my singing voice is perpetually trapped between two notes with no way to get out."

Jimmy pulled on Daddy's sleeve. "Mama says it's time to go."

"There is the true voice of authority in our society, gentlemen," Mr. Robinson said. "I may hold sway in my courtroom for a few hours a week, but what is that compared to the perennial power of a woman?"

Jimmy and Daddy found Mama talking to Grandma.

When Jimmy came close, he heard Mama say, "We need a plan. I'll talk to you later in the week."

They got into the car, and Daddy turned the air conditioner up as high as it would go. Jimmy glanced sideways and saw Mr. Morton leave the parking lot with his car window down and a red kerchief pressed against his brow. People leaving the church caused five minutes of busy traffic on the otherwise empty streets.

They drove home but didn't change clothes. Sunday dinner with relatives was part of the day's religious activities, and everyone wore nice clothes. Only after the dessert plates were carried to the kitchen did the men take off their jackets and go into the den to watch sports on TV.

Jimmy held the front door open while Mama carried out hot casseroles. Daddy arranged the dishes in a large cardboard box in the trunk of the car and wedged them in with towels to keep them from sliding around and spilling.

It took about five minutes to drive to Uncle Bart and Aunt Jill's house. Daddy pulled into the driveway and parked in front of the two-car garage. Several other cars were in the driveway.

"Look at Bart's lawn," Mama said. "It's so green."

"He put in a sprinkler system that runs at night," Daddy responded.

"Does Walt cut the grass?" Jimmy asked.

"No, his father hired a company to do it."

As they walked to the front door, Jimmy spoke to Mama.

"Can I stay with you? I don't want to play with Walt."

"You have been getting along fine recently, and I'm sure you don't want to hurt his feelings. I'll make sure not to let you wander off together."

"Sometimes he's nice, but mostly he's mean."

"I'll keep an eye out for you," Mama said. "Have a good attitude."

Jimmy followed his parents.

"Do you want to ring the doorbell?" Mama asked.

"No, ma'am."

Aunt Jill opened the door. She was taller and heavier than Mama with blond hair and brown eyes. Uncle Bart, Mama's younger brother, shared his sister's reddish-brown hair but had a bigger nose.

"Come in," Aunt Jill beckoned. "Everyone else is here."

Inside were friends whom Uncle Bart and Aunt Jill considered close enough to invite for Sunday dinner. In addition to the adults, there were several very small children and three teenage girls. Walt wasn't in sight. None of the other guests were relatives of the Mitchells. Jimmy kept close to Mama's side during the round of greetings and hugs.

"Where's Walt?" he whispered.

Mama glanced around and then turned to Uncle Bart, who was carrying a basket of rolls to the dining room table. "Bart, where is Walt?"

"Upstairs in his room. He's being punished until we sit down to eat."

Jimmy wanted to know what his cousin had done wrong, but Uncle Bart offered no explanation.

There were three tables set up for the meal: adults only, children who could eat unsupervised, and children who needed parental assistance. Jimmy, the teenage girls, and Walt were in the second group.

When the food was ready, Uncle Bart called upstairs. "Walt! Come eat!"

There was no answer. Everyone grew quiet. Uncle Bart walked partway up the stairs.

"Walt! Can you hear me? Come eat!"

Walt appeared at the top of the stairs and slowly came down. He was a male version of his mother, tall and slightly overweight with sandy-blond hair. He would be a junior at the high school in the fall.

"Walt, you've grown an inch or two in the past month," Daddy said. "Has Coach Nixon seen you recently?"

"Football bores me," Walt answered.

"I've tried to encourage him," Uncle Bart said. "In a few months he could bulk up enough to make varsity. He's a lot stronger than he realizes. His arms are busting out of his shirt."

Jimmy looked at Walt's arms. They were definitely getting bigger. Jimmy knew that special boys weren't allowed to play high school football; however, Daddy had told him that he might be able to serve as a manager. Jimmy wasn't sure what that meant, but Daddy had promised to explain it to him during the upcoming season. The Mitchell family, like many residents of Cattaloochie County, never missed a Friday night game.

Daddy spoke. "In my day, it would have taken a medical excuse for a big healthy boy like you to avoid going out for football."

"I like football," Jimmy added in a soft voice.

"Then why don't you play?" Walt asked.

"Walt!" Uncle Bart said. "Do you want to go back upstairs?"

Walt didn't answer but walked past his father toward the kitchen. Daddy and Uncle Bart moved toward their seats at the table for grown-ups. Mama helped Jimmy pour a glass of iced tea. He took it to a table set up in a wide hallway between the dining room and den. A hand gripped his left arm.

"What's up, squirt?" Walt asked.

Jimmy didn't answer. He tried to pull away. Walt's grip tightened, and he spoke into Jimmy's ear.

"Don't ignore me when I'm talking to you. It's not good manners."

Jimmy looked for Mama, but the adults were not in sight.

"Stop it," Jimmy said. "I want to get my food and eat."

Walt released his hold. "Of course; we'll go together."

Jimmy knew it was useless to complain. Adults had decided that Walt would be his tablemate, and there was nothing he could do about it.

Dinner was served buffet-style with the smaller children going first. Mama helped Jimmy fill his plate.

"Walt is in a bad mood," Jimmy whispered after his cousin had left the line.

"That's because he got in trouble before we arrived. It will be better after we eat." Jimmy sighed and went back to his table.

"Do you want me to cut up your meat?" Walt asked.

"No, thank you," Jimmy said.

Walt picked up the table knife and rubbed it against his thumb. "Are you safe to use this? You might cut yourself."

"No. I have a real knife at home."

"I'd like to see it. I can do lots of things with knives."

"I'd have to ask Mama. It's not a toy."

Walt leaned over close and said, "I know you're a mama's boy, but there isn't anything wrong with that. I think it's kind of cute."

One of the girls at the table spoke to Walt, and they began to talk about school. Jimmy wasn't very hungry, but he picked away at his food, keeping his head down and trying to think about something happy, like washing Deputy Askew's car. He finished eating without any more trouble from Walt, who seemed to like talking to the girls.

Aunt Jill rang a little bell, signaling that the dessert table was open. Jimmy didn't need Mama's help in choosing dessert. Everyone rushed into the room, creating momentary chaos around the banana pudding bowl. Jimmy liked Aunt Jill's banana pudding but didn't try to force his way to the large round container. He waited his turn and took a piece of Mama's pineapple upside-down cake along with a thin sliver of German chocolate cake. He stopped by to show Mama his plate.

"How are you doing with Walt?" she asked.

"Okay," he answered. "Are we going to stay a long time?"

Mama patted him on the arm. "We can't eat and run. It would be bad manners."

Jimmy had an idea. "Can I help clean the dishes?"

Mama looked down at the nice china. "You would have to be very careful."

"I'll hold each one with both hands," Jimmy promised.

"We'll see. Go enjoy your dessert. Thanks for selecting my cake."

Jimmy returned to the table. Walt had a massive portion of banana pudding that threatened to spill onto the tablecloth. He looked at Jimmy's plate.

"Hey, I can't eat all this. Why don't you have some?"

"Uh, thanks."

Walt scraped some pudding onto Jimmy's plate. Jimmy saw a salt shaker near Walt's hand and took a small bite of the pudding. Several times in the past, Walt had given Jimmy bad food and then laughed at his reaction. Today it tasted fine.

"What do you want to do after we eat?" Walt asked.

"I'm going to help with the dishes."

"Are you in trouble?"

"No."

"Then skip it."

Jimmy didn't answer. He finished his dessert and took his plate into the kitchen. Aunt Jill, wearing a white apron trimmed in pink, stood at the sink scraping excess food down the disposal.

"I'm here to help," Jimmy announced.

Jill looked over her shoulder. "That's sweet, Jimmy, but the ladies will take care of it. You'll just be in the way. Check with Walt. I'm sure he has something you can do together."

Jimmy remained planted in the middle of the kitchen floor.

"I'm here to help," he repeated. "I'll be careful not to break anything."

Aunt Jill dried her hands on her apron and turned toward him.

"No, thank you," she said in a voice that left no room for debate.

Walt stuck his head in the kitchen door. "There you are. I told you not to mess with the dishes. You'll break more than you clean."

"Don't be mean," Aunt Jill said. "You should offer to help sometime."

Mama came into the kitchen.

"Jimmy wanted to clean the plates, but I told him to go have fun," Aunt Jill said.

"I'll read to him," Walt suggested.

"Go ahead," Mama said. "I'll help clean up."

"Come up to my room," Walt said.

Jimmy followed his cousin upstairs. Walt had a large bedroom. He, like Jimmy, did not have any brothers or sisters. A computer workstation filled one corner of the room. A large-screen TV with surround-sound speakers sat in another.

"How does it feel being retarded?" Walt asked as soon as they entered the bedroom. "I mean, what is it like to be inside your stupid head?"

Jimmy stopped. "I'm going to tell Mama what you said."

Walt stepped around him and blocked the door. "I'm kidding. Can't you take a joke?"

Jimmy wanted to push the larger boy aside.

"Be nice, or I'll tell," he responded.

Walt held up his hands. "I'm terrified."

Walt closed the door and locked it. He opened the bottom drawer of his computer desk and took out several magazines. He flipped through them and handed one to Jimmy.

"This is a good one," Walt said.

Jimmy pulled back at the picture on the cover. A huge man with a bloody board in his hand stood over another huge man lying on the floor. Bright red blood covered the face of the second man. They were both wearing bathing suits.

"What's wrong?" Walt asked. "Don't you like wrestling? There are better pictures inside, but it's all fake. That's not real blood."

"No," Jimmy said. "I don't like it."

Walt jerked the magazine from his hand. He opened another drawer and took out a clear plastic box.

"The pictures in here are real," he said.

Jimmy liked photographs. It was fun to stare at a moment in time that never changed and think about what he was doing in the picture. Walt dug through the photos and handed one to Jimmy. A strange woman with brown hair was standing next to Daddy on the porch in front of the Mitchell home.

"Who is that with Daddy?" Jimmy asked.

"Your mama," Walt said.

"No, it's not," Jimmy replied. "Her face and hair isn't right, and she's too tall."

Walt laughed. "If you don't like her face, you should check yourself out in the mirror. You look just like her. Haven't you ever seen any pictures of your real mama?"

Jimmy's eyes grew big. "Where did you get these?"

"I think your mama wanted them out of the house because she was jealous, so she gave them to my dad." Walt picked up another one. "This one is in front of the Christmas tree at your house."

Jimmy stared at the familiar scene. Daddy and the woman stood beside a Christmas tree in their living room. Jimmy recognized ornaments on the tree.

"This is my favorite," Walt said, handing him another one.

The woman lay in bed cradling a tiny baby in her arms. Daddy stood beside her.

"That's you in the hospital after you were born," Walt announced. "See how happy they are? At first, they didn't know you were retarded."

Usually, Jimmy ran out of the room when Walt talked like that, but today he couldn't pull away from the picture. He stared into the woman's eyes. She seemed happy. Daddy was smiling too. He'd seen baby pictures of himself, but never one that included his other mom.

"Here's a goofy one," Walt said.

The woman was holding a toddler's hands in the air as he stood in front of the coffee table in the living room at their house.

"Her name is Vera. That's a creepy name, isn't it? She's trying to teach you to walk. My mom says it took you a long time to learn how to walk. That's one way they realized you were dumb."

Jimmy had heard Mama and Daddy say Vera's name, but he'd never seen her face.

"Can I have the pictures?" he asked.

Walt snatched them from his hand. "No way. I'm keeping them forever."

Walt put the photos in the box and slammed the drawer shut. Jimmy stared at the drawer.

"Now, get a kid's book to read," Walt said. "The stuff you might like is on the bottom shelf."

Jimmy sat on the floor, unmoving.

Walt spoke. "You still can't walk very well, can you? I'll guess I'll have to get a book."

Walt retrieved a book from the bookcase. "*The Story of Edward*," he said. "I know you like this one. The story of a talking donkey for a real-life dumb—"

A loud knock at the door interrupted him.

"Who is it?" Walt called out as he unlocked the door.

The door cracked open. It was Mama.

"Are you boys okay?"

Before Jimmy could answer, Walt held up *The Story of Edward.* "Yes, I'm going to read this book to Jimmy."

"That's a good choice. Please leave the door ajar so I can call Jimmy if I need him."

"Sure."

Mama left, leaving the door wide open.

"Your mama watches wrestling on TV after you go to bed," Walt said after Mama's footsteps faded. "I bet she has the same magazine in her bedroom."

"No, she doesn't," Jimmy managed.

"How would you know? You're asleep."

Jimmy could not think of an answer.

"Come sit on the bed, and I'll read the book," Walt said.

Jimmy reluctantly sat next to his cousin. Walt opened the book and began to read. Jimmy knew by heart the story of the donkey's adventures across the French countryside; however, today the words and pictures didn't take him to the place of imagination. The woman with the baby filled his mind. When Walt finished, he patted Jimmy's knee.

"You're kind of cute in a weird way," he said.

"HOW WAS YOUR TIME WITH WALT?" MAMA ASKED DURING the drive home.

"He showed me some of my baby pictures but wouldn't let me keep them."

"Why not?" Daddy asked.

"Because of my other mama." Jimmy paused. "I don't know what to call her."

Mama turned in her seat. "Was your birth mother in the pictures?"

"Yes, ma'am."

"What was Walt doing with pictures of Vera and me?" Daddy asked.

"Uh, I think I showed some to Bart when we first married," Mama answered.

"Walt has no business dragging that up." Daddy put his foot on the brake. "Let's go back and—"

"Please, Lee," Mama said. "Not now."

Daddy grunted and didn't say anything but stepped on the gas.

"Jimmy," Mama said as the car picked up speed. "We'll talk about it later, okay?"

"Yes, ma'am."

THAT NIGHT WHEN MAMA CAME INTO JIMMY'S ROOM TO PRAY and tuck him into bed, she had something in her hand. Turning on the light near his pillow, she handed him a photograph. It was his birth mama in a white dress standing next to Daddy.

"This is the day your birth mother and Daddy got married."

"They look happy," Jimmy said.

"They were for a while."

Mama handed him a photo of a baby in a stroller being pushed by his birth mama. The baby was wearing a tiny blue cap.

"This is when you were six months old. I think this is your first cap."

Jimmy studied the picture. "I wish I still had the cap. I couldn't wear it, but I could put in on a shelf."

"I don't know what happened to it."

Mama handed him a third picture. In this one, the baby was sitting in a sandbox in the backyard. The woman was sitting on the grass beside him with a tree behind her. She had her hand behind Jimmy's back.

"I know that tree," Jimmy said. "It's the one with the tire swing on it."

"Yes."

Jimmy looked at the three pictures again. This time he studied the woman's face but learned nothing.

"Where does she live now?" he asked.

"We don't know," Mama said. "Your daddy hasn't heard from her for almost eleven years."

"Why did she go away?" Jimmy asked. "Was it because of me?"

In an instant, Mama had her arms around him and brought his head into her shoulder.

"Don't ever say or think that again," she said. "You are a wonderful boy. Anyone would be proud to have you as a son."

Jimmy enjoyed the hug but wasn't sure why Mama did it. She stroked the back of his head, kissed him on the forehead, and released him.

"I love you," she said.

"I love you too," he answered.

"Do you want to keep the pictures?" she asked.

Jimmy held the photos lightly in his hand. "Is it okay with Daddy?"

"Yes, we talked it over and decided you were old enough to have them."

"I'll put them in my desk drawer but not on my board."

"That's fine."

Mama prayed for him then stood up.

"Good night," she said.

"Good night, Mama."

As Mama turned to leave, Jimmy spoke. "If I ever meet the woman in the pictures, what should I call her? I can't call her Mama, because you're my mama."

Mama was still for a second.

"I'm not sure," she answered in a slightly shaky voice. "Maybe you should call her Ms. Horton. Her name is Vera Horton."

− Eight −

The first week of summer vacation, Jimmy helped Mama around the house. Each morning they worked in the backyard vegetable garden. By early June the Georgia sun had coaxed tomatoes, green beans, yellow squash, okra, and three rows of corn from the red clay. Jimmy enjoyed routine, repetitive tasks that most people found boring and was an expert at pulling weeds. Mama taught him the difference between the good plants and the bad plants, and he carefully worked his way down each row, leaving weed-free soil behind him.

Buster enjoyed having Jimmy home from school and often interrupted by begging for a stomach scratch. Mama wore a broad-brimmed straw hat while she worked. Jimmy wore an Atlanta Braves cap with a big *A* on the front. Mama told him he received an A as a weed puller.

One morning as Jimmy finished the last row, Mama came across the yard with two glasses of lemonade.

"Are you thirsty?" she asked.

"Yes, ma'am."

They sat down, leaned against a large tree, and stretched out their legs. The late-morning air was still. It was as quiet as only a small town in the summer can be. Drops of water ran down the outside of the glasses. Buster lay down beside Jimmy.

"I'm glad you're my mama," Jimmy said.

"Me too."

"You chose me, didn't you?" Jimmy asked.

"You know I did."

"Tell me again."

Mama smiled. "Do you like that story?"

"Yes, ma'am."

"How old were you when I first met you?" Mama asked.

"Four years old."

"Do you remember the first time I saw you?" Mama asked.

"I pretend that I can."

"Well, you were the cutest four-year-old boy in Piney Grove. I worked in the clerk's office at the courthouse and knew your daddy because he was a lawyer."

"The best lawyer in Piney Grove."

"That's right."

"One day he picked you up from the babysitter and brought you to the clerk's office. I looked up from my desk, and there you were, standing in front of me."

"Was I wearing glasses?"

"Yes, and you blinked your eyes several times and stared at me."

Jimmy chuckled. "Why was I staring and blinking my eyes?"

"I'd like to think it was because you knew I was going to be your mama, but I think you wanted me to give you a lollipop from the jar I kept on my desk."

"Did you give me a lollipop?"

"Not until I asked you to tell me your favorite flavor. You said 'grape,' which was my favorite too. We each ate a lollipop."

"Where was Daddy?"

"He was watching us. We'd been talking on the phone and eating dinner together for several months, and he wanted me to meet you."

"What did you think?"

"I liked your daddy a lot."

"No, about me," Jimmy said, smiling.

Mama took a sip of lemonade. "I loved you the first time I saw you. Now I love you with my whole heart. I couldn't love you any more if I tried."

Jimmy felt doubly warm—from the sun above and the love sitting beside him.

"A few months later, I planned your five-year-old birthday party," Mama said. "The next week your daddy asked me to marry him, and I said yes."

"Because you loved both of us."

"Yes. And we got married at Christmastime."

Jimmy had a picture in his room of Mama and Daddy in front of a Christmas tree. Mama was wearing a white dress. They got married at the house and both looked happy.

"Where was I when they took the picture of you in the white dress in front of the Christmas tree?"

"Probably eating wedding cake in the dining room."

"Do you still have some of the cake in the freezer?"

"Yes, your daddy and I will eat it after we've been married ten years."

"Can I have some too?"

"Yes, we'll give you a bite."

Jimmy rolled a piece of ice around in his mouth, then put it in his hand for Buster to lick.

"Why don't I have any brothers or sisters?" he asked.

Mama lowered her glass from her lips. "What made you think about that?"

"Max has a sister. Denise has a brother and a sister."

Mama turned slightly and rested on her arm so that she faced him.

"Some people love their own children; others get to love a child who's already been born. Daddy and I wanted to have more children, but the doctors said that we can't. I'm happy to have you to love. That's enough for me."

Jimmy looked closely into Mama's face.

"Did I make you sad?" he asked.

Mama reached over and stroked his hand. "No, but it was a serious question. Do you understand my answer?"

"I think so."

"Tell me."

Jimmy was used to this. It was how he learned best.

"You and Daddy went to the hospital to get a baby, but the doctors told you there wasn't one for you, so you came home and kept loving me."

"Yes, that's right."

They finished their lemonade. Jimmy carried the tools back to the rear of the house and leaned them against the wall. Mama followed with the empty glasses.

"You're a good worker," Mama said. "On Monday you're going to help your daddy at the office."

"But I don't know what to do."

"There are weeds that need to be pulled at a law office too."

ON MONDAY MORNING, JIMMY PUT ON A NICE PAIR OF PANTS and a collared shirt. He went downstairs to the kitchen and watched Mama remove a crisp strip of bacon from the skillet and place it on a paper towel.

"Lawyers' helpers need to eat a good breakfast," she said with a smile.

Daddy lowered the newspaper. "I eat prosecutors for breakfast, insurance companies for lunch, and government agencies for supper."

Jimmy gave Daddy a puzzled look. "I like bacon and eggs."

Mama placed four slices of bacon on a plate beside a mound of fluffy eggs. Daddy had a single piece of bacon and a smaller portion of eggs.

"Lawyers' helpers don't have to worry about cholesterol," he grunted.

Jimmy sat at the table and methodically ate his breakfast. Daddy glanced at his watch.

"Hurry, so you can brush your teeth. We need to leave in a few minutes. I have a hearing at nine o'clock in front of Judge Robinson."

Jimmy ate faster, then ran upstairs and brushed his teeth. He coated the toothbrush with so much toothpaste that in a few seconds the foam spilled from the corners of his mouth and made him look like a rabid dog. He carefully kept his face over the sink. Mama called upstairs.

"Rinse out your mouth! It's time to go!"

Jimmy splashed water on his face and into his mouth. He pulled his lips away from his teeth and inspected his work. Mama and Daddy were waiting for him at the bottom of the stairs.

"You're only going to be at the office until eleven o'clock," Mama said. "I'll pick you up, and we'll make a few stops before coming home to eat lunch. You'll spend the rest of the afternoon with me."

"What about Grandpa?" Jimmy asked. "I didn't get to see him this weekend because he was sick."

"It's time to go," Daddy said. "You can sort out the rest of the day later."

Mama hugged Jimmy, holding him longer than she did when he left for school.

Jimmy followed Daddy out the door. The June air was cool and the grass damp. By late July there wouldn't be enough moisture in the air to spare for dew. They rode in silence. Jimmy glanced over at Daddy several times. They parked in the spot marked "Reserved for James Lee Mitchell, Esq."

DADDY'S OFFICE WAS IN A HOUSE ONCE OWNED BY THE GRAND-mother of a local surgeon. Two blocks from the courthouse, the one-story brick house had an archway over the front door. Daddy claimed it was in better condition than when it was first built. Mama especially liked the pretty yard and said it was the nicest law office in Piney Grove.

To reach the front door, Jimmy carefully stepped from one paving stone to the next. Daddy glanced back at him.

"You can't be looking down if you want to work for me."

"I was checking for weeds."

Jimmy, hopping on one foot, hit the center of three more pavers before reaching the front door.

In the room where people waited to see Daddy, fancy chairs sat in front of a fireplace that could be turned on with a switch. Pictures in thick frames of men on horseback with dogs hung on the walls. Jimmy's favorite picture was of a pack of dogs running beside some horsemen after a red fox that was climbing a wall in the far distance.

A lady who worked for Daddy sat at a shiny wooden desk. A fancy red rug covered the center of the wooden floor. Daddy stood beside the lady's desk and flipped through a stack of pink papers.

"I have to go to court in a couple of minutes," he said to her. "Call David Gallegly and tell him the closing on his new building has been changed to Wednesday at three o'clock. Warn Bryce Thomas that the insurance company may hire a private investigator to spy on him and not to be doing anything inconsistent with the doctor's recommendations."

Daddy glanced up and saw the lady staring at Jimmy.

"Oh, yeah," Daddy continued. "You know my son, Jimmy. He is going to help us this morning. You and Delores need to find something for him to do until I return from the courthouse. My hearing shouldn't take more than half an hour."

Daddy left the room and went into his office. Jimmy stood in the middle of the red carpet. The pretty lady with yellow hair gave him a little smile. She'd been working for Daddy for six months. Jimmy had met her briefly a couple of times when Mama brought him by, but he couldn't remember her name.

"Hi, Jimmy," she said. "I'm Kate."

"Hi," he responded.

"Would you like something to drink?" she asked.

Before Jimmy could answer, Daddy reentered the room. He had his briefcase.

"Jimmy can do more than you might think. Just make sure you show him specifically what you want him to do, and check on him."

"Yes, Mr. Mitchell."

The front door closed behind Daddy.

"We have coffee, water, soft drinks," Kate said. "But I guess you don't drink coffee, do you?"

"No, ma'am. I'm not thirsty."

"You don't have to call me ma'am."

"Yes, ma'am."

Kate laughed. It was a friendly sound. She stood up. She was short like Mama but skinnier. Her straight hair fell to her shoulders.

"Do you know Delores?"

"Yes, ma'am."

"Let's ask her if she has a project for you."

Daddy relied on Delores Smythe for everything except telling him what to say in court. She'd been his secretary since before he met Mama. She didn't have a husband, but she had three cats. Jimmy didn't know how old she was, but Mama said Delores had reached the place in life where she never got any older.

Jimmy and Kate went into a small office across the hall from Daddy's big office. Small paintings of her three cats hung behind Delores's desk, and photographs of the cats, singly and together, surrounded her work area. Delores was wearing a white blouse with a bright yellow scarf around her neck. Reading glasses hung from a chain that disappeared under the scarf. She looked up when they entered the room and removed earphones from her ears.

"Jimmy," she said in surprise. "Is your mother sick?"

"No, ma'am."

"I haven't seen you since Christmas. You're getting taller and taller."

Jimmy wasn't aware of this, but he'd heard similar comments from several people.

"Yes, ma'am."

Jimmy glanced at the pictures of the cats.

"How is your dog doing?" Delores asked. "Buster, isn't it?"

"Buster is the best dog in the whole world," Jimmy answered. "He'd like to play with your cats if you want to bring them over to the house sometime."

"That's probably not a good idea. My babies spend most of their time indoors." Delores picked up a photograph of a brown tabby. "Do you remember this one?"

Jimmy squinted at the picture. He'd met the cats several times when Daddy dropped work papers off at Delores's house. All three cats walked around on tip-toe with their backs arched when strangers visited and didn't reveal enough about their personalities to make a name stick in his memory.

"No, ma'am."

"This is Otto," Delores replied. She reached for a large photo in a silver frame of a fawn-colored Siamese and a long-haired white Persian lying together on a fancy green pillow and showed it to him. "And here are Maureen and Celine."

Jimmy looked at the cats. He couldn't understand cats. They didn't seem to care about anything. Except in storybooks, Jimmy had never known a cat to join in an adventure like Buster's trips with him to Grandpa's house.

"Pretty cats," he managed.

"Doesn't Jimmy have the best manners?" Kate interjected. "He even calls me 'ma'am,' and I'm barely out of high school. He's going to help us this morning."

"Help us do what?" Delores asked.

"Work here at the office."

"What does Lee want him to do?"

"That's up to us," Kate responded. "Uh, to you."

The phone rang, and Kate returned to the reception area. Delores tilted her head to the side and put the end of her glasses to her lips.

"So this isn't a fun visit to your daddy's office?"

"No, ma'am. The other night at supper Daddy said he needed help, and I told him I'm a good worker. Mama thinks it would be good for me to spend time at the office so Daddy and I can do things together."

Delores raised her eyebrows. "Jimmy, I've never heard you put that many words together in your whole life. I guess you're growing up in more ways than inches. What would you like to do? Did you talk with your daddy about it?"

"No, ma'am, but I'm good at pulling weeds from the garden. I can vacuum the floor, put dishes in the dishwasher—"

"Hold on. That's what you do with your mother, but it gives me an idea."

Delores pointed to a large white box in the corner of her office.

"I was going to ask Kate to organize the papers in that box, but it might be something you can handle. Do you know the months of the year in correct order?"

Jimmy gave her a puzzled look.

"You know, January, February, March." Delores stopped and waited.

Jimmy continued the sequence. "April, May, June, July, August, September, October, November, December."

"Good enough. Bring that box into the conference room."

Jimmy picked up the heavy box and followed Delores to the rear of the office.

"Is that box too heavy for you?" she asked.

"No, ma'am. I'm getting stronger every day."

At the end of the hall they entered a rectangular area that had once been a sunroom. Solid walls had been added, but two skylights remained. In the middle of the room was a glass table surrounded by six chairs.

"Put the box on the table," Delores said.

Delores took out a stack of letters and documents. She picked up a letter and pointed to the top of the sheet.

"Read this," she said.

"October 8, 2004."

"Good."

She selected several other sheets, and Jimmy correctly identified the date.

"Now, put these five letters in order beginning with the oldest one on the bottom."

Jimmy stared at the letters for several seconds before shaking his head. "I don't understand."

Delores placed all five letters on the table. "Which one was written first?"

"I don't know. I wasn't there."

Delores didn't get upset. "You don't have to be there to know when a letter was written. That's why the date is at the top. Which comes first every year, your birthday or your mama's birthday?"

"My birthday."

"Is July before December?"

Jimmy didn't answer but glanced at the letters. "So this letter with January on top is before the one with May on top."

"That's right. It's older. But you have to look at the year, not just the month. This is an old case that has information in it from several years ago. There are letters in this box written in 1998."

Overwhelmed, Jimmy backed away from the table. "I can't do this. But please don't tell Daddy. Maybe I could work in the yard? I'm a good weed-puller."

"Don't give up so easily."

Delores took out a pen and wrote a different year on several yellow Post-it notes. She stuck the notes in a horizontal row across the glass table.

"First, all I want you to do is look at the year on each letter. Put the letter in front of the correct date. After that's done, we will talk about the months. Do you understand?"

Jimmy nodded. "I think so."

Delores took out a thick stack of papers. "Let me watch you do it."

Jimmy looked at each sheet for several seconds before placing it on the table. Delores watched without comment. After he'd done twenty, she touched him on the arm.

"You haven't made any mistakes. I'm going back to my desk. Let me know when you've sorted every letter in the box. If you have a question about one, set it aside and we'll talk about it later."

To Daddy, the correspondence told a fascinating story of corporate intrigue and sophisticated financial fraud, but Jimmy stayed focused on the year listed at the top of each sheet, reviewing the data with computerlike detachment. Within an hour, he had several neat piles of letters on the table. He went into Delores's office.

"I'm done," he announced.

Delores looked at her watch. "Your daddy should have been back from court by now. I'll come check your work."

They returned to the conference room, and after quickly flipping through the letters, Delores expressed her satisfaction.

"Now, sort them by day and month, and then you can—"

Jimmy's puzzled expression stopped her.

"Let's back up," she said. "We'll keep it simple."

Delores made notes for each month of the year and stuck them to the table. By the time she finished, Jimmy was nodding his head.

"I know what to do. This time I look at the month."

"Correct. But don't go to the next year until we sort them by day."

The work went slower. Jimmy walked up and down the table putting sheets of paper under the right months. Working for Daddy was more fun than he'd imag ined. He finished the first year and ran down the hall to get Delores. She returned and made thirty-one stickers for the days of the month. She watched while he completed January and placed it to the side in a neat stack.

"Do the same thing for each month, and then for each year. Do you understand?"

"Yes, ma'am."

By 10:00 a.m., Jimmy had organized all the papers in the box by year, month, and date. He was straightening up the stacks for the final year when Daddy came to the door of the conference room.

"I'll be back in a minute and give you something to do," he said hurriedly. "I have to take an important phone call."

"Yes, sir," Jimmy replied, glancing up from his work.

Jimmy finished and then got Delores. She surveyed the neat stacks of documents, checked several for accuracy, and pronounced her blessing.

"Good job. This is a lot more help to your daddy than pulling weeds. There is another box containing pleadings filed in the case. Let's get it, and I'll show you what to do."

By the time Daddy returned to the conference room, Jimmy had started his second project.

"I got stuck in court because a special hearing backed up the judge's calendar," Daddy said. "It's almost time for your mama to pick you up. I appreciate you making neat stacks of paper, but next time, I'll make sure you have something worthwhile to do."

"I did the year, month, and day," Jimmy said.

Daddy stopped and stared again at the papers on the table.

"What?" he asked.

Jimmy pointed to the completed correspondence files. "Those are letters."

Daddy picked up the nearest stack and turned over the sheets. "This file was a mess. Now, they're organized in chronological order."

"Year, month, day," Jimmy repeated. "Delores made it easy. She would be a good teacher in school."

"That's very nice of you," Delores said from the doorway. "But you're the one who did such careful work."

Daddy shook his head. "I knew he could do routine tasks but never considered it might be so useful to us."

He turned to Jimmy and stuck out his hand. Jimmy stared down at it.

"Shake my hand," Daddy commanded. "You've got a job."

THAT NIGHT AT THE SUPPER TABLE, DADDY GAVE MAMA THE full story. Jimmy listened between bites of broccoli casserole, carrots cooked in butter with brown sugar, and sliced ham.

"According to Delores, the key is to give him tasks in small increments," Daddy said. "I never realized the importance of structure in what he can do."

Mama squeezed some lemon into her tea. "I've known that for years. He's a great helper around the house so long as I don't try to load too much on him at once. It takes him a long time to do the job, but he doesn't leave a single weed in the garden. If you spent more time one-on-one with him, you wouldn't be so surprised."

Jimmy chewed a bite of carrots.

Daddy continued. "There are future vocational implications to all this. Jimmy could have a degree of independence—"

"Lee," Mama interrupted. "Jimmy could work in sheltered workshop programs, but that wouldn't provide enough money to live on. Surviving on his own is not a goal we need to set for Jimmy."

Jimmy swallowed. "What do you mean, Mama?"

Mama's voice softened. "That you are going to live here with us for as long as you want."

Jimmy scooped up a perfect portion of broccoli. "That's good. I never want to be anywhere else. You cook good food, and this is my home."

— _Nine_ —

Jimmy's favorite summer activity, except for playing with Buster, of course, was pole climbing. Almost every Saturday, he and Grandpa waited for Grandma to go to the beauty shop and then headed into the backyard for a practice session. Part of the training included lessons in what Grandpa called "utility-pole anatomy."

"What is the black sticky stuff on the pole called?" Grandpa asked one morning in July.

"Creosote," Jimmy answered promptly.

"Right, and we don't want you to get it on your clothes or your skin. That's why you always wear gloves when you're on the pole."

Grandpa's extra pair of work gloves swallowed Jimmy's hands. Jimmy wiggled his fingers in the gloves while he sat on the step in front of the toolshed. Grandpa knelt at his feet attaching a climbing hook around Jimmy's left boot and the straps to his calf.

"How does that feel?" Grandpa asked.

"Tight," Jimmy answered. "But it's supposed to be tight. When are you going to teach me how to put on the hooks?"

"Later. I still want to do it myself. You've got enough to think about."

Once both hooks were firmly in place, they walked across the yard to the pole. Garbed in his climbing gear, goggles, and heavy work gloves, Jimmy looked like a pint-sized medieval knight preparing to enter the lists.

"Tell me about this pole you're about to climb," Grandpa asked.

"It's a forty-five-foot, class-B pole made from a south Georgia pine tree."

"What does the forty-five mean?"

"That it's forty-five feet tall."

"What does the class-B mean?"

"That it's thicker than a class-C pole and thinner than a class-A pole."

They reached the pole. The coating of creosote produced a pungent odor in hot weather.

"Why doesn't the pole get eaten by termites?" Grandpa asked.

"Because they don't want a stomach full of creosote."

"Tell me what you're going to do," Grandpa said.

Jimmy stepped close to the pole. "I'm going to put my safety strap around the pole."

He put the thick leather strap around the pole and fastened it on his belt.

"What next?"

"I'm going to lean back against the strap."

This had been hard for Jimmy to learn. Every instinct urged him to hug the pole, not push away from it. Grandpa stood behind him, and Jimmy leaned back until he felt Grandpa's thick hands in the middle of his back. Jimmy dug his right hook into the face of the pole a few inches above the ground. Leaning against the belt, he dug his left hook into the wood. He was now suspended in air. He moved his right hook up a few inches and dug it into the wood. He matched the movement with his left hook. He repeated the process until he was now about two feet above the ground.

"Move the safety strap," Grandpa said.

Putting his weight on the hooks, Jimmy leaned slightly forward and scooted the strap up the pole. This maneuver had taken many times of trial and error. On several occasions, he'd grabbed the pole without thinking and banged the side of his face against the dark wood. He pulled out the right hook and moved it upward.

"That's good spacing," Grandpa said, keeping his hands against Jimmy's back.

Up Jimmy went, the hooks cutting into the wood and the belt squeaking as it rubbed against the far side of the pole. He passed several white spots painted on the black surface. The white spots marked a new height he'd achieved during the past few months. In a utility belt around his waist, Jimmy carried a can of white spray paint.

Buster ran to the bottom of the pole and looked up at Jimmy before scampering to another corner of the yard to investigate an interesting smell. Grandpa's hands remained in place until they were on the back of Jimmy's thighs. An additional upward positioning of the strap brought Jimmy above the highest white mark and beyond the range of Grandpa's help.

"You're on your own," Grandpa said.

Jimmy glanced down over his right shoulder and froze. He was about eight feet above the ground. Grandpa's strong, reassuring hands hung at his side.

"No!" Jimmy called out.

Grandpa spoke in a calm voice. "You can keep going higher or come down the way I've taught you."

Jimmy shook his head. "I need you holding me up!"

"I've not been holding you up for weeks," Grandpa replied. "You're holding yourself by the hooks and the belt."

Jimmy's right leg began to tremble.

"Something's wrong with my leg!"

"It's just that your leg is getting tired. Come down slowly."

Jimmy jerked his right hook from the pole, but instead of keeping tension on the safety belt, he leaned toward the pole and wrapped his arms around it in a tight grip. A woman's voice screamed across the yard.

"Jim! What are you trying to do to that boy?"

Still hugging the pole, Jimmy looked toward the house and saw Grandma standing on the steps beside the back door.

"I'm getting the ladder!" Grandpa called out as he left the pole and jogged toward the toolshed.

Grandma walked briskly across the yard, exposing her fresh, perfect hairdo to the hot August sun. She reached the pole and looked up at Jimmy.

"Hold on!" she commanded.

Jimmy had a tight grip on the pole, but he was getting used to the height. He pulled up his right leg up and dug the hook into the pole. Pushing upward, he put weight on the climbing hooks and leaned back against the safety belt.

"Be careful!" Grandma called out.

"Don't worry. I'm learning how to climb the pole," Jimmy responded. "I got scared when I couldn't feel Grandpa's hand on my back, but now I'm getting used to it."

Breathing heavily, Grandpa arrived with a six-foot ladder. He put his hand to his chest.

"Keep calm," he managed between breaths. "I'll have him down in a second."
Grandpa opened the ladder.

"Wait, Grandpa," Jimmy said. "Let me show Grandma what I can do."

"I don't want to see you fall off that pole," Grandma began.

"I won't fall," Jimmy interrupted. He took a step down. "All I have to do is remember what Grandpa taught me. Lean back against the safety belt and don't get in a hurry."

Grandpa opened the ladder but didn't climb it. Jimmy kept talking.

"Pull out one hook at a time. It's like coming down a ladder only in smaller steps. Make sure the hook is in the pole before moving lower."

Grandma watched in surprise as Jimmy descended the pole. Grandpa scooted back the ladder so it would not be in the way. When Jimmy reached chest height, Grandpa put his hand on Jimmy's back.

"That's perfect, Jimmy," he said.

Jimmy reached the ground and looked up the pole.

"Uh-oh," he said.

"What?" Grandma managed.

"I forgot to paint the place on the pole where I stopped."

"That's okay," Grandpa replied. "You'll have another chance."

"Not so fast," Grandma shot back. "His parents need to know what you've been doing before he sets foot on that pole again. He's okay today, but you don't have any right to put him in such a dangerous situation."

Jimmy patted the safety belt.

"I have on a safety belt."

Grandpa held up his hand. "We'll save the discussion until later."

"And I can't believe you've been sneaking around behind my back," Grandma said to Grandpa. "Waiting until I went to the beauty shop!"

Grandpa didn't answer.

"Tell her about the surprise," Jimmy said.

"What surprise?" Grandma asked.

"That it was going to be a surprise for everyone when I learned to climb the pole. If I ever want to work for the Georgia Power Company, I have to be able to climb a forty-five-foot, class-B pole."

"Get him out of that rig," Grandma said as she turned back toward the house. "I'm going to call Ellen right now."

Jimmy watched the back of Grandma's gray head as she returned to the house. Not a hair on her head moved. Grandpa picked up the ladder and turned toward the toolshed. Jimmy followed, the hooks making tiny holes in the dirt beneath the grass. He sat on the step while Grandpa released the straps that held the climbing hooks. Grandpa's thoughts seemed to be somewhere else.

"Are you mad at me?" Jimmy asked.

"No."

"I got scared."

"But you got over it and came down the pole like you've been doing it for years. There are a lot of things you could do if someone would be patient and give you a chance."

Jimmy wasn't sure exactly what Grandpa meant, but he could tell by his voice that he was proud of him.

"Yes, sir. And I didn't tell anyone what we were doing. I wanted to, especially Mama, but remembered what you told me about it being a surprise and a secret. I've never kept a secret before."

Grandpa gave him a wry smile. "It's not a secret anymore. If your mama is at home right now and we're real quiet, we might be able to hear her reaction to our surprise."

Jimmy and Buster walked home without any problems. Grandma and Mama had a system. Grandma would call Mama when Jimmy left his grandparents' house. That way Mama could figure the time it would take him to get home.

Today, because Grandpa said he should, he marched straight home. He put Buster in the backyard and entered the house. Mama was nowhere in sight. He entered the kitchen and found Mama on the phone.

"They're coming over after supper to talk," she said. "Can't the committee let you make your report first?"

Jimmy turned on the faucet and filled a glass with water. Mama always told him to drink plenty of water in the summer.

"Then you'll just have to leave. This is important. No later than seven thirty. Bye."

Jimmy took a big drink of water. He gave Mama a hug.

"How are you?" he asked.

"Glad you're not in the hospital with a broken bone or paralyzed from the neck down," she replied.

Jimmy nodded. "Me too. Do you think Max could come over this afternoon?"

"No," Mama replied sharply.

"Why not?"

Mama started to speak, then stopped.

"Maybe that's a good idea," she said. "I'll call his mother."

Max arrived in early afternoon. Mama and Jimmy greeted him on the front porch.

"You boys have several hours until we eat an early supper and Max's mother comes to pick him up. Are hamburgers okay with you, Max?"

"Yes, ma'am."

Mama left, and Jimmy turned toward his friend.

"What do you want to do?" Jimmy asked. "I got a new baseball glove for my birthday. You can use my new glove, and I'll use my old one."

"No, I've been playing so much baseball that I'm tired of it. Let's mess around with Buster."

Jimmy smiled. He wanted to be a good baseball player like Max, but playing with Buster sounded like more fun to him too.

"Buster would like that."

Max didn't own a dog. His little sister, Tiffany, was allergic to animal hair and couldn't be around a dog for more than a couple of minutes without beginning to sneeze and rub her eyes. After playing with Buster, Max would have to change clothes as soon as he entered his house. Jimmy felt sorry for Tiffany. She was a good reader, but not being able to have a dog was one of the worst things that could happen in life.

Max suggested they build an obstacle course for Buster. He'd seen a TV show on which dogs ran up ramps, crawled through tunnels, jumped across water, and zigzagged between cones. Using boards, bricks, an old wading pool, and other items, they created a makeshift course for the dog.

"It's good," Max announced when they finished.

Max led Buster to the bottom of the ramp that stretched as high as a slide on an old swing set. Jimmy stood at the far end and called to him. Buster obeyed the easy way by running around the ramp. The boys overcame this problem by using a ladder. Jimmy climbed to the midpoint of the ramp and called Buster's name. The dog scampered up the ramp, received a treat, and ran down the other side to Max. The water barrier created a different type of problem. Buster immediately jumped into the pool but wanted to stay and play, not move on to the next task. Jimmy didn't want to get in even six inches of water, so Max took off his shoes and entered the pool with Buster. After a few seconds of splashing, Max hopped out of the pool and ran to the next obstacle. Buster joined him in the excitement of the moment and learned two new commands: "in water" and "out water."

The final step involved coordinating all the tasks into a race against the clock. The boys didn't have a stopwatch, so they found an old windup alarm clock with a large second hand. When the second hand reached twelve, they started the competition. The first time, Buster became so worked up by their cries of encouragement that he left the course to run around the yard barking at the squirrels in the tree.

"On the TV shows, the owners of the dogs are very calm," Max said. "They walk alongside the dogs acting as if they don't care what's happening."

Max then directed Jimmy, who communicated with Buster, who eventually overcame all obstacles. The last station was a broomstick that the dog had to jump over. When he landed on the other side, Max called out the time.

"Twenty-one minutes, fourteen seconds."

"Is that good?" Jimmy asked as he knelt down to rub Buster's head.

"I think on TV they do it in about two minutes."

Jimmy gave Buster one more big scratch. "Did you hear that, Buster? You did great."

"Do you want to let him do it again?" Max asked.

"Sure," Jimmy said.

They did several more rounds on the circuit. Mama watched the last one when she came outside to start the fire for the hamburgers.

"Ten minutes, thirty-one seconds," Max announced.

"Very good," Mama said. "Buster is a smart dog, but he couldn't perform without the help of good trainers."

"Thanks, Mrs. Mitchell," Max replied. "Do you want us to put everything away?"

Mama surveyed the yard.

"Jimmy, do you know where you got everything?"

Jimmy shrugged. He'd spent most of the construction time tagging along behind Max as his friend rummaged through the yard and the crawl space underneath the house.

"No, ma'am."

"Would you like to keep it up?" Mama asked.

"Yes, ma'am! Buster and I could do it some more tomorrow."

"If it's okay with your daddy, it's fine with me. You're going to be spending more time at home, and it will give you something else to do."

— Ten —

Hamburgers cooked on the grill were one of Jimmy's favorite foods. He liked the smoky flavor the charcoal gave the meat. On Saturday evenings the smell produced by charcoal grills was a common aroma in the neighborhoods of Piney Grove. Daddy was a staunch believer in the superior cooking qualities of charcoal. He vowed that the day he switched to a gas grill would be the day he joined the Methodist church. Jimmy assumed all Methodists cooked on gas grills.

To eat his hamburger, Jimmy first cut the meat and bun in half. He left one half bare—meat and bun only so he could enjoy the meat without other flavors. He loaded the other half with ketchup, mayonnaise, mustard, cheese, pickles, lettuce, onions, and tomato until it was a challenge to open his mouth wide enough to take a bite.

Mama could cook hamburgers just as good as Daddy. Jimmy and Max each ate two, followed by a piece of apple pie. Jimmy pushed away his empty plate like Daddy did when he finished a big serving of fried catfish.

"That was good," he said.

"Yes, Mrs. Mitchell," Max added. "Delicious."

"Thank you, boys," Mama replied with a smile. "Take your plates to the sink and rinse them off."

Jimmy stood beside Max while he ran water over his plate. He looked over his shoulder at Mama, who was still eating a piece of pie.

"Can Max spend the night? He could wear a pair of Daddy's old pajamas."

"No," Mama answered. "He needs to sleep in his own bed. In a few minutes, I'll call his mother to come pick him up."

Max nudged him on the elbow and whispered in a low voice. "Save it for next weekend."

Mama left the kitchen.

"What do you mean?" Jimmy asked.

"I'll invite you to come to my house Friday night. My uncle Mike is going to be visiting from South Carolina, and he's going to take my dad and me skeet shooting on Saturday. Maybe you can go with us."

"What's a skeet?"

"It's a piece of round pottery about the size of this dessert plate," Max said. "A machine throws it into the air, and you try to shoot it with a shotgun. It's a lot of fun."

Grandpa had a shotgun in the closet in his bedroom. Jimmy had peeked at the shiny wooden stock and dark black barrel. He could stick two fingers in the end of the barrel. The thought of holding a gun in his hands and pulling the trigger was a heady yet fearful thought.

"Does anybody ever get killed?" Jimmy asked in a hushed voice.

"No," Max scoffed. "It's safe. You never point a gun at another person."

Jimmy put his plate in the dishwasher.

"I'm not sure Mama would let me go. She doesn't like guns."

Mama returned to the kitchen.

"Ask her," Jimmy said.

"What?" Mama said.

"I'd like to invite Jimmy over to my house next weekend," Max responded casually. "But I need to check with my mom first."

Mama picked up the phone receiver. "Okay. We can discuss it later in the week."

While Mama called Max's mother, the boys went upstairs to Jimmy's room.

"Don't say anything about the skeet," Max said.

"I know," Jimmy replied with a sigh. "It's the same as climbing the pole."

"Climbing the pole?"

Jimmy described his pole-climbing lessons with Grandpa. Max's eyes grew wide. "That is awesome. Could I come over and watch sometime?"

"I'll ask Grandpa."

"Maybe he could let me try."

"Max!" Mama called out. "Your mother is here."

Jimmy pointed to the rows of caps. "Do you want to take a cap?"

"Are you sure?"

"Yes, you're my best friend."

Max smiled. "Okay, but not one you care about. I might lose it or get it dirty."

Jimmy thoughtfully surveyed his collection. He selected a white cap with gold trim and handed it to his friend. Max inspected it. The letters *GT* were embroidered on the front. A tiny yellow jacket sat on the end of the *T*.

"That's a nice Georgia Tech hat," Max said. "Are you sure you don't want to keep it?"

"No, my uncle Bart gave it to me. He went to school at Georgia Tech. On the way home from their house, Daddy told me Georgia Bulldogs don't like Georgia Tech Yellow Jackets and that I shouldn't wear it outside the house. He said Uncle Bart gave it to me to make Daddy mad. It's not doing any good staying in my room."

Max slipped on the cap, and the boys ran downstairs. After Max left, Jimmy gave Mama a hug.

"Thanks for letting him come over. We had fun."

JIMMY WAS UPSTAIRS IN HIS ROOM LOOKING AT THE PICTURES in a magazine about bass fishing when he heard heavy footsteps on the stairway. Daddy was home. When the steps reached his bedroom door and stopped, Jimmy looked up. To his surprise, Grandpa stood in the doorway.

"Hey, Grandpa!"

"Hi, Jimmy."

Jimmy ran over to Grandpa, gave him a hug, and put his head against his Grandpa's chest. When he started to pull away, Grandpa held him close for a few more seconds before releasing him.

"Your heart is fine," Jimmy said.

"It feels a little heavy to me."

"We have apple pie," Jimmy replied. "That will make you feel better. And there is ice—"

"I'm not hungry," Grandpa interrupted.

They went downstairs. Grandma and Mama were already in the kitchen. Jimmy could hear them talking, but they stopped when he and Grandpa entered the room. Grandpa sat down at the kitchen table. Mama was making a pot of coffee. None of the adults were talking. Puzzled, Jimmy glanced around. Nobody was smiling. Daddy entered. He was wearing a white shirt with his tie loosened around the neck. He, too, looked serious.

"Go to your room," he said to Jimmy without another greeting. "We have something to discuss."

"No," Mama interjected. "There's part of this I want to get straight with Jimmy too."

Jimmy saw Daddy's cheek muscles tighten.

"All right," he said after a moment's pause. "You called this meeting."

"Would anyone like coffee?" Mama began in a more cheerful voice.

Jimmy raised his hand. "I would."

"You're too young to drink coffee," Mama answered.

Jimmy laughed. "It was a joke. Everyone seems sad."

The adults looked at one another. Grandpa spoke.

"I'll have a cup," he said.

Jimmy sat in his chair, swinging his legs underneath the seat. His feet struck the floor with each pass. Grandpa sipped his coffee. Everyone except Mama was sitting at the kitchen table. She leaned against the counter with her arms folded across her chest.

"Jimmy," she said. "Look at me."

Jimmy stopped swinging his legs, his feet flat on the floor.

"Yes, ma'am."

"Why didn't you tell me about climbing the pole?"

Jimmy looked at Grandpa, who spoke.

"Ellen, I told him to keep quiet about it."

"I want to hear from my son."

"It was going to be a Christmas surprise," Jimmy said hopefully. "Grandpa and I talked about it. Everyone was going to come watch me climb the pole. I'm not sure how high I could go, but I would do my best. After I climbed the pole, we would eat hamburgers and hot dogs." He stopped and looked at Grandpa. "How long is it until Christmas?"

"About four months."

"And everyone would be proud of me," Jimmy concluded.

For Jimmy it was a long speech, albeit in front of close family. Daddy rubbed his chin.

"We've talked about Jimmy's need to use self-restraint in what he says," Daddy said. "I'm not sure we should fault him. He had a plan—"

"To deceive," Mama cut him off. Raising her voice, she gestured toward Grandpa. "Involving an activity that could have gotten him killed! Talk about setting a bad precedent! I've worked hard for eight years to gain Jimmy's trust. For you to tell him to keep a secret from me is inexcusable. His body may be getting bigger, but he's not mature enough to exercise proper judgment about information to keep to himself."

Mama paused. Jimmy rarely saw Mama get upset, and when it happened, it shook his world to the core.

Grandpa looked down at the floor. "I was wrong," he replied. "I shouldn't have told him to keep quiet. I knew you would be worried."

"And for good reason!" Mama replied, her eyes still flashing.

Grandpa raised his head, and his voice became more intense. "Ellen, I'm trying to apologize. I may not be a churchgoer, but I know what it means to admit a mistake. I'm sorry. It won't happen again."

Daddy looked at Grandpa in surprise. Mama unfolded her arms.

"Why did you do it?" she asked in a softer tone.

"So you wouldn't worry," Grandpa replied.

"No, I mean risk Jimmy's life by putting him on that pole."

Grandpa rubbed his thick hands together. "I thought it would increase Jimmy's self-confidence. I doubt any other boys his age have ever climbed a power pole, and I saw it as a chance for him to do something that could set him apart from the crowd in a good way."

"Did you consider the fact that other thirteen-year-old boys don't climb poles because their parents realize it's not a safe thing to do?" Mama asked.

"Max thought it sounded like fun," Jimmy interjected. "He wants to learn."

"That's what I mean." Mama looked toward Daddy. "We've got to stop this now. What if Max Cochran fell from the pole and broke his leg? We could all get sued for encouraging a boy to do something like this."

"If a child was hurt due to negligence of a third party, the parents could file suit." Daddy paused. "Unless they signed a waiver of liability."

"Lee, this is serious!" Mama shot back.

"I don't intend to open a pole-climbing school and don't need a legal paper." Grandpa spoke softly. "This was between me and Jimmy. He wasn't in any danger. In fact, yesterday was the first time he climbed beyond the reach of my arms."

"Which means we put a stop to this foolishness just in time," Mama answered.

The meaning of Mama's words suddenly hit Jimmy. He raised his hand.

"What is it?" Daddy asked.

Jimmy's voice trembled slightly. "Do I have to stop climbing the pole?"

"Yes," Mama answered emphatically. "If you won't take swimming lessons in a pool with a certified lifeguard, you're not going to climb a pole."

"But Grandpa is with me," Jimmy protested.

Mama looked at Grandpa. "I never liked you giving him rides in that crazy rig you fixed up, but I was new to the family and kept quiet. This is entirely different. There's no safety net. You're not going to hurt Jimmy."

Jimmy wanted to speak, but Mama's reference to swimming lessons scared him into silence. He'd made several trips to the large swimming pool maintained by the Cattaloochie County Recreation Department but never got in the water. Nothing could convince him to get in the water. Mama had tried groups of children happily splashing in the shallow end, private lessons with a smiling teacher who held out a kickboard, even taking Max, who promised there were no sharks in the water. Nothing worked. When Jimmy stepped onto the pool deck, the flood of tears and involuntary shaking that racked his body convinced everyone present that Jimmy's time to enter the water had not arrived.

Grandpa stood and left the room. The adults looked at one another in silence. Finally, Grandma spoke.

"Ellen, you know I was in the dark about this, but after I cooled down, I realized Jim didn't mean any harm. Ever since he retired, I've felt like I've got a child all over again. He does his chores around the house, but he's always off fishing or trying to get one of his buddies to go walking in the woods in search of a new place for a deer stand."

"You don't expect him to take up knitting, do you?" Daddy asked.

"No, but Jimmy isn't an ordinary playmate," Grandma answered. "He's a delight to have around the house, and at times he does so well that it lulls you into thinking he's more independent than he really is. However, none of us can ever forget the seriousness of our responsibility to look out for him."

"Amen," Mama said soberly.

Grandpa returned with a cardboard box. He put it on the floor and lifted the top. Jimmy leaned over to peer into the box. Inside was a jumble of ropes and pulleys. Grandpa spoke in a level voice.

"Ellen, I never intended to put Jimmy at risk of injury. When I realized that he was going to start climbing beyond my reach, I called the district office and asked if they had a training harness I could borrow. The line foreman is an old friend whom I taught to climb about twenty-five years ago. He located an extra unit they were going to throw away and offered it to me. It had a broken rope that I replaced, and now it's as good as new."

"How does it work?" Daddy asked, picking up one of the ropes.

Grandpa held up a thick metal bolt with an eye hook on one end. "This piece attaches to the top of the pole. A rope is secured to the eye bolt and then connected to a safety belt around the climber. A man on the ground holds the other end of the rope, which runs through a simple pulley system. As the climber ascends the pole, the man on the ground keeps proper tension on the line. If the climber slips, the rope stops him from falling. Because of the pulleys, the helper can handle a heavy climber without straining. Jimmy is so light that it will be easy to keep him from falling."

"Until the rope breaks again or you're not able to hold on to your end or Jimmy unhooks the rope or any of a hundred other things happen." Mama looked at Daddy. "Lee, back me up on this."

Grandpa spoke again. "Every time Jimmy goes higher, he marks the spot with white paint. If you could see how proud he is of the marks on that pole, I think you would reconsider. The rope is new, and the latch on the belt can't be accidentally opened. I agree that we need increased safety measures as he goes higher, and I've taken care of it. Because the equipment is industrial grade, it's safer than a climbing wall at a summer camp."

"But your heart," Daddy said. "If you had another attack, it could be dangerous for both of you. You could drop the rope, and Jimmy might panic."

Grandma nodded. "He's right, Jim. You didn't look so well when you had to hurry across the yard to get the ladder this morning."

Jimmy got up and ran over to Grandpa.

"Let me check Grandpa's heart," he said.

While everyone watched, Jimmy put his head against the old man's chest. After listening for a moment, Jimmy glanced up and smiled.

"Thump, thump, thump."

Grandpa hugged Jimmy, who reciprocated. No one spoke for a few seconds.

"I know he loves you," Mama said to Grandpa. "And I don't want to hurt your relationship, but pole climbing isn't a good idea. There are other ways you can spend time together. Just the two of you at the pole is too great a risk."

Grandpa stared at the rope in his hand.

"Maybe you're right," he admitted.

He returned the safety device to the box. As he shut the top, Jimmy looked at Daddy.

"You could help," he said.

"What?" Daddy asked.

"You could help me learn to climb the pole." Jimmy turned toward Mama and held up three fingers. "If Daddy comes, there would be three people in the backyard."

Daddy gave a short laugh. "You heard your mama. There are other reasons why this isn't a good idea. Besides, Saturday is my golf day."

Grandpa spoke. "The only reason we've been doing it on Saturdays was because of your mother's appointment at the beauty shop. Now that everything is out in the open, we could change the day to suit your schedule. You could be my backup and get a chance to watch Jimmy's progress."

Daddy looked at Mama. "Didn't you mention a hundred things that could go wrong? It's your turn to back me up."

Mama crossed her arms. "I don't recall that you came to my rescue when I asked for help. But before I make up my mind, I'd like to see how this safety device works. The idea of the three men in Piney Grove named James Lee Mitchell spending time together is the first part of this scheme that sounds like a good idea to me."

Jimmy thought Mama had just called him a man, but he wasn't sure.

— Eleven —

For the rest of summer vacation, Jimmy worked two mornings a week at Daddy's office. He learned how to put files in the correct alphabetical order in the filing cabinets and how to run the copy machine. Delores declared him an indispensable asset to the office. Jimmy had no idea what she meant, but when she said the words, she looked at him the way she looked when showing someone pictures of her cats.

One day when Daddy was out of the office for a few minutes, Kate let Jimmy answer the telephone.

"When it rings, push this button and say, 'Good morning, Mitchell Law Office.'"

In a few seconds, the phone rang. Kate excitedly pointed to the button. Jimmy pressed the button and announced, "Good morning, Mitchell Law Office."

Kate picked up the receiver and repeated the greeting. After listening for a moment, she passed the call to Delores and gave Jimmy a sheepish grin.

"I should have told you to pick up the receiver before you press the button. The caller couldn't hear you."

On the next call, Jimmy coordinated picking up the receiver and pressing the button, but the precise greeting escaped him.

"Hello, the Mitchell office. What do you want?"

Kate grabbed the receiver, but the caller had already hung up.

"Uh, why don't you sort your daddy's mail?"

Kate picked up the mail at the post office each morning on her way to work. Daddy got a lot of letters. Jimmy would put the regular envelopes in one stack, the larger envelopes in another stack, and any boxes or packages in another. He made sure they were neatly placed on Daddy's desk so he could open and read them.

He finished his task and returned to Kate's desk. Slumped in one of the leather chairs in the reception area was Jake Garner. He'd grown a scraggly beard, and Jimmy didn't recognize him until he saw the snake on his arm. When Jimmy came into the room, Jake Garner glanced up and grinned.

"The boy with the bulletproof testimony. What's the sheriff been saying recently? Oh, I guess you don't see him much now that you ran him out of the county."

Jimmy didn't say anything.

"I'm here to pick up a big check," Jake continued. "Then I'm going to ask Kate here out on a date."

"Mr. Mitchell will be back in a minute," Kate said.

"I've learned my lesson," Jake continued. "I'm going into business. The next time you see me, I'll be driving a new car and living in a big house." He touched his dirty T-shirt. "I'm also going in for a complete makeover and won't have to get on TV to do it."

The front door opened and Daddy entered.

"Jake, sorry I'm late," he said. "Come into my office. Everything is ready for your signature."

Jake walked past Kate and Jimmy. He winked at Kate.

"He's nasty," Kate said after the door to Daddy's office shut. "I'm glad he settled his case so he won't be coming in here anymore. I don't ever want to see him again."

Jimmy stared down the hallway at the closed door. His curiosity about Jake Garner and the snake coiling up his arm was gone.

"Yes, ma'am," he said softly.

That night at the supper table, Jimmy left the kitchen after dessert and went upstairs to his room. He was straightening his caps when he remembered that he'd left a cap on the extra chair in the kitchen. Returning downstairs, he went into the kitchen and found Mama was standing in front of the stove with her hand over her mouth and a shocked expression on her face. In her other hand was a sheet of paper.

Jimmy stopped. "What is it?" he asked.

Mama held up the sheet of paper.

"Not now," Daddy said sharply. "We need to talk first."

Jimmy stood still, confused.

"Go back to your room, son," Daddy said. "We'll talk later."

"Can I get my cap?" Jimmy asked.

Daddy picked up the cap and tossed it to him. Jimmy backed out of the room and walked slowly up the stairs. He sat on his bed and tried to figure out what he'd done wrong. He decided it probably had to do with climbing the pole but didn't know why.

AFTER SATISFYING HERSELF ABOUT THE RELIABILITY OF THE safety ropes, Mama had given her stamp of approval to additional pole-climbing lessons. Jimmy, Daddy, and Grandpa all promised not to have a lesson unless everyone was present. Together with Mama and Grandma, the three Mitchell men stood in a circle around the pole and prayed that Jimmy would be kept safe and learn the lessons God had for him in climbing the pole. Jimmy kept his eyes shut until Mama said, "Amen."

Since then, Daddy held the end of the safety rope while Grandpa called out instructions. Daddy had never climbed a pole and didn't seem interested in learning now, but he never criticized Jimmy. After each session, he patted Jimmy on the head and told him that he'd done a good job. Daddy usually drove his car to Grandpa's house and left as soon as Jimmy returned to the ground. Jimmy would stay and spend time with Grandpa.

JIMMY WAITED FOR THE SOUND OF FOOTSTEPS ON THE STAIRS. He went to his door and peeked out. He couldn't hear anything. He returned to the bed and sat down. He tried to be patient, but it was hard to wait. He went to the doorway and into the hallway. He moved slowly to the top of the stairs. He strained to listen and could hear Mama's voice but did not understand her words. She and Daddy were sitting in the living room. They almost never sat in the living room unless company came over. Jimmy hadn't heard anyone arrive.

He started down the steps. When he reached the halfway point, Daddy came out of the living room. Jimmy saw him first and took off up the stairs.

"Jimmy! Stop!" Daddy called out.

Jimmy had already reached the top of the stairs. He turned around.

"I didn't hear anything," he said. "I'm going back to my room."

"Come down. It's okay," Daddy said. "We're ready for you."

Jimmy entered the living room. Mama was holding a tissue in her hand. Her eyes were red.

"Give me a hug," she said as soon as she saw Jimmy.

Jimmy put his arms around her neck. She kissed him on the cheek.

"Sit down, son," Daddy said.

Jimmy sat in a chair. Daddy sat beside Mama on the sofa.

Daddy spoke. "When you sorted the mail for me this morning, you put a letter on my desk from a lawyer in Atlanta. He represents your birth mother. She wants you to visit her. She remarried a long time ago and has two little girls. We're not sure why this is coming up after all these years, except she may be sorry that she abandoned you."

"The woman in my baby pictures?" Jimmy asked.

"Yes," Daddy replied.

"No phone calls, gifts, visits, or cards for eleven years," Mama said, shaking her head.

"Or child support," Daddy added.

Jimmy looked at Mama. It hurt him when she hurt.

"I already have a mama," he said.

"Which is a big reason why we don't think it would be a good idea for her to come back into our lives," Daddy said. "We have a happy family."

"Yes, sir."

Mama leaned forward. "Do you remember anything about her?"

"No, ma'am. Only what she looks like in the pictures Walt showed me and the ones you gave me."

"Do you ever get them out and look at them?" Mama asked.

"Yes, ma'am."

"How do you feel when you see her face?" Mama asked.

"I'm not sure."

"Do you want to meet her?" Mama asked.

"Ellen, I thought we agreed not to—"

"No, I need to know," Mama responded firmly. "It's one thing to be curious and look at a few photos. But this letter raises an entirely different issue." Mama turned toward Jimmy. "Son, look me in the eye and tell me the truth. Do you want to meet your birth mother?"

Jimmy swallowed. "You're my mama."

"And I'll always be your mama. I just want to know how you feel—"

"This isn't fair," Daddy interrupted. "We should be making the decisions for him at this point in his life. Don't put him under this kind of pressure."

Mama stared at Daddy for several seconds before sitting back. "Okay. You answer the lawyer. I'm going to concentrate on loving Jimmy."

SUMMER VACATION ENDED AND JIMMY RETURNED TO SCHOOL. It rarely snowed in Piney Grove, but it was often cold and rainy from December through February. One Saturday in early December the temperature warmed up, and Daddy had an early afternoon tee time. Shortly before noon, he drove Jimmy to Grandpa's house. In a routine familiar to all three of them, they walked to the storage shed, where Grandpa made sure Jimmy properly attached the climbing hooks to his boots and strapped on the safety belt.

"Grandpa, do you remember the black place on the pole?"

"It's black from top to bottom," Daddy said.

"No, he's right," Grandpa said. "There is a darker spot about twenty-five feet up on the side facing away from the house."

"Am I getting close to it?" Jimmy asked.

"No," Grandpa shook his head. "It's eight feet or more from the highest white mark."

Grandpa snapped the training rope to a harness that wrapped around Jimmy's chest. Since installing the safety lines, there had been several instances in which Jimmy became unstable and Daddy had to pull the rope tight to help him regain his position. Before he dug his right hook into the pole, Jimmy turned toward Grandpa.

"If I climb all the way to the black spot, will you go to church with Grandma on Sunday?"

Grandpa chuckled. "Christmas will be here in a few weeks, and I'll be there for the Christmas Eve service."

"But I want you to come *this* Sunday."

Grandpa tilted his head to the side.

"Why?"

Jimmy pointed to the line of trees at the rear of the lot. "A Watcher sitting in the tree with the squirrel's nest in it told me to ask you."

Grandpa looked at Daddy, who shrugged his shoulders.

"What do you do when he says something like that?" Grandpa asked.

"It doesn't happen very often, but I send him to his mother. Wherever the thoughts come from or what he sees, it's real to him."

Grandpa grunted. "What if a Watcher told him that you should buy him a bike?"

"Could I get a bike for Christmas?" Jimmy asked. "Max showed me a picture of a good one."

"Climb the pole," Grandpa said. "If you reach the black spot, I'll be in church on Sunday. In trying to reach your goal, don't forget to climb the right way."

"Yes, sir."

Jimmy dug his right hook into the pole and leaned back against the belt. He moved steadily up. Jimmy kept his feet positioned in front of him, resisting any urge to let them creep to the side of the pole. Within a few minutes, he reached his previous best height.

"That's record time," Grandpa said. "If you have the strength, you can go higher. How do you feel?"

"Good."

"Can you still see your Watcher friend?"

Jimmy turned his head toward the line of trees. "No, sir. He's gone."

He continued climbing. He looked down at Grandpa and Daddy. They had their heads tilted back watching him and seemed smaller than he could ever remember.

"You're little," he started up, then his left hook slipped loose. He swung to the side and heard the sound of the safety rope shooting through the pulleys. He leaned back against the safety belt and came to a stop. He looked down. Daddy had stepped away from the pole and was pulling on the rope.

"I'm okay," Jimmy said, digging his left hook into the pole. "Can you see how much higher I have to go?"

"Not from where I'm standing," Grandpa replied. "Do you want to come down?"

"No, sir. I want you to go to church on Sunday."

Jimmy moved farther up the pole. He'd positioned himself on the proper side so that the dark spot would be in line with his climb. He dug his hooks into the wood several more times. Looking up, he saw the blacker area of the pole.

"I'm almost there!" he cried out.

In a few more digs, he came up to eye level with his goal. A double dose of creosote had created the dark stain. He took his can of white paint from his utility belt and shook it. The metal ball in the can rattled back and forth.

"That's enough," Grandpa said. "Mark the spot and come down."

Jimmy looked at the arrow on top of the spray button. Twice he'd gotten a face-full of paint when he didn't point the can in the right direction. Aiming the can at the pole, he released a quick burst of white. He returned the can to his belt and descended. Closer to the ground, Grandpa reached up and put his hand against Jimmy's lower back. Jimmy came down until there was only a foot of pole showing above the grass, then hopped to the ground. Grandpa patted him on the shoulder. There was a big smile on the old man's face.

"Jimmy, that was unbelievable. You looked as good as the men who worked with me at the power company."

"I'm glad I got to watch you today," Daddy added simply.

After returning the gear to the toolshed, they went into the house to get a drink of water.

"I'll drive you home today," Daddy said to Jimmy. Turning to Grandpa, he added, "And I'll see you tomorrow morning with a suit and tie on."

When they arrived home, Daddy quickly changed clothes and left for the golf course. Sitting at the kitchen table, Jimmy told Mama about seeing the Watcher and Grandpa coming to church. She shook her head in disbelief.

"I never imagined God could use that pole for his glory," she said.

"What?"

"You did a good thing," she reassured him. "Now we need to pray that God will speak to Grandpa during the church service. He's not getting any younger and needs to get saved while he still has a chance. It would make your grandma so happy if he trusted in Jesus."

"Yes, ma'am," he replied.

SUNDAY ARRIVED, AND JIMMY WAS MORE EXCITED THAN USUAL about going to church. Mama let him wear his University of Georgia tie. Driving to church, he bounced up and down in his seat until Mama told him to fasten his seat belt.

"What will it be like for Grandpa to get saved?" he asked.

"Don't get your hopes up too high," Daddy answered. "He went to church when he was a boy, and he's had plenty of chances to walk the aisle. I don't want you to be disappointed."

"But you should pray," Mama added. "Just like anyone else in the congregation, your grandpa will have a chance at the end of the preaching to go forward and give his life to Jesus."

"Will Brother Fitzgerald pray for him?"

"Or one of the deacons helping in the service," Mama replied.

"I hope it's not Jesse Langston," Daddy said. "I wouldn't trust him to give me directions to the bathroom, much less point me toward heaven."

"Lee, don't say that," Mama said. "I know you're not serious, but it sends the wrong message to Jimmy."

"Can you make sure Grandpa gets to talk to Brother Fitzgerald?" Jimmy asked anxiously.

"It will work out fine," Mama said. "Don't worry."

With the start of another school year, Jimmy's Sunday school class had moved to a new room and new teacher. Mrs. Goodwin was a nice lady with no interest in Studebaker automobiles. She never strayed far from the curriculum sent from Nashville and only allowed prayer requests at the end of the class time. Jimmy thought about Grandpa while she read the lesson. He sat between Max and Denise, who passed notes back and forth to each other behind his back. At the end of class, Mrs. Goodwin looked at her watch.

"We have a couple of minutes for prayer requests," she announced.

Jimmy immediately thrust his hand in the air. Before Mrs. Goodwin could call on him, he blurted out, "Please pray for my grandpa! He coming to church because I did a good job climbing the pole."

The teacher gave him a puzzled look.

"Jimmy's grandpa used to work for the power company," Max explained. "He's teaching Jimmy how to climb a pole using those boots that have hooks on them."

"The hooks aren't on the boots," Jimmy corrected. "There is a thing that goes around my leg—"

"That's enough," Mrs. Goodwin interrupted. "Does anyone have another prayer request?"

Several sick relatives and an ailing rabbit made the list. When Mrs. Goodwin prayed, she forgot to mention Grandpa, then dismissed the class. Max continued talking to Denise as they walked out of the room at a slow pace. Jimmy sped past them so he could wait for Mama and Daddy at the doorway to their class. He grabbed Mama's hand.

"Let's go!" he said. "I want to see Grandpa."

Mama smiled and let him drag her along. They stepped outside onto the sidewalk connecting the educational wing with the sanctuary. Jimmy peered up and down the throng of people but didn't see Grandpa.

"Where is he?" he asked.

"He might not be feeling well and stayed home," Daddy suggested. "He's been having more chest pains recently."

"No! He promised," Jimmy said.

They wound their way through the crowd and up the broad steps to the sanctuary.

"Maybe they're already inside and sitting in our pew," Mama said.

Still holding Mama's hand, Jimmy entered the sanctuary and anxiously looked toward their pew. A man and a woman with gray hair were sitting beside each other in the center of the pew.

"He's here!" Jimmy exclaimed in a loud voice that caused several people to turn around and stare.

Releasing Mama's hand, he ran down the aisle. He slid into the pew and greeted Grandpa with a quick hug and smile.

"Good morning, Grandpa!" he said.

Grandma touched her index finger to her lips. "You don't have to yell."

Grandpa held out his arms, and Jimmy scooted next to him as close as when he was a little boy and Grandpa read a book to him.

"Thanks for coming," Jimmy said in a softer voice.

Grandpa smiled. "A promise is a promise."

Daddy and Mama joined them. Mama sat on the other side of Jimmy, who happily watched familiar faces enter the room and take their accustomed seats. The choir entered, followed by Brother Fitzgerald, who strode to the platform and sat in a big chair with a high back and large arms.

"Don't let me bother you," Jimmy whispered to Grandpa. "I want you to listen to Brother Fitzgerald."

"You're not bothering me," Grandpa replied. "I promise to pay attention if you do too."

"Yes, sir."

Jimmy had never concentrated so intently on a worship service. He followed along with the hymns and listened to the prayers in hope that his actions could somehow pull Grandpa into the flow of the meeting. When Brother Fitzgerald stood and read the Scripture passage for the day, Jimmy slowed his breathing to focus on the words that so often proved difficult for him to understand.

In his best preacher's voice, Brother Fitzgerald proclaimed, "Our Scripture today is found in John 3:16."

"I know what that says," he whispered to Grandpa.

"Me too."

Jimmy glanced sideways in surprise. He wanted to ask Grandpa a question, but the preacher's voice stopped him.

"'For God so loved the world, that he gave his only begotten Son, that whosoever believeth in him should not perish, but have everlasting life.'"

The preacher shut the Bible and let his eyes roam across the congregation. Jimmy felt the minister's gaze pause for a second when he reached the people sitting on the Mitchell family pew.

"Many of you have known the familiar words in this verse since before you could read," the preacher continued. "But knowing the words is not the same as believing the good news they proclaim."

For the next few minutes, Brother Fitzgerald spoke in a conversational tone so different from his usual preaching style that the sanctuary felt eerily quiet.

When he began to warm to the task and his words began to roll like distant thunder, Jimmy sat mesmerized, his eyes fixed on the minister and his attention drawn into the message, not the preacher's method of delivery.

"In conclusion, I want to share my own journey to the wells of salvation." The preacher once again spoke in a normal tone of voice. "Picture a cool, north Georgia evening in the fall of the year after the corn and the soybeans have been harvested. My favorite uncle took me to a revival meeting beneath a brown tent on the outskirts of Dawsonville. It was a Thursday night, and there weren't many people. My uncle marched down a sawdust aisle to the front row. We sat so close to the platform that I thought the preacher was going to jump into my lap. I'd been to church a few times in my life, but I'd never heard anything like this."

The preacher paused. "The speaker was an auto mechanic who sold his business and bought a tent so he could tell people about Jesus. As a thirteen-year-old boy, I heard a similar message to the one I've preached today. The call of God came to my soul, and the Son of God came into my heart. I've been preaching the gospel for over twenty-five years, and that revival preacher whose name I've forgotten has a stake in every soul I've led to Jesus. Whether you're thirteen or seventy-three, today can be your day of salvation. Don't ignore the inner witness of the Holy Spirit calling you to give your life to Jesus. Obey God! Come forward and find mercy and grace for your time of need."

Jimmy licked his lips. His heart was pounding, and he felt shaky on the inside. He'd heard about salvation his entire life, and belief in Jesus had never been a problem for him. But the preacher's message caused new thoughts and emotions to swirl in his head. He felt an ache, a longing for something he didn't have but wanted with all his heart.

Jimmy had never been encouraged to respond to an altar call. The important people in his life assumed his low IQ qualified him for a free pass into heaven. But at that moment, the theology of salvation for those with borderline intellectual ability didn't apply to Jimmy Mitchell. The call of God came to his soul. Brother Fitzgerald prayed; Jimmy closed his eyes. The choir started to sing softly. Jimmy leaned over to Mama.

"I want to go up front," he said.

"Why?" Mama asked in surprise.

"To get saved."

Mama leaned over and whispered in his ear. "You're already saved. Pray for your grandpa."

"Yes, ma'am."

Jimmy peeked sideways at Grandpa, who sat with his eyes closed. Jimmy tried to get his mind off himself and think about Grandpa, but his own uneasiness didn't lift. He tapped Mama on the arm.

"I want to go up front," he repeated.

Mama put her hand on his arm and leaned over to Daddy. Jimmy couldn't hear what she said, but she turned back to him and spoke in a quiet but firm voice.

"Jimmy, it's not necessary. You're just worked up over your grandpa."

Jimmy tried to settle back into the pew. The choir finished the third verse of the closing hymn. So far, no one had come forward. Brother Fitzgerald usually stopped the music to give another plea before the start of the fourth verse. If no one responded, the service ended. The choir grew silent. Brother Fitzgerald spoke.

"I have a sense in my heart there are least two people who need to respond to the message this morning. If you feel that tug of God in your heart, please don't resist his great love. There will never be a better opportunity for you to come to Jesus than this moment."

Jimmy's anxiety increased. The choir started to sing the fourth verse. He couldn't stand the thought of staying in his seat. Without saying anything to Mama, he slipped from the pew and moved so fast that Daddy's hand fell off his shoulder before he could slow Jimmy down. Once he'd set his feet in motion, the distress Jimmy felt while sitting in the pew lifted, and upon reaching the aisle, he walked quickly toward the front of the sanctuary. A thirteen-year-old boy responding to the invitation at the conclusion of a service wasn't an unusual event. But Jimmy Mitchell wasn't a usual boy. Whispers on each side accompanied his journey. Brother Fitzgerald saw him coming and moved from behind the pulpit to the floor of the sanctuary. He held out a beefy hand with a welcoming smile on his face. They shook hands. Brother Fitzgerald didn't let go.

"What do you want Jesus to do for you?" the preacher asked, leaning close to Jimmy's face.

Jimmy looked at Brother Fitzgerald, saw the choir behind him, and suddenly realized that he'd left the security of the family pew. He started to turn around and flee to safety. Only the preacher's grip on his right hand prevented him.

"Do you want to get saved?" Brother Fitzgerald asked.

Jimmy managed a weak nod. The preacher flipped the switch for the wireless microphone clipped to his tie.

"People of God!" the minister boomed. "Jimmy Mitchell wants to give his heart to Jesus this morning. Pray for us, while I pray with him."

Brother Fitzgerald got on his knees and pulled Jimmy down with him.

"Repeat after me," the preacher said.

Brother Fitzgerald prayed three or four words at a time. Jimmy repeated the words. It was a standard prayer, probably used by the preacher on hundreds of occasions, but on this day, for Jimmy Mitchell, it wasn't rote; it was real. As he repeated the words of the prayer, something changed.

"In the name of Jesus, amen," he repeated.

Brother Fitzgerald pulled Jimmy to his feet and turned him around to face the sanctuary.

"Everybody welcome our new little brother in Christ."

There was polite applause. A smile on his face, Jimmy peered through his glasses in the direction of his family. Mama held a tissue to her eyes. Daddy was looking around the sanctuary. Grandpa sat with his arms crossed.

The preacher bustled down the aisle, leaving Jimmy alone for a second before a congratulatory crowd of people descended upon him. Jimmy felt overwhelmed and did not know what to say. He felt a hand on his shoulder and turned. It was Mama, with Daddy close behind her. They'd worked their way down the aisle to reach him. Mama leaned over and hugged him.

"I'm proud of you," she said. "I didn't realize the Lord was really calling you."

Mama and Daddy took over management of the crowd. All Jimmy had to do was smile and shake hands with the men and allow the women to give him a hug. Several lipstick-laden kisses smudged his forehead and both cheeks. The informal reception lasted only a few minutes, but it seemed much longer to Jimmy. When the crowd thinned, he turned to Mama.

"Where are Grandpa and Grandma?"

"They had to leave. Grandpa wasn't feeling well."

"He should have come down with me. I didn't feel well either, but I'm a lot better now."

Mama nodded. "Yes. You led the way. All he had to do was humble himself like a little child and follow. He missed a great opportunity."

— Twelve —

Jimmy and his family ate lunch at the Springdale Restaurant. The restaurant featured a Sunday buffet that united all God's children. Baptists, Methodists, Presbyterians, and Pentecostals might not be able to gather in the same sanctuary, but they had no problem fellowshipping around roast beef, pan-fried okra, and creamed corn.

Mama always helped Jimmy select the food for his plate. Otherwise, he had a tendency to load up with meat and potatoes, leaving little room for anything green, yellow, or orange. He reached the end of the line with a plate heaped high with roast beef, mashed potatoes, carrots, green beans, and a cornbread muffin perched on top of the pile. Daddy waited for them at a table toward the rear of the restaurant. He clicked off his cell phone as they joined him.

"He's having chest pains, and he went to lie down as soon as he took off his shoes," he said to Mama.

"Should he go to the hospital?"

"He claims it's not any worse than usual, but I don't trust his self-diagnosis. I'm going over to see him after we eat."

Jimmy knew they were talking about Grandpa.

"I could listen to his heart," he volunteered.

"That always makes him feel better," Mama replied, "but he needs to see a doctor to make sure he's okay."

In public places, Daddy prayed a very short blessing over the meal. After he finished, Jimmy cut off a juicy piece of meat and chased it with a bite of mashed potatoes. It was one of his favorite flavor combinations.

"Jimmy," Daddy said, "tell me in your own words what happened to you today. Don't try to sound like a preacher."

"Are you going to cross-examine him?" Mama asked. "I told you at the church we shouldn't try to challenge what the Holy Spirit—"

"No," Daddy interrupted. "I'm willing to listen. Go ahead."

"Can I eat another bite of food?" Jimmy asked. "Getting saved made me real hungry."

Daddy smiled. "Okay, but don't forget your carrots and green beans."

They waited in silence until Jimmy swallowed his bite. "Something inside made me want to go up front," he said.

"Did you see anything?" Daddy asked.

"Yes, sir. Everyone in the choir was staring at me, and I wanted to go back to my seat, but Brother Fitzgerald held on to my hand. Then he prayed, and I repeated the words."

Daddy lowered his voice. "Did you see a Watcher in the sanctuary?"

"No, sir. Did you?"

"No. I've never seen one."

"Neither have I," Mama added. "But I believe they're real."

"Even if that's true," Daddy said, "I don't understand why he would claim divine revelation to take my father to church. It seems like the wrong person went forward. You've claimed for years that Jimmy was already saved, and I agreed with you. He's always been a good boy who prays and tries to be good most of the time."

Mama shook her head. "It's not about being good enough. We don't know everything in his heart. You saw me. I tried to hold him back, but when I saw him walk down the aisle, something inside me jumped for joy." She turned toward Jimmy. "Did you mean it with all your heart when you prayed with Brother Fitzgerald?"

"Yes, ma'am. And the bad feelings went away. I felt happy and then hungry."

"Maybe it's another step in growing up," Mama said. "A child starts out relying on his parents' faith but at some point has to believe because it's his or her choice to do so. I wasn't sure that would ever happen with Jimmy, but it has, and we should be glad about it."

"Oh, I'm glad," Daddy answered. "I guess there's just a part of this I won't be able to understand."

As they neared the end of their meal, Brother Fitzgerald came over to their table. The preacher had loosened his tie and unbuttoned the top button of his shirt.

"May I join you for a minute?" he asked Daddy. "I was going to call you later but wondered if we could talk now."

"Sure," Daddy replied.

The preacher sat in the extra chair and placed his large hands on the edge of the table.

"I'm so proud of Jimmy stepping out and coming down front to receive Jesus into his life. It will be a memory I carry with me for a long time."

"Thank you," Mama said. "And we appreciate the sensitive way you treated him."

"He's a fine boy," Brother Fitzgerald said, patting Jimmy on the shoulder. "God works in mysterious ways his wonders to perform. I've led lots of people to the Lord, but you're one of the most special."

Jimmy winced.

Brother Fitzgerald continued. "I'll have to double-check the church calendar, but I think we're going to have a baptismal service on Sunday night in two weeks. I realize it's close to Christmas, but it's a great time of year to follow the Lord under the water. If your family is going to be in town, I'd like to put Jimmy on the list. He'll be in a group with the Cole family. They were Methodists before moving to Piney Grove, and all six of them are going to be baptized. I'm also talking to a young man who works as an industrial engineer at Southwire. He wants to be baptized and join the church. All in all, it will be a nice assembly. The sooner, the better, is my theology of baptism. Philip baptized the Ethiopian at the first sign of water." Brother Fitzgerald winked at Jimmy. "And no matter how cold it is outside, our baptismal pool is a pleasant eighty degrees."

"That should work fine," Daddy replied. "We don't have any plans to be out of town until after the holidays."

"Good." Brother Fitzgerald pushed away from the table and stood to his feet. He smiled down at Jimmy. "God bless you, son. Your baptism will be one of the greatest days of your life."

Jimmy didn't respond. He'd seen many baptisms. Watching and participating were two entirely different matters.

"Do either of you want dessert?" Daddy asked. "I think there's a piece of coconut pie with my name on it."

"Lee," Mama replied in a low but intense voice. "What were you thinking? Do you really believe Jimmy is going to let Brother Fitzgerald baptize him?"

"Uh, it shouldn't be a problem. The baptismal pool isn't any bigger than a bathtub."

"When was the last time Jimmy took a bath?"

Daddy didn't answer but looked at Jimmy. "Tell your mama that you're not afraid to be baptized."

Jimmy kept his eyes down and spoke in the direction of his plate. "I don't want to do it."

"The water is less than four and a half feet deep," Daddy answered, trying to keep his voice calm. "There will be children in the Cole family younger and smaller than you getting baptized. It will all be over in a few seconds. The preacher is holding you steady the entire time. Brother Fitzgerald is strong enough not to let anything bad happen to you."

Jimmy couldn't close his ears, but he could shut his eyes. He hid in the self-imposed dark.

"Don't try to argue with him," Mama said. "Leave him alone."

"You should have kept quiet," Daddy retorted. "You put fear in his head."

There was silence at the table for a moment. Jimmy opened his eyes, but the image of the water closing over his head seeped into his mind.

"No," Mama said in a steely voice. "I think there is someone else to blame for that."

Daddy didn't eat any coconut pie.

THE SUBJECT OF BAPTISM DIDN'T COME UP DURING THE SILENT drive home. Daddy dropped off Jimmy and Mama then continued to Grandpa and Grandma's house. Jimmy walked up the steps beside Mama. Inside, Mama stopped him before he could run upstairs to change clothes and gave him a heartfelt hug.

"Don't let anything ruin this day," she said. "The angels in heaven are rejoicing over what you did at the church."

"What would that look like?"

Mama smiled. "You probably know more about that than I do. Someday we'll both find out. Now go upstairs and change clothes. Be sure to hang up your pants and jacket in the closet."

JIMMY PUT ON A FLANNEL SHIRT AND BLUE JEANS SUITED TO the cool December afternoon. Before going outside to play with Buster, he lay on the bed and looked out the window that gave him a broad view of the front yard. It was a familiar sight viewed from a safe place, and he often liked to lie on the bed and stare out the window. Today no one passed by on the sidewalk. No breeze blew. The scene was as still as a painted landscape.

But today his world looked different.

Jimmy took off his glasses, rubbed them with the corner of his soft shirt, and returned them to their place. The sense that he was seeing things in a new way didn't go away. Puzzled, he remained on the bed, unable to understand a reason for the difference. The green grass, the texture of the bark on the trees, the rich brown of the fallen leaves. Everything seemed more alive. Then a message came into the stillness of his heart.

"Behold, I make all things new."

To Jimmy, the words sounded like something from the Holy Bible, but he had no idea where the verse might be found. He glanced over his shoulder, half expecting to see a Watcher standing in the doorway. But he was alone. He repeated the words.

"Behold, I make all things new."

Jimmy propped his elbows on the bed and thought about the meaning of the sentence. He didn't know what "behold" meant, and that made the rest of the message fuzzy. Over and over, he repeated the words. As he did, a sense of understanding came.

First, he knew the words were linked to the events of the morning as a personal message from God. Second, he felt excitement and fear: excitement that God was doing something and fear that it would be new and therefore unfamiliar.

Sliding from the bed, he went to his desk and carefully wrote the words on a sheet of paper. When he finished, he found a tack and stuck the sheet on the small corkboard where Mama placed family photos she thought he would enjoy. The message rested beside a picture of Grandpa holding a stringer of fish he and

Jimmy had caught at a small pond owned by one of Grandpa's friends. The sight of Grandpa triggered a prayer. Jimmy didn't pray long prayers. He made his point and moved on.

"Jesus, please make all things new for Grandpa, amen."

He reached out and touched the stringer of fish. They'd felt cold and slimy when caught, but the photograph left them dry. Jimmy enjoyed fishing but stayed away from the edge of the water. That had been his way as long as he could remember.

Jimmy had an idea.

Going into the guest bathroom, he found a white drain stopper and took it to his bathroom. He covered the drain with the stopper and turned on the water. He watched as it slowly crept up the sides of the tub. When the water reached six inches, he touched it with his right index finger. It was cool, so he increased the flow of hot water into the mix. By the time the water was a foot deep, he'd stepped away from the tub. He watched until the water came dangerously close to sloshing over the side then hurriedly turned off the knobs and retreated to his room.

He took down the sheet of paper from the corkboard and marched into his bathroom. He put the paper on a small shelf above the toilet and stared at it for several seconds, rereading the message. If all things were new, then he should no longer have a fear of water.

He could step into the bathtub. He could be baptized. Jimmy slipped off his blue jeans. Wearing his shorts, he stared at the water. His legs begin to tremble. He bit his lip and tried to will his feet forward.

"Jimmy! What in the world are you doing? I heard the water running and came upstairs to check on you."

Mama stood in the doorway.

"Uh, I was going to try to get into the tub." Jimmy backed away from the water and picked up the sheet of paper and handed it to her. "What does *behold* mean?"

Mama took the paper from his hand. "When did you write this?"

"When I got home from church."

"Did you copy it?"

"No ma'am, I heard it in my head."

"From a Watcher?"

"No, ma'am."

Mama was silent for a second before she spoke. "It was the Holy Spirit. This is part of a verse from the Bible."

"What does *behold* mean?" Jimmy repeated.

"Oh, it means 'look.' Another way to write the verse would be, 'Look, I make all things new.' *Behold* means to pay attention, like a teacher telling the class to look at something written on the blackboard."

"Okay."

"But what does the verse have to do with filling the tub with water?" Mama asked.

"I wanted to see if I was still afraid of water."

"Oh, I think I understand. If everything in your life is new, then the old things that bothered you should be gone."

"Yes, ma'am."

Mama held up the sheet of paper. "All right. If you want to step into the tub, I'll stand here and watch. I know that with God's help you can do it."

Jimmy faced the water. All the ripples caused by the process of filling the tub had ceased, and the water was completely still. He took a small step forward. He advanced another step.

"Behold, I make all things new," Mama said softly.

Jimmy shuffled his feet forward across the tile floor and stopped. He repeated the process until his toes touched the cool side of the tub. His breathing increased. He began to feel slightly dizzy.

"Stay calm," Mama's soothing voice reassured him. "Behold, I make all things new."

Jimmy started to lift his left leg, but it didn't rise more than an inch before it returned to the floor.

"Use your right leg," Mama suggested. "When it touches the water, you won't feel anything except wetness."

Jimmy took a couple of quick breaths. He raised his right leg until his foot was level with the top of the tub. He stared at his foot as it moved toward the water. He lowered it to the surface. The ball of his foot and the end of his toes went into the water. Mama was right: it was wet. His foot went deeper. The water crept up his leg to his calf.

"No!" he screamed, jerking away his foot so violently that he stumbled backward.

In an instant, Mama had her arms around him. Jimmy leaned against her, his chest heaving up and down.

"No," he repeated. "I don't want to do it."

Mama stroked his head. "It's okay. It's okay. You don't have to. It's good that you made as much progress as you did."

"I don't feel very good."

"Do you want to lie down?"

"Yes, ma'am."

Mama kept her arm around him as he walked to the bed. Jimmy sat on the edge of the bed. Mama stood beside him.

"Will you take care of the water?" he asked.

"Of course, in just a minute."

"Will you do it now?"

"Yes, I'll be right back."

Jimmy heard the water began to drain from the tub and sighed. He heard Daddy come in the front door.

"Ellen!" he called out.

"I'm up here with Jimmy," Mama answered.

Daddy appeared in the doorway as Mama returned from the bathroom with Jimmy's blue jeans.

"How's your father?" she asked.

"Resting, so I didn't wake him up. I'll talk to him tomorrow about seeing the cardiologist."

Daddy looked at Jimmy with concern. "Are you sick? You look pale."

Mama handed Jimmy his pants. "Put those on while I show your father what you wrote."

Jimmy slipped on his blue jeans. Mama brought the sheet of paper from the bathroom and handed it to Daddy.

"Jimmy wrote this," she said.

Daddy read it with a puzzled look on his face.

"Let me tell you what happened," Mama said. "Sit on the bed with your son."

Jimmy listened as she told Daddy the story. At first Daddy asked a few questions, but then he grew silent and didn't interrupt. When Mama reached the part about Jimmy putting his foot in the water, Jimmy spoke.

"Why didn't it work?" he asked.

Mama reached over and patted him on the knee.

"It was a beginning. Before today you wouldn't have thought about filling the tub with water and stepping into it. God makes all things new, but sometimes it takes awhile for us to learn how to live in the new world he has for us."

"So, will I stop being afraid of the water?"

"Yes, be patient. And God may use other people to help."

"Is that right, Daddy?" Jimmy asked.

"I hope so. You mama is the theologian."

"What's that?"

Mama turned toward Daddy. "I think we should call the child psychologist and then talk to Brother Fitzgerald."

"About what?" Daddy asked.

"Everything. Perhaps you're right that I've been overprotective. After what happened today, Jimmy may be mature enough to begin dealing with the truth. Knowledge could be a part of his healing."

– Thirteen –

Jimmy asked Grandpa about his visit to the heart doctor.

"As long as I have you to check me out, I really don't need to see a doctor," the old man said. "But I went anyway because it made your daddy and grandma happy."

"Did he listen to your heart through one of those things?"

"Yes, and a stethoscope is a lot colder than your ear, even when you've been outside in the middle of winter."

Jimmy and Grandpa were sitting in the kitchen. It was late afternoon on Thursday. The weather had been cold and rainy for several days, but today a winter sun ruled the skies. Jimmy looked out the window into the backyard. He could see some of the white paint splotches that marked his ascent of the power pole.

"Could you call Daddy and ask him to come home early so I can climb the pole?" Jimmy asked.

"I already talked to him. He has a late appointment and can't leave the office until supper time. Would you like to look at a fishing catalog?"

"Yes, sir."

"I'll get it. It's in the bedroom."

Jimmy sat in one of the extra chairs and watched the second hand move forward on the clock near the back door. He could tell time on a digital clock, but not on a clock face.

"What time is it?" Jimmy asked when Grandpa returned.

"Five fifteen, which is a perfect time to look at a fishing-equipment catalog."

They moved into the living room and sat on the couch together. Grandpa didn't rush through the pages. They looked at rods, reels, lures, and other angling gear. There were many photographs of fishermen and fish. Grandpa pointed to a picture of a man casting a lure into a mountain lake that reflected with mirror-like quality the snowcapped peaks that surrounded it.

"I bet this fellow spent the night in a tent about fifty feet from the water. When he woke up in the morning, he stepped outside to stretch and saw a grizzly bear drinking on the opposite side of the lake. A grizzly bear can be ten feet tall when it stands on its hind legs." Grandpa flipped to a different part of the catalog. "The man would have used binoculars like these to watch the bear from a safe distance. After the bear drank plenty of water, it walked back into the woods."

"Are grizzly bears mean?"

"They can be mean and ornery."

"How tall is ten feet?"

Grandpa set aside the catalog. "I'll show you. Put on your jacket."

As they walked across the grass, Grandpa reached out and took Jimmy's hand in his thick fingers. Grandpa's hand was different from Mama's. Grandpa's grip was rough. Mama's touch was tender. Love flowed freely from both. They reached the pole, and Grandpa pointed upward with his free hand.

"Do you see the mark that looks like the letter *C*?"

"Yes, sir."

"That's about ten feet. With his front paws up in the air, it would be even higher than the mark. Can you imagine what it might look like?"

Jimmy thought about the massive bear. "Are there grizzly bears in Piney Grove?"

"No. You don't have to worry about running into one around here."

Jimmy's eyes climbed higher up the pole. The next mark had a different shape.

"Look at that paint spot," Jimmy said, pointing. "It looks like a cross."

Grandpa tilted back his head. "Yes, I see it."

"How high up in the air was Jesus when they put him on the cross?"

"I don't know, but I doubt it was that high."

Still hand in hand, they returned to the house. When they reached the back step, Grandpa let go of Jimmy's hand, touched his chest, and grimaced slightly.

"Does your heart hurt?" Jimmy asked.

"A little bit."

Jimmy put his hand on top of Grandpa's hand. "I'll ask Jesus to give you a new heart. He can make all things new. Mama says it might take awhile, so you have to be patient."

THE FOLLOWING WEEK, JIMMY HAD A SESSION AT SCHOOL WITH Dr. Paris. While waiting for her to review his answers to a short test, he sat at his desk with a smile on his face.

"What's going on?" she asked. "You seem extra happy today. Has something good happened in your life?"

"Yes, ma'am."

Jimmy told her about going forward to be saved. The blond-haired doctor listened closely.

"I joined the church when I was about your age," she said.

"Which one?"

"A Methodist church in Macon, where I grew up. I haven't gone to church much in Piney Grove."

"You could come to the First Baptist Church and sit on the pew with my family. We have plenty of room."

"Thank you."

Jimmy's face grew more serious. "I wish I could invite you to watch me get baptized on Sunday night, but I don't think I'm going to be able to do it."

"The water," Dr. Paris said.

"Yes, ma'am. Could you help me? Mama said God will use other people to help me stop being afraid of water so I can be baptized."

Dr. Paris patted Jimmy on the shoulder with a red-tipped hand. "My job at the school is to help with subjects like math and spelling. I could get in trouble if I give you advice about religious beliefs or practices."

Jimmy couldn't imagine Dr. Paris getting into trouble. She told the teachers what to do.

"What kind of trouble?" he asked.

"I won't try to explain it. But you should talk to your parents and the pastor of your church about what to do. They're the ones God will use to steer you in the right direction."

"Yes, ma'am. Mama and Daddy are going to take me to see Brother Fitzgerald about it this afternoon."

"Good."

Jimmy continued. "Max told me some churches put a few drops of water on your head and call it baptism. I wouldn't be scared of a few drops of water, but it doesn't sound right to me. What do you think?"

"That's what most Methodist churches do. It's called *sprinkling* or *christening*. I was baptized by sprinkling as a baby, but I can't give you my opinion about what you should do."

Jimmy shook his head. "You were lucky. I wish I'd been baptized as a baby. Even if the preacher put me all the way under the water!"

JIMMY, MAMA, AND DADDY SAT IN THE LARGE WAITING AREA outside Brother Fitzgerald's office. Like the sanctuary, the church office suite had white walls and dark burgundy carpet. Several potted plants rested in brass containers. The two sofas in the waiting area were covered in a bold print fabric. Side chairs rested in the corners.

Sitting at a desk near the door to the preacher's office was Mrs. Kilmer, a middle-aged woman who also served as church bookkeeper. Daddy said the fireproof filing cabinet behind her desk held top-secret financial information about how much money people put into the offering plate. Jimmy stared at the brown cabinet for a few seconds and then nudged Daddy.

"Is that the filing cabinet that wouldn't be burned up in the lake of fire?"

"Yes. A lot of people would like to know what's in it, but it is sealed until the last trumpet."

Mama reached over and pressed down Jimmy's cowlick.

"You're overdue for a haircut," she said.

The phone on Mrs. Kilmer's desk buzzed, and she picked it up.

"You can go in," she said.

Jimmy followed Mama and Daddy. They stepped into a large rectangular office lined from floor to ceiling with books. A wooden desk occupied the left-hand side of the room. Brother Fitzgerald stood from behind it to greet them as they entered. Jimmy eyed the number of books in wonder.

"Have you read all these books?" he asked.

Brother Fitzgerald smiled. "No, but I've read most of them. I like to collect books."

"I collect hats," Jimmy replied.

"So I've heard. Which one is your favorite?"

"My John Deere hat, or the white one from the University of Georgia."

"Go, dawgs," the preacher responded. "I spent four years at Prince Avenue Baptist when I was a student at the university. Football on Saturday and church on Sunday. It was a good life. Have a seat."

There were four chairs in a circle on the other side of the room. Everyone sat. Jimmy sat between Mama and Daddy.

"How have you been doing since you got saved?" the preacher asked Jimmy.

"Good."

Mama opened her purse and took out a sheet of paper and handed it to Brother Fitzgerald.

"He wrote this down the afternoon after he came forward in the service."

"Behold, I make all things new," the preacher read. "Very nice. I'd like to mention that verse when you're baptized."

"Uh, that's why we're here," Daddy said. "There is a problem with Jimmy and baptism. He's afraid of water."

The preacher waved his hand in the air. "Oh, I've worked with folks who didn't like to get their head wet. One woman in Douglasville wore a pink swim cap to keep her hair dry. I'm flexible."

"This isn't a case of dislike," Daddy replied. "Jimmy experiences a full-blown panic attack when faced with the possibility of being in the water. He won't go wading in a stream or step into a bathtub full of water. He's never been in a swimming pool or the surf at the beach."

Brother Fitzgerald sat back in his chair. "I see. What do you think caused the problem?"

They sat in silence for several seconds.

Mama spoke. "Lee, are you going to say anything?"

"Go ahead," Daddy said. "You're the one who did the research."

"Do you want Jimmy to step outside?" Brother Fitzgerald asked.

"No," Mama replied, her face serious. "Before coming to see you this afternoon,

I talked to a child psychologist in Atlanta who is familiar with our situation. He suggested it might be time to discuss it with Jimmy. We thought you could counsel and pray with us."

Brother Fitzgerald sat up straighter in his chair. "All right. I'll be glad to listen. What happened?"

"Lee, you have to do this part," Mama said.

Daddy sighed. "I can't verify all the details because I wasn't there, but it involves my first wife, Vera, Jimmy's birth mother."

Jimmy's eyes opened wide. Daddy looked directly at Brother Fitzgerald. Mama reached over and took Jimmy's hand. Usually, her hand was soft and cool. Today it felt hot and sticky. Daddy spoke.

"When Jimmy was about eighteen months old, Vera was at home giving him a bath. Instead of a modern, plastic baby bath, she insisted on using an antique washtub that had been in her family for generations. It was a hot day, and she put more water than usual in the tub. The phone rang—"

"The tub was on a small back porch that we tore down when we built our sunroom," Mama interjected. "It was directly next to the kitchen."

Daddy continued. "Vera claims she ran inside to grab the phone and slipped in water that had sloshed from the tub when she carried it to the porch. She crashed to the floor and hit her head. I don't know whether she was knocked unconscious or not. Ten seconds, thirty seconds, a minute passed. I don't know. But when she came around and tried to stand up, she fell down again. Eventually, she crawled to the back porch and found Jimmy underneath the water. She pulled him out, but he wasn't breathing. One of our neighbors at the time was the chief of the fire department. Vera saw his car in the driveway and ran over to his house. Fortunately, he was home and came running. He started CPR, then Jimmy coughed up water and began breathing again. We have no idea how long he'd stopped breathing. An ambulance took Jimmy to the hospital, where he spent a couple of days under observation."

"Is that why he has, uh, problems?" Brother Fitzgerald asked.

"That's been a matter of disagreement among the professionals who've evaluated him," Mama replied. "I have a folder full of reports at the house. I could let you read them. There's so much more to this than we're telling you."

"It's not necessary," Daddy said. "To answer your question, Vera and I already knew developmental issues existed. Jimmy was slow to develop age-appropriate motor and verbal skills, but at eighteen months it's hard to categorize the severity of those types of problems. Some of the challenges Jimmy faces aren't typically caused by anoxic injury following a near-drowning incident—"

"Anorexic?" Brother Fitzgerald asked.

"No, anoxic. That is, a diminished flow of oxygen to the brain. Depending upon the length of time a person stays underwater, the loss of oxygen to the brain can affect many cognitive functions, including short- and long-term memory. Jimmy's memory is spotty; however, at times, he exhibits a remarkable memory."

"Which makes me think he had an extraordinary memory that was partially destroyed by the lack of oxygen to his brain," Mama said. "He's a smart boy—"

"Only one of the doctors in Atlanta gave any credence to that theory," Daddy interrupted, holding up his hand. "And we're not going to debate it here."

Mama pressed her lips tightly together.

Daddy continued. "All the doctors and psychologists agree on one thing—a near drowning can open the door to significant anxiety. In Jimmy's case, it involves a fear of water, which makes sense given what happened to him."

As Mama and Daddy talked, Jimmy felt less and less part of the conversation. He couldn't remember any of the events Daddy talked about, and it seemed the adults were talking about someone else—another boy named Jimmy with a different mama named Vera. He didn't understand the strange words Daddy was using. Mama squeezed his hand, and her voice called him back to the moment.

"Are you okay?" she asked.

"Yes, ma'am."

"Obviously, I'm not a psychologist," Brother Fitzgerald said.

"But you're our pastor, and I"—Mama paused—"*we* would like to ask you to pray for Jimmy. With his limited insight, we've been told that he's not a good candidate for psychotherapy, and I'd prefer a spiritual solution anyway. We'd like to see him helped for a lot more reasons than just so he can be baptized. Before you give us your opinion, there is one other thing that should be mentioned in private."

Daddy said, "I can tell you in a couple of minutes."

"Could Jimmy sit in the chair behind your desk?" Mama asked the preacher. "That should allow Lee to speak confidentially."

"Of course," Brother Fitzgerald replied with a wave of his hand.

Still holding Jimmy's hand, Mama led him to the far end of the room. Brother Fitzgerald's desk was nice but not as big and fancy as the one in Daddy's office. Jimmy sat in a soft chair with a high back, and Mama slowly turned it around. When he faced Daddy and the preacher, Jimmy could see them leaning forward with their heads close together as they talked. The next time Jimmy came around in the chair, he reached out, grabbed the desk, and stopped the spinning.

"What is it?" Mama asked.

Jimmy pointed to the corner of the room behind Brother Fitzgerald.

"It's a Watcher," he whispered.

Mama put her fingers to her lips and leaned close to Jimmy's ear.

"What does he look like?"

Keeping his eyes fixed on the corner of the room, Jimmy answered, "A Watcher. He stays here at the church."

"All the time?"

"Yes, ma'am."

"Is he talking to you?"

"Just inside my head. Is that where my brain stays?"

"Yes."

Jimmy nodded. He remembered the diagram of the human body on the wall in Mr. Jenkins's science class. It was beside Jimmy's desk, and Jimmy would stare at it while the teacher talked to the regular students.

"Daddy was talking about my brain, wasn't he?"

"Yes. Is the Watcher still there?"

"Yes, ma'am. He's watching Daddy and Brother Fitzgerald."

"Do you know what he thinks?"

Jimmy glanced up at Mama. "About what?"

Mama hesitated. "Can you ask him a question without saying it out loud?"

"I don't know."

"Try it. Ask him if you're going to get over your fear of water and be baptized."

"How do I do that?"

"Repeat the words in your head—'Am I going to get over my fear of water and be baptized?'"

Jimmy looked at the Watcher, who continued to look at Daddy and Brother Fitzgerald. He forgot the order of the words.

"Can you say it again?"

"Are you talking to me?" Mama asked.

"Yes, ma'am."

Mama repeated the words into Jimmy's left ear. He moved his lips without making a sound.

"We're done!" Daddy announced in a loud voice.

"What did he say?" Mama asked anxiously.

"We're done!" Jimmy exclaimed.

Mama stayed close to Jimmy's ear. "No, the Watcher."

Jimmy paused for a second, looked up into Mama's eyes, and gave her a slight smile.

"Yes," he said.

"Anything else?"

"No, ma'am. That's all he said. He said yes."

"Ellen, we're ready," Daddy said.

MAMA AND JIMMY RETURNED TO THEIR SEATS. BROTHER FITZGERALD rubbed his large hands together. Jimmy had seen the same gesture when the preacher spoke to the congregation before taking up the offering.

"I appreciate the sensitivity of this information and will of course respect your request for confidentiality."

He smiled at Jimmy. Up close, Brother Fitzgerald's smile was even bigger than Jimmy had noticed from the pew. His white teeth sparkled.

"You have white teeth," Jimmy said. "How many times a day do you brush them?"

Brother Fitzgerald laughed. "After every meal if I can. I even keep a toothbrush at the church and brush them on Sunday morning after eating a donut and drinking a cup of coffee during the fellowship hour."

Jimmy looked up at Mama. "Should I bring my toothbrush to church?"

"No," Daddy replied. "And don't get us off the subject with your questions."

Brother Fitzgerald held up his hand. "It's my fault. I led him on. I had no idea Jimmy was such an interesting conversationalist."

"He'll definitely challenge your usual way of thinking," Mama replied. She leaned over and whispered in Jimmy's ear. "Is the Watcher still here?"

Jimmy peered past Brother Fitzgerald.

"No, ma'am. I can't see him."

"I'm right here," Brother Fitzgerald replied.

"Not you," Mama said. "While we were at your desk, Jimmy saw an angel standing in the corner of the room. He calls them Watchers."

Daddy groaned. Brother Fitzgerald's eyes grew large as he spoke.

"Mrs. Mitchell, are you telling me Jimmy claims to see angels?"

"Yes, it's been going on for a long time."

The preacher turned in his seat and looked at the corner of the room.

"Where was it?" he asked Jimmy. "Show me."

"Preacher—," Daddy began.

"Humor me, Lee," Brother Fitzgerald replied. "I'll keep this just as confidential as everything else."

"Secrecy doesn't matter," Daddy grunted. "This all came out in court last year when Jimmy testified in a case before Judge Robinson. I'm surprised you haven't heard some of the jokes that come my way."

Mama patted Jimmy on the knee. "You heard Brother Fitzgerald. Go stand where you saw the Watcher."

Jimmy slipped out of his chair and walked to the corner of the room. Bookshelves rose on either side of him. He faced the chairs and held his right hand out in front of him with his palm toward the adults.

"Why is your arm like that?" Brother Fitzgerald asked.

"That's what he was doing," Jimmy replied.

"You didn't tell me that," Mama said.

"No, ma'am. You didn't ask me."

"Where is he now?" Brother Fitzgerald asked.

Jimmy slowly scanned the room. The adults followed his gaze.

"I can't see him," Jimmy said when he completed the circuit.

"Is he still here, only invisible?" Brother Fitzgerald asked.

"He's always here."

"In my office?" the preacher asked in surprise.

"At the church. I don't know where else he goes. But he always stays at the church. This is his home. I've seen him in the room where the babies stay, and once he whispered in your ear while you were preaching the sermon."

Brother Fitzgerald let out a big breath of air. "I've never encountered anything like this in thirty years of ministry! You say he spoke to me while I was preaching?"

"Yes, sir."

"What did he say?"

"I don't know," Jimmy replied. "He whispered in your ear, not mine."

Daddy looked at his watch.

"If we're going to pray, we need to get started. I have a conference call scheduled with a judge in Douglas County in less than thirty minutes."

"Sure," Brother Fitzgerald replied. "Jimmy and I can talk about angels another time."

"Watchers," Jimmy corrected.

"I believe they're angels, and I've explained to Jimmy—" Mama stopped when Daddy made a swift downward motion with his hand.

Brother Fitzgerald cleared his throat. "Let us pray," he said, lowering his voice.

Jimmy bowed his head and closed his eyes. The preacher's words rolled from his lips. He talked about God's power, love, mercy, and holiness. Jimmy was amazed at how much Brother Fitzgerald knew about God. The preacher identified the people in the room: Daddy, Mama, Jimmy, and himself. He then used as many big words as Daddy when describing what the doctors said about Jimmy. The prayer went on a long time. Jimmy could tell the end was coming by the way the preacher talked.

"And all God's people said . . ." Brother Fitzgerald paused.

"Amen," Mama and Daddy said.

"Amen," said Jimmy.

Brother Fitzgerald stood and shook everyone's hand. Mama and Daddy thanked him for his time. When he reached Jimmy, he flashed another of his trademark grins.

"Young man, I look forward to further theological discussions with you. I'll be watching you, and you be watching me."

"Yes, sir."

MAMA TURNED SIDEWAYS IN HER SEAT SO SHE COULD SEE Jimmy's face.

"Did you understand what we told Brother Fitzgerald about your birth mama giving you a bath, answering the phone, and then finding you underwater?"

"I don't remember it."

"Of course you don't, but there is a place inside your brain that does. That place is what makes you afraid of the water."

Jimmy wrinkled his brow. "Can the doctor cut it off like he did the wart on Max's finger?"

"No, problems like this one can't be fixed by an operation. That's why we asked Brother Fitzgerald to pray and ask God to take away your fear."

"I didn't feel anything while he was praying."

"Neither did I," Daddy added as he glanced toward Mama. "I swear that preacher flips a switch and out comes a prayer that sounds like a twenty-page brief I'd file with the Court of Appeals. I'm more moved when you pray before we go to sleep than by—"

"Lee, don't," Mama interrupted. "We went for help and shouldn't criticize Brother Fitzgerald's efforts."

They rode in silence for a minute.

"You're right," Daddy sighed. "I guess I'm trying not to get my hopes up and then be disappointed."

"We'll fill up the tub when we get home and see what happens," Mama said.

— Fourteen —

An hour later Jimmy hadn't gotten a toe wet, and Mama removed the stopper from the tub. Jimmy sadly stared at the water as it swirled down the drain. He kept his head lowered.

"I'm sorry," he said. "I know I should be able to get in the water but won't do it. I'm a bad boy."

"No, no," Mama replied. "You can't control the fear. If this problem were simply a matter of willpower, I know you could do it, but you're wrestling with something bigger than your ability to conquer."

"I don't understand."

"Don't think about it any more today," Mama said. "Do you believe Jesus loves you?"

"Yes."

"Why?"

"For the Bible tells me so."

Mama touched his heart. "That's right, but do you know it in here?"

"Yes, ma'am."

"Then don't let anyone or anything take that love away from you. I don't understand why the fear is still there. We're all weak and fearful in some ways and need God's help."

"You and Daddy aren't afraid of anything."

"Adult fears are hidden."

Jimmy was puzzled. "Then how do you know what they are?"

Mama put her arms around his shoulders and walked him into his room.

"Because sometimes they come out of hiding and scare us."

DURING SUPPER, DADDY LISTENED TO MAMA TELL ABOUT THE afternoon's efforts beside the bathtub. Jimmy gnawed a fried chicken leg and didn't contribute to the conversation.

"I'll call the church and tell Mrs. Kilmer not to put Jimmy on the list to be baptized next week," Daddy said. "If things change, he can be baptized in the future."

Jimmy took a bite of peas mixed with carrots. Suddenly, he had an idea.

"I could be sparkled," he suggested as soon as he swallowed.

Daddy gave him a puzzled look. "What does that mean?"

"Dr. Paris told me she was sparkled at her church when she was a baby, and in the restroom at school, Max showed me how they do it."

"Sprinkled," Daddy corrected. "The minister or priest puts a few drops of water on your head, and they call it baptism."

"Yes, sir," Jimmy said. "I'll show you."

Jimmy jumped up from his chair and ran to the sink. He turned on the water, cupped a small amount in his right hand, and dumped it on his head. The drops ran down his cheeks to his chin.

"See, that isn't a problem," he said. "Could Brother Fitzgerald do that to me?"

Mama and Daddy looked at each other.

"If he refuses, we could always become Presbyterians." Daddy replied.

"It wouldn't hurt to ask," Mama said.

"Okay," Daddy said. "I'll see what I can find out."

IT WAS A COLD, CLEAR NIGHT WHEN THE SIX MEMBERS OF the Cole family and the young engineer who worked at Southwire were baptized in the warm interior of the First Baptist Church. Jimmy sat in the Mitchell pew and watched with more than usual interest. He marveled as each person stepped into and then under the water. A girl much younger than Jimmy did nothing more than sputter. Brother Fitzgerald had said no when Daddy asked that Jimmy be sprinkled.

THE RAINY, COLD WEATHER OF THE GEORGIA WINTER INTER-fered with pole-climbing lessons, but in the few days available, Jimmy extended the white marks higher and higher. Grandpa's heart seemed fine, and he returned to his usual activities.

During the Christmas holiday, Jimmy spent several days working at Daddy's office, where his ability to sort documents without becoming bored earned the increased admiration of Delores Smythe. One day he carried a neat stack of papers into her office and put them on a small table beside her workstation.

"Here they are," he announced. "All of these papers are for the same year."

"Sorted according to the month and day?"

"Yes, ma'am."

Delores picked up a photograph of Maureen, her fawn-colored Siamese cat.

"I'm going to be out of town for several days after Christmas and need someone to check on my cats and make sure they have enough food and water. Would you be interested in doing it for me? I'd be glad to pay you."

Jimmy stared at the picture of the cat. It was standing with its front paws wrapped around a stuffed mouse.

Delores continued, "Your daddy says you do a good job with your dog, and cats are much easier to take care of than dogs because they use a litter box. I already have a special feeder that drops the correct amount of food into their dishes twice a day and a watering station that dispenses water. But I hate for my babies to have nothing to eat except that boring dry food. It would be sweet if you could open a can of cat food and feed them every afternoon around five o'clock. After they eat and do their business, you could dump the litter box and freshen it up. My garbage can is next to the back door."

Jimmy, stuck at the point of trying to decide if he liked cats enough to do the job, didn't take in all the directions.

"Could you tell my mama about it?" he managed.

"Of course, but I wanted to make sure you were interested in helping."

"Uh, yes, ma'am. If Mama says it's okay."

"Great." Delores pointed to a stack of folders on the floor beside her desk. "Those files are ready to be returned to the filing cabinets."

"Yes, ma'am."

CHRISTMAS DAY ARRIVED WITHOUT A BICYCLE FOR JIMMY. However, his disappointment was temporary. He received a lot of neat fishing stuff, two new caps, a new sleeping bag, and a picture book about angels. Jimmy sat on the floor and turned the pages. Mama stood behind him and looked down.

"What do you think about the angel book?" she asked.

"Is this what angels look like?"

"I don't know. Do any of them look like the Watchers you've seen?"

Jimmy kept turning pages until he reached the end of the book.

"No, ma'am. I don't see any Watchers."

"How are the Watchers different from the pictures in the book?"

"Do you have him on cross-examination?" Daddy asked from the recliner where he was reading the instructions for a pair of digital binoculars.

"I'm just curious," Mama answered. "And I thought the book would give us a point of reference for discussion." She turned back toward Jimmy.

Jimmy furrowed his brow. "Watchers are different like people are different."

"What do you mean?"

"The Watcher at the school looks different from the one I saw in Grandpa's backyard."

Jimmy glanced down at a picture of a smiling cherub perched on the end of a child's bed. He held up the book so Mama could see it.

"And they're more serious than this. Being a Watcher means taking, uh . . ."

"Responsibility," Daddy suggested.

"Yes, sir. Responsibility for things."

"Where did you learn that word?" Mama asked.

"Mrs. Gilman has been teaching us about responsibility in class. She told me that it has to do with my job of feeding Buster and making sure he has water. Buster is my responsibility."

"It's as plain as can be," Daddy added. "We think the county commissioners are running Cattaloochie County, but it's the Watchers who are really in charge."

"Lee, that's sacrilegious."

"I'm as serious as a Watcher," Daddy answered. "I believe God is in charge, and he's delegated some of his authority to underlings who do his bidding. What's sacrilegious about that?"

"It's the way you said it."

Daddy handed the binoculars to Jimmy. "Am I right?"

Jimmy wasn't sure about the question, but he could tell by the tone of Daddy's voice what the correct answer should be.

"Yes, sir."

"There you have it from the expert."

"I'm going to the kitchen before lightning strikes in the living room," Mama said.

Daddy handed the binoculars to Jimmy.

"Take these to the window, hold them up to your eyes, and see how big the fake reindeer in Mr. Perdue's front yard looks. Push this button, and it will take a picture."

Jimmy looked through the binoculars, but everything was fuzzy.

"I can't see very good."

Daddy knelt beside him. "Let me adjust them for your eyes. Tell me when it looks clear."

He turned the knobs. The reindeer came into focus. Jimmy pressed the button. Together they checked the image.

"Would you like to take these up the pole and take a picture?"

"Yes, sir!"

Mama always made homemade donuts for breakfast on Christmas morning. Jimmy's job was to apply a thin coating of sugar to the tops of the donuts while they were still hot from the vegetable oil.

"Speaking of responsibility, today is the first day for you to take care of Delores Smythe's cats," Mama said.

Jimmy carefully held a spoonful of sugar over a donut and tilted it from side to side so that just the right amount of sugar slipped over the edge.

"Do you have the sheet of paper she gave me?" he asked.

"Yes. She gave more detailed instructions than a parent leaving a child for a week with his grandparents."

"Could we take Buster with us? He could play with the cats."

Mama's eyes narrowed. "Are you kidding?"

"Yes, ma'am." Jimmy smiled mischievously. "Buster would scare them."

"That's right, and you would lose your job before you got started."

IT WAS A SHORT DRIVE TO DELORES'S HOUSE. SHE LIVED IN the same area of town as Grandpa and Grandma but on a different street. Along the way, Jimmy saw children playing with toys received earlier in the day. Two children had new bicycles. One was a dark-haired girl riding a pink bike with plastic flowers in the ends of the handlebars. Her bike didn't appeal to him, but the next one grabbed his attention. It was a mountain bike with a water-bottle holder and a rack on the rear. The boy riding it was wearing a camouflage helmet. Jimmy turned and looked out the back window of the car as they passed by. When they arrived at Delores's house, Mama handed the instruction sheet to Jimmy.

"You read the sheet to me."

Jimmy put his finger on the first item on the paper. He could often sound out complex words that he didn't understand. However, there was nothing fancy about his job duties.

"Clean out litter box in kitchen. Dump old litter in garbage can." He looked up from the list. "What's a litter box?"

"It's a restroom for cats."

Mama took a key from her purse and unlocked the front door. Otto, Maureen, and Celine were in a cluster mewing in the small foyer. Maureen immediately rubbed herself against Mama's leg. Celine stepped backward toward the dining room at the sight of strangers. Otto bolted toward the door.

"Shut the door!" Mama yelled.

Jimmy pulled the door shut, striking Otto on the end of his nose. The cat squalled in pain. Mama reached over to pick him up, but he hissed and moved away from her.

"We're not getting off to a good start," Mama said. "The kitchen is this way."

Mama showed Jimmy the litter box. He leaned over and wrinkled up his nose.

"It doesn't smell good."

"That's the way it's supposed to smell. Pick it up. The garbage can is outside this door."

Mama opened the back door, and Jimmy dumped the dirty cat litter into the can. Returning to the kitchen, he swept up little pieces of litter on the floor, then poured in fresh material. After he read each task, Mama told him the best way to perform it. She left the work up to him. He moved down the list. All three cats walked in circles around his feet.

"Look out, Otto," he warned when he almost stepped on the cat's tail. The cat ignored him.

"Doesn't he know his name?" Jimmy asked.

"Probably, but cats don't respond like dogs. They're smart but don't let you know it."

Jimmy shook his head.

"Don't feel bad," Mama said. "People have been trying to figure out cats for thousands of years."

Jimmy opened the cabinet that contained row after row of canned cat food. Each cat began loudly mewing.

"What are they saying?" he asked.

Mama listened for a second. "Feed me the liver dinner."

"Are you sure?"

"No, but if you feed them the liver dinner, they will get quiet."

Jimmy read the labels on several cans before finding the right one. Each cat had an eating bowl with its name on it. Jimmy scooped food into the three dishes. All noise stopped as the cats ate. When they finished, he let them into the fenced-in backyard. While they were outside, he refilled the water and dry-food containers. They scratched at the door, and he let them inside.

"How do you like taking care of cats?" Mama asked.

"I can see why Mrs. Smythe works for Daddy. Staying in the house with cats all day would make her tired and upset."

JIMMY WAS GLAD TO BE IN THE QUIET OF THE CAR FOR THE ride home. The boy on the bicycle was not in sight, but the girl was still riding on the sidewalk.

"Let Buster sniff your legs when you get home," Mama said. "He will be very curious about the smell left by the cats."

"How will he know where I've been without seeing the cats?"

"A dog's nose can tell a story."

Jimmy thought about Mama's comment as they pulled into the driveway. The idea that a story was hiding inside Buster's black nose made him smile. They walked into the house together. Daddy wasn't in the living room.

"I'll get Buster a treat," Jimmy said.

They entered the kitchen. Daddy was on the telephone.

"I'm not going to commit to anything on the spur of the moment," Daddy said with obvious tension in his voice. "You can't call me up out of the blue on Christmas Day and expect me to give an answer. I wrote your lawyer last summer. There are legal obligations you haven't kept—"

Daddy stopped talking. Jimmy walked over to the jar where they kept Buster's treats. They came in different colors. He didn't know the dog's favorite, but Jimmy liked the red ones. He stirred through the treats until a red one came into view. Mama came into the kitchen and opened the refrigerator door.

"No, you can save your breath," Daddy said. "I'm not going to let you barge in and disrupt our lives."

Jimmy picked up the treat. The corner was broken off, but Buster wouldn't care. The dog crunched down on the biscuit as soon as it touched his teeth.

"That's up to you," Daddy said. "He can send me a proposal in writing, but I won't commit to anything."

Daddy hung up the phone with a serious look on his face.

"What was that about?" Mama asked. "Did somebody you sued call you on Christmas Day?"

"No. It was Vera. She's threatening to take us to court."

— Fifteen —

Mama stepped back and fell into one of the kitchen chairs. The dog treat still in his hand, Jimmy stopped and watched.

"She wants to see Jimmy with regular visitation at her home in Atlanta. Her husband recently got a big promotion, and she says paying child support isn't a problem."

"Child support?" Mama said, raising her voice. "We don't need her money! We don't want her money!"

"Of course we don't. She blurted out a bunch of information. I'm simply letting you know what she said."

"How can you act so calm? Imagine the trauma this is going to be for Jimmy! Trying to drown him in the bathtub was bad enough—"

"Ellen, please," Daddy interrupted. "Not in front of Jimmy."

Mama looked at Jimmy as if noticing his presence in the room for the first time.

"Take Buster his dog treat," Daddy said. "Mama and I need to talk."

"What does, uh, Vera want to do in Atlanta?" Jimmy asked.

"We'll explain it later," Daddy said more firmly. "Now, go. I'll let you know when you can come inside."

As HE WALKED DOWN THE HALLWAY, JIMMY COULD HEAR MAMA'S voice but couldn't make out her words. He quietly closed the door. Buster ran up and began sniffing his legs. Jimmy put the treat in the dog's mouth and sat on the back steps. He put his elbows on his knees and his chin in his hands. Buster lay at his feet and crunched the treat.

Jimmy understood that Vera wanted to see him. After that, Mama's emotions made it difficult for him to follow the conversation. He reached down and scratched the top of Buster's neck.

"Be nice to Mama," he said. "She's upset today. If she comes outside to feed the birds, make sure you wag your tail."

The dog stretched out his head in satisfaction.

"And there's a woman who used to live here who wants to see me. She's my other mama. Her name is Vera, but I'm not sure what to call her."

Jimmy sat on the steps, scratched Buster's neck, and watched the squirrels in the trees until the door opened.

"You can come inside now," Daddy said in a soft voice. "Your mama is upstairs. She doesn't feel well and went to bed."

"Can I give her a hug and a kiss?"

"Later, she wants to be alone for a while."

BOTH DADDY AND MAMA WERE ON THE PHONE A LOT DURING the rest of Christmas vacation. When Jimmy brought up the subject of Vera's call, Mama and Daddy told him not to worry about it.

"I'm not worried," he replied.

"Good," Daddy answered.

"But I didn't understand why Mama got upset," Jimmy said.

"Don't worry," Mama repeated.

Jimmy couldn't escape from the circle of words.

ON A SUNNY SATURDAY BEFORE JIMMY WAS TO RETURN TO school on Monday, he and Daddy went to Grandpa's house for a pole-climbing lesson. The air was brisk, and Jimmy wore an old jacket over his shirt. He strapped on his climbing hooks, stopped for Grandpa's inspection, and walked across the yard to the pole. Buster ran alongside until a noise in the bushes at the rear of the property sent him flying off to investigate. Grandpa hooked on the safety rope, and Jimmy moved slowly but steadily up the pole. He stopped to rest a few feet below his previous best height. He looked down at the ground. Daddy was still holding the safety rope, but his attention was on Grandpa. Daddy's words drifted up to Jimmy.

"Nothing has been filed, and she may not follow through. She claims to be a new Christian, but I didn't recognize the kind of church she attends. Ellen suspects it's a cult and that she wants to get Jimmy, take him away, and never bring him back."

Grandpa answered in a softer voice that Jimmy couldn't hear.

"No," Daddy replied. "It doesn't make any sense to me either, but there is no reasoning with Ellen. I've never seen her like this. I don't think she's slept through the night since we got the phone call. I wake up, and she's not in the room. When I ask her about it in the morning, she tells me she was making sure that Jimmy was still in his bed."

Jimmy dug his hooks into the pole and continued higher. Not far past his previous best climb he would be able to see over the top of Grandpa's house to the world beyond. He glanced down and saw Daddy scratch his head. He still held the safety rope loosely in his left hand.

"I'm more worried about Ellen than concerned about Vera," Daddy continued. "There's no use talking to Brother Fitzgerald. Our meeting with him about Jimmy was a bust. He prayed a fancy prayer but, in the end, stiff-armed us back to the professionals. That avenue is closed. I'd like to suggest she go to a psychologist or psychiatrist herself, but I'm not sure how she'll react. It's one thing for Jimmy to get help; it's another for her to admit a problem."

Jimmy stretched up straight. He could see Buster weaving his way back and forth around the trees along one side of the yard. Jimmy touched the pole. He didn't feel like trying for a new record today.

"Yes," Daddy said. "I thought about that too. Matt McMillan could prescribe something to help her sleep and while he had her in the office, probe into the cause for her insomnia. However, if she thinks I manipulated the situation, I'll be in hot water. The uncertainty of the whole situation could last for months."

"Is this high enough?" Jimmy called out. "I'd like to come down."

Grandpa shielded his eyes and looked up. "That's a good climb. Smooth and steady. Remember not to come down too quickly. Keep tension on your safety belt."

Jimmy leaned back against the safety belt as he descended. He didn't remember

Mama coming into his room in the middle of the night to check him. Dr. McMillan was a nice man. He talked in a soft voice. If Mama was sick, she should go see him, even if he gave her a shot.

DELORES SMYTHE CAME BY THE HOUSE AFTER STOPPING BY to check on her cats. Mama answered the door and called for Jimmy to come downstairs. To his surprise, Delores gave him a quick hug.

"I won't stay long because I have to get back to my babies, but I wanted to tell you how much I appreciated you taking care of Maureen, Otto, and Celine. They looked great, and the house was neater than when I left on my trip. Did you vacuum the living room?"

"Yes, ma'am. Mama taught me how to run the vacuum cleaner. I also cleaned the kitchen counters and put the cans of cat food together so I could find the chicken dinner, liver dinner, beef dinner, fish dinner—"

"I saw that, too, and I'll try to keep it organized. If you want any other cat-sitting jobs, I'll recommend you to all my friends."

Jimmy heard Mama sniffle and saw her get out a tissue.

"Uh, that's okay," Jimmy said. "I have a big responsibility with Buster. He needs me every day."

Delores opened her purse. "Well, here's forty dollars. Is that enough for all you did?"

Jimmy took the two crisp twenties and handed one to Mama. "Mama helped, so I want to share the money with her."

Mama blew her nose on the tissue.

"Ellen, what's wrong?" Delores asked.

"I can't talk about it," Mama said. "Lee will fill you in at the office on Monday. I'm pretty fragile right now, and your kind words about Jimmy touched me." She handed the twenty back to Jimmy. "Keep this, son. You deserve it."

IT RAINED THE FOLLOWING WEEK; HOWEVER, SATURDAY MORN-ing dawned clear, cold, and sunny. His University of Georgia cap on his head, Jimmy released Buster from the backyard and they started walking toward Grandpa's house.

Jimmy had forgotten to bring any gloves and thrust his hands into the pockets of his jeans to keep them warm. His fingers felt paper.

It was the money Delores Smythe had given him. The formerly crisp twenties had survived a trip through the washing machine. He carefully folded the bills, planning to show them to Grandpa.

Reaching the corner of Ridgeview Drive, he came to a house with a line of cars and pickups parked along the curb. A large, handmade sign on a piece of brown cardboard announced "Three-Family Yard Sale." People in coats and sweaters were looking at the items for sale.

"Stay close," Jimmy said to Buster.

They walked up the driveway, passing by a CB radio with antenna, a table with four rickety chairs, a wooden gun rack with deer antlers glued to the top, and four large boxes of children's clothes. Small pieces of brown cardboard set the price for each item or group.

Jimmy stopped at the one-dollar table, amazed at what a dollar could buy. There was a slightly rusty toaster, a hammer, an alarm clock, a green telephone, and other household goods. Near the garage were lawn and garden items. There was a wheelbarrow for five dollars and a lawn mower for ten dollars. Leaning up against the lawn mower was a candy-apple red bicycle.

Jimmy caught his breath. Looking around, he slowly stepped closer. It was a mountain bike with knobby tires. On the handle bars he saw the gear mechanism. Max had explained how the gears worked. Jimmy had listened carefully and nodded whenever Max asked a question, but he still couldn't see how moving a tiny lever a fraction of an inch could make a difference in how easy or hard it was to push the pedals. He leaned over and touched the front tire. It didn't look worn at all. He eyed the frame. There was only one bad scratch across the top connecting bar. He pushed down on the seat. It was firm but broad. He squeezed one of the brakes and watched the calipers close snuggly on the front rim.

"Go, dawgs," a male voice said.

Jimmy looked up into the face of a young man who was wearing a University of Georgia cap exactly like Jimmy's. He had dark hair and a neatly trimmed goatee.

"Go, dawgs," Jimmy answered.

"How do you like the bike?" the man asked, squatting down beside Jimmy.

"It's a very nice bike."

Buster sniffed the back tires. Jimmy reached out and pulled the dog closer to him.

"Is that your dog?"

"Yes, sir."

The man laughed. "Do I look old enough to be called *sir*?"

"Yes, sir."

The man stared at Jimmy's face for a few seconds. "What's your name?"

"Jimmy Mitchell."

"And your dog?"

"That's Buster."

The man motioned toward the bike. "Are you shopping or just looking around?"

"I'm looking at this bike. Is it yours?"

"Yes, sir."

Jimmy stood up. The young man seemed nice.

"Thanks for letting me look at it."

"Would you like to ride it?"

Jimmy's jaw dropped open. "Uh, I can't ride a bike."

"How old are you?" the young man asked in surprise.

"Thirteen years old."

"And you can't ride a bike?"

"No, sir."

"Have you ever tried?"

"No, sir. I don't have a bike."

"Would you like one?"

"Yes, sir."

"What kind?"

Jimmy looked at the red bike. It was an easy question.

"Just like yours," he said.

"Well, anyone who has a UGA cap and a dog like Buster should have a bike." The young man looked around. "Where are your parents?"

"My mama went to the grocery store, and my daddy is playing golf."

"You came to the yard sale alone?"

"Yes, sir. I'm going to see my Grandpa. He lives on this street."

"And you stopped to browse along the way." The young man put his hand on the bike.

Jimmy started to move away.

"Wait a minute," the young man said. "I bought a new mountain bike and want to sell my old one to someone who will take good care of it. Do you see anyone who might be the right person to buy this bike?"

It was Jimmy's turn to look around at the crowd of people. None of the people in sight seemed to be the mountain-bike type.

"No, sir."

"Then, maybe you're the one to buy it," the young man announced.

Jimmy stepped back. "I don't know about that."

He put his hands in his pockets, felt the two twenties, and took out the money.

"How much do you have there?" the young man asked.

Jimmy held up the two bills.

"Is that your money?"

"Yes, sir. I earned it taking care of Mrs. Smythe's cats—Otto, Maureen, and Celine. She was out of town for the Christmas holidays."

"Anyone who can take care of cats while the owner is out of town must be a very responsible individual."

"Yes, sir. I'm responsible for Buster too."

The young man picked up the bike with one hand. "Do you see how light it is?"

"Yes, sir."

"Pick it up."

Jimmy used two hands to hoist the bike. It was light.

"It's a mountain bike, but weight is still important. Every ounce counts."

"Yes, sir."

"Would you like to buy this bike for forty dollars? It cost about four hundred and fifty dollars when it was new."

Jimmy looked down at the money in his hand. The thought that two pieces of wrinkled green paper with a man's picture on them could buy a beautiful red mountain bike was hard to imagine.

"Yes, sir," Jimmy managed.

"I think you're the perfect new owner for this bike, but to make sure it's okay with your parents, I'm going to give you a money-back guarantee. Do you know what that means?"

"No, sir."

"If your parents tell you that you can't keep the bike, you can bring it back here, and I'll give you back your forty dollars. I'm visiting friends who live in this house and will be here for a few more days."

The young man held out his hand, and Jimmy shook it.

"We have a deal," the man said. "Now, give me the money."

Jimmy handed him the two bills.

"Enjoy the bike," the young man said. "You should be proud of yourself for earning the money to buy it. Don't forget to buy a helmet before riding it."

"Yes, sir."

In a daze, Jimmy rolled the bike down the driveway to the street. The other people at the yard sale seemed unaware of the importance of the event. Buster wasn't sure where to walk and so ran around Jimmy and the bike in a tight circle. They reached the sidewalk and continued toward Grandpa's house. Jimmy had trouble keeping his eyes off the spinning wheels of the bike and almost ran into a tree before swerving at the last second. He reached Grandpa's house and leaned the bike against a tree while he rang the doorbell. When Grandpa opened the door, Jimmy gave him a hug and listened to his heart. Grandpa was wearing a scratchy gray sweater.

"Did you see the boy who left the bike?" Grandpa asked, looking over Jimmy's head. "The neighborhood kids should be more responsible with their property."

Jimmy released the old man and turned toward the bicycle. "That's my bike. I'm responsible for it," he replied. "I bought it from a man wearing a University of Georgia cap."

"Where was this man?" Grandpa asked in surprise.

"At the yard sale."

"What yard sale?"

"I'll show you."

Jimmy took Grandpa by the hand and led him out to the sidewalk.

"There," he said, pointing toward the vehicles. "Buster and I stopped to look at all the stuff for sale and found this bike."

"What did you pay for it?"

"I gave the man the forty dollars I earned taking care of Mrs. Smythe's cats. He'd bought a new bike and didn't want this one anymore. It has a scratch on it, but I think it's perfect."

They returned to the tree, and Grandpa gave the bike a closer inspection.

"That's a nice bike for forty dollars," he agreed. "Does your mama know about it?"

"No, sir. The man gave me a money-backwards thing in case Mama and Daddy won't let me keep it."

"A money-back guarantee?"

"Yes, sir." Jimmy's voice grew more anxious. "But I thought you could talk them into letting me keep it. You got Mama to let me take pole-climbing lessons, and you could explain why I need a bike."

"You don't know your mama," Grandpa said. Then he paused. "Or maybe you do. Have you tried to ride it?"

"No, sir. I don't have a helmet."

"I never wore a helmet when I was a kid."

"The man who sold me the bike said I needed a helmet, and all the bike riders on TV wear helmets. They come in all sorts of colors, but I want a red one, just like the bike."

"Do you have any money left?"

"No, sir."

Grandpa rolled the bicycle across the grass. "It has a nice motion. The wheels don't wobble and the frame seems straight."

"Yes, sir," Jimmy said hopefully.

Grandpa handed the bike to Jimmy. "Put Buster and the bike in the backyard while I get the keys to my truck. We'll go to the store and look for a red helmet. Before trying to convince your parents to let you keep the bike, it would be good to show them that you can safely ride it."

– Sixteen –

Jimmy and Grandpa returned from the store with more than a red helmet. Also included in the bag of bicycle accessories were a new plastic water bottle and a large horn with a bright red bulb. When he saw the horn and squeezed the bulb, Jimmy burst out laughing so hard that it made Grandpa chuckle too. He put the horn in the shopping cart without being asked.

Grandpa installed the horn and a bracket for the water bottle. He then washed the water bottle, put in a couple of ice cubes, and filled it with water.

"Take a drink," he said, handing the bottle to Jimmy. "And tell me how the water tastes."

Jimmy tilted up the bottle, swallowed, and made a face.

"Like soap."

"I'll rinse it out more."

Grandpa repeated the process, and Jimmy took another drink.

"That's good," he said.

Grandpa snapped the water bottle in place. He checked the brakes and made sure the seat was secure.

"Do you mind if I ride it first?" Grandpa asked.

"You can ride a bike?" Jimmy asked, his eyes big.

"It's one of those things you never forget."

"What about a helmet?"

"Your red helmet won't fit me, but if all modern-day bike riders wear helmets, I can fit right in."

Grandpa went to the shed and returned with a scuffed yellow Georgia Power Company helmet on his head.

"This helmet has saved my life a couple of times. It should be able to handle a ride around the yard on a bicycle."

Grandpa threw his leg over the bike and after a wobbly start leveled out and rode to the rear of the lot. He turned and made a tight circle around the power pole. Buster kept pace, barking in excitement. Jimmy watched in amazement.

"It's very smooth!" Grandpa called out. "You won't have to use all these gears just to ride around town."

Grandpa slowed to a stop in front of Jimmy.

"That's the limit of my bike riding for the year," the old man said. "I'm not sure if my cardiologist would approve, but I'm not going to ask him. This is a very nice bike for you. Learning how to ride it should be easy."

Grandpa held the bike upright while Jimmy, red helmet in place, perched on the seat like a jockey in the lists and received his final instructions.

"All you do is pedal and go straight. Don't try to do anything with the gears. Squeeze both brakes at the same time when you want to stop."

Jimmy turned the pedals once, stopped, and fell on his side. Only the black strap holding his glasses in place kept them from flying through the air.

"You have to keep pedaling," Grandpa said. "Try it again."

Jimmy made it a few more feet before jerking the handlebars to one side, causing another minor crash.

"Why did you do that?" Grandpa asked.

"I don't know."

Even though it was chilly outside, Grandpa rubbed his forehead with the sleeve of his sweater.

"When I taught your daddy to ride, I ran alongside him and held up the bike. I know my cardiologist doesn't want me to do that, so you're going to have to learn with me simply telling you what to do."

Jimmy found many ways to fall from the bike. He did not complain, however, because he wanted to ride more than anything. His best attempt lasted about fifteen feet before ending all of a sudden when he squeezed the front brake but not the back brake, causing the bike to hop up on its front wheel. He landed close to a prickly holly bush.

"Look out!" Grandpa shouted as he walked briskly toward him. "Are you okay?"

"Yes, sir," Jimmy replied, getting to his feet and holding the bike upright. "Can we wash the bike after we finish the lesson? It's getting dirty."

"Yes, and I want to show you pictures of Orville and Wilbur Wright, the first people to fly an airplane. You're as determined as they were."

Grandma's voice from the back step interrupted them.

"Jim! What are you doing with that boy?"

"What does it look like?" Grandpa replied. "Teaching him to ride a bike!"

"You know what I mean!"

Jimmy turned to Grandpa. "She's going to call Mama."

"Leave that up to me." Grandpa said in a low voice. "I hear you!" he said to Grandma. "We're done for now."

They reached the house. Grandpa told Grandma the whole story of the bicycle.

"And I'm going to call Ellen and let her know what happened so they can make up their minds about it. Jimmy has a money-back guarantee on the bike."

"From a yard sale?" Grandma asked. "It sounds to me like someone took advantage of him. He's never had forty dollars in his pocket before."

"No, it's a quality bike, but I'll talk to the seller if it becomes necessary. If there's a problem, Lee can step in. After all, the boy's father is a lawyer."

Jimmy washed the dirt from his hands and face while Grandpa phoned Mama. He wasn't sure what Grandpa told Mama, but when he came out of the bathroom, Grandpa was nodding and smiling.

"I agree," he said. "He shouldn't be riding on the street or unsupervised in the yard. I'll bring him home in the back of my truck."

Grandpa hung up the phone and gave Jimmy a thumbs-up.

"You're not going to have to test your money-back guarantee. I've worked everything out with your mama. Come into the kitchen, and we'll talk about it. Your grandma is fixing hot chocolate, and I know where there are some little marshmallows to put on top."

FOR THE NEXT MONTH, JIMMY TOOK A BREAK FROM POLE climbing to learn to ride the bike. Grandpa and Mama let Jimmy ride in grassy areas away from traffic, but he had to walk the bike to and from Grandpa's house. Grandpa's backyard was too small for riding, so Grandpa would put the bike in the back of his truck, and they would go to a grassy meadow owned by one of Grandpa's fishing buddies. The rolling field used to be a cow pasture but had been cow-free for a couple of years. Making it to a large tree in the middle of the field became the goal. Over and over Jimmy would pedal a few feet toward the tree before crashing to the ground.

"It would be a lot easier to learn to ride on a smooth surface, but as much as you fall, it would be tough on your knees and elbows," Grandpa said. "Anyway, you bought a mountain bike and should learn how to ride it off-road."

Jimmy didn't complain. He'd wanted a bike for so long that any chance to try was a dream fulfilled. Even the January weather didn't stop him. The sky might be filled with clouds ready to splash the ground with cold drops, but Jimmy asked Mama if he could have a bike-riding lesson. Grandpa didn't always feel like going outside for an hour on a wintry afternoon. Several times he reminded Jimmy that the Wright brothers didn't try to fly their plane in the rain.

One Friday in February, Jimmy made it all the way to the tree. The next day, he rode to the tree and returned without losing his balance. Grandpa, wearing his yellow hard hat in case he wanted to take a short ride himself, grabbed the handlebars with one hand and gave Jimmy a big hug with the other arm. Jimmy squeezed the horn several times in celebration.

His cheeks burning from exposure to the wind, Jimmy arrived home and parked the bike at the far end of the front porch. Even though it was Saturday, Daddy had gone to the office for the morning. He drove up as Jimmy sat on the porch steps taking off his slightly muddy shoes before entering the house.

"I did it!" Jimmy proclaimed as Daddy got out of his car. "I rode all the way to the tree and back without falling down!"

Daddy rubbed Jimmy's head as he climbed the steps.

"That's good. Come into the house so I can talk to you and Mama."

Jimmy followed Daddy. Mama was reading in the sunroom. She liked thick books about men and women who fall in love and get married. When Daddy and Jimmy entered the sunroom, she slipped a bookmark into her book and placed it on a glass table beside her chair.

"How are my men doing?" she asked with a smile.

Grinning, Jimmy announced, "I rode the bike all the way to the tree and back!"

"And I picked up the mail from the post office and received the papers from

Vera's lawyer," Daddy said with a serious look on his face. "She's filed for visitation and joint custody."

"Oh, no!" Mama said.

"And followed through on her offer to begin paying child support. Seeing it in print was a slap in the face. To insinuate that we're not already providing everything Jimmy needs—"

"Like a bicycle," Jimmy interrupted. "Did you hear me, Mama? I rode all the way to the tree in the middle of Mr. Anderson's field and back to Grandpa without falling over. Next week, Grandpa is going to teach me to change gears."

"I heard you," Mama managed. "Now go to your room and change clothes. Even if you didn't fall off, you still managed to get dirty."

Jimmy turned to leave.

"No, stay here," Daddy commanded. "You need to understand what is going on. We've protected you from the correspondence and phone calls, but with the filing of suit, you'll have to understand what's at stake when you testify."

"Does he have to testify?" Mama asked in alarm. "Can't we rely on Dr. Meyer's recommendations?"

"That's only part of our proof."

"But *she* will be there!" Mama replied. "Vera has no right to see him, talk to him, touch him—"

"Please, Ellen," Daddy interrupted. "Let me work with Jimmy for a minute. Son, sit beside your mama."

Jimmy slid into the chair next to Mama. She gently stroked his back.

"I need to explain what is going on," Daddy began. "No, I want to hear from you. How much of this do you understand? What does your birth mother want to do?"

Jimmy pressed his lips together before he spoke. "Her name is Vera. She bathed me when I was a baby, and that's why I'm afraid of water. She left our house a long time ago and moved away after she found out that I was"—he paused—"retarded."

"You're not retarded," Mama said sharply.

"Who told you she left for that reason?" Daddy asked.

"Walt."

Daddy muttered for second. "Go ahead. Do you understand what is going on now?"

Jimmy took a deep breath. "I know Mama has been sad and worried, because I can see it in her eyes. After she tucks me in at night and kisses me on the head, I get out of bed and pray that she will smile again. I also pray for Grandpa that his heart will be okay and that he will go back to church and get saved. Usually, I pray in a soft voice so I won't bother you, but I know that God hears my prayers even if I say them inside my head. I've tried to be extra good to make Mama happy, but I know that my room isn't as clean as it should be because I've been with Grandpa learning how to ride my bicycle. I promise to clean it this afternoon."

Jimmy paused and glanced back at Mama for affirmation.

"That's very sweet, Jimmy," she said. "But remember that none of this is your fault. You're a wonderful son."

Daddy cleared his throat. "Here's what is going on. Vera wants you to come to her house and visit. Mama and I want you to stay here with us."

Jimmy knit his brow. "If you and Mama don't want me to go, then I won't go. You're my parents. I'm your responsibility."

"I wish Judge Robinson would make it that simple," Mama said with a sigh.

"Robinson won't be allowed to hear the case," Daddy said. "Because I'm personally involved in the case as Jimmy's father, Vera's lawyer will ask Judge Robinson to recuse himself, and a superior court judge from a neighboring circuit will come in for a specially set hearing."

"Will Judge Robinson allow that to happen?"

"Yes. But I will seek to delay any hearing until after Jimmy's birthday."

"Does she want him to visit her on his birthday?" Mama asked in dismay.

"No, that's not in the pleadings, but his birthday has legal significance. Once a child turns fourteen, the judge has to consider the child's wishes when determining visitation. Jimmy's testimony will be one of the most important aspects of the case. If he doesn't want to visit Vera, the judge will have to give a lot of weight to his preference."

Mama tapped Jimmy on the back.

"Do you want to see your birth mother and spend the night at her house?"

"Spend the night with someone I don't know?"

"Yes."

"No, ma'am. It's fun going over to Max's house, but I like sleeping in my own bed."

"I don't think Jimmy's testimony will be a problem," Daddy said. "When you add that to Dr. Meyer's opinion, our family life, and Vera's complete abandonment for the past eleven years, I don't think it will be much of a contest."

"I hope you're right." Mama sighed. "Who will be our lawyer?"

"Dean Stanley is a possibility."

"No," Mama replied sharply. "I've heard you talk about his shaky ethics too many times to trust him myself, and I didn't like him when I dealt with him at the clerk's office."

"He only bends the rules to try to help his clients, and he's one of the most aggressive litigators in the area. He'll go for the jugular and not let go."

"No," Mama repeated.

Daddy rubbed his left cheek with his hand. "Well, there's Bruce Long. He's young, but he's smart and quick on his feet in the courtroom. Hiring him would also give me a close look at him as a future law partner."

"Talk to him. I've met his wife and liked her. They go to Deep Springs, and I'd rather have someone like him than a shyster with a long list of courtroom victories. Besides, you'll be telling anyone who helps us what to do. They'll just be your mouthpiece for the day."

"Yeah. I'll call Bruce first thing Monday morning. I'm also going to file a counterclaim to Vera's petition."

"A counterclaim? What do we want from her?"

"I'm going to ask the judge to terminate her parental rights. That will end any possibility that she will cause us trouble in the future. The judge can end parental rights if there hasn't been any personal contact or financial support for a twelve-month period. I think we'll have a strong case."

"Good," Mama replied. "Once this is over and I know Jimmy is safe, I'll be okay."

"And be able to smile?" Jimmy asked.

Mama forced a wan smile. "If you clean your room, I'll promise you a big smile."

— Seventeen —

Delores asked Jimmy to sort a thick stack of documents, and he laid them out in neat rows on the conference table. While Jimmy was working, a stocky, blond-haired man came into the room with Daddy.

"Jimmy, this is Mr. Long."

Mr. Long extended his hand to Jimmy, who shook it.

"What are you doing in here today?" Long asked.

Jimmy explained how he sorted the sheets of paper by day, month, and year. Long listened closely.

"He files, makes copies, and does other routine, repetitive tasks," Daddy added when Jimmy finished. "He enjoys jobs considered tedious by most people. He keeps focused and does excellent work."

"Could you do that at my office?" Mr. Long asked. "I'd be glad to pay you to help me organize some of my files."

Jimmy looked at Daddy.

"We can discuss it later. He's in the inclusion program at the middle school and occasionally has modified homework assignments, so I don't want to interfere with his schoolwork. That's one reason why he only works here a couple of afternoons a week. But it might be good for him to spend time with you so he will be comfortable with you in the courtroom."

Mr. Long spoke. "Before going to law school, I taught theater for three years in high school but never worked with a student like Jimmy. I think getting to know each other would be helpful."

"If you're able to delay the hearing until after his birthday, we should have plenty of time."

WINTER GAVE WAY TO AN EARLY SPRING THAT SPLASHED THE west Georgia landscape with cherry blossoms. Close on the heels of the cherry trees, the pear trees burst forth like huge white ice-cream cones. Winter coats were returned to closets, and windows were raised to allow in fresh air before air-conditioning became necessary.

Jimmy continued riding his bike. Daddy came along on several trips to Grandpa's house until Mama agreed that Jimmy could ride alone from home to Grandpa's house but nowhere else.

The sound of the oversized horn on Jimmy's handlebars became his calling card. At every intersection and stop sign, even if no cars or pedestrians were present, he sounded the horn before crossing the street. He also used the horn to say hello and good-bye. When the windows of the house were open, Grandpa could hear Jimmy's horn as he pedaled down Ridgeview Drive and would come to the door before Jimmy rang the doorbell.

Mama and Daddy made reservations for a weekend getaway to Callaway Gardens, a resort about an hour from Piney Grove. Mama began to cry when Daddy told her about the trip, and Daddy had to quickly assure Jimmy that her tears were happy ones.

Jimmy wanted to spend the weekend his parents would be gone with Max, but the Cochran family was hosting relatives from out of town and wouldn't have room for an extra houseguest. Grandpa and Grandma were going to visit Grandma's sister in Jacksonville. Their trip had been planned for months and couldn't be changed. So Jimmy would have to stay with Uncle Bart and Aunt Jill. On Friday afternoon, Mama helped Jimmy pack a suitcase and drove him to their house.

"We'll be back in time Sunday morning to take you to church," Mama said as they pulled into the driveway.

"Where will I sleep?" Jimmy asked.

"Either in Walt's room or the guest room."

Jimmy ground his teeth together.

"Guest room, please," he managed.

Mama glanced sideways at the tone in his voice.

"Of course. I'll tell Aunt Jill. If Walt bothers you, let her know so she can take care of it. Now that he's older and more mature, I don't think you have anything to worry about."

Jimmy wasn't so sure about that. Aunt Jill greeted them at the door.

"Where's Walt?" Mama asked after they'd deposited Jimmy's things in the guest bedroom.

"He's running around in the new car we bought him Monday night. He's already burned over a tank of gas without leaving the county."

Mama and Aunt Jill walked into the kitchen. Jimmy joined them.

"I'm staying home all weekend," Aunt Jill said. "Barr won't be around much except to eat and sleep. He has to prepare for an important presentation when the CFO of the company arrives next week. Walt will probably be showing off his car to anyone who will take a look."

"Jimmy is able to entertain himself. Will you have time to take him by the house to feed and water Buster?"

"Sure."

Mama gave Jimmy a tight hug and a big kiss on the cheek.

"This kiss and hug will last until I see you on Sunday," Mama said. "We'll be home before you know it."

Jimmy gave her a game smile. "I love you."

"I love you more," Mama replied.

AFTER MAMA LEFT, AUNT JILL TURNED ON A SMALL TV ON the kitchen counter and began watching a soap opera. Jimmy wandered upstairs to Walt's room and looked at the cases of his cousin's video games. Jimmy had never been interested in computers. He liked the world in which his family and Buster lived. On Walt's bed was a rolled-up poster. Jimmy straightened it out and saw members of a music group with a strange name. Aunt Jill's voice at the bedroom door interrupted him.

"Would you like to watch a movie?" she asked.

Jimmy didn't watch much TV, but he didn't want to be rude to his aunt.

"Yes, ma'am."

"What do you want to see?"

"I don't know."

Aunt Jill smiled. "Stay here. I'll find something."

In a minute, she returned with a movie called *Old Yeller* and put it in the player. Jimmy sat on the floor of the room.

"It's a story about a dog. I think you'll like it," she said.

"What if Walt comes home?" he asked.

"I'll tell him to let you finish the movie."

At first, Jimmy liked the movie. The dog didn't look anything like Buster, but Jimmy could easily understand how the boy could love the dog. But then all sorts of bad things started to happen. Jimmy became upset and fidgety. He got up to leave the room but didn't want Aunt Jill to get mad at him for not watching the entire movie, so he sat back down. The story got worse and worse until the dog died. As he watched tears stream down the boy's face, Jimmy imagined how sad he would be if Buster died. He wished he could meet the boy and tell · him how sorry he was about his dog.

"Old Yeller! Please come home!" a voice called out, causing Jimmy to jump. It was Walt.

"That's a sappy story, isn't it?" he asked as he clicked off the movie. "I'll tell you what happens so you don't have to watch it. The boy gets another dog."

Jimmy asked the question that remained on his mind.

"Do you know where the boy lives?"

"Just over the line in Alabama. The sad thing is that his new dog died too. A neighbor killed it. Shot it in the head while the boy was watching. Blood and brains went everywhere."

Jimmy started for the door. He'd heard enough. He'd rather sit in the kitchen and watch Aunt Jill cook supper. The thought of the boy losing two dogs was more than he could bear. Walt put his arm around Jimmy's shoulders and stopped him.

"Don't run off. I'm kidding. The boy got another dog that looked exactly like Old Yeller, and they lived happily ever after."

Jimmy tried to squirm free, but his cousin tightened his grip.

"Do you want to wrestle?" Walt asked.

Jimmy shook his head. He didn't know what Walt meant, but it didn't sound like fun. Walt didn't release him.

"This is how it works. I'll hold you down on the floor and you try to get up.

Or, you can hold me down, and I'll try to get up. Which one do you want to do? You pick."

"No," Jimmy answered.

Walt leaned over close to Jimmy's face.

"Then go to the kitchen and peel potatoes, but be careful not to cut your finger."

Walt released him, and Jimmy fled to the guest bedroom. He sat on the bed and stared at the wall, waiting for his heart to slow down. He heard footsteps in the hall. He'd forgotten to close and lock the door. He looked up in alarm. A head appeared in the doorway.

It was Uncle Bart.

"Hey, Jimmy," he said. "We're glad you can stay with us. It's almost time for supper. Wash your hands and come to the kitchen."

"Yes, sir."

When Jimmy went downstairs, Walt was getting a soft drink from the refrigerator. Uncle Bart was filling four glasses with tea.

"Did you finish the movie?" Aunt Jill asked Jimmy.

"No, ma'am."

Aunt Jill set a bowl of peas on the table. She'd fixed fried chicken. The sight of the chicken lifted Jimmy's spirits. Aunt Jill made very good fried chicken—crisp and slightly spicy on the outside and hot and juicy on the inside. They all sat down, and Bart prayed the blessing.

"Tell us what you've been up to," Uncle Bart said as Jimmy selected a golden drumstick. "Are you still learning to ride your bike?"

Jimmy took a bite from his chicken leg. It was delicious.

"Yes, sir."

"Tell us about it."

Jimmy wanted to focus on the chicken leg but knew Uncle Bart's question had to be answered first. He gave a brief report of his progress with special emphasis on bike safety. Jimmy had learned that no matter what he did, adults were always interested in safety.

"Have you seen Walt's car?" Uncle Bart asked.

"No, sir."

"I hope he thinks as much about safety as you do."

Jimmy saw Walt roll his eyes. The conversation shifted to Walt, leaving Jimmy free to remove every speck of meat from the chicken leg. When he finished, Aunt Jill gave him another one before he could ask for seconds.

THE REST OF THE EVENING PASSED WITHOUT INCIDENT. UNCLE Bart returned to the office, Walt mercifully disappeared into his room, and Jimmy stayed close to Aunt Jill. In a small storage room adjacent to the kitchen, she'd set up a craft room, where she spent many hours making wreaths and Christmas tree ornaments.

Aunt Jill's wreaths weren't simple circles decorated with a few plastic berries. She placed hand-painted figurines into the greenery and made every wreath different. Jimmy was amazed at her ability to paint with the tiny brushes neatly lined up in a wooden rack on her worktable.

Aunt Jill brought an even greater eye for detail to her Christmas tree ornaments. For several years, she'd given Mama a new ornament on which she'd painted a member of the nativity scene. This past Christmas, a whole section of the tree in the Mitchell living room was occupied by shepherds, angels, animals, and members of the holy family. Most recently Aunt Jill had painted the wise men riding camels, one each on three ornaments. Mama placed them in a row moving up toward the star at the top of the tree.

"Let me show what I'm working on for your mother," Aunt Jill said to Jimmy.

She opened a drawer and took out a gold-colored ornament with a delicate winged figure on it.

"What do you think of my angel?" she asked.

Jimmy leaned closer but remembered not to touch. He could see fluffy detail in the creature's wings. It reminded him of the pictures in the angel book.

"It's very pretty," he said.

"Would you like to help me?"

"No, ma'am. I'm not a good painter."

"I'm not talking about this type of work. There is something I'm sure you could do very well. Will you give it a try?"

"Yes, ma'am," Jimmy answered reluctantly.

Aunt Jill taught him how to paint small Styrofoam balls. The first three turned out messy, but Jimmy thought his fourth wasn't so bad.

"I paint a spot on the pole I climb in Grandpa's backyard," Jimmy said, liking his work. "But I don't have to be so careful because nobody sees it up close."

Wearing half-frame magnifying glasses, Aunt Jill carefully finished the dark eyes and nose for a miniature sheep.

"How far have you climbed?"

"I'm not sure, but Grandpa says it's a lot higher than Goliath's head."

"Is that close to the top?"

"No, ma'am. It's a forty-five-foot, class B pole, and I'm not going to stop until I go all the way up."

"That's amazing. I could never do that."

"Oh yes, you could. I'm sure Grandpa would teach you if you asked him. You could borrow my climbing hooks. We're about the same size, so they would fit you."

Aunt Jill shook her head. "I think I'll stick to painting angels."

THAT NIGHT JIMMY CRAWLED INTO BED MISSING HIS MAMA. He stared at the closed door with the narrow band of light beneath it and sighed. Rolling onto his left side, he faced the darkness and felt an aching loneliness. At home, Mama slept out of sight in the bedroom at the other end of the hall, but Jimmy knew she was there. If he didn't quickly fall asleep, he would imagine her cleaning the kitchen counters, drinking a glass of water, reading a book in the living room, or turning off the downstairs lights.

Jimmy was afraid he'd stay awake all night feeling sad, but the next thing he knew the morning sun was dancing around the sides of the curtains. He dressed and went downstairs to the kitchen. Aunt Jill, a cup of coffee in her hand, leaned over the counter reading the newspaper.

"Would you like pecan pancakes for breakfast?" she asked.

"Yes, ma'am."

"Your mother told me how much you like them. Bart has already left for the office, and I don't expect to see Walt for another hour or so."

Jimmy sat at the kitchen table and watched Aunt Jill make the pancakes. When she put a steaming stack in front of him, he bowed his head and offered a brief, silent prayer before coating the hot disks with butter and syrup. He took a monstrous bite.

"How are they?" Aunt Jill asked.

Jimmy chewed and swallowed. "They're good. Not as good as Mama's, but I like them."

Aunt Jill smiled. "I'll take that as a high compliment."

Jimmy finished breakfast, washed his plate off in the sink, and put it in the dishwasher. Aunt Jill stood back and watched.

"Do you always do that?" she asked.

"Unless the dishes in the washer are clean. Then I leave my plate in the sink."

"That's good. Would you like to watch TV?"

"No, ma'am. I'd like to help you."

Jimmy helped Aunt Jill perform her morning tasks. She watered her indoor plants on Saturday. Jimmy carried the watering can and filled it up with water from the sink when it ran dry.

"Do you always stay this close to your mother?" she asked.

Jimmy nodded. "Yes, ma'am. I love her a lot. When you love someone, you want to be with them all the time. I like seeing Grandpa too."

Walt made his first appearance of the morning as Jimmy, a load of dirty clothes in his arms, followed Aunt Jill to the laundry room.

"When you finish the laundry, vacuum my room," Walt said.

"You should hang around and learn a few things," Aunt Jill responded. "Jimmy knows more about taking care of a house than a lot of grown men."

"Do you want me to vacuum Walt's room?" Jimmy asked.

"No, there's too much stuff on the floor. It wouldn't do any good."

Walt went back to his room and closed the door. When he appeared a half hour later, he called out to his mother, "I'm going out for a ride to see some friends. I'll be back by supper."

A few minutes later, Aunt Jill received a phone call.

When she hung up, she said, "A woman in our church is in the hospital, and I'm going over to see her for a few minutes. Will you be okay by yourself?"

"Yes, ma'am. Mama leaves me alone at the house, but I'm not supposed to leave the yard or answer the door."

"That's a good rule for here too."

"I usually play with Buster."

"We'll go over later today and make sure he has food and water."

After Aunt Jill left, Jimmy wandered around the house. He missed his bike and Buster. After looking at the pictures of a forest in a magazine, he went upstairs. He slowed when he came to Walt's door. He tried the knob. It was unlocked. After looking both ways, he slowly pushed the door open and entered. A trash can was in front of the drawer where Walt put the pictures of Jimmy and Vera. Jimmy moved the trash can and opened the drawer. It was filled with broken pencils, rubber bands, CDs without the cases, and photographs. Jimmy grabbed a handful of pictures and flipped through them. Most were of Walt playing baseball and opening Christmas presents. Jimmy took out more pictures. In the second batch, he found the photo of Vera holding him in the hospital. He took it to a window and held it in the light. The scene was as he remembered. Both Vera and Daddy looked happy. Jimmy studied his own face more closely. He couldn't tell much. He looked red and wrinkled. It was hard to believe that he had been so tiny. He put the picture on top of the desk and continued to look through the drawer. He found the picture of Vera and Daddy beside the Christmas tree but not any others. The drawer was a mess.

Jimmy held a picture in each hand. He wanted to put them in his suitcase and take them home. He hesitated. He remembered the commandment against stealing. But then, Walt wasn't in the pictures. Photos should belong to the people who were in them. And Walt wasn't taking good care of them. One had suffered a tear in the corner since the first time Jimmy saw it.

Suddenly, he knew what he would do.

He would borrow the photos. Borrowing wasn't stealing, because the pictures would be returned. Jimmy could look at them for a few weeks then give them back to Walt so he could look at them. Sharing was a good thing. Mama encouraged him to share.

Jimmy left the room, took the pictures to the guest bedroom, and put them in his suitcase. If he put tape on the back of the torn photo, he could keep it from ripping more.

Going downstairs, he wandered around until he reached the craft room. Under the counter was a small bag filled with the white balls Aunt Jill had showed him how to paint. Beside it were cans of red, green, and gold paint. He shook the green paint, listened to the little ball rattle inside, and slowly counted to sixty. Grandpa said that the little ball stirred the paint from the inside. Jimmy wasn't sure what needed to be stirred since only one color could fit in a can, but he'd shaken his can many times before spraying a white spot on the pole.

He placed a white ball on the end of a long needle that held it up in the air. He held the can the right distance and pressed the button. He carefully moved the spray back and forth. In less than a minute, he finished a perfect green ball. No runs; no drips. He blew on it and waited for it to dry. Setting it aside, he pulled out another one.

He was on his seventh ball, a red one, when the phone rang. Startled, he turned toward the kitchen, and his hand followed his eyes. He didn't release the spray button on the paint, and the result was broad racing stripe across a wreath Aunt Jill had almost finished. Jimmy lifted his finger from the button and stared. He looked again at the balls he'd painted. Seven perfect balls, even without drips or runs, wouldn't equal the damage to the beautiful wreath. He touched the red paint on the wreath with his finger. It was already dry. He heard the front door open. He quickly put another wreath on top of the ruined one.

Walt came into the kitchen and saw him in the craft room.

"What are you doing?" Walt asked. "You'll mess up her stuff."

Jimmy sat still. Walt came over to him.

"Did you paint these balls?" he asked.

"Yes."

"You might have a future as one of Santa's elves."

Jimmy adjusted the wreath to hide his mistake. Walt reached across him and picked it up.

"What's this? Got a little carried away with the red paint?"

"The phone rang, and I forgot to let go of the button."

"At least you didn't paint a line all the way across the kitchen." Walt held up the wreath. "This was her favorite one. She's going to be very upset."

Jimmy felt a hot tear in the corner of his left eye. He rubbed it away with the back of his hand. Walt patted him on the back.

"Don't cry. I have an idea."

"What?" Jimmy asked, his voice shaking a little.

"My mom uses a lot of artificial stuff, but she also likes to make wreaths with live plants. The only problem with collecting plants is she hates going into the woods, because she has a terrible reaction to chigger bites. If you could find some good plants and give them to her, she wouldn't get too mad at you for messing up her best wreath."

Jimmy still felt sad. "But I don't know what kind of plants to get, and I don't have a way to get to the woods. Mama and Daddy aren't coming back until tomorrow morning, and then we have to go to church."

Walt reached in his pocket and pulled out his car keys.

"That's where I come in. We can go in my car and be back before supper. I'll leave her a note on the refrigerator."

Jimmy hesitated.

"Do you have a better plan?" Walt asked. "I don't really care. I just stopped by to get something to drink before going over to a friend's house."

Jimmy couldn't let his chance go. "No, let's go. I need to put on some blue jeans if we're going to be in the woods."

While he changed clothes, Jimmy had an idea. He rejoined Walt in the foyer. "Could we go by my house? I need to give Buster his food and water."

"Sure. That's on the way."

JIMMY DIDN'T KNOW MUCH ABOUT CARS, BUT HE COULD TELL Walt was excited about his new transportation. To Jimmy, it was simply a small black car.

"It's four years old and only has thirty thousand miles on it," Walt said as they got in. "I've already had it up to a hundred."

Jimmy had to move two bags of fast-food leftovers in order to sit. Walt reached into one of the bags and took out a french fry. It was so hard that it snapped when he broke it off in his mouth. Jimmy buckled his seat belt.

"You don't have to buckle up. I'm a good driver."

Jimmy left the seat belt in place.

"I guess you always buckle up, don't you?" Walt asked.

"Mama won't start the car if I'm not buckled."

"Suit yourself, but I'm not your mama."

Walt backed out of the driveway. When he did, the car swerved slightly to the left, and he barely missed the mailbox. After that, he settled down, and they arrived without problems at the Mitchell home. The sight of the house made Jimmy miss Mama again. He wished he could have stayed at home by himself. He and Buster would have managed just fine. When he opened the door of the car, Jimmy could hear Buster was barking furiously.

"Do your dog thing," Walt said. "I'm going to wait here."

Jimmy called out, "It's me, Buster!"

The dog stopped barking. When Jimmy opened the gate, Buster jumped up and put his paws on Jimmy's leg to receive a welcoming pat on the head. The dog's water bowl was almost empty.

"What happened to your water?"

Jimmy looked down at his jeans and saw wet paw prints.

"It's to drink, not for swimming," he scolded.

Buster did not seem at all sorry. Jimmy turned on the water hose and filled the bowl. Buster lapped up the cool water. There wasn't much dry food in his bowl, either.

"Did the squirrels steal your food?" he asked.

Jimmy refilled the dog's bowl. Walt honked the horn. Jimmy patted Buster on the head. He hated leaving the dog so quickly. He picked up Buster and carried him to the car. Walt rolled down the window and yelled at him.

"What are you doing with that dog?"

Jimmy came closer before answering.

"Could Buster go with us?"

"No, I don't want a dog making a mess in my car."

"He rides with Mama and me and stays on the floor. He won't jump on the seat if I tell him not to. I promise that he'll be good."

Buster lifted his head and licked Jimmy's chin.

"How cute," Walt said. "Get in. I'll give him a chance, but if he causes any trouble, you'll have to do a lot more than vacuum my room to make up for it."

Jimmy opened the car door and carefully placed Buster on the floorboard.

"Stay!" he commanded in his strongest voice as he fastened his seat belt.

Buster curled up in a ball at Jimmy's feet. Walt left town heading west and turned on the radio so loud that Jimmy put his fingers in his ears and looked out the window. He felt a tap on his shoulder and turned toward his cousin.

"Do you want me to turn down the music?" he asked.

Jimmy nodded. "It hurts my ears. And dogs can hear better than we do, so it's probably bothering Buster too."

ON THE WEST SIDE OF TOWN, THE RESIDENTIAL NEIGHBORHOODS of Piney Grove ended not far from the city limits. Rows of nicer homes were replaced by scrubby wooded areas with small dwellings spaced farther apart. They passed several dirt roads that disappeared into the woods. Walt turned down a paved side road and sped up.

"Why are you going so fast?" Jimmy asked as the trees began to flash by.

"There is a straight stretch of road ahead. Let's have some fun."

− Eighteen −

Jimmy leaned over and patted Buster on the head. The small, lightweight car began rocking back and forth as the speed increased. They went around a sweeping curve, and Jimmy felt his body strain against the seat belt. Walt let out a yell.

"Here it comes!"

A long, straight section of road lay before them; however, the road wasn't flat. It went up and down. Jimmy could see a farmhouse far ahead. A barbed-wire fence ran along both sides of the road. They topped the first little hill, and Jimmy felt his stomach jump inside his body.

"Oh!" he exclaimed.

"Wait until you feel the next one!" Walt responded.

Buster was trying to stand up on the floorboard. They went over the next hill with such speed that they almost became airborne. Buster skidded around on the floor, losing his balance. Jimmy's stomach jumped to his throat.

"Stop!" Jimmy called out.

"Yahoo!" Walt exclaimed.

Jimmy looked out the window and saw a man standing on the front porch of the farmhouse. There was a frown on his face, and Jimmy saw his mouth move in anger as he raised his fist. Walt barreled past the house and over a final small hill that again caused Jimmy's stomach to lurch. Walt took his foot off the gas. The car began to slow, and he braked as they entered another curve. By they time they came out of the curve, he'd returned to a more normal speed.

"I bet you've never done that before," Walt said.

Jimmy didn't answer.

"Do you want to do it again?" Walt asked.

"No. I want to get the plants and go back to your house."

"Don't be such a baby."

"I'm not a baby. I'm almost fourteen years old."

They drove a few more minutes. The paved road ended and became gravel. It hadn't rained in the area for several weeks, and a cloud of reddish-gray dust floated behind the car.

"You'll have to help me wash the car when we go home," Walt said.

"I'm good at washing cars."

They crossed a one-lane bridge over a narrow stream and drove a couple of miles. Walt pulled off the road and parked behind a massive oak tree.

"This is a good spot. No one coming from town can see the car."

Jimmy opened the door and let Buster jump out.

"Will he run off?" Walt asked. "I'm not going to chase a stupid dog through the woods."

"He'll come when I call."

Walt reached under the front seat of the car and pulled out a pack of cigarettes. He knocked the pack against the palm of his hand, then took one out and lifted it to his nose.

"Ah, smell this," he said, handing the cigarette to Jimmy. "There is nothing like the smell of fine tobacco."

Jimmy sniffed the cigarette. No one in his family smoked, and he'd never held a cigarette. Walt was right. The tobacco had a rich, sweet smell. His cousin took out another cigarette and pushed in the car's lighter. When it popped out, he showed Jimmy the glowing coils.

"Quick! Hold the cigarette up to the coils and breathe in."

Jimmy didn't move. Walt touched the lighter to the end of his cigarette and took a deep drag. Wide-eyed, Jimmy watched the smoke roll from his cousin's mouth. Walt pushed the lighter in and when it popped out, held it out to Jimmy.

"Go ahead. You're almost fourteen."

"I'd have to ask Mama. She doesn't like cigarettes."

Walt took another puff. "Your grandpa used to smoke like a chimney. That's why he had a heart attack."

Jimmy didn't know that Grandpa had smoked.

"Are you going to have a heart attack?" he asked.

Walt laughed. "No. This is just for fun."

Buster barked, and Jimmy looked out the window as the dog approached a hole in the ground and sniffed around the edges.

"Do you know why I brought you here?" Walt asked.

Jimmy turned away from Buster. "Yes, so we can find some plants for Aunt Jill."

Walt laughed. "What kind of plants? Marijuana?"

"What's that?"

"They use it to make another kind of cigarette that really makes you feel good."

"But what about the plants she likes to use in the wreaths? You said you would show me."

"Get out of the car."

Leaving the unlit cigarette on the seat, Jimmy did as he was told. Walt took a final puff from his cigarette and dropped it to the ground. Jimmy shut the car door. No other cars had passed by since they stopped, and the air was still. Jimmy could hear Buster rustling through the underbrush that grew beyond the shade of the tree.

"Before we go looking for plants, I'd like to play a game," Walt said. "Is that okay with you?"

"What kind of game?" Jimmy asked suspiciously.

"It's an escape game."

Jimmy stood still. Walt took off his belt and held it up.

"There was a famous guy named Houdini who could get out of anything. People would tie him up with ropes, put handcuffs on his wrists, and even put chains around his legs, but he could always get free."

"Deputy Askew put handcuffs on me to show me how they work, and I couldn't take them off. He had to use a key to unlock them."

"You're not Houdini."

Jimmy looked at the belt in Walt's hand. "I don't want to play that game. I want to get the plants."

Walt moved closer until he was directly in Jimmy's face. "You can tie me up first if you want, or I can tie you up. Then we'll see who can wiggle free. There are other parts of the game that I can't tell you about until we start playing."

Jimmy looked in his cousin's eyes and saw evil. A wave of fear washed over him. He spun and started to run. In a few steps he was into the woods surrounding the clearing. Buster barked and ran after him.

"Come back here!" Walt commanded.

Jimmy didn't slow down or look back. He could hear Walt's footsteps close behind him. Buster barked excitedly at the mad dash through the woods. Jimmy tore through a small grove of trees but didn't slow down even when skinny branches scratched his face and arms.

"If you don't stop, I'm going to beat you bloody!" Walt called out.

Jimmy ducked under a large branch. When he did, his glasses fell off. For a split second, he hesitated, but the sound of Walt crashing through the underbrush seemed more important than finding his glasses. He kept running, holding his hands before his face to try to clear a way through the blurry branches and tree trunks.

Jimmy reached the top of a rise and turned. He didn't see the drop-off until he'd run over the edge and found himself falling through the air. He landed in a bush that crackled beneath him. Buster scampered around and down the rocks.

Dazed, Jimmy stood up. He could hear Walt cursing and making threats. Jimmy shook his head to clear it and then continued running down the hill. He didn't stop until the pain in his lungs became so great that he had to grab a small pine tree and hold on. His chest pumped up and down while he caught his breath. When the sound of his breathing quieted, he listened. He heard Walt's voice, but it was farther away now. Jimmy couldn't tell if his cries were the sound of rage or pain. Buster barked.

"Quiet!" Jimmy commanded.

Jimmy continued running but at a slower pace. He didn't know where to go or what to do. All he knew was that he needed to get as far away as possible from the evil he'd seen in Walt's eyes. The next time he stopped to catch his breath, the only sound that reached his ears was the chirping of a bird perched on a limb above his head. He waited longer. Still no sound of Walt. He looked around. He could see things within a few feet of his face, but beyond that, his surroundings were fuzzy. Buster had wandered off, and Jimmy couldn't see or hear him.

"Buster," he hissed out.

He heard a crunching in the leaves behind him. He whirled and strained to see who or what was approaching. In a moment, the dog returned to his side.

Jimmy slumped down on the ground at the base of the tree. Buster jumped into his lap and licked his chin.

Jimmy began to cry.

He sobbed. His whole body shook. To avoid wailing out loud, he stuffed the bottom of his shirt into his mouth. Buster laid his head on Jimmy's leg. Jimmy bit down on his shirt until the crashing waves of sadness went away. He sniffled a few more times and stroked Buster's back.

"What am I going to do?" he asked in a shaky voice.

He rubbed his eyes and wished he had his glasses. He couldn't think of anything to do except to keep walking. Standing up, he continued in what he hoped was the direction away from Walt. The underbrush thickened and slowed him. He pushed aside small limbs with his arms and shuffled his feet along the ground. In a few minutes, the ground cleared up again and stayed like that for a long time. Jimmy went on without hearing the sound of another person or any sight of Piney Grove. The sun sank lower in the late-afternoon sky. Buster roamed to one side or another of Jimmy's route. Several times, Jimmy called him back.

The trees opened, and Jimmy stepped into a clearing. In the center of the open space was a run-down house built of weathered gray boards. Jimmy came closer and saw that one side of the roof was caved in. The front porch had fallen to the ground, and the bottom of the front door was chest high. He pushed on the door, but it didn't budge. Standing on the ground, he couldn't reach the rusty doorknob. The windows had been boarded up with plywood that was also gray.

He was very thirsty and his mouth felt dry. He walked around to the back of the house and found an outhouse. Beyond the outhouse at the edge of the woods was a large piece of tin. Buster was sniffing the edges of the square piece of metal. Jimmy moved the tin out of the way. When he did, he saw that it covered a hole in the ground. Jimmy got down on his knees. It was an open well. He could smell the water. It smelled like rotten eggs, but if he'd had a cup, Jimmy would have taken a big swallow. Buster twitched his nose.

"There is water in there, but we can't get it."

Jimmy picked up a small rock and dropped it in the well. Almost immediately he heard a small splash.

"It's close to the top."

Jimmy lay on the ground and stuck his arm into the hole as far as he could reach. He touched nothing except the sides of the hole. He began to look around for something to dip into the water. He found an old coffee can with blue paint on the outside, but the bottom was rusted out. He kicked around in a small mound of trash near a large metal drum. His shoe uncovered pieces of aluminum foil that hadn't rusted. He stepped away from the large drum and heard the crunch of plastic beneath his feet. Looking down, he picked up a plastic milk jug. He'd smashed one corner, but it was still usable. He shook it. It was empty.

"Grandpa would know what to do," he said, sorry that Grandpa wasn't with him.

He returned to the well, lay on the ground, and tried to reach the water with the jug. He pushed himself forward so that more of his body went into the hole. He inched forward and teetered at the edge, in real danger of losing his balance and falling headfirst into the well. He heard a sound behind him, and when he shifted his body, he slipped forward. In an instant, he realized he was going into the water.

He screamed.

His hand slammed into the side of the well, where it struck a small stone protruding from the wall. The rock slowed his slide, and he reached out with his other hand and grabbed a tangle of roots. For a second he didn't move, suspended over the pit. Then, holding the roots as tightly as he could, he shoved himself off the rock. His fingers scratched across the dark surface and found a thicker root. He grabbed the root and pushed himself away from the hole.

In a few seconds, he was out of the well and lying facedown on the grass. He sucked air into his lungs as if still threatened with drowning. He couldn't remember ever being as tired as he was now. He closed his eyes and lay still. Buster came over and licked his ear. Jimmy didn't move. Several minutes passed before he rolled over and looked up.

At his feet stood a figure framed by the setting sun. Without his glasses, Jimmy couldn't make out his exact form, but he immediately knew who it was.

It was a Watcher.

Jimmy held up his hand, and the Watcher lifted him to his feet. Never before had Jimmy touched one of the Watchers. His touch gave Jimmy warm strength. He showed no emotion. Buster, now sitting on the other side of the well, looked past Jimmy with his head tilted to one side.

"Thank you, sir," Jimmy said.

He wasn't sure if he was supposed to say anything, but Mama had taught him that good manners were always the right thing to do. The Watcher turned and began to walk away from the well. Jimmy knew to follow. They walked to the other side of the house. The Watcher stopped beside an old washing machine. There was a metal pipe sticking up from the ground with a spigot attached to it. A small tin cup on a slender, rusty chain hung down from the spigot. Jimmy held up the cup and understood.

"It's a way to get water," he said, nodding his head.

He looked around and saw a long, sturdy stick in the grass near the washing machine. He picked up the stick and grabbed the chain. He could use the chain to tie the cup to the end of the stick. It would be like one of the old cane poles he used as a little boy when he went fishing with Grandpa. Before Jimmy could yank the chain free, the Watcher stretched out his hand and placed it firmly on Jimmy's wrist. Once again, Jimmy felt the warmth of his touch. He dropped his hand.

"What do I do?"

Still not understanding, he looked again at the pump. He touched the handle and pushed down. It moved. He grabbed the handle and pulled it up. He repeated the movement and heard the hissing sound of moving air. Several more times he pumped up and down. He heard a gurgling noise, and a tiny stream of water dripped from the spigot. He stopped and looked up in surprise.

The Watcher was gone.

Jimmy pumped the handle hard until water gushed from the spigot. He grabbed the cup and held it underneath while it quickly filled. He took a long drink. The water from the pump didn't smell at all like rotten eggs. It had the sweetest taste of any liquid that had ever passed his lips. Buster joined him, licking up water that splashed onto the ground. Jimmy kept pumping and filled the cup again. He drank it to the bottom, then held a cupful in front of the dog's nose. Buster greedily lapped it up.

"It's good water," Jimmy said. "He knew where to find good water."

THEY DRANK ALL THEY WANTED. THEN JIMMY SPLASHED HIS neck and rubbed his face, washing away the grime and dirt from his flight through the woods and close call at the well. Afterward, he felt better inside and out. He poured water on Buster's back and laughed as the dog shook himself dry. The sound of his own voice caused Jimmy to glance around. The sun had sunk below the trees. He looked at the old house. He could probably find a way to get inside, but spending the night in an abandoned house in the middle of the woods didn't seem like a good idea. He stepped away from the pump and stood in the front yard. Trees surrounded the house, but even with his blurred vision, Jimmy could tell that at one place the trees were much smaller and less developed.

"The driveway," he said to Buster. "Grandpa says all driveways lead to roads. Whoever lived here had to have a way to come and go."

He walked toward the smaller trees. There was no mistaking a narrow road leading away from the house. He started to follow it, then stopped.

If he found the road, he might also find Walt. He'd spent the past few hours running away from his cousin. Did he want to return to an area where he might run into him? Jimmy looked back at the house and the pump. He could stay and drink the sweet water in safety or leave and risk what was waiting for him in the woods. He wished the Watcher had stayed.

"What do you want to do?" he asked Buster.

The dog didn't move. Jimmy knelt and stroked his back.

"That's not your job, is it?"

Suddenly, tears welled in Jimmy's eyes. It wasn't the same crushing sadness he'd felt in the woods. He wasn't sure what caused it. After a few moments, he rubbed his eyes.

"Now that I've had a drink of water, I can cry," he said.

Jimmy stayed on his knees, rubbing the dog's back and wishing for an answer. The shadow of a tall pine tree reached the edge of his foot. He stared at the shadow for a few seconds, then stood up.

"Let's go," he said. "If we wait much longer, it will be too dark to see what's up ahead."

After about thirty minutes, the shadows deepened, and the possibility of spending the night alone in the woods became more likely. Buster pattered alongside him.

"This sure is a long driveway," he said.

He stepped across a narrow ditch. Growing on the opposite side of the ditch was a band of wild azaleas sprinkled with lavender blossoms. At the sight of the flowering bushes, Jimmy remembered his plan to find fresh plants for Aunt Jill. He snapped off several limbs and clutched them in his right hand. He hoped Aunt Jill would be happy.

A few feet farther, he crossed another ditch and stumbled onto the edge of a gravel road. He looked one way and could tell the road climbed a small hill. In the other direction, the road seemed flat.

"Let's not climb any hills," he suggested to Buster. "I bet you're tired."

They walked along the gravel surface. The last gray light from the sun slipped away, and the first stage of night arrived. On nature's cue, hundreds of crickets and katydids began to call out. The road stayed flat. They passed an old mailbox with faded numbers on its side. Not much farther off, Jimmy saw another mailbox knocked from its post. No houses were visible in the dark. No welcoming lights shone through the trees. Jimmy heard the sound of a car coming down the road behind them. He stepped back into the woods.

"Come here," he called to Buster.

He knelt and held the dog while the vehicle approached. When it came level with them, Jimmy could tell it was a pickup truck. Loud country music blared from the open windows. He scrambled into the road and waved his arms.

"Hey!" he called out. "Stop!"

The red taillights of the truck disappeared in a haze of dust. He ran a few steps, then stopped.

They continued walking. Jimmy was thirsty and tired. The good water from the pump was a happy memory that began to make him grumpy. His tired and hurting feet slowed. They walked around a curve. It was now totally dark. He looked up and saw a blue light flashing against the sky. He stopped and stared. In a few moments he heard the sound of an approaching car. He moved to the edge of the road as the lights came around a bend.

It was a police car.

Jimmy stepped into the road and began to wave his arms. The car slowed to a stop, and the door flew open.

"Jimmy! Are you all right?" a familiar voice called out.

It was Deputy Askew. Jimmy let his hands drop to his side.

"Yes, sir!" he said. "It's me and Buster!"

The deputy came over to him. Jimmy's shoulders slumped, and he leaned against the officer as he led Jimmy to the car. Buster barked and ran around them.

"Walt," Jimmy began.

"I already know," Deputy Askew interrupted. "He's at the hospital with a broken ankle. It was brave of you to go for help, but you should have stayed with him. We've been looking for you since four o'clock this afternoon. I was making one more pass up this road before heading home for the night."

Jimmy felt light-headed. The officer opened the passenger side door of the car and helped him inside. Jimmy reached for a bottle of water, then stopped.

"Go ahead," Deputy Askew said. "I know you must be dying of thirst after so many hours without a drink."

Jimmy started to tell about the pump but stopped.

"Do you have a cup for Buster?" he asked.

"Sure."

Askew took a paper cup, tore off the top half, and poured water for the dog. Buster stood beside the vehicle and lapped up the water. Jimmy took a few good swallows from the blue plastic water bottle.

"You took time to pick flowers?" the deputy asked, shaking his head at the rapidly wilting bouquet on the front seat of the patrol car.

"Yes, sir. They're for my Aunt Jill so she won't be mad at me."

"Why would she be mad?"

Jimmy told him about the wreath.

"After what's happened today, I don't think some stray red paint on a wreath is going to be very important."

"He chased me," Jimmy said, leaning back against the seat.

"I know. I talked with him at the hospital just before they took him back for surgery."

"Surgery?"

"Yeah. The bone was almost popping out of the skin. It was a bad break, but I radioed the hospital a few minutes ago, and he's already back in a regular room. We knew you had to be in the area, and he told me you tried to take a shortcut through the woods. If you ever go for help in the future, always stay near the road. That's how they found Walt. He crawled to the edge of the road. A driver saw him, stopped, and called an ambulance."

"Is he in trouble?"

"Yes, but I'm sure his parents are glad that he didn't spend all night in the woods with a broken ankle."

"My parents are out of town."

"Your uncle's been trying to reach them. They may already be on their way back."

"I want to go home."

"Do you need to go to the hospital?"

"No, I'm not sick. Just tired."

Deputy Askew radioed the other patrol cars that he'd located Jimmy and told the dispatcher to get in touch with his parents and Uncle Bart. Jimmy settled into the seat as they drove down the gravel road. Buster was already asleep on the floorboard. Jimmy's eyelids fluttered, and he leaned his head to the side.

His eyes popped open with a start when the gravel road ended and they hit a bump that marked the beginning of a smooth surface. It wasn't the same road with the hills that made Jimmy's stomach jump. The events of the day already seemed a week old. Deputy Askew didn't have on his blue lights anymore, but he seemed to be driving fast toward town. Although fuzzy and out of focus, Jimmy could distinguish familiar sights as they crossed into the city limits. A female voice came over the radio.

"Jimmy's parents are at the house waiting for him. They know he's okay and won't be going to the hospital."

"It looks like you're going to sleep in your own bed tonight," the deputy said. "Are you hungry?"

Jimmy hadn't thought about food.

"I'm so tired, I don't really know," he answered.

Deputy Askew reached over and patted him on the shoulder.

"Your appetite will be back tomorrow. What's your favorite breakfast?"

"Pecan pancakes with link sausage."

Jimmy remembered that Aunt Jill had fixed his favorite meal that very morning. She'd been very nice to him, and he hoped she wouldn't be disappointed that he didn't find more flowers. Askew turned onto Jimmy's street.

"If you ever have something like that happen again, what are you going to do?" the deputy asked.

"Run as fast as I can," Jimmy answered.

"Are you going to leave the road?"

"Yes, sir."

Deputy Askew sighed. "We'll talk about it later."

Jimmy saw the front door of the house open and could make out Mama and Daddy walking rapidly down the steps. Deputy Askew stopped the car. Buster stretched for a second before jumping out of the car onto the grass and running toward the backyard. It had been a great day in the woods for a dog.

Jimmy followed him from the car into an enveloping embrace from Mama. She was crying. Jimmy had cried in the woods. Now that he was home, he didn't feel sad at all. Daddy stood behind Mama.

"I'll be going, Mr. Mitchell," Deputy Askew said.

"Thanks for staying out there until you found him," Daddy said. "We're forever grateful."

"Oh, he found me. He was walking down the road and flagged me down. He knows his way in the woods better than a lot of normal—"

The deputy stopped.

"It's okay," Daddy said. "We're just thankful to have him home in such good shape. I'll send you boys something as a thank-you the first of the week."

Mama released her hold and blew her nose on a tissue.

"We were so worried. Are you sure you're not hurt?"

"I don't think so. I lost my glasses, but I found these flowers for Aunt Jill."

Buster ran back to where they stood.

"Oh, I need to give him some food and water," Jimmy said.

"I'll do it," Daddy replied. "Go inside with your mama."

Mama kept her arm around Jimmy as they climbed the steps to the front porch. Inside the house, she gave him another pair of glasses. He slipped them on and sighed in relief as his world came into focus again. Jimmy washed his hands in the kitchen sink while Mama poured him a glass of lemonade. The lemonade tasted good, but he wondered if anything would ever be sweeter than the water from the pump beside the old house. Daddy returned from taking care of Buster.

"I pulled a tick from Buster's ear, but he seems no worse for wear," Daddy said.

"You've got some scratches on your face and arms," Mama said, examining Jimmy more closely in the light of the kitchen.

"I ran though the woods for a long time," he said.

"Do you want to talk about it now?" Daddy asked.

Jimmy shook his head. "No, sir. I'd like to go to bed."

"Do you want to take a shower?" Mama asked.

Jimmy hesitated.

"Yes, ma'am, but it better be short. I think I could go to sleep standing up."

As the water cascaded over him, Jimmy let the pain and stress of the day run down the drain. He put on his pajamas and brushed his teeth. Returning to his nightly routine brought peace to his soul and made the memory of the evil in Walt's eyes seem far away.

Mama was waiting for him in his bedroom. She'd pulled back his top sheet and fluffed up his pillow. He crawled into bed. She covered him up to his chin and began to pray. It was not the usual prayer of nightly blessing. There was more in Mama's heart tonight than could be spoken in a few words. Jimmy nestled into the soft mattress as the familiar voice spoke thanks to God for preserving his life and watching over him. Jimmy forced his eyes open.

"Mama," he said.

She stopped praying. "What is it?"

"I know I'm not supposed to talk when you're praying, but a Watcher helped me today. He kept me from falling into a well and showed me where to get a drink of water."

"Tell me more," she said.

Jimmy turned over on his side and closed his eyes.

"It was the best water I've ever tasted," he said with a yawn. "I wish I could get some for you to—"

His voice faded, and his breathing became regular. Mama wiped away a tear and continued praying.

— _Nineteen_ —

When Jimmy awoke, the morning sun had filled his bedroom with light. He started to jump out of bed, but his aching body reminded him of yesterday. He sat on the edge of the bed and stood up as stiffly as Grandpa getting up from his easy chair after a long afternoon nap. After a few steps, Jimmy's muscles loosened, and he went downstairs. Mama, wearing her blue robe and white slippers, sat in the kitchen drinking a cup of coffee.

"Good morning, sunshine," she said.

Jimmy rubbed his hand through his hair.

"What day is it?" he asked.

"It's Sunday."

"Aren't we going to church?"

"Daddy and I weren't sure you'd feel like it and decided to let you sleep late."

"What time is it?"

Mama glanced at the clock on the microwave oven. "It's almost ten. Sunday school has already started."

"We could still go to the church service, couldn't we?" he asked.

Mama put down her cup of coffee.

"I guess we could if you want to. We'd have to hurry to get ready."

Jimmy nodded. "I think today would be a good day for me to go to church."

Mama stood. "I'll tell Daddy that you want to go. Drink a glass of orange juice and then get dressed."

Jimmy opened the refrigerator. The sight of food and drink available at any time made him remember how hard it had been to get a cup of water in the woods. He poured a glass of orange juice and sat at the kitchen table. Before taking a sip of the juice, he bowed his head and spoke a silent word of thanks.

"What are you doing?" Daddy interrupted him.

Jimmy looked up. Daddy, too, was still in his pajamas.

"I'm thanking God for the orange juice."

"Are you feeling all right?"

"Yes, sir, except I know how Grandpa feels when he says his knees don't want to work. My legs hurt when I got out of bed."

"You walked a long way in the woods," Daddy's voice was softer than normal. "Mama says you want to go to church."

"Yes, sir. I think I need to thank God for taking care of me. Did Mama tell you about the Watcher I saw?"

"She did."

Jimmy picked up a banana and peeled it. He couldn't tell if Daddy wanted to talk more or not.

"We'll go," Daddy said after another moment of silence. "Finish eating and get ready as soon as you can."

JIMMY ATE A SECOND BANANA RIDING IN THE BACKSEAT OF the car on the drive to church. Every normal thing about his life made him happy. He looked in the rearview mirror and saw that Daddy was smiling too.

"Did you have a car take you to church when you were a boy?" he asked Daddy as the church came into view.

"No, son. I had to ride a mule without a saddle."

"Lee," Mama said.

Daddy corrected himself. "No, that's my grandfather I'm thinking about. Grandpa bought his first car several years before I was born."

"Was it a Studebaker?" Jimmy asked.

"No, a beautiful blue Chevrolet."

They arrived as the Sunday school crowd was leaving the educational building. They slipped into the throng, but not unnoticed.

Several men came over to Jimmy, patted him on the head, and congratulated him on his survival in the woods. One man spoke to Daddy.

"From where they found Walt, I calculate Jimmy walked between eight and ten miles."

"I'd say closer to twelve," another man said.

Jimmy listened and learned that Walt, a white cast on his right leg, was going to come home from the hospital on Monday. Jimmy spoke to Mama as they climbed the steps to the sanctuary.

"I don't want to ride in Walt's car anymore."

Mama put her arms around his shoulder. "Yes, it was foolish of him to drive you that far away from town, but you shouldn't have asked him to take you and Buster to the woods."

"But, Mama—," Jimmy began.

"Not now," Mama interrupted. "You're not in trouble, and Walt won't be driving anywhere for a while. I'm just glad you're home."

JIMMY SNUGGLED CLOSE TO MAMA ON THE PEW. DADDY ALSO moved closer to him than normal. Between the two of them, Jimmy felt secure. During the announcements that came before the prayer, Brother Fitzgerald looked directly at Jimmy.

"We should be thankful today that no harm befell young Jimmy Mitchell, who was lost in the woods for several hours yesterday after his cousin, Walt Dunhill, fell and broke his ankle. Jimmy bravely went for help and was found by the sheriff's department shortly after dark. Walt is fine and recuperating in the hospital. Jimmy is with us in God's house this morning."

It seemed to Jimmy that the entire congregation turned in his direction. Jimmy peeked out from behind Daddy's shoulder and saw a sea of curious eyes.

When the minister moved on to the next topic, Jimmy whispered to Daddy, "Who told him?"

Daddy leaned down. "It's hard for anything to escape Brother Fitzgerald's attention. He has to know about things. It's part of his job."

Jimmy thought finding out about events in Piney Grove was the job of the people who worked at the newspaper. Daddy had given him a copy of the newspaper article that mentioned Jimmy's testimony in Jake Garner's trial. It stayed on Jimmy's corkboard until it turned yellow around the edges.

"Will there be a story in the newspaper?" he whispered.

"I don't know," Daddy responded. "If a reporter calls the house, I'll talk to him."

"Quiet, you two," Mama said.

Jimmy relaxed. He didn't want to tell a stranger what Walt tried to do, and he had no idea why everyone thought he ran away from Walt to find help. If Walt had been nice, they would have found more pretty plants for Aunt Jill and gotten home in time for supper, and Walt wouldn't be in the hospital with a broken ankle.

Brother Fitzgerald cleared his throat. It was time for the long prayer. Right at the beginning, he heard his name.

"And we thank you, this day, O Lord, for your watch over young Jimmy Mitchell, and your mercy in sparing him from the dangers of the wild, bringing him safely home to his family."

AFTER CHURCH, A LOT OF PEOPLE CAME UP TO JIMMY AND started asking him questions. It was a bigger crowd than when he was saved. He couldn't understand all the questions fired at him and simply started saying, "Thank you," "Yes, sir," and "Yes, ma'am." Daddy took over and steered him through the crowd. Jimmy held Mama's hand. They didn't break free from the people until they reached the bottom of the steps in front of the sanctuary.

"Let's go before someone else corners us," Daddy said.

They walked briskly toward the car. Just as they reached it, Jimmy heard Max's voice calling out to him.

"Jimmy Mitchell!"

"Tell me what happened," Max said, out of breath from running across the parking lot. "I want to hear about it before you forget anything."

"Sorry, Max, we've got to go," Daddy said.

Jimmy turned to Mama. "When can Max come over to the house?"

Mama turned to Max. "Ask your mother if tomorrow afternoon works for her."

THEY LEFT THE CHURCH PARKING LOT BUT DIDN'T TURN IN the direction of home.

"Where are we going?" Jimmy asked.

"To the hospital to see Walt and then to lunch at Springdale," Mama replied. A frown crossed Jimmy's face. "Why do we have to see Walt? I don't want to go."

Mama turned sideways in her seat.

"Why not?"

Jimmy took a deep breath. "I didn't run through the woods to get help for Walt. I didn't know he had a broken ankle. I ran from him because he scared me. He wanted to play a game, and I didn't want to do it."

"What kind of game?" Daddy asked, looking in the rearview mirror.

Jimmy tried to remember. "It was a Hindu game."

"Hindu?" Mama asked.

"He took off his belt and wanted to tie me up and see if I could escape."

"Houdini," Daddy responded.

"Yes, sir. That's what he called it. I told him that I didn't want to play and then ran into the woods. He chased me and yelled, but I got away."

"You didn't know his ankle was broken?" Mama asked.

"No, ma'am, not until Deputy Askew told me."

"Did he hit you or hurt you?" Daddy asked.

"No, sir. I'm a fast runner, but it was hard because I lost my glasses and didn't know where to go. Buster stayed right with me."

Daddy looked across the seat at Mama. "What are we going to do? He's your nephew."

Mama pressed her lips together. "Do you believe Walt cooked up a story to make Jimmy look like a hero and hide the fact that he scared him?"

"I'd say that sums it up," Daddy answered. "Quick thinking for a sixteen-year-old with a broken ankle. I've always thought that boy had a sneaky—"

"Let's skip the hospital," Mama interrupted. "I'm going to have to think about this before I talk to Bart and Jill."

"Or I see Walt," Daddy added grimly.

TUESDAY EVENING, JIMMY AND HIS PARENTS WENT OVER TO see Uncle Bart, Aunt Jill, and Walt. Aunt Jill gave Jimmy a big hug as soon as he entered the house. Mama had put the wild azalea stems in a vase, but the blossoms were almost completely wilted. Jimmy nervously handed her the vase.

"I picked these for you," he said.

"Thank you, Jimmy," Aunt Jill responded. "Come into the living room. Walt is set up in there."

Walt, his lower leg in a white cast, sat with his foot propped up on a low chair brought in from the foyer. He avoided meeting Jimmy's eyes. Jimmy stood so close to Mama that he was touching her.

"I made some cherry cobbler," Aunt Jill said. "Who would like some with a scoop of ice cream on top?"

"I would," Jimmy blurted out, glad for a chance to leave the room.

"No, let's wait on the cobbler," Mama said. "We need to discuss what happened in the woods on Saturday."

Uncle Bart spoke. "Oh, I've already told Walt that he shouldn't have taken Jimmy so far out of town. After his ankle heals, I'm going to ground him for a month before he can drive his car."

"That's not what we're talking about," Daddy responded. "Jimmy told us—"

"You need to tell the truth, Jimmy," Walt interrupted.

"I did."

"Did you tell about spraying red paint on the wreath and ruining it?"

Jimmy looked at Aunt Jill, "No."

"What does that have to do with going to the woods?" Daddy asked.

"Everything, Uncle Lee," Walt replied. "That's why we left the house, isn't it Jimmy?"

Jimmy nodded. "Yes."

"Jimmy was here alone for a few minutes and sprayed red paint all over a wreath my mom was making. It's still in the craft room. Mom, would you get it, please?"

Aunt Jill left and in a moment came back with the marred wreath. Jimmy gave Mama a sheepish look.

Walt pointed at the wreath. "To make things right before she got home, Jimmy and I decided to go to the woods and find something she could use in another project. We drove to a place that has a bunch of sweet gum trees. I thought we could pick up a sack of those prickly balls and bring them home so she could paint and use them."

"You didn't tell me that," Jimmy protested.

"I did, but you weren't listening. All you seemed interested in was your dog. If we hadn't taken him with us, none of this would have happened."

"Wait a minute," Daddy said. "Jimmy told us you wanted to tie him up."

Walt looked confused. Then he said, "Oh, I know where he got that idea. When we got out of the car, Jimmy ran off to play with his dog, and I started picking up sweet gum balls. I didn't want to do all the work and yelled that if he didn't come over and help, I was going to put him and his dog on a leash. I was kidding."

"Jimmy said you wanted to play a game called Houdini," Daddy said. "You were going to tie him up and see if he could escape."

"Houdini?" Walt asked. "What is that?"

"An escape artist," Uncle Bart answered. "He lived a long time ago."

"I've never heard of him," Walt said.

"Why would Jimmy mention his name?" Mama asked.

Walt shrugged. "I don't know. He didn't hear it from me."

"He could have seen something on TV," Aunt Jill suggested.

Jimmy turned his head from side to side as he followed the conversation. The more he listened, the more confused he became. Aunt Jill turned toward him.

"Have you ever seen a TV show about Harry Houdini?"

"No, ma'am," Jimmy answered.

"Lee, I resent your insinuations," Uncle Bart said, his face slightly red. "We didn't realize you were coming over here to cross-examine Walt as if he were a criminal. He's done nothing wrong, and we should all be thankful the boys are alive and well."

"We are," Mama said. "But Jimmy says he didn't know Walt's ankle was broken until a sheriff's deputy told him about it. Jimmy didn't leave Walt to seek help. He ran away from Walt because he was scared."

"Scared of what?" Uncle Bart seemed angry now. "Picking up a few sweet gum balls?"

"I think I can explain," Walt said in a softer voice.

Everyone looked at him.

Walt spoke in a level voice. "After I asked him to help me, Jimmy threw a stick for his dog to fetch and went into the edge of the woods. I ran after him and stepped in a hole. That's when I broke my ankle. I cried out in pain. Jimmy turned around and saw me, and I guess the look on my face scared him. He took off running. I thought he was going for help. I started yelling for him to come back, but he left me alone."

Daddy turned to Jimmy. "Did the look on Walt's face scare you?"

"Yes, sir."

"Did he yell for you to come back?"

"Yes, sir."

"That's enough," Uncle Bart said. "This is exactly what Walt told us the first time we talked about it. I'm sorry Jimmy misunderstood what happened, but I'm offended that you would come over here and accuse Walt like this. We're all part of the same family."

"It's okay," Walt said. "I thought it was strange that Jimmy ran into the woods instead of down the road, but I guess he's easily confused and didn't think about it. He panicked."

Daddy glanced at Mama. Mama spoke.

"Walt, we owe you and your folks an apology. We're protective of Jimmy because of his limitations and overreacted to the information he gave us. Now that I know what actually happened, I can see the whole picture."

Aunt Jill reached over and patted Jimmy on the knee. "And don't worry about the wreath. It doesn't matter, so long as you're safe and sound. You're worth a lot more to us than a wreath or a few sweet gum balls."

Daddy looked at the floor and didn't say anything.

"Let's have cobbler and ice cream," Aunt Jill added brightly. "It will make everyone feel better."

Jimmy sighed with relief. He'd rather enjoy cobbler than argue with Walt and Uncle Bart. Aunt Jill's cobbler was as good as her fried chicken. It had a flaky crust with slightly sweet cherries underneath that popped in his mouth when he bit down on them. And it was easier to eat the delicious dessert than try to argue with Walt and the adults.

AS SOON AS THEY GOT IN THE CAR TO GO HOME, DADDY SPOKE.

"I don't believe Walt. Something in my gut tells me he's still lying."

"But you heard Jimmy admit everything that came up. It was a big misunderstanding."

"I've seen clever liars like Walt. They know how to manipulate facts and rework them so they come out looking squeaky clean."

"Just because your clients lie doesn't mean your nephew isn't telling the truth," Mama responded. "Why would Walt want to hurt Jimmy in the first place? He has a smart mouth, but he's never hit or hurt him during all the time they've been growing up."

Daddy grunted. "Not all my clients lie. Just the guilty ones."

"Maybe so, but after tonight, we can't dwell on it with Bart and Jill." Mama paused. "However, there is one thing I want to avoid in the future."

"What's that?" Daddy asked.

"Jimmy will not be left alone with Walt for any length of time under any circumstances."

"Or ride with him in the car."

"Agreed. There's no need to mention anything for a few weeks, because Walt is out of commission."

"Thank you," Jimmy interjected.

"And we'll need to change our estate plan," Daddy added. "Bart and Jill are designated as Jimmy's guardians in case something happens to us."

Mama raised her eyebrows. "I'd forgotten about that."

"I'll modify the papers this week and let you know when to come by the office and sign them."

"Who will take their place?"

"My parents. And we'll hope nothing happens to us or them until we come up with an alternate plan."

Mama was silent for a second. "What about Vera? Could she come in and try to take him?"

"She would have an argument. That's another reason why we're countersuing to terminate her parental rights."

Mama sighed. "It's complicated, isn't it? And beyond all this is the idea of Jimmy trying to live independently as an adult."

Jimmy didn't understand exactly what she meant.

THE FOLLOWING WEEK MAX CAME OVER FOR A VISIT BUT got nothing more than a short account of Jimmy's adventures in the woods. He forced Jimmy to stop when he came to the part about the Watcher at the well.

"Why can't I see them?" Max asked.

"I don't know."

"Why do you get to see them?"

Jimmy smiled. "Because I'm special."

Max's mouth dropped open in surprise. He knew how Jimmy didn't like that word.

"Jimmy, did you mean that as a joke?"

"Was it funny?"

"Yes."

"Then why aren't you laughing?"

Max laughed. "Because I didn't want to hurt your feelings if you didn't mean it that way. Does that mean there is a good kind of special?"

"Yes," Jimmy said. "I've been thinking about it, and you're a special football player. When we go to high school, you're going to be the most special quarterback ever."

— Twenty —

The school year ended, and Jimmy was promoted to the eighth grade. Two days later he celebrated his fourteenth birthday. The night before the big day, he lay in bed wondering about his presents. With Buster in the backyard and his red bicycle leaned against the railing of the front porch, Jimmy had everything a boy could possibly want.

Jimmy didn't like big birthday parties. When he turned six, Mama invited his whole first-grade class to a party at the local roller-skating rink, but after thirty minutes, Jimmy went to the car.

Jimmy went downstairs for breakfast. Mama was fixing pecan pancakes with link sausage. Birthdays were different from Christmas. On birthdays he had to wait until the afternoon to open his gifts.

"Happy birthday," she said.

"Good morning, Mama. Where's Daddy?"

"He had to go to work early so he can come home for your party."

After breakfast Jimmy and Mama spent two hours working in the flower beds. Mama raised flowers in broad bands across the front and side of the house. The plants needed a lot of watering and weeding. Daddy had spread several dump-truck loads of river-bottom dirt over the red clay, and Jimmy liked the feel of the rich soil between his fingers. He kept a plastic cup beside him, and as he pulled up the weeds, he searched for earthworms. He put moist soil in the bottom of the cup and dropped the worms on top. When he had a few wiggling creatures in a pile, he added another layer of soil and repeated the process. Grandpa believed homegrown earthworms, so long as they were fresh, caught as many fish as the ones bought at the bait store.

Buster liked to dig in the flower beds too, but he couldn't tell the difference between a daisy and a dandelion, so one of Jimmy's jobs was to keep the dog entertained. Jimmy brought two tennis balls outside and threw them across the yard for Buster to fetch. The black-and-white dog was tireless, and even on the hottest days he never stopped returning the balls and waiting for another one. Sometimes Jimmy would reach over and scratch Buster's belly. A certain place Jimmy scratched caused the dog's hind leg to twitch rapidly back and forth. Watching the dog's leg shake made Jimmy laugh. Buster didn't mind. He closed his eyes and let his tongue hang out the side of his mouth.

MAX ARRIVED MIDAFTERNOON CARRYING A LARGE PRESENT wrapped in yellow paper. Jimmy saw his friend's arrival from his bedroom window and ran downstairs to greet him. As he threw open the front door, he saw Max lifting his bicycle from the back of his mother's van.

"Happy birthday!" Jimmy called out.

Max rolled his bike up to the porch and leaned it against the steps.

"That's what I'm supposed to say. It's your birthday."

"But I want you to have a happy day on my birthday."

Max came into the house and handed Jimmy the present. "Guess what it is."

Jimmy took the box and shook it. It didn't make any sound.

"It's light. Is it a really small gift that you put in a big box to fool me?"

"You'll have to find out later."

Max walked into the foyer and slipped off a backpack. Mama entered.

"What's in the backpack?" Jimmy asked.

"My clothes. I'm going to spend the night."

"Yes!" Jimmy exclaimed, glancing up at Mama in appreciation.

"And I asked Max to bring his bike," Mama added.

"We can ride in the yard!" Jimmy exclaimed.

Max smiled. "I thought we might take a longer trip."

"To Grandpa's house?"

Mama spoke. "No, I'm willing to let you ride downtown so long as Max is with you. You'll have to promise to stay right beside him and do what he tells you about traffic. Leave Buster home for this trip."

"Yes, ma'am."

Ten minutes later, the two boys were pedaling down the sidewalk with Max in the lead and Jimmy's eyes glued to his friend's back. At the first intersection, they slowed to a stop. Jimmy honked his horn twice. Walking the bikes across the street, they continued toward Hathaway Street and the center of town. At each stop sign or light, Jimmy pressed the bulb for his horn at least two times.

"You sure like that horn, don't you?" Max asked.

Jimmy honked in response. Let the world know he'd arrived.

They reached Hathaway Street, named for the family who owned the first general store in the area. It was the center of business activity.

"We'll walk our bikes down the sidewalk," Max said.

Jimmy passed the barbershop where he went for haircuts. Mr. Griffin, the barber, looked out the big plate-glass window. Jimmy proudly pointed at his bike, and Mr. Griffin waved. Next to the barbershop was an insurance agency, a small café, and then a two-story office building at one corner of the courthouse square.

The Cattaloochie County Courthouse never appeared on calendars featuring historic Georgia courthouses, Daddy said, because it was built in the 1950s under the supervision of a board of county commissioners who knew more about concrete-block hog pens than courthouses. Built of dingy brown brick, it had two entrances framed by white columns much too small for the size of the structure.

"That's where you'll be next week," Max said as they passed in front of the courthouse. "I hope everything goes okay."

"Daddy doesn't send me to the courthouse. I stay at his office and work."

"No, I mean the court hearing with your birth mother."

Jimmy stopped pushing his bike. Max kept going a few feet, then glanced back.

"Uh-oh," Max said, turning his bike around so he faced Jimmy. "My mom told me about the hearing before the school year ended. I thought you knew about it."

Jimmy swallowed. "What is a hearing?"

Max shook his head. "Your parents should explain it to you, especially since your daddy is a lawyer."

"No. I want you to tell me. Mama starts to cry when anyone says anything about my birth mama, and Daddy doesn't want to upset her."

Max pushed his bike closer. "All I know is that your birth mother wants to spend time with you, but my mom says she didn't care about seeing you for a long time, and it wouldn't be right for her to change her mind now. My dad told me it also has to do with her not buying presents for you on your birthday and at Christmas. There will be a hearing at the courthouse next week in front of a judge who will decide if you have to visit your birth mother or not. My mother is going to be one of the witnesses."

"Does she know my birth mama?"

"A little bit, but I think she is going to tell the judge what good friends we are and that it wouldn't be right for us not to see one another."

"Why wouldn't I see you?" Jimmy asked in alarm.

"Because your birth mother wants you to live part of the time with her in Atlanta. My dad says no judge in the world would make that happen. He's not a lawyer, but he's smart about lots of stuff."

"Are you going to be at the hearing?"

"No, I don't think so."

"Why not?"

"I haven't been invited."

"Well, I want you to come."

"Listen, Jimmy. I'm sorry I brought this up. It's your birthday, and I don't want to ruin it. Everything is going to be all right."

A man exited the courthouse and walked down the sidewalk toward them. It was Mr. Long. He saw Jimmy and smiled.

"Happy birthday!" he called out as he came closer to them. "How does it feel to be fourteen?"

"Okay," Jimmy replied.

"What's wrong?" Mr. Long asked.

Jimmy didn't respond, and the man turned to Max.

"You're Max Cochran, aren't you?"

"Yes, sir."

"I'm a lawyer helping Jimmy's father. Your mother showed me a picture of you and Jimmy taken at your house. I think you were standing in front of a small barn."

"Yes, sir. That's the day Jimmy came over and helped me rake leaves. We worked most of the day and finished a lot quicker than if I'd been doing it alone. Jimmy is like a machine with a rake. He almost never takes a break."

Mr. Long smiled at Jimmy. "If you like to rake leaves so much, I'd like to invite you to my house in the fall."

Jimmy stared at the sidewalk. "Yes, sir."

"I just told Jimmy about the hearing," Max said. "I don't think he knew about it."

Mr. Long nodded his head to a concrete bench in front of the courthouse. "Come over here," he said to the two boys.

They leaned their bicycles against the end of the bench. Mr. Long sat down. Jimmy and Max stood before him.

"Jimmy, I'm going to meet with you and your parents tomorrow and talk to you about the hearing. We thought it would be better to let you enjoy your birthday without thinking about anything else. Can you forget about the hearing for now?"

Jimmy stuck out his lower lip. "No, sir. I want to stay with Mama, Daddy, Grandpa, Buster, and Max."

"And that's exactly what you're going to tell the judge. Now that you're fourteen, the judge has to pay attention to what you think should happen about visitation and custody. He'll also listen to your parents and the other witnesses we'll have in court."

"Visitation and custody?" Jimmy asked.

"Visiting your birth mother and spending a lot of time with her at her house. Your birth mother wants the judge to make your parents let her see you."

"Judge Robinson goes to our church," Max said. "He'll do what Mr. Mitchell wants him—"

Mr. Long interrupted. "Judge Robinson won't be deciding the case. There will be a visiting judge from Harrelson County. But no more talk about the hearing. This is Jimmy's special day. You boys finish your bike ride. Jimmy, I'll see you tomorrow."

Mr. Long got up and continued down the street. Max spoke.

"Jimmy, everything is going to be okay. My dad told me you don't have anything to worry about."

Max's father was an expert shot with both a pistol and a rifle and could fix a lawn mower engine that wouldn't start.

"What exactly did he say?"

"That your parents are in the right, and your birth mother is in the wrong. You'll have to come to the courthouse for the hearing, but nothing is going to change. All that talk about visitation and custody is just a bunch of lawyer talk that won't amount to anything."

Jimmy nodded. "I want to be nice to my birth mama, but I don't want to go to a strange place and not see my family or you."

"My dad says that won't happen. The judge is going to throw it out of court."

"I hope he doesn't throw it at me."

Max laughed.

"Do you want to ride over to your daddy's office?" he asked. "We could show him how far we've ridden our bikes today."

"No, I want to go home. I don't want to miss my party."

"Don't worry about that either. The party can't start without you. You're the birthday boy."

They went back the way they'd come. Jimmy honked his horn, but with less gusto, at all stop signs and traffic lights. He couldn't figure out how he should feel about his birth mama. He was fascinated by the five pictures he kept in his desk, but his curiosity didn't make him want to leave home to spend time with someone he didn't know. And, of course, he didn't want people to fight over him.

The two boys turned into Jimmy's driveway behind a brown UPS truck. The driver stepped from the vehicle. Jimmy recognized the man as a member of the First Baptist Church.

"Just the person I need to see," the driver said as Jimmy and Max stopped beside him on their bikes.

The man handed Jimmy a long, narrow box.

"This has your name on it."

Jimmy read *James Lee Mitchell III*, followed by his address.

"I bet it's a birthday present," Max said.

Jimmy thanked the driver and took the box. He and Max carried it to the front porch and sat on the steps.

"Open it," Max said.

"Not until after we eat the cake."

"Don't worry. It will be wrapped on the inside."

Jimmy hesitated. Max took the box from him and turned it so he could read the label.

"Who is Mrs. Lonnie Horton?" he asked. "Is she one of your relatives?"

"I don't know. Let's go ask Mama."

Mama was not in the kitchen. Max leaned the box against the kitchen counter. While the boys were drinking water, Mama came into the room.

"How was the bike ride?" she asked.

"Fine," Max replied before Jimmy could answer. "Jimmy stayed right with me, and we didn't have any problems with traffic. He must have honked the horn on his bike at least thirty or forty times. We went all the way to the courthouse before we turned around."

"Who did you see downtown?"

"Lots of people," Max said.

"I guess you know most everybody," Mama said with a smile.

"Yes, ma'am." Max picked up the long, narrow box. "But I don't know Mrs. Lonnie Horton. Is she one of Jimmy's out-of-town relatives?"

The smile on Mama's face vanished. She jerked the box from Max and examined the label.

"Where did this come from?" she asked sharply.

"We followed the UPS driver up to the house, and he gave it to us," Max replied. "Isn't it a birthday present for Jimmy?"

"If it is, he doesn't want it."

"Why not?" Jimmy asked. "It might be a BB gun. It feels about the same weight as the one Max has at his house. The last time I spent the night with him, he showed me how to shoot it, and I hit a can sitting on a fence."

"We're careful, Mrs. Mitchell," Max began. "My dad taught me all about gun safety, and Jimmy follows the rules—"

"You're not going to open this box no matter what it is," Mama interrupted. "You don't want any gifts from Mrs. Horton."

Recognition flashed across Max's face. "Is it from Jimmy's birth mother?" he blurted out.

"Yes," Mama replied curtly. "And this is no time to start accepting gifts from her. I'll call UPS and have it sent back."

Jimmy, fascinated by the possibility of a BB gun, eyed the brown box.

"Could we find out what it is? It has my name on it."

"No!" Mama answered with such force that Jimmy stepped back. "This is not a true gift. It's something she's doing to help her case in court."

"Max told me about the hearing," Jimmy said.

Mama stared hard at Max.

"I'm sorry, Mrs. Mitchell," Max said, looking at his shoes. "I didn't realize that you hadn't told Jimmy about it and opened my big mouth when we got to the courthouse. Then Mr. Long came up and explained some stuff to us. He didn't seem worried."

"He didn't?" Mama asked.

"Uh, he seemed confident."

"I hope he's not overconfident," Mama replied. "You boys go into the backyard and play with Buster. He's been barking since you left on your bike ride."

Jimmy eyed the box. "It might be a BB gun."

Mama gave him a fierce look. Jimmy fled from the kitchen with Max close behind him.

JIMMY AND MAX TOSSED A FOOTBALL BACK AND FORTH WITH Buster playing the role of defensive player. Max could throw a perfect spiral that landed softly in Jimmy's arms. Jimmy's passes were much less predictable; however, Max enjoyed diving for the ball and pretending that he was stretching for the goal line. Buster would jump on Max's head or back to tackle him.

Daddy got home and started a fire in the grill. At Jimmy's request, hamburgers and hot dogs were the birthday menu. Jimmy wanted to ask Daddy about the package from his birth mama but wasn't sure how to bring it up. Max went inside to go to the bathroom. When he returned, he came up close to Jimmy.

"Your parents are talking about the gift from your birth mother," he said.

"What are they saying?"

"Oh, they're talking about why she sent it and deciding when to send it back. It's not complicated, but parents have to make a big deal out of stuff. They'll talk for hours about something that should be over in thirty seconds."

"Wasn't it nice of her to send me a birthday present?" Jimmy asked.

"I thought you didn't want to see her or spend the night at her house. Now you're saying she's nice. What's going on with you?"

"People don't send birthday presents unless they like you."

"But she's never sent you a Christmas or birthday gift before."

Jimmy paused. "Maybe she did."

"No way," Max scoffed. "Your mama is right. Your birth mother just wants to make herself look good in front of the judge at the hearing. If your parents return the gift, she can't claim that she's done anything nice for you. My mom says it's not right for a parent to abandon a child and then come back years later and try to get involved."

Jimmy shook his head. "I wish I was smarter."

"You're plenty smart about the things that matter," Max answered. "Go out for another pass. I'll throw it close to the tree beside the garden."

GRANDPA AND GRANDMA ARRIVED AS DADDY TOOK THE hamburgers and hot dogs off the grill. Jimmy stacked their two gifts carefully beside Max's present. The package from his birth mama was nowhere in sight. They ate supper in the sunroom that was shaded by trees in the late afternoon and cooled by the house's air-conditioning system. While they ate, Grandpa answered Max's questions about pole climbing. The subject of the missing gift didn't come up.

Mama had baked a chocolate cake with white icing, Jimmy's favorite cake. On top, she'd written, "Happy Birthday, Jimmy," and beneath his name drawn a crude picture of a boy and a dog.

"That's me and Buster," Jimmy said.

"I'm glad you can tell," Mama said. "I'm not as talented as Aunt Jill."

Walt's family hadn't been invited to the party this year.

After devouring a healthy slab of cake, he opened his presents—a soccer ball from Max, a shirt from Grandma, a tackle box from Grandpa, a retractable leash from Buster, a backpack with his initials on it from Mama, and a new University of Georgia cap from Daddy.

That night Mama fixed a soft mat on the floor for Max. After she left the room, Jimmy took out the pictures of Vera and showed them to Max.

"Where did you get these?" Max asked.

"Mama gave me these three, and I borrowed the other two from Walt."

Max studied the faces in the light. "You can tell from her face that she's your birth mother."

"What do you think about her now?" Jimmy asked.

Max looked up at Jimmy. "You want to meet her, don't you?"

"I'm not sure."

After they turned off the lights and lay down, Jimmy stared at the ceiling. It was made of hundreds of tiny, thin boards. A full moon cast a pale light into the room.

"Max," he whispered, "are you awake?"

"Yes."

"What do you think about me climbing the pole?"

"I think it's awesome," Max said.

"What does that mean?"

"That you're a great pole climber."

Jimmy smiled into the darkness. Max always told him the truth.

"Do you want to see how far I've climbed?" he asked.

"Yes. Could we go over to your grandpa's house sometime? I'd like to do it too."

"I'll ask Mama."

They lay silent for a minute.

"Do you think there was a BB gun in the box from my birth mama?" Jimmy asked.

"Maybe, but you'll never know."

"Where do you think they put the box?"

"Underneath their bed. That's where my parents put stuff they don't want me and my sister to find."

"Do you think my mama's still mad about it? She didn't seem upset when we said our prayers."

"It's hard to tell with parents," Max replied. "Lots of times they hide what they're really thinking."

Jimmy counted the tiny boards until he fell asleep.

— Twenty-one —

Jimmy was wearing his Sunday clothes. Only it wasn't Sunday. He and Mama sat in Daddy's office while Mr. Long and Daddy talked in the conference room to the other people who were going to testify at the hearing. On the credenza behind Daddy's desk was a small piece of equipment about the size of a TV remote. Jimmy picked it up and showed it to Mama.

"What is this?" he asked.

Mama was sitting in a chair tapping her foot rapidly against the carpet. She'd spent more time getting dressed today than when they went to church on Easter.

"It's a tape recorder," she answered briskly. "Daddy talks into it, then gives it to Delores so she can type letters for him."

"Can I talk into it?"

"Uh, sure. I'll make sure the tape is blank."

Mama checked the tape and showed him how to push down a red button on the side of the unit.

"Now talk," she said.

"Where?"

"Into the end of the recorder. It has a tiny microphone in it."

Jimmy held it up to his lips and smiled at Mama.

"I have the prettiest, nicest mama in the whole world. I love her very much."

"Stop, Jimmy," Mama said. "If you make me cry, it will ruin my makeup."

"I know you feel sad today, so I want to make you happy."

"I'll be happy once this day is over and we've won the case."

She took the recorder from him.

"Do you want to hear what you said?"

"Yes, ma'am."

"Press the *rewind* button."

Mama positioned Jimmy's finger on the correct button. He pushed down, and the tape quickly wound back to the beginning.

"Now press the *play* button."

Mama moved Jimmy's finger up.

"Push here to play and here to stop."

Jimmy pushed down. There was silence for a couple of seconds, then a voice spoke.

"I have the prettiest, nicest mama in the whole world. I love her very much."

Jimmy pushed the stop button.

"Who is that?" he asked.

"That's you."

"It doesn't sound like me."

"It sounds different because you hear yourself inside your head. To everyone else, your voice is like the sound on the tape. Push the *play* button again."

Jimmy pushed the button.

"Stop, Jimmy. If you make me cry, it will ruin my makeup."

"That's you!" Jimmy exclaimed.

"Yes. And you're a very sweet boy to say such a nice thing about me."

Jimmy returned the recorder to its place on the credenza. Max's mother, Mrs. Cochran, came into the room.

"Are you ready?" she asked Mama.

"I hope so."

Mrs. Cochran smiled at Jimmy. "How about you? What are you going to say today when Mr. Long asks you questions?"

Jimmy raised his right hand high in the air.

"The truth, the whole truth, and nothing but the truth. We've been practicing every day this week. Mr. Long asks me questions, and then Daddy pretends he is the other lawyer and tries to trick me. Mr. Long says I'm doing great and don't have to worry about saying the wrong thing."

Mama's foot started tapping up and down again. "I wish I could be so confident."

"Are Lee's parents going to be here?" Mrs. Cochran asked.

"No, his father's heart isn't in the best shape."

Daddy stuck his head into the office. He'd put on his fanciest suit and neatly combed his hair.

"We need to leave in five minutes."

"Are the other witnesses ready?" Mama asked.

Daddy nodded. "Bruce and I have mock-tried this hearing over the past three months more than a million-dollar personal-injury case."

"There's more than a million dollars at stake," Mama responded.

The group set out for the courthouse. It was a cloudless, sunny morning that promised a scorching afternoon. Daddy, Mr. Long, and Dr. Meyer, the psychologist from Atlanta, led the way. Mama, Mrs. Cochran, Dr. Paris, and Jimmy followed.

"Did you bring any vanilla wafers with peanut butter on them?" Jimmy asked Dr. Paris as they waited for the crosswalk light to turn green.

Dr. Paris patted her purse with a red-tipped finger. "There might be something in here to eat when we take a break."

They crossed the street and turned right toward the courthouse. Mama positioned Jimmy between herself and Max's mom.

"Sue, if she tries to come up and talk to Jimmy, put him behind us until Lee can intervene," Mama said to Mrs. Cochran. "She doesn't have any legal right to communicate with him. If she tries to touch him, I'm not sure what I'll do."

"You'll keep cool," Mrs. Cochran responded. "This is a one-day challenge. Try to imagine how relieved you'll be by this time tomorrow. Letting the pressure of the moment overwhelm you is the greatest danger you face. Lee and Bruce have assured us the law is on your side."

"I know. Lee has tried hard to reassure me. He even brought home some appellate court decisions for me to read, but no matter how a judge in Atlanta interprets the law, it doesn't erase the fact that she's trying to take away my baby."

They reached the courthouse steps. Mr. Long held the door open for everyone to enter.

"We're in courtroom two," Daddy said. "It's down this hall on the right."

The interior of the courthouse was as plain as the outside. The hallway, with its tile floors and its concrete-block walls painted a cream color, reminded Jimmy of the area near the science labs at the middle school. Small brown signs were glued to the wall beside each door. They passed the office for the clerk of probate court and approached the magistrate court area. Chairs lined the wall on both sides of the entrance. A dozen or so people in work clothes were sitting in the chairs or milling around the door. Everyone looked up as the well-dressed people came by. A man came out of a door and touched Daddy on the arm. Daddy shook his head and kept walking. Jimmy saw that the man had a snake tattoo coiling up his arm. When Jimmy passed by him, they locked eyes. The man didn't smile.

"Mama, the man with the tattoo is here."

"Who?"

"From the other time I came to court."

Mama glanced around. The man stared down the hall after them.

"That's Jake Garner," Mama said. "He was Daddy's client in the case."

"Yes, I know. Why is he here?"

"I have no idea. All I care about are the people involved in our case."

They reached the double doors for courtroom two and went inside.

COURTROOM TWO WAS THE SAME PLACE WHERE JIMMY offered testimony in the Jake Garner trial. Fifteen long wooden benches, split down the middle by a broad aisle, provided seating. The bar, stained the same color as the benches, stretched across the courtroom and separated the witnesses and any spectators from the parties and their lawyers. No one else was present. Daddy looked at his watch.

"Everyone sit on this bench," he said, motioning to the front bench on the left side of the room. "We can all be here for the preliminary discussions, but once we start the hearing, all the witnesses except for Jimmy and me will be sequestered."

Jimmy sat next to Mama and scooted close to her like he did at church.

"I won't be able to be with you," she said. "You'll sit next to Daddy at the table with Mr. Long."

"Why can't you stay?"

"Because I've never adopted you."

"Why not?"

"I wanted to, but we would have had to notify your birth mama and take her to court to terminate her parental rights. Now that she's dragged us here, we're going to ask the judge to do it."

When Mama was nervous or upset, she sometimes used words Jimmy didn't understand. He wasn't sure what she meant by "terminate her parental rights," but it sounded like something a doctor might say. A door opened behind the place where the judge sat, and a deputy sheriff entered the courtroom.

"Is everyone here, Mr. Mitchell?" he asked. "Judge Reisinger is in chambers with Judge Robinson and wants to get an early start."

"The petitioner hasn't shown up," Daddy answered. "The hearing isn't set to begin for another five minutes."

"I'll tell the judge."

"Why aren't the other people here?" Jimmy whispered.

"I don't know," Mama answered.

"Maybe my birth mama is sick and couldn't come."

"Don't call her that. Her name is Mrs. Horton."

"Yes, ma'am."

Jimmy decided it best not to talk any more to Mama. He looked around the courtroom. Daddy and Mr. Long were arranging papers on a table. A woman with a little black box in front of her sat in a chair near the witness stand. The back door opened, and everyone turned around.

It was Jake Garner. He came forward and stood by Jimmy and Mama. Daddy left the table.

"What are you doing here?" Daddy asked.

"I have to be in court for a preliminary hearing on a misdemeanor assault charge in five minutes," Garner said. "I got in a fight at a bar on the west side. I didn't start the fight, but I finished it. I'd like to be able to tell the judge that you'll represent me."

"I can't talk about it now."

"I've called your office every day this week, and you didn't return my calls."

"That ought to tell you something," Daddy said. "Look. I don't have time to take your case. Check with someone else. You've got money to hire a lawyer. Dean Stanley would be a good choice."

"So that's how it is," Jake said angrily. "You get what you want out of me and then kick me into the street."

"Not now," Daddy said firmly. "I don't have time to help you."

The deputy returned.

"Any word from the other side?" he asked.

Daddy turned away from Jake.

"No," he said.

The deputy closed the door.

Daddy faced Jake. "I'm not doing any criminal defense work unless appointed by the judge. Call Stanley. His number is in the phone book."

Garner stared hard at Daddy for a second, then turned around and left the courtroom. Daddy returned to the table.

"Why was he mad at Daddy?" Jimmy asked.

"He's gotten into trouble again, and Daddy doesn't want to help him."

"Why not?"

"Not now," Mama whispered.

A young, athletic-looking man with dark, curly hair entered the courtroom. Everyone in the courtroom stood up.

"I'm Judge Reisinger," the man said. "Please be seated. Will the lawyers approach the bench?"

Daddy and Mr. Long went forward and shook the judge's hand. Jimmy couldn't hear what they were saying, but the judge pointed at the clock at the back of the courtroom. Jimmy turned around to look, and when he did the back doors opened and a well-dressed woman entered. Walking beside her with his hand on her back was a man. Behind the man and woman were two men dressed in suits. One of the men wearing a suit opened the waist-high gate in the bar.

"Your Honor," he announced. "I'm Bob Jasper, counsel for Mrs. Lonnie Horton, the petitioner in this case. Sorry we're late. There was a wreck on I-20, and we sat in traffic for thirty minutes while it was cleaned up."

Jimmy turned sideways as his birth mother reached the end of the bench where he sat. She looked like the woman in the photographs, only older. Her hair was wavy, and she was taller than he thought. She was slender and wore red lipstick.

Their eyes met, and Jimmy saw recognition flash across her face. She moved toward Jimmy along the open space in front of the bench behind him. Her lips turned up in a nice smile, and she raised her hand in a simple wave.

The judge spoke. "Ladies and gentlemen, *Horton v. Mitchell* is the only case on the court's calendar. I've reviewed the petition filed by Mrs. Horton, the child's biological mother, requesting visitation and joint custody, and the counterclaim filed by Mr. Mitchell, the child's natural father, seeking denial of visitation and custody as well as termination of Mrs. Horton's parental rights. Mr. Mitchell, it is my understanding that Mr. Bruce Long will be representing your interests today."

"That's correct, Your Honor," Daddy said.

"How many witnesses does each side intend to call?"

"We have three witnesses," Mr. Jasper replied.

"We have four, possibly five, witnesses," Mr. Long said.

"All witnesses, please rise," the judge said. "And raise your right hand for the administration of the oath."

Everyone in the courtroom except Mr. Long and Mr. Jasper stood up. Jimmy raised his hand high in the air. He saw his birth mother turn and watch him. He tried to look straight ahead as Mr. Long had instructed him. As the judge spoke the words of the oath, Jimmy silently mouthed them along with him.

"I do!" he said in a loud voice at the end.

"Your Honor, we invoke the rule of sequestration," Mr. Long said.

"We have no objection to the witnesses remaining in the courtroom," Mr. Jasper responded. "It might save time on cross-examination if all testimony is brought out in open court. Otherwise, it will require more extensive hypothetical questions."

"If one party invokes the rule, the court will grant it," the judge said. "All witnesses except Mr. Mitchell, Mrs. Horton, and the child, please follow the bailiff."

Mama leaned over to Jimmy. "I'll see you in a few minutes. Remember what Daddy and Mr. Long told you."

"Yes, ma'am."

The witnesses followed the deputy through a door on the opposite side of the courtroom from the way the judge entered. Mama looked back and held her hands together in prayer before she disappeared.

"Come sit with me," Daddy said to Jimmy.

As he passed through the gate in the bar, Mrs. Horton reached out and touched his arm.

"Hi, Jimmy," she said in a friendly voice.

Up close, his birth mama looked like the kind of person Mama would invite over to the house to talk and drink coffee.

"Mr. Jasper," the judge said. "Your client is the moving party on the petition. Proceed with your first witness."

"Judge, before we begin, Mrs. Horton would like to spend a few minutes privately with her son. She's not had an opportunity to tell him why she wants to reestablish contact, and it's important that he have a chance to hear it from her lips without the formal trappings of the hearing as a distraction."

"We oppose the request," Mr. Long said, rising to his feet. "The petitioner has had eleven years to communicate but chose not to do so. I assume she'll testify today and provide an excuse or explanation for the lack of contact as well as the reasons why she filed the petition. Jimmy is in the courtroom and can hear it along with the rest of us."

"Mr. Long, is it your intention to call the child as a witness?" the judge asked.

"Yes, Your Honor. He's fourteen and wants to express his preferences as to visitation with a noncustodial parent."

Mr. Jasper spoke. "Judge, there is no dispute that Jimmy is laboring under a mental disability, and we submit his impairment will affect his ability to comprehend the ramifications of these proceedings. His father has had ample opportunity to influence his son's responses to questions, and we're concerned the boy's preference on any issues will thereby be tainted. My client only requests a brief chance to talk to Jimmy and explain in simple terms why we're here today. No one would be present except mother and child."

Daddy shifted in his chair but didn't speak.

"Your Honor, this sounds like an attempt to—," Mr. Long began.

"Request denied," the judge interrupted. "I'll be the one making the decisions today, and any private conversations with the child will be conducted by me in chambers. Proceed for the petitioner."

Mr. Jasper leaned forward on his feet for a second. "Very well. We call Mr. Lonnie Horton."

The bailiff opened the door to the witness room, and the man who had arrived beside Jimmy's birth mother emerged. He was balding with a fringe of dark hair and a thin mustache. He sat in the witness chair.

"Please state your name," Mr. Jasper said.

"Lonnie Vinson Horton," the witness replied in a soft-spoken voice.

"What is your relationship to Vera Horton?"

"I'm her husband. We married shortly after her divorce from Mr. Mitchell."

"Tell the court about your personal and professional background."

The witness mentioned the names of a lot of companies and places unfamiliar to Jimmy.

"Currently, I'm president of Horton Risk Management in Atlanta. We provide workers' compensation and human-resources consulting services for several Fortune 500 companies as well as many smaller corporations across the Southeast."

"How is your wife employed?"

"She is on the board of directors for the company and owns twenty-five percent of the stock. She doesn't work outside the home but spends her time caring for our two daughters."

"Does she have a source of income to pay child support for Jimmy?"

"Yes. She receives an annual director's fee of fifty thousand dollars and stock dividends that range between seventy-five and a hundred thousand dollars a year."

"If allowed to establish a relationship with Jimmy, what plans have you and your wife made to provide for his needs?"

"Knowing his limitations, we're prepared to fund a trust designed to take care of him for the rest of his life."

Mr. Jasper walked forward and handed Horton some papers. "What are these documents?"

"An irrevocable trust naming my wife and her parents as co-trustees. The purpose of the trust is to provide money for Jimmy's educational, medical, and day-to-day needs."

"Your Honor," Mr. Jasper said. "I've marked the trust documents as Exhibit A."

"Are you tendering them into evidence?" the judge asked.

"Not yet."

"How much will be deposited with the trustees?" Mr. Jasper asked the witness.

"Initially, five hundred thousand dollars, with an additional million dollars payable in ten equal installments over the next ten years."

Mr. Jasper handed Mr. Horton some more papers.

"What are these records?"

"This is a letter from my bank confirming that the half million dollars has been placed in a designated account. The funds will be transferred to the irrevocable trust pending the outcome of this hearing."

"What about current child-support assistance?"

"That will come from my wife's resources."

"We'll ask her about that in a few minutes," Mr. Jasper said.

The lawyer returned to his table. "Mr. Horton, do you support your wife's desire to reestablish contact and develop a relationship with Jimmy?"

"Objection. Leading," Mr. Long said.

The judge looked at Mr. Long and narrowed his eyes. "This is a bench trial, Mr. Long. I think I can properly evaluate the evidence regardless of the form of the question. Please keep that in mind as we proceed. Overruled."

Mr. Long sat down. Daddy leaned over and said something to him that Jimmy couldn't hear.

"Please answer the question," Mr. Jasper said.

"Yes. I wholeheartedly believe this is the right step for Jimmy and our family. I believe my financial commitment proves the sincerity of our decision to file the petition. My hope is that Jimmy can have a healthy relationship with both his parents and the financial resources to take care of him in the best ways available in the future."

Mr. Jasper turned toward Mr. Long. "Your witness."

— Twenty-two —

Mr. Long stood with a yellow legal pad in his hand. One afternoon at the office, Jimmy had asked Daddy about the yellow paper.

"My teachers at school only let us use white paper," he said. "If I did my homework on yellow paper, she'd make me do it over."

"Lawyers can use any color they want," Daddy replied. "The judges don't care. There's a female lawyer in Macon who uses a pink legal pad. She waves it around the courtroom every time she wants to distract the jury from listening to evidence that hurts her client."

Daddy had given Jimmy a yellow legal pad of his own and written, "Property of James Lee Mitchell III," across the top. Jimmy showed it to Delores and Kate, and they promised never to use it by mistake. Jimmy left his pad at the office. So far, he hadn't written anything on it except to copy his name in block letters underneath Daddy's handwriting.

"Mr. Horton, is today the first time in your life that you've seen Jimmy Mitchell?" Mr. Long asked.

"Yes, except for pictures."

"To your knowledge, has your wife had any personal contact with Jimmy since she abandoned him eleven years ago?"

"She didn't abandon him. She phoned Mr. Mitchell several times after their divorce was finalized, but he never returned her calls."

"Approximately how far is it from your house in Dunwoody to Piney Grove?"

"About eighty or ninety miles."

"How many trips did you make during the past eleven years to see Jimmy?"

"None. Mr. Mitchell never returned my wife's calls."

"Did Mr. Mitchell prevent you from getting into your car and driving to Piney Grove to see Jimmy?"

"I saw no need to waste a trip."

"Mr. Horton, you testified that Exhibit A is an irrevocable trust, didn't you?"

"Yes."

Mr. Long set the papers on a narrow ledge in front of the witness. "Where is the signature line?"

Mr. Horton didn't touch the exhibit. "On the last page."

Mr. Long picked up the sheets of paper and flipped to the final page. "Here it is. Everything is in order except your signature, isn't it?"

"As I mentioned, I will fund the trust once we are able to resume contact with Jimmy."

"Resume? Have you ever met Jimmy or spent one minute with him in your life?"

"Objection. Argumentative," Mr. Jasper said.

The judge turned to Jasper. "My comments to Mr. Long also apply to you. I don't want to hear an objection unless it goes to substantive matters appropriate for appellate court review. Opposing counsel has the witness on cross-examination, and I will allow the question."

"Answer," Mr. Long said.

"I've never had the opportunity to meet Jimmy, but I'd like to do so."

"And if the judge's order in this case doesn't suit you and your wife, you won't waste your time setting up a trust to help Jimmy, will you?"

"It wouldn't be right for me to pay money if we can't have a relationship."

"Won't Jimmy have educational, medical, and day-to-day needs for the rest of his life regardless of the judge's decision?"

"Yes; however, I don't apologize for making the trust contingent on the opportunity to develop a relationship with Jimmy. If the judge grants our petition, I've instructed Mr. Jasper to include a requirement that we establish the trust I've described this morning. This is a tremendous chance to secure Jimmy's future as well as allow him to get to know his mother better."

Mr. Long was standing beside Daddy, who tapped him on the arm and then whispered into his ear.

"Do you have any evidence that Mr. Mitchell is not financially capable of providing for Jimmy's educational, medical, and day-to-day needs?"

"I don't know anything about Mr. Mitchell's financial status."

"Would you be willing to name Mr. Mitchell as co-trustee of the trust?"

"No. I think that would be a prescription for conflict."

"You know a lot about conflict don't you, Mr. Horton?"

The witness didn't answer.

Judge Reisinger spoke. "Mr. Long, I've told Mr. Jasper to refrain from objecting, and I'm going to ask you to be specific, not accusatory, in your questioning. No theatrics. It's not going to impress me."

Mr. Long stepped closer to Horton. "How many times have you been divorced?"

"Four."

"Who was your first wife?"

"Cindy."

"Second?"

"Pam."

"Third?"

"Sara."

"Fourth?"

"Vera."

"Isn't it true that you divorced Vera Horton three years ago?"

"Yes, but we reconciled last year and remarried. Now our relationship is stronger than ever."

"Would you characterize your marital history as stable?"

"Those problems are behind me. We're ready to open our hearts and home to Jimmy."

Mr. Long looked at Daddy, who shook his head.

"Nothing further," Mr. Long said.

Mr. Jasper stood. "Petitioner calls Dr. Bertrand Poitier. We also ask that Mr. Horton be allowed to remain in the courtroom."

"No objection, so long as he's not going to be recalled to the stand," Mr. Long said.

Horton sat on the bench behind his lawyer. Jimmy saw him take out his handkerchief and wipe his forehead. His birth mama turned in her seat, and Jimmy could see her mouth the words "thank you" followed by "I love you." After all the negative things he'd heard about Vera Horton, the thought that she loved someone was a surprise to him. He leaned over to Daddy.

"She told him, 'I love you.' Isn't that good?"

Daddy grunted. "She said that to me but didn't mean it."

Jimmy sat back in his seat and tried to get a handle on the fact that a woman besides Mama once told Daddy that she loved him.

Dr. Poitier entered the courtroom. He was a short man, younger than Daddy, with neatly combed brown hair and dark eyes. In his hand he carried a thick book.

"Please state your name and occupation," Mr. Jasper said.

"Bertrand Poitier, clinical psychologist, Palo Alto, California."

"Would you summarize your professional and educational background for the court?"

Dr. Poitier talked about where he grew up, the schools he attended, and the places he'd worked. He spoke in a monotone voice, and Jimmy's mind began to wander. He watched Judge Reisinger take notes. Once, the judge picked up his legal pad, and Jimmy could see that is was yellow, just like his own. In response to a question by Mr. Jasper, Dr. Poitier held up the book he'd brought into the courtroom.

"This is *Adolescent Bonding—Studies in Resumption of Severed Parental Relationships.* I spent eight years researching and writing this book, which is currently being used as a text by practicing psychologists and in graduate-level education courses at Columbia, Stanford, University of Michigan, and several other schools across the country. I found that genetic links, especially between birth mothers and their children, are surprisingly durable."

"The title suggests you evaluated real-life situations," Mr. Jasper said.

"That's correct. Over half of the studies involved a mother who placed a baby for adoption and then didn't have any contact with the child for ten years or more. For a variety of reasons, interaction was reestablished during the child's adolescence. I monitored the restored relationship over a period of years and documented what took place."

"Is the book limited to maternal restoration?"

"No, I also studied paternal separation; however, the most common scenario involves the mother. This has long been the case with adults adopted as infants who later engage in a search for their birth parents. In over ninety percent of those cases, the adopted individual's primary goal is to find the mother. The bond formed in utero endures at a subconscious level for a lifetime."

"What conclusions did you reach about the vitality and importance of adolescent bonding between a mother and child?"

The witness held up the book. "The conclusions, with supporting data, are contained in chapters fourteen through sixteen of the treatise, but as it relates to the facts of this case, I can state there is a high likelihood of positive adolescent bonding between Mrs. Horton and Jimmy."

"What is the basis for your specific opinion?"

"I've interviewed Mrs. Horton and read information provided to me about Jimmy's psychological and mental status."

"What can you tell us about Mrs. Horton?"

"She is the mother of two daughters and is the primary caregiver for her daughters with assistance from her husband during the evenings and on weekends. Mr. Horton is often away on business trips, at which time Mrs. Horton assumes sole responsibility for the children. The Fulton County Department of Family and Child Services performed a home evaluation of the Horton household two months ago and found no negative factors present. I privately interviewed the two girls, ages ten and seven, and found no indication—"

"Objection," Mr. Long said. "Hearsay as to statements made by these girls."

The judge stopped taking notes and put down his pen.

"Mr. Long," he said with a hint of frustration in his voice. "Are you aware that this type of out-court information is universally admissible as the foundation for an expert opinion?"

"Yes, sir."

"Objection overruled. If you know the law, I expect you to help the Court, not mislead it."

Mr. Long sat down.

The judge spoke. "Proceed, Doctor."

The witness repositioned himself in his chair.

"The information I obtained from the daughters revealed nothing that would hinder introduction of Jimmy into their family matrix. Both Mr. and Mrs. Horton are enthusiastic about the opportunity and have spent a considerable amount of time learning about Jimmy's needs and the best way to respond to them. Mrs. Horton is a loving mother to her daughters, and there is no indication that she would have a problem including Jimmy in the sphere of her affection."

"What can you tell us about Jimmy?"

"I reviewed all the reports supplied to me from the treating and evaluating psychologists and doctors, beginning with his pediatrician."

"Before you continue," Mr. Jasper said, "let me show you Exhibits B through F and ask you to identify this information."

The psychologist leafed through the thick stack of papers. "These are Jimmy's medical and psychological records supplied to you by Mr. Mitchell's attorney in response to discovery requests."

"In addition to reviewing these records, did you have opportunity to personally evaluate Jimmy?"

"No, it is my understanding that Mr. Mitchell refused your request that I have the opportunity to do so."

"Would a personal evaluation be necessary to render an opinion about Jimmy's ability to reestablish a relationship with his mother?"

"Helpful, but given the extent of available data, not necessary."

"What can you tell the Court about Jimmy?"

"The results of multiple IQ tests and academic evaluations are in the file and establish that he functions in the lower end of the dull-normal range. However, more important than his IQ deficits are the personality traits that will affect whether he would benefit from renewed contact with his mother."

"What can you tell us about those traits?"

"Jimmy is a resilient, determined young man with a strong work ethic. He has adapted remarkably well to his status at school and within the local community. These strengths are coupled with a trusting, loyal, and affectionate nature. He has a particularly close relationship with his stepmother and paternal grandfather. He views his father as aloof, distant, and difficult to please."

Jimmy saw Daddy grip the arms of his chair so hard that his knuckles turned white.

"Would reestablishment of contact with his birth mother threaten the strong bond that exists with his stepmother?"

"I don't think so, unless either woman sought to poison his attitude toward the other. Jimmy is slow to criticize or judge others, but he could be influenced to do so by significant authority figures in his life."

"Would it be fair to say a mutually supportive relationship would work best?"

"Absolutely. Jimmy is willing to trust others if they prove trustworthy to him. I think after any initial obstacles are overcome, he would enjoy interaction with the Horton family, and serving as an older brother to the Horton girls would be a maturing process for him."

"Are there any negative factors that should be mentioned to the Court?"

Dr. Poitier held up his book. "If visitation and partial custody are granted to Mrs. Horton, I believe the results could be included in the success section of my next revision of this book."

Mr. Jasper smiled and turned toward Mr. Long. "You may ask."

"Dr. Poitier, how much are you being paid by Mrs. Horton for your evaluation and testimony?"

"My standard expert-witness fee of five hundred dollars per hour out of court and nine hundred in court."

"Plus expenses?"

"Yes."

Long looked at his watch. "What would that total be as of this moment?"

Dr. Poitier glanced up at the clock at the back of the courtroom. "That will be affected by the length of your cross-examination, but the approximate figure would be around eighteen thousand dollars."

"Plus expenses?"

"Yes."

"In how many cases have you provided expert-witness services, either as an evaluator or via in-court testimony, over the past two years since your book was published?"

"About ten or eleven."

"I realize you live in California, but have you worked with Mr. Jasper before?"

"Yes, on three occasions."

"Did you perform evaluations in those cases?"

"Yes."

"Did you reach conclusions and recommendations?"

"Yes."

"Did you testify in all three cases?"

"Yes."

"Did you reach conclusions and recommendations consistent with the position advocated by Mr. Jasper and his clients?"

"I don't know what you mean."

"Did you testify for or against Mr. Jasper's clients?"

"I gave my opinion."

Mr. Long held a yellow pad in his hand, but he wasn't reading from it.

"Was your opinion favorable to Mr. Jasper's clients?"

"Only to the extent I believed appropriate."

"And now Mr. Jasper has hired you for a fourth case, is that correct?"

"Yes."

"Any other cases on your horizon as an expert witness involving Mr. Jasper and his clients?"

"I'm performing another evaluation next month."

Jimmy turned slightly sideways so he could see his birth mama. She was sitting with her husband behind the table for the other lawyers. She seemed to be paying attention to what the witness said. She turned her head toward Jimmy, saw him, and waved. He spun to face forward again.

"Do you always bring your book to court?" Mr. Long asked the witness.

"No, but my research for this project especially qualified me to testify in this case."

"Let's talk about your research, not for the book, but related to the Horton family. Are you aware that Mr. and Mrs. Horton were divorced three years ago and only remarried last year?"

"Yes."

"Did you administer any psychological tests to Mrs. Horton?"

"No, but I conducted an extensive clinical interview."

"Which in layman's terms means you talked with her for a few hours, isn't that correct?"

"*Evaluated her* would be a more accurate term."

"And what independent verification for her answers did you obtain?"

"The interview with her two daughters and the Fulton County DFACS report."

"Which involved talking to a couple of minors and reading a report by an overworked county agency, correct?"

"I considered the report professional, and the girls corroborated their mother's statements."

"In reviewing Jimmy's records, did you note the presence of any profound fears?"

"Yes, he has a form of aquaphobia, or fear of water. He's not afraid of all water, just the possibility of being submerged in it."

"Did you try to inquire into the cause of that fear?"

"As I stated earlier, Mr. Mitchell would not allow me access to the child."

"Did you have access to Mrs. Horton?"

"Yes."

"Did you ask her about it?"

"No."

Mr. Long turned away from the witness. "No further questions."

MR. JASPER STOOD. "AT THIS TIME, WE CALL VERA HORTON."

Jimmy glanced sideways at Daddy. His face was rigid and his jaw tight, like the way he looked when he found out about Walt and what really happened in the woods. Jimmy watched his birth mama walk slowly to the witness stand. When she sat down, she smoothed her dress and nodded toward Judge Reisinger.

"Please state your name," Mr. Jasper said.

"Vera Horton," she replied in a voice that sounded like one of Jimmy's teachers who'd grown up in south Georgia. She looked at Jimmy as she answered.

"What is your relationship to James Lee Mitchell III?"

"He is my son. I was married to his father for eight years. Jimmy was our first and only child."

"How old was Jimmy when you and Mr. Mitchell divorced?"

"Two years and one month."

"What was the reason for the divorce?"

"The papers listed irreconcilable differences, but it was the result of constant disagreements and a breakdown in communication with no interest on either side to correct the problem."

"Why did you agree to leave Jimmy in the sole custody of his father?"

"I was tired of the daily battles for control that existed throughout my relationship with Lee Mitchell and didn't have the emotional strength to keep on fighting. I knew issues related to Jimmy would have become the focus of future conflicts. I'd met Lonnie Horton while separated from Jimmy's father and decided the best course for everyone would be for me to withdraw from the scene. My relationship with Jimmy was a casualty of that decision, a choice I've come to regret."

"Prior to filing this petition, what efforts did you make to reestablish contact with Jimmy?"

"I wanted to set up an amicable arrangement for me to see Jimmy, so I phoned Lee at the office several times. He never took my calls or returned my messages. When I learned that he'd remarried, I left him alone, not wanting to disrupt his chances to form a good relationship with his new wife. I know how Lee reacts. If he's threatened in one area, he'll lash out in others."

Jimmy felt Daddy tense.

"What's wrong?" Jimmy whispered.

"Quiet!" Daddy responded. "We'll talk later."

The judge looked at Daddy. "Mr. Mitchell?"

Daddy stood. "Excuse me, Your Honor. Jimmy had a question about Mrs. Horton's comment, and I told him he would have to wait until later to discuss it."

"Proceed," the judge said.

Mr. Jasper walked closer to the front of the courtroom. In the process, he temporarily blocked Jimmy's view of the witness stand. Jimmy craned his head to the side in an effort to see. Listening to his birth mama talk and watching the way she moved her head and hands gave him a lot of new information to go along with the still images in the photos. Mr. Jasper looked down at a sheet of paper in his hand and stepped toward the jury box. Jimmy could see again.

"Are you prepared to pay child support?"

"Yes."

Mr. Jasper handed her some papers.

"Please identify what has been marked as Exhibits G through I."

"These are tax returns and financial statements. I'll pay child support at the level determined by the judge."

"And serve as co-trustee of the trust mentioned by your husband?"

"Yes. We've prospered financially, and I would like Jimmy to share in that blessing."

"Mrs. Horton, why did you decide to file a petition seeking visitation and custody rights with Jimmy?"

"It's a step I should have taken long ago. My fear of conflict with his father was not a legitimate reason to abandon my relationship with my son." She paused, and it seemed to Jimmy that she looked directly at Daddy. "About a year and a half ago, I experienced a religious conversion that transformed my whole outlook on life. As a result of the changes in me, I reconciled with my current husband, and our family has been restored. Jimmy is the missing piece. I would like to bring him home to my heart."

Mr. Jasper stood still for several seconds. The room was quiet.

"Your Honor, that's all from Mrs. Horton."

"Mr. Long," the judge said. "You may conduct your cross-examination."

Mr. Long stood and walked around to the front of the table.

"Mrs. Horton, isn't it true that you haven't seen Jimmy in over eleven years?"

"Yes. It's too long."

"Who's been taking care of Jimmy while you were trying to figure out if you ever wanted to see him again?"

"I assume his father."

"Do you have any evidence that someone else has been taking care of Jimmy?"

"I believe his grandparents do a lot for him."

"And his stepmother?"

"Yes, that's what I read in the psychological reports."

"All of the people who have invested their time, money, and love into Jimmy live here in Piney Grove, don't they?"

"Yes, and it's time I shared that obligation and opportunity."

"Do you believe you can waltz into this courtroom, wave around a big check, and expect—"

"Don't go there, Mr. Long," the judge interrupted. "Keep to the statutory criteria applicable to the issues before me."

Mr. Long cleared his throat. "Yes, sir."

"Mrs. Horton, does Jimmy reside in the same house where you lived when you and Mr. Mitchell were married?"

"I believe so."

"When is Jimmy's birthday?"

"June 5."

"And how many gifts have you sent Jimmy on his birthday and at Christmas since you left town eleven years ago?"

"I sent him a birthday present last week, but it was returned unopened. I'd learned that he liked the University of Georgia football team, and Lonnie was able to get a poster signed by all the players and coaches. I thought Jimmy would enjoy putting it up in his room."

Jimmy's eyes grew big. Though not as spectacular as a BB gun, the poster would have been an awesome present. Daddy would have liked it too.

"You would like that poster," Jimmy whispered to Daddy.

Daddy didn't answer.

"Before this year, how many presents have you sent Jimmy since you left Piney Grove?"

Jimmy sat up in his chair to listen closely.

"None."

"Have you paid for any medical care?"

"No."

"Bought Jimmy any clothes?"

"No."

Mr. Jasper stood to his feet. "Your Honor, we can stipulate that there has not been any child support provided by Mrs. Horton since her divorce from Mr. Mitchell. This list could go on and on without proving anything else."

"So noted," the judge said. "Move on."

"Speaking of divorce," Mr. Long said. "What was the gap in time between your divorce from Mr. Mitchell and your first marriage to Mr. Horton?"

"A couple of months."

"Does three weeks sound more accurate?"

"Maybe. It was a long time ago."

Mr. Long walked back to the table and stood beside Daddy. "Were you in the courtroom when Dr. Poitier testified about Jimmy's fear of water?"

"Yes."

"Do you remember an occasion when you were bathing Jimmy and he almost drowned?"

"Of course. It was one of the worst days of my life." She looked directly at Jimmy. "And I'm very, very sorry it happened."

Jimmy's eyes widened.

"Didn't he have to be resuscitated by a neighbor and rushed to the hospital?" Mr. Long asked.

Mrs. Horton began to cry. She reached into her purse and pulled out a tissue.

"Do we need to take a recess?" the judge asked her.

"No."

"Please answer the question," Mr. Long said.

"A neighbor helped me, and an ambulance took Jimmy to the hospital."

"Do you still maintain that you left Jimmy unattended because you had to answer a phone call?"

"Yes. That's exactly what happened."

"Have you considered the possibility that some of Jimmy's mental challenges are the result of oxygen deprivation during the time he was left unattended and submerged?"

"I've been told the accident didn't do any permanent brain damage or add to his developmental problems."

"Are you qualified to make that determination?"

"Not necessarily, but I trust the people I talked to about it."

"How soon after this happened did you abandon Jimmy and his father?"

"I didn't abandon them. His father and I separated, and I moved home to be with my parents."

"When did that happen? Within a month of the incidence of neglect?"

"It wasn't neglect. It was an accident."

"Whatever the reason, are you aware some of the psychologists who have evaluated Jimmy relate his fear of water to this trauma?"

"Yes."

"Did you discuss this near-drowning episode with anyone?"

"Quite a few people knew about it. It was embarrassing, but I didn't try to hide it. I wanted to make sure I hadn't done anything to hurt Jimmy, so I talked to all the doctors."

Mr. Long stepped closer to the witness. "Did you try to hide the fact that you intentionally left Jimmy alone?"

"That's not true!"

Jimmy saw a flash of anger in her eyes.

"Was there a police investigation of this incident?" Long asked.

"I wouldn't call it that. Lee sent a detective friend over to the house to harass me. It was the final straw that drove me to seek a divorce. There was no need to make me feel any worse than I already did."

"Do you know the results of the investigation?"

"They tried to claim that there wasn't a phone call because I didn't know who called me. I was so upset that it slipped my mind."

"Did you tell the detective who might have phoned you?"

"Objection," Mr. Jasper said. "This happened eleven years ago and is irrelevant to the issues before the Court."

"Not to me," the judge replied. "Overruled. The witness will answer the question."

"This was before we had caller ID on phones, so I gave the detective the names of several friends who might have called. Lee claimed none of them remembered phoning the house that day."

"Did you try to find out yourself?"

"Yes."

"Were you successful?"

"No. I decided the trauma created a mental block or something."

"Have you since resurrected the identity of the mystery caller?"

"No."

"Mrs. Horton, did you also try to hide the fact that you were ashamed of Jimmy due to his mental handicap?"

"No. I mean, yes." Mrs. Horton began to cry. She took a tissue from her purse and put it to her face. "Your Honor, I need to take a break."

"We'll take a five-minute break," the judge said. "Mrs. Horton may go to the restroom, but she shall not consult with her attorneys. Mr. Long still has her on cross-examination."

Jimmy's birth mama didn't look at him as she passed by on her way out of the courtroom. Her husband followed her. Jimmy leaned over close to Daddy.

"Why is she crying?"

"Mr. Long's questions are making her face something inside that she'd forgotten existed."

"Oh," Jimmy answered without understanding.

Mr. Long came over to them. Daddy spoke.

"That's it, Bruce. No more questions."

"But I still have two lines of attack. She's on the run. If we push—"

"No," Daddy repeated. "Enough."

"Okay," Mr. Long shrugged. "You're the boss. But if we back off, it's no guarantee that Mr. Jasper will do the same when his chance comes."

"I know. You're doing a good job, but I don't want to hurt her anymore. She's made mistakes—just like the rest of us."

— Twenty-three —

You're not rethinking your position?" Mr. Long asked in surprise.

"No, of course, not. It's not in Jimmy's best interests to allow Vera back into the picture, but I want to avoid any further bloodletting. Let's prove our case and get out of the courtroom."

"What do you want me to do?" Mr. Long asked.

"Put on the evidence we've prepared, but don't push her face into the dirt."

"Okay. Same order of witnesses?"

"Yes."

Jimmy's birth mama returned to the courtroom. As soon as everyone was settled, the judge looked down at her.

"Mrs. Horton. Are you ready to continue?"

"Yes, sir."

The judge nodded toward Mr. Long, who was standing beside Daddy at the counsel table.

"Mr. Long, proceed with your questioning."

"Mr. Mitchell and I consulted during the break, and I have no other questions for this witness."

"Very well. Mrs. Horton, you may step down. Any other witnesses for the petitioner?"

"None, except for rebuttal pending the testimony offered by the respondent."

The judge looked at Mr. Long. "You may call your first witness."

"We call Dr. Susan Paris."

For the second time, Jimmy watched the school psychologist take the witness stand. She smiled at him several times while she talked. She talked about his good relationship with Mama and how hard he worked in school. There was no mention of his ability to remember what he heard people say.

"Dr. Paris," Mr. Long said, "based on your repeated evaluations of Jimmy, do you have an opinion about his cognitive ability to express a bona fide preference as to custody and visitation?"

"Yes."

"What is that opinion?"

"If stated in simple terms, he will understand the issue and tell the truth."

"That's all from this witness," Mr. Long said.

Mr. Jasper stood behind the table.

"Dr. Paris, during your direct testimony, did you express a preference about the custody or visitation issue?"

"No, sir."

"How old is Jimmy?"

"Fourteen."

"Have you found Jimmy to be a compliant child?"

"Yes."

"With a high desire to please those in authority?"

"Yes."

"Would this desire to please authority figures be stronger than normal?"

"*Normal* is not a word I use in that context. There are common understandings of the term *normal* that do not fit within recognized diagnostic criteria. I don't have anything to add to my previous answer, other than to say Jimmy likes to please people: parents, teachers, adults, peers."

"Who has the greatest personal influence on Jimmy?"

"His mother—uh, I mean, stepmother. The bond between them is very strong."

"And his father?"

"Is important as well."

"Does Jimmy fear his father?"

Dr. Paris hesitated. "I'd say he holds him in awe from a distance. However, during the past year, he has been working at his father's office for a few hours a week. I think this is a good idea because it brings him into his father's world and gives them another avenue for interaction outside the home."

"If Jimmy's father told him to do something, would he do it?"

"If it's a reasonable request consistent with Jimmy's ethical framework, I believe that he would. Jimmy believes obeying his parents is a good thing."

"If his father wanted Jimmy to say something, would he do it?"

"Same answer, so long as he understood the request."

Mr. Jasper stepped closer to Dr. Paris and raised his eyebrows.

"Don't your last two answers contradict your testimony about the significance of authority figures in Jimmy's life?"

"No."

Mr. Jasper glanced up at the judge. "Your Honor, please take note—"

"I heard the testimony," Judge Reisinger replied. "But you'll have to save your argument until later."

Mr. Jasper came forward until he stood to the side of the witness stand.

"Dr. Paris, are you telling the Court that Jimmy Mitchell possesses an unfailing moral compass from which he never wavers?"

Dr. Paris turned away from Mr. Jasper and looked up at the judge.

"His moral compass is consistent, not perfect. For example, Jimmy believes it is right to tell the truth and wrong to lie. He believes it is wrong to physically hurt another person and right to be kind to everyone. He has incorporated these beliefs in a simple, concrete way. Like anyone, there are many ethical issues he has not yet confronted. In those areas, an authority figure such as his father could potentially lead him astray."

Mr. Jasper hesitated. "Has Jimmy told you what his father wants him to say in this hearing?"

"No. Once I was contacted about being a witness, I purposely avoided the subject with Jimmy. Recently, I haven't seen him because of summer vacation."

Mr. Jasper looked down at this notes.

"Dr. Paris, I know you don't like the word *normal,* but what is a normal IQ?"

"*Normal* has an appropriate use in this area. Normal would be an average score of 100 on the verbal, performance, and full-scale components. Most people have variations, but the scores usually cluster together."

"Does Jimmy have analytical abilities comparable to a fourteen-year-old with an IQ of 100?"

"No."

"Does that deficit affect his decision-making process?"

"On a test at school?"

"No, when faced with options in day-to-day life."

"Yes."

"How?"

"He would have trouble evaluating the implications of the choices presented and would almost always select the familiar over the new. He'll try something different if it takes place in an environment in which he's comfortable or if he has the support of his parents."

"Doesn't that illustrate the increased importance of Mr. and Mrs. Mitchell's influence as compared to a typical fourteen-year-old?"

"Perhaps."

"Do you work with other fourteen-year-olds on a regular basis?"

"Yes."

"Are you aware that the laws of this state allow a fourteen-year-old to express preferences as to visitation and custody issues?"

"Yes."

"Would Jimmy's overall ability to evaluate his options and make a decision be the same as for a child with an IQ of 100?"

"No."

"No further questions."

Mr. Long stood to his feet. "I have a brief redirect, Your Honor."

"Proceed."

"Did any of Mr. Jasper's questions change your opinion about Jimmy's ability to evaluate his options as to the visitation and custody issues pending before the court?"

"Objection. Asked and answered," Mr. Jasper said.

"Sustained."

"No other questions," Mr. Long said.

Mr. Long plopped down in his chair. Daddy said something to him that Jimmy didn't hear. Dr. Paris came down from the witness stand. She walked past Jimmy, smiled, and patted her purse. The vanilla wafers with peanut butter were still waiting for him. Daddy leaned over to him.

"No Watchers," he said.

Jimmy glanced around the courtroom.

"No, sir. I don't see any. Do you want me to let you know if one comes?"

Daddy shook his head. "I meant no questions about the Watchers for Dr. Paris. That would have kept her on the witness stand an extra thirty minutes and distracted the judge."

Max's mother testified. Jimmy liked listening to her talk about his friendship with Max. When she told the story about Max and Jimmy playing hide-and-seek in the cornfield, he laughed before she got to the funny part about him falling asleep. Mrs. Cochran mentioned some of the problems that came up when Jimmy was with children who didn't understand him. Mr. Jasper didn't ask her any questions.

"Let's take a ten-minute break," Judge Reisinger said when she finished testifying.

As soon as the judge left the courtroom, Dr. Paris leaned across the bar and tapped Jimmy on the shoulder.

"Are you ready for your snack?"

"Yes, ma'am."

"No food in the courtroom," Daddy said.

Jimmy followed Dr. Paris into the hallway. She took a plastic bag from her purse and handed it to him. Inside were three perfectly formed pairs of vanilla wafers with peanut butter between them. When Jimmy took a bite, the peanut butter oozed out the sides.

"Good," he said. "You make them the best."

He happily munched the treat.

"There is a water fountain around the corner," Dr. Paris said.

"Yes, ma'am. Peanut butter makes me thirsty."

As Jimmy turned the corner, he saw his birth mama returning from the restroom. He slowed down as she approached. She slowed too. They stopped and stared at each other. Jimmy had the uneaten vanilla wafer with peanut butter in his right hand. He held it out to her.

"Would you like one? Dr. Paris made them for me."

"That's nice of you to offer. I'd love to have one."

His birth mama took it from him. When she did, Jimmy could see that she had big rings on several of her fingers.

"Thanks," she said. "Your fingers look like mine."

Jimmy shook his head. "No, ma'am. I don't wear any rings."

"That's true," she replied with a laugh. "Dr. Paris says you always tell the truth."

"Yes, ma'am. Lying is a sin."

His birth mama took such a tiny bite of the snack that no peanut butter oozed out.

"Jimmy, are you happy?" she asked.

"When?"

"Right now."

Jimmy thought for a moment.

"I'm happy to talk to you and share my snack. I have five pictures of you in my desk drawer."

"Do you like to look at them?"

"Yes, ma'am."

"Would you like to visit me and meet your sisters?"

The question reminded him of one Mr. Long had asked over and over when practicing for the hearing. Jimmy knew what to say.

"I want to stay in Piney Grove with Mama, Daddy, Grandpa, and Buster."

"Who is Buster?"

"My dog."

"We have a dog. Her name is Peaches."

Jimmy smiled. "I like to eat peaches. Why would you name a dog Peaches?"

"Because she has peach-colored fur on her back."

Jimmy couldn't imagine such a strange looking dog. Before he could ask another question, he heard a voice calling his name.

"Jimmy!"

He turned around. It was Bruce Long.

"Come back into the courtroom."

"Can I get a drink of water?" he asked.

"Yes. I'll stand here and watch."

Jimmy's birth mama continued toward the courtroom. Jimmy drank a few quick sips of water and joined Mr. Long.

"What did she say?" Mr. Long asked.

"She told me about her dog named Peaches. Have you ever seen a dog with peach-colored fur on its back?"

"No. Is that all she said?"

"I shared my snack with her."

"Did she try to get you to say anything in court?"

"No, sir."

"Do you want to visit her in Atlanta or live part of the time in her house?"

"No, sir. I want to stay in Piney Grove with Mama, Daddy, Grandpa, and Buster."

"Good. Let's go."

They reentered the courtroom. Jimmy took out his handkerchief, wiped his mouth, and sat down beside Daddy.

"She has a dog named Peaches," he said in a soft voice.

"She talked to you?"

Mr. Long leaned over. "They passed in the hallway. Nothing substantive. He's still firm."

Before Daddy said anything else, Judge Reisinger entered the courtroom.

"Gentlemen, I reviewed psychological reports during the break. Are there other reports coming into evidence?"

"Dr. Meyer has a report," Mr. Long answered. "We intended to submit it during direct examination of the witness."

"Does the other side have a copy?" the judge asked.

"Yes, sir."

"Mr. Jasper, are you going to object to its admissibility?"

"No, Your Honor. We don't agree with his conclusions but will stipulate his qualifications as an expert witness."

"Let me have it after the court reporter marks it as an exhibit," the judge said. "Is he your next witness?"

"No, sir. I intended to call Ellen Mitchell."

"The stepmother?"

"Yes, sir."

"I'd like to hear from Dr. Meyer while the reports are fresh in my mind."

Mr. Long glanced at Daddy, who nodded. "We call Dr. Nathan Meyer."

Jimmy liked Dr. Meyer. He had white hair and kind eyes like Grandpa's. Mr. Long called Dr. Meyer to the witness stand and started with the same types of questions he'd asked the other expert witnesses.

Then Mr. Long asked, "How many times has Jimmy Mitchell come to your office?"

"I've had three sessions of two hours each with Jimmy, and a three-hour session with his father and stepmother."

"What was the primary purpose of these sessions?"

"Determining the effect of any reintroduction of Jimmy's birth mother into his life."

"What information did you have about Mrs. Horton?"

"The results of Dr. Poitier's interview and the Fulton County DFACS report."

"Did you have copies of Dr. Poitier's interviews with Mrs. Horton's daughters?"

"No."

"Was the information at your disposal about Mrs. Horton sufficient to form an opinion as to the suitability of Jimmy resuming contact with her via visitation and shared custody?"

"Not by itself, but when coupled with what I've learned about Jimmy and his current family situation, I can render an opinion."

"Is that opinion set forth in the report prepared for this hearing?"

"Yes."

Mr. Long looked up at Judge Reisinger, who was flipping through papers.

"I'm reading and listening at the same time," the judge assured him. "Go ahead. I'll follow along."

"Please tell us your opinion."

"At this point in Jimmy's life and stage of development, the risks outweigh any possible benefits. The rationale for my opinion is contained in my report, but it's clear that stability is a key component of Jimmy's emotional health. In fact, stability is much more important for him than for a typical fourteen-year-old. The instability inherent in sending him back and forth between two competing households is likely to upset the equilibrium that exists. Jimmy is a sensitive young man for whom conflict is highly traumatic. Due to the influence of his parents and grandparents, he has a surprisingly positive outlook on a difficult world. Undermining this perspective will adversely affect his emotional well-being."

"What about the nurturing benefits available from his birth mother?"

"That need has been ably filled by his stepmother. They have one of the best relationships of this type I've ever observed."

"I don't need to hear anything else," the judge said, glancing up. "Any cross-examination?"

Mr. Jasper stood up. "Yes, Your Honor, if I might have a moment to collect my notes."

Mr. Long retreated and sat down beside Daddy.

"What on earth did that mean?" Mr. Long asked Daddy. "Cutting me off like that?"

"Either very good or very bad," Daddy answered drily.

Mr. Jasper's questions for Dr. Meyer sounded a little bit like Mr. Long's questions for Dr. Poitier. However, Dr. Meyer had charged less than six thousand dollars for his evaluation and never worked with either Mr. Long or Daddy. He didn't have a book to show the judge.

"Doesn't your opinion assume the presence of conflict if Mrs. Horton is granted visitation and shared custody?" Mr. Jasper asked.

"Yes, because it is the only realistic conclusion that can be supported by the parties' history and my practical experience. I've treated hundreds of adolescent patients who manifested problems caused or exacerbated by this type of scenario."

"Have you read Dr. Poitier's book about successful adolescent bonding?"

"Yes, and if you read pages 234 through 238, you'll find similar comments to those I offered earlier. Of the cases studied by him, a positive result more often occurred when the absent parent reentered the picture without the presence of other significant parental figures. Dr. Poitier also notes that a strong grandparent connection can adversely affect delayed parental bonding with adolescents. In this case, very strong grandparent relationships exist between Jimmy and his paternal grandparents."

Mr. Jasper stepped back and looked at his notes.

"Doesn't Dr. Poitier document successes?"

"Yes, but I don't consider the number statistically significant, and the ones cited are completely inapplicable to this case."

"Uh, no other questions, Your Honor."

Mr. Long rose to his feet. "Your Honor, do you want to hear from another witness before lunch?"

The judge tapped his pen against the bench. "I want to hear from all witnesses before lunch."

"Yes, sir. We call Ellen Mitchell."

Mama didn't look at Jimmy as she came into the courtroom. Her face was tense, and her expression made Jimmy's stomach tie up in a knot.

"Please state you name for the record."

"Ellen Mitchell."

No witness captured Jimmy's attention like Mama. Even his birth mama hadn't made him as interested in what was happening as much as watching and listening to the person more familiar to him than any other. She looked smaller than normal in the big courtroom. At first, her voice shook. But as she talked, it evened out. Her message to the judge was simple. She loved Jimmy and believed he needed the stability of a single home.

"I've devoted the past eight years to creating a home where Jimmy could thrive in safety," she said. "He's a wonderful boy, and if we're allowed to continue what we're doing, he's going to blossom even more in the future."

"What have you done to better equip yourself as a parent?"

"I've read several books about raising a special-needs child, attended seminars, and completed three college-level courses about child development."

"How did you do in the college courses?"

Mama smiled. "I made an A in each one. No one was more motivated to learn than I."

"We hear about problems between stepmothers and stepchildren. How would you describe your feelings for Jimmy?"

"I love him with my whole heart," Mama said. "He is the sunshine of my life. In fact, that's one of my nicknames for him."

She looked at Jimmy, and the sunlight of their smiles united.

"That's all from this witness," Mr. Long said.

Jasper picked up a manila envelope from the table and approached the witness stand. He slid out a single sheet and handed it to Mama.

"Mrs. Mitchell, who is in this photograph?"

"Objection," Mr. Long said. "We haven't been furnished any photos."

"Show it to Mr. Long," the judge said.

Mr. Jasper retrieved the picture and handed it to Mr. Long, who passed it to Daddy. Jimmy couldn't see it, but Mama's face flushed red. Mr. Jasper returned to the witness stand and handed it back to Mama.

"Have you been spying on us?" Mama asked indignantly.

"Please answer my question," Jasper replied.

Mama put the photo on the ledge in front of the witness stand.

"That's Jimmy."

"What is he doing?"

Mama looked at Daddy as she answered. "He's learning how to climb a utility pole at his grandfather's house."

"He has a pole at his house?"

"In the backyard. There aren't any wires on it. It was a gift given to him when he retired."

"How tall is this pole?"

"I'm not sure," Mama responded through clenched teeth.

"I'm sorry, I couldn't hear you," Jasper said.

"I'm not sure," she repeated.

Jimmy whispered to Daddy. "It's a forty-five-foot, class-B pole."

Daddy didn't respond.

"Do you believe this is an appropriate activity for a boy like Jimmy?" Mr. Jasper asked.

"No."

"How often does Jimmy climb this power pole?"

"Once a week or less, depending on the weather. He's not made it to the top."

"Do you realize he could be killed or seriously injured if he fell from this pole?"

"Yes, but they use a safety harness. His grandfather worked for Georgia Power for over thirty years."

Jimmy whispered again. "He was a lineman and foreman."

"I know. Be quiet," Daddy replied.

"Do you believe there is greater risk in allowing Jimmy to climb a power pole or in getting to know his mother, who wants to nurture a positive, healthy relationship with him?"

"Objection, argumentative," Mr. Long said.

"Sustained. You've made your point, Mr. Jasper," the judge said.

"His father is there to make sure Jimmy doesn't fall," Mama blurted out.

"Oh, so Mr. Mitchell directly supports this activity?" Mr. Jasper asked in surprise.

"Yes."

"Is the whole family in on this educational project?"

Mama frowned but didn't speak. Mr. Jasper retrieved another photo from the envelope and handed it to Mr. Long and Daddy. Jimmy craned his neck and saw Grandpa's pickup truck. The lawyer handed the photograph to Mama.

"Who is in this picture?"

"Jimmy."

"What is he doing?"

"He's riding in the back of his grandfather's pickup truck with a few fishing poles. It's just a couple of miles to the pond where they like to fish."

"Do you consider this a safe way to transport Jimmy?"

"No."

"Are you aware that most motor accidents occur within four miles of a person's home?"

"No."

"Does Mr. Mitchell consider this a safe way for Jimmy to ride in a truck?"

"No."

Jimmy whispered. "You let me ride in the back of the truck all the time."

"Quiet! I mean it," Daddy responded.

"How often does Jimmy ride without use of a seat belt in the back of a pickup truck?"

"He would only do it for short trips in warm weather."

"Do you believe there is greater risk in allowing Jimmy to ride unrestrained in the back of a pickup truck, or in getting to know his mother, who wants to nurture a positive—"

"No need, Mr. Jasper," the judge interrupted.

"Yes, sir."

Mr. Jasper took out another picture. Jimmy could hear Mama's sigh all the way across the courtroom. Mr. Jasper handed the photo to Mr. Long and Daddy, who shielded it from Jimmy's curious gaze.

"Mrs. Mitchell, is this Jimmy in this photo?"

"Yes."

Mama set the picture on the ledge before her.

"What is in his hands?"

"A BB gun."

Mr. Jasper picked up the photo and looked closely at it.

"Would you agree that it looks like a rifle?"

"It's a BB gun. He shot it at Max Cochran's house. They live out in the country."

"Is this the family of the Mrs. Cochran who testified earlier?"

"Yes."

"Is their son, Max, Jimmy's best friend?"

"Yes."

"Does Jimmy often spend the night at their house?"

"Occasionally."

"If Mrs. Cochran mentioned that Jimmy spends quite a bit of time at their house during the summer, would she be correct?"

"Yes."

"Does Mr. Cochran keep guns in his house?"

"Yes, he's a deer hunter."

"Did you inspect the gun in this photo to make sure it wasn't a deer rifle?"

"I wasn't present."

"How often does Jimmy shoot guns at the Cochran house?"

"I don't know."

"Did you give permission for Jimmy to shoot any kind of gun at the Cochran house?"

"No. I didn't learn about it until Jimmy's birthday party last week."

"Does Mr. Mitchell support Jimmy playing with guns?"

"No."

Mr. Jasper looked up at the judge. "Same question, Your Honor."

"Duly noted," Judge Reisinger replied.

"Thank you, Mrs. Mitchell. That's all the photographs and questions I have at this time," Mr. Jasper said.

Mama left the witness stand and walked past the table without looking at Daddy. She had a serious look on her face. Jimmy turned around and saw her sit down next to Max's mother and shut her eyes.

"We call Lee Mitchell," Mr. Long announced.

Daddy straightened his tie as he walked up to the witness stand. Daddy was so smart that Jimmy knew he would be a good witness.

— Twenty-four —

First, Daddy talked about being a lawyer in Piney Grove. Daddy couldn't do everything Max's father could do around the house or in the woods, but Jimmy was still proud of him.

"Where and when did you and Mrs. Horton meet?" Long asked.

"While I was in law school at the University of Georgia, but we didn't marry until several years later."

"Did you hear her description of your marriage and divorce?"

"Yes."

"Do have a different perspective?"

"Somewhat. I have faults, but our problems weren't as one-sided as she claims. Neither of us worked as hard as we could have to salvage the marriage. I hope we both learned lessons that will help our current marriages be more successful."

"How long have you and Ellen Mitchell been married?"

"Eight years. She's a great wife and wonderful mother to Jimmy."

Jimmy wanted to say "amen" like in church when the preacher said something that was true.

"Do you recall Mrs. Horton trying to contact you after the divorce?"

"I remember two occasions. Both times I was out of the office, and she left a message with my secretary."

"Do you have proof of the date and time of those calls?"

"Yes. I saved the slips and put them in our divorce file."

Mr. Long handed Daddy two slips of pink paper.

"Are these the message slips?"

"Yes. One call came about a year after the divorce and the other three months later."

"Did you return the phone calls?"

"No."

"Why not?"

"She'd walked out on us without looking back, and I wanted to go on with my life."

"Did you receive any other verbal or written contact from her?"

"Not for ten years."

"Any child support during that time period?"

"No."

"What about contact by her with Jimmy?"

"None."

"Why didn't you file to terminate her parental rights during this time?"

"I knew the law would allow me to petition the court to do so after a year passed without contact or payment of child support, but I didn't want to stir up controversy. Ellen has always wanted to adopt Jimmy, but like Vera, I was tired of fighting and didn't want to start another war."

"Why do you want to terminate her rights now?"

"She brought the war to us, and I believe adequate grounds exist to end her right to disrupt our family in the future."

Mr. Long handed Daddy the three photographs used by Mr. Jasper.

"What is your perspective on the activities depicted in these pictures?"

"Jimmy has limitations, but I haven't raised him in an overprotective bubble. He's a fourteen-year-old boy growing up in a small town. If that means riding in the back of a pickup truck a few miles to a fishing hole on a hot summer day, it's okay with me. The Cochrans and my father are reliable folks, and there have been no incidents of injury or improper supervision of Jimmy while he's been with either of them. All three of these pictures taken by Mr. Jasper's private detective were shot within the past two or three months."

"Objection. Speculation by the witness," Mr. Jasper said.

"I doubt you found these photographs lying on the street," the judge responded drily. "Mr. Mitchell can testify as to the approximate time period during which they were taken and the activities depicted. You can offer rebuttal evidence if you choose to do so. Overruled."

Daddy continued, "And I'm proud of Jimmy learning how to climb the power pole. It's been a tremendous confidence builder for him to engage in an activity that none of his peers have attempted. My father was a lineman with the Georgia Power Company and trained many young men to climb. The harness he rigged up on the pole makes it as safe as climbing a step ladder, and I'm always present to assist if needed. So far, that hasn't been necessary."

Daddy's speech made Jimmy feel good. It was nice to find out what Daddy really thought about things.

"When Vera left, I resolved to be the best father I could to Jimmy," Daddy said. "I've not been perfect, and I realized earlier today that I've not been as accessible to Jimmy as I should have been. I'm looking forward to being his father more than ever."

"That's all I have from Mr. Mitchell," Mr. Long said.

"Mr. Jasper, you may cross-examine," the judge said.

Bob Jasper was an experienced lawyer, but he made a first-year-associate mistake and replowed ground tilled by Bruce Long in hope that he might unearth something new. Daddy turned every question into an opportunity to reemphasize the points he wanted the judge to remember. Jimmy could see Mr. Jasper's frustration level rising. The Atlanta lawyer pulled out the photographs that cut so deeply during cross-examination of Mama.

"Mr. Mitchell, did you hear your wife state under oath that she considers these activities inappropriate for Jimmy?"

"Yes, and I don't agree with her. Like every couple, we have different perspectives on some issues, but we're a unified team when it comes to providing a good home for Jimmy. On all major matters we're in agreement."

"Don't you consider Jimmy's safety a major matter?"

"Absolutely, but there's no indication that anything you've brought up is a true danger. It's all speculation."

"What about leaving Jimmy in the custody of your sixteen-year-old nephew, who took Jimmy out into the woods and didn't watch out for him?"

Jimmy could see Daddy's jaw stiffen.

"We left him with my brother-in-law and his wife, not the nephew."

"Were any adults present when the nephew took Jimmy into a remote area of Cattaloochie County a few months ago?"

"No."

"One last matter, Mr. Mitchell," Jasper said. "Has Jimmy ever been lost in the woods?"

"Yes."

"Did this occur while you and Mrs. Mitchell were out of town and Jimmy was left with a sixteen-year-old cousin who'd just gotten his driver's license?"

"Yes."

Jasper held up a sheet of paper. "I have the police report, but would you tell us in your own words what happened?"

Daddy turned toward Judge Reisinger.

"They were going to collect flowers and plants. My nephew stepped in a hole and broke his ankle. Jimmy walked through the woods to a road where a deputy sheriff picked him up."

"How long was Jimmy alone in the woods?" Jasper asked.

Jimmy leaned over to Mr. Long. "I wasn't alone. Buster was with me."

"He doesn't count," Mr. Long replied in a soft voice.

"About six or seven hours," Daddy said.

"Was it getting dark by the time they rescued him?"

"Yes."

"If he'd not been rescued, would he have spent the night alone in the woods?"

"Yes."

"Do you consider this a minor incident?"

"No, but except for a few scratches, Jimmy came out okay."

Mr. Jasper paused before asking his next question.

"Mr. Mitchell, do you believe there is greater risk of danger in allowing Jimmy to accompany a sixteen-year-old nephew to a remote area in the woods where he's lost for several hours than in getting to know his mother, who wants to nurture a positive relationship with him?"

Mr. Long stood up. "Objection. You previously instructed Mr. Jasper—"

"Overruled," the judge interrupted. "I'll let him answer the question."

"I don't think either option is a good one."

Mr. Jasper stood still for a second as if searching for another question.

"That's all," he said.

Mr. Long stood. "We call Jimmy Mitchell."

"I won't receive any testimony from the boy in the courtroom," the judge said. "I'll talk to him in Judge Robinson's chambers."

"I'd like the Court's indulgence to be present during that process," Mr. Jasper said.

"I would like to observe as well," Mr. Long added.

"No need for either of you to join us," the judge responded. "I've perused the psychological reports and feel comfortable talking to Jimmy alone."

"We could stand at the back of the room without making any comments," Mr. Jasper offered.

"I want you to stay in the courtroom."

Daddy leaned over to Jimmy. "Go with Judge Reisinger and remember what we told you."

"Yes, sir."

"Jimmy, please come with me," the judge said.

Jimmy rose to his feet. Although he'd done nothing wrong, he felt as if he was going to the principal's office at school. He nervously followed Judge Reisinger from the courtroom. The door closed behind them with a loud click.

"Judge Robinson's chambers are this way," the judge said.

Jimmy followed the judge down a hallway to a door marked "Honorable Jack B. Robinson—Superior Court Judge." They stepped inside. A woman sat behind a desk typing on a computer keyboard. She looked up as they entered.

"Go on in," she said. "Judge Robinson is out for the rest of the day."

Beyond her desk was an open door. Jimmy followed the judge into the office and immediately connected the room with Mr. Robinson. On one wall were pictures of Sunday school classes taught by the judge. In every photo, a group of young people stood in front of a mountain cabin. Jimmy could identify the faces of high school students who had been part of the class in the past.

"Sit down, Jimmy," the judge said, motioning to a chair in front of a large wooden desk.

The judge didn't sit behind the desk but beside Jimmy. Up close the judge didn't look much older than Mr. Arnold, the eighth-grade science teacher.

"May I ask you some questions?" the judge asked.

"Yes, sir."

"Will you tell me the truth?"

"Yes, sir. The truth, the whole truth, and nothing but the truth."

"Good."

"What is this hearing about?"

"She wants me to visit her in Atlanta."

"Who?"

"Mrs. Horton, my birth mama. I'm not sure what to call her."

"Let's call her your birth mama."

"Yes, sir."

"Do you know that your birth mama wants you to live with her part of the time in Atlanta?"

Jimmy said, "I want to stay in Piney Grove with Mama, Daddy, Grandpa, and Buster."

The judge tapped the ends of his fingers together. "Is that what your father and Mr. Long told you to say if someone asked you that kind of question?"

"Yes, sir."

"Who is Buster?"

"My dog."

"What do you think about visiting your birth mama in Atlanta?"

"I want to stay in Piney Grove with Mama, Daddy, Grandpa, and Buster."

"Would you like to get to know her?"

"Do you mean talk to her?"

"Yes."

The conversation in the hallway had been pleasant. She liked vanilla wafers with peanut butter too.

"It would be nice to talk to her and ask her questions," Jimmy said, but then quickly added, "but it would be a problem."

"Why?"

Jimmy took a deep breath. "Since my birth mama called our house, my mama has been sad. If I started talking to my birth mama, it would make Mama cry, and I don't want to do that."

"Do you think of your stepmother as your mama?"

"She's my mama."

"Okay, but you seem like a fine young man. Do you think your birth mama should get to know you too?"

"That's for you to decide," Jimmy responded.

"Why do you say that?" he asked.

"You're the judge. It's what judges do."

Judge Reisinger laughed. "Thank you for the respect; however, because you're fourteen years old, I have to listen to what you want to do."

"It doesn't make sense that you should listen to me."

"But you're the reason we're here today. I want to know your opinion. Do you understand what I mean by that?"

Jimmy sighed. "Yes, sir. I just wish there was two of me."

"Why?"

"One could live in Piney Grove and make everyone happy here. The other one could visit my birth mama in Atlanta and make her happy."

"A different solution to Solomon's dilemma," the judge said thoughtfully.

"What?"

"Another judge who had a difficult decision to make about a child. He's mentioned in the Bible."

"I believe every word in the Holy Bible," Jimmy said. "Did the judge in the Holy Bible pray about what he should do?"

"I suppose so."

"Have you prayed?"

The judge sat back and his eyebrows went up. "About this case?"

"Yes, sir."

"No, I haven't."

"I pray about stuff all the time," Jimmy said. "That would be a lot better than asking me questions."

"You think I should pray?"

"Yes, sir."

Before the judge said anything else, Jimmy bowed his head and closed his eyes. Judge Reisinger briefly glanced up at the ceiling before closing his own eyes. After a few seconds, he spoke slowly and deliberately.

"God, please show me what I should do in this case. I want to make the right decision for Jimmy and his family, amen."

Jimmy opened his eyes. "That was a lot shorter than when Brother Fitzgerald prays, but I think it will work."

"I hope so, Jimmy," the judge said. "I sincerely hope so."

They returned to the courtroom. Jimmy sensed all eyes on him as he returned to his seat. Daddy leaned over.

"Did you tell him what we told you to say?"

"Yes, sir."

"What did he say?"

"He prayed."

"He prayed?" Daddy asked in surprise.

"Yes, sir, I closed my eyes, but I heard every word."

"YOUR HONOR, MAY WE TAKE A SHORT RECESS BEFORE CLOSING arguments?" Mr. Jasper asked.

"That won't be necessary," the judge said.

Mr. Long and Daddy were whispering and suddenly stopped.

"Are there any unusual legal issues presented in this case?" the judge asked.

Mr. Jasper cleared his throat. "I thought it might be helpful to summarize my client's position for the Court."

"I think I know what each side wants me to do, and I'm very familiar with the appropriate statutes. My question relates to appellate authority that supports your client's position. What cases will give me guidance?"

"Uh, we believe *Patterson v. Patterson* sets out a good summary of the law," Mr. Jasper said. "In that case, the Supreme Court—"

"I'm familiar with the case," Judge Reisinger interrupted. "In fact, I was trial counsel for the mother of the child and handled the appeal before I became a judge."

The judge turned toward Mr. Long. "Are there any unusual legal issues on your side?"

"The long passage of time without contact or support by Mrs. Horton makes it clear—"

"That sounds like facts, not law, to me," the judge said. "We've been here long enough. I'm going to close the hearing and release the parties and their witnesses. I'll consider the testimony, exhibits, and applicable case law and issue a decision," the judge said.

"Do you want us to submit written briefs?" Jasper said.

"That won't be necessary. I'm going to decide the case before I leave the courthouse today. If each of you will provide a phone number, I'll verbally notify you of my ruling. The prevailing party will draft findings of facts and conclusions of law consistent with my decision."

Mr. Jasper told the judge a phone number. Mr. Long gave the number for

Daddy's office. The judge banged the gavel and left the courtroom. Mr. Jasper and Mr. Long shook hands. Daddy grabbed Jimmy by the arm.

"Let's go."

As they stood and moved toward the bar, Jimmy's birth mama stepped from behind Mr. Jasper.

"Lee," she said. "Please wait."

Daddy stopped. Jimmy could see Mama coming toward them.

"What is it?" Daddy asked.

"Uh, I'm sorry about the past."

"Forget it."

Mama arrived but stopped short of the gate in the bar.

"No, I mean it," Mrs. Horton said. "I'm deeply sorry."

Mama spoke. "Then why have you tried to ruin our lives now?"

"That's not what I'm doing. I believe this can work."

"But you don't know anything about Jimmy," Mama said.

"He likes vanilla wafers with peanut butter on them," Mrs. Horton said.

"Which I've fixed for him hundreds of times since you left. If you really cared about Jimmy, you'd let him live in peace. Bouncing him back and forth will tear him apart emotionally. Is that what you want?"

Jimmy saw tears in his birth mama's eyes as she turned away. He and Daddy joined Mama and walked out of the courtroom.

"What an ordeal," Mama said with a sigh. "I'm glad it's over."

"Me too," Jimmy added.

"What is the judge going to do?" she asked Daddy. "You heard all the evidence."

"He's going to pray about it," Daddy answered.

"Pray?"

"Yes, that's what he and Jimmy did when they went into Judge Robinson's chambers."

"And then what?"

"We'll go to the office and wait to find out what God tells him."

THE WITNESSES AND MAX'S MOM DIDN'T GO WITH THEM TO Daddy's office. Kate and Delores peppered Daddy with questions as soon as the smaller group entered the reception area; however, Daddy refused to predict the judge's decision. They turned their focus to Mr. Long.

"The law is clear," he said. "Mrs. Horton's current wealth or change of heart after ten years shouldn't be determining factors."

"Is that right, Lee?" Delores asked.

"Bruce did a good job," Daddy answered. "Especially with their expert witness. We put up a good case but couldn't keep them from scoring some points too."

"I'll wait in the conference room," Mr. Long said to Kate. "I have some work to do in another file. When Judge Reisinger calls, direct it to me."

The Mitchell family went into Daddy's office. Mama sat down in a chair and closed her eyes.

"How do people go through this day after day?" she asked.

"Not very well. It's one reason I've stayed away from domestic work," Daddy replied.

Jimmy picked up the dictation unit he'd played with earlier.

"Listen to this," he said, pushing the *play* button. "Do you think it sounds like me?"

"I have the prettiest, nicest mama in the whole world. I love her very much."

Daddy smiled. "I agree with your opinion of your mama."

"Thanks," Mama replied. "But I don't feel very pretty. Do you think I was too harsh with Vera after the hearing? I've been so upset and worried—"

"I'm not going to criticize you," Daddy said. "Right before you came up, Vera apologized about the past to me, but I have no way of knowing if she was sincere. The only way we'll find out if she's telling the truth about a change of heart is if Reisinger grants her visitation or partial custody. Then her true character will come out."

"What will that do to my character?" Mama asked with a sigh.

"I love you, Mama," Jimmy said.

Mama looked at him and smiled. Jimmy fiddled with the buttons on the dictation device.

"I love you, Mama," the tape repeated.

"You can keep that tape. It's an extra," Daddy said to Jimmy. "Put it with your legal pad and record anything you want Mama or me to hear."

There was a knock on the door.

"Come in!" Daddy said.

Mr. Long opened the door and stuck his head inside.

"The judge called. He's reached a decision."

— Twenty-five —

"What is it?" Mama asked anxiously.

Mr. Long smiled. "He denied the petition. He's going to terminate Mrs. Horton's parental rights for failing to maintain regular contact with Jimmy or pay child support. Basically, he applied the statute and wants a *de minimus* order that mentions his consideration of the expert testimony but doesn't try to over-analyze it."

"To make it harder on appeal," Daddy said.

"Exactly."

"What about Jimmy's preferences?" Daddy asked.

"All he mentioned is a finding that he met with the child, who asked him to rule as he deemed appropriate."

"Is that right?" Daddy asked Jimmy.

"I don't understand," Jimmy answered.

"Didn't you tell Judge Reisinger that you wanted to live with us in Piney Grove?"

"Yes, sir. I want to stay in Piney Grove with Mama, Daddy, Grandpa, and Buster."

"It doesn't matter," Mama said, taking a tissue from her purse to wipe away the tears flowing from her eyes. "We got what we wanted and prayed for. Peace."

Daddy stood and shook Mr. Long's hand.

"Good job, Bruce. I'd like to review the order before you submit it to the judge."

"I'll get on it as soon as I get back to my office."

Mr. Long left. Daddy buzzed Delores and Kate and gave them the news. Jimmy could hear their screams through the telephone speaker.

"Why are they yelling?" he asked.

"They're happy. It's like winning a big football game, only more important."

Jimmy nodded, then a thought came to him.

"How will she feel?" he asked.

"Who?"

"My birth mama."

Mama wiped away a tear. "She'll be upset," she said softly. "But we have to believe that God helped the judge to make the right decision for everyone. She has two daughters to love. You're the only child we have, and all our love belongs to you."

Jimmy picked up the dictation unit. "Could you say that again?"

SATURDAY MORNING, JIMMY PEDALED STEADILY DOWN THE street as Buster ran alongside on the sidewalk. Not very many cars took the roads to Grandpa's house, but Jimmy stayed close to the curb anyway. He'd added a rearview mirror to his handlebar, but the sound of an approaching car proved more reliable than a glance into the piece of glass. Jimmy came to the first stop sign and stopped. He looked in both directions and honked his horn. No cars were in sight, but he honked the horn again. Buster barked. They continued to Ridgeview Drive.

It was hot, and Buster's tongue was hanging out the side of his mouth by the time they reached Grandpa's house.

Jimmy rang the doorbell. It took almost a minute for Grandpa to open the door. When he did, Buster scooted past on his way to the kitchen. Jimmy hugged Grandpa and listened to his heart.

"I can hear it better," Jimmy said raising his ear from Grandpa's chest. "It's getting louder."

"I think that's because it's working harder doing ordinary activities," Grandpa replied.

They went to the kitchen. Buster was already in the backyard barking at a squirrel that had run up the power pole. Jimmy gave Grandma a hug.

"Not too hard," she protested. "You don't know how strong you're getting."

Grandpa squeezed Jimmy's upper arm. "Wiry but tough," he said.

"What does that mean?" Jimmy asked.

"You're getting a man's body."

"How is your mama doing?" Grandma asked.

"She's happy again."

"I heard you had a prayer meeting with the judge," Grandpa said.

"Yes, sir."

"It's been a long time since Vera left," Grandpa said, shaking his head. "What did you think when you saw her? Did you remember anything about her?"

"I don't think you should bring this up with Jimmy," Grandma said. "It's not right to put him on the spot."

"It's okay," Jimmy said. "I told everyone that I wanted to stay in Piney Grove with Mama, Daddy, Grandpa, and Buster."

"Don't ask him anything else about it," Grandma said. "I'm sure he's been through enough. Let's be thankful everything is going to stay the way it is."

Jimmy and Grandpa went into the backyard. By the time they reached the shed, the heat caused Grandpa to wipe the sweat from his forehead with the red bandanna he kept in his back pocket. Sitting on the single step in front of the shed, Jimmy glanced up at the power pole. The white marks striped the pole like a giant black-and-white candy cane.

"Is today the day?" Grandpa asked.

Jimmy strapped on the climbing hooks without assistance.

"I don't know, Grandpa. I've been thinking about it all morning."

"What were you thinking?"

"Inside my head, I saw myself touch the top of the pole and feel a cool breeze."

"If that happens, send it down to me. What time will your daddy get here?"

"He was reading the paper and drinking a cup of coffee when I left."

"I hope he doesn't give up on us because of the heat."

Grandma opened the back door.

"Lee is on the phone!"

"Wait here while I talk to your daddy. Don't try to climb that pole on your own."

"Yes, sir."

Jimmy called Buster, and the dog came running. Grandpa kept a can of old tennis balls in the shed. Jimmy threw all three balls at once and waited while Buster retrieved them as fast as he could.

Grandpa returned.

"Your daddy can't come, but he said for us to go ahead without him."

"Are you sure?" Jimmy asked.

"Yes."

"Did he ask Mama about it?"

"She's at the grocery store."

They approached the pole. Grandpa grabbed the safety rope and attached it to Jimmy's utility belt. On two occasions the safety device had proved its worth. Neither time resulted in more than a slight scrape.

Jimmy began to climb. He passed the now fading marks of his early progress. He continued to the midpoint he'd reached after several months of climbing. He slowed as he approached three-quarters of the pole's height and looked down. Grandpa had shrunk in size. Buster looked smaller too.

"How are you?" Grandpa yelled.

Jimmy put his gloved hands against the black surface of the pole.

"I feel strong."

"Then keep going!"

Five more digs into the wood brought Jimmy to his previous best. From this spot he could see the sights he'd first observed during his days resting in Grandpa's arms. The top of the pole was in sight. Jimmy adjusted the safety belt and leaned closer to the pole so he could climb monkey style. He looked up after four more digs, but the top of the pole seemed as far away as before. Sweat streamed down the back of his neck, and his shirt stuck to his chest and back. He wanted to rub his eyes but couldn't because a piece of creosote on his glove might get in his eye and sting. He reached to the side and felt the can of paint in his utility belt. He looked down at Grandpa. The old man stood still, holding the safety rope.

"Are you going to stop?" Grandpa called out.

Jimmy left the paint in its place, blinked the sweat from his eyes, and kept climbing. Twice more he moved the safety belt upward. Staring at the pole in front of him, he dug in and raised himself higher. He leaned forward and slipped up the safety belt. Leaning back, he managed to rub his eyes on his shirt sleeve. He looked up.

Just above his head was the top of the pole.

He strained to reach up and touch it. When he did, he lost tension on the safety belt, and his left hook came loose.

"Ride it!" Grandpa shouted.

Jimmy knew what he meant. They'd rehearsed this many times two feet above the ground in case it became necessary to do it at forty feet in the air. He rode the momentum of the belt to the right and then let it take him back to the left. Waiting a split second longer than instinct urged him to, he reached the correct distance, solidly planted his left hook in the pole, and leaned back against the belt. He stopped swinging and looked down.

"How was that?" he asked.

Grandpa gave him thumbs up. "I'm very proud of you. That's very good. Come on down."

"No, sir."

Grandpa didn't answer for a second, then called out, "Four more digs! Keep tension on the belt!"

Jimmy stepped down a few inches, regained the proper form, and slowly went up the final four digs. His head cleared the top of the pole. He leaned back against the belt and put his hand on top of the pole.

Closing his eyes, he felt a cool breeze.

When he looked down, Grandpa was dancing around the pole, whooping and yelling. Buster had joined the old man and barked and barked and barked.

An explorer reaching the top of a mountain knows it is a moment to savor. Jimmy didn't know anything about mountain-climbing rituals, but he didn't want to depart the summit too quickly. He patted the top of the pole and inspected the place where the safety harness screwed into the wood.

"Paint the top of the pole!" Grandpa cried out.

Jimmy looked down, puzzled. "But no one will see it!"

"But you'll know it's there! That's all that counts."

Jimmy took out the can of paint and shook it. He could hear the little ball inside rattling around. Checking the spray arrow on the button to avoid a face full of paint, he quickly coated the top of the pole in white. Returning the paint can to his utility belt, he took a last look around and descended the pole. When he reached the ground, Grandpa stood back while Jimmy took off the safety belt. Then the old man stepped forward to give him a big hug. When he released him, Grandpa put his ear to Jimmy's chest.

"Why are you doing that, Grandpa?" Jimmy asked.

"I'm listening to your heart."

"Why?"

"Because I want to listen to the heart of a champion."

Jimmy returned to the step in front of the utility shed and began taking off his gear. He handed the climbing hooks to Grandpa.

"I wish Daddy had been here," Jimmy said.

"Me too."

They stowed the climbing gear in the shed.

"What am I going to do now that I've climbed the pole?" Jimmy asked.

Grandpa stopped, put his hands on Jimmy's shoulders, and looked directly into his eyes. "Anything you want. Do you believe that?"

"Yes, sir."

They walked to the house.

"I'm thirsty," Jimmy said. "It was hot up there."

"A glass of lemonade to celebrate sounds good to me," Grandpa said.

Grandpa poured Jimmy's drink, then left the room. In a minute, he returned with a medium-sized paper sack.

"This is for you," he said, handing the sack to Jimmy. "I didn't wrap it up fancy, but I've been saving it for you."

Jimmy opened the bag and pulled out an old red cap. A stick figure with lightning bolts for arms and legs danced across the front. Underneath were the words, "A Citizen Wherever We Serve."

"It's a Ready Kilowatt hat!" Jimmy said in an excited voice. "Is this your hat—"

"No," Grandpa interrupted. "I found it on the Internet and bought it to give you when you climbed to the top of the pole. It's yours. You've earned it."

Jimmy slipped the cap on his head and looked up at Grandpa with a big grin.

"My very own Ready Kilowatt hat!"

WHEN HE RETURNED HOME, JIMMY PUT HIS READY KILOWATT cap in the middle of his collection. Mama watched from the doorway.

"How do you like my new cap?" he asked.

"It's very nice. What did your daddy think about your accomplishment?"

"I don't know. He wasn't there."

"Why not?"

"I'm not sure, but he told Grandpa it was okay."

Mama pressed her lips together. "We'll discuss that when he gets home."

Jimmy continued. "I'm going to wear my new cap when Grandpa and I go fishing. There is a big carp contest in a few weeks at Webb's Pond. Can I go?"

"Maybe. I don't want you climbing the pole anymore without your daddy there."

"Yes, ma'am. If I'm ever going to be a Georgia Power Company lineman, I have to be able to climb a lot better than I do now."

"Has Grandpa told you that you could be a lineman?" Mama asked in surprise.

"No, ma'am, but he told me I could do anything I want. I'm not afraid of being up high in the air, and now I have my own Ready Kilowatt hat."

— Twenty-six —

Twenty-nine days after Judge Reisinger signed the order prepared by Bruce Long, Jimmy's birth mama filed an appeal.

Daddy, Mama, and Jimmy were eating supper in the kitchen. Mama had fixed veal parmesan, rice, and fried okra. Jimmy liked veal parmesan but not as much as meat loaf.

"I wish she'd given up." Mama sighed. "What are her chances on appeal?"

"Slim and none," Daddy replied.

"What does appeal mean?" Jimmy asked.

"She wants some other judges to change Judge Reisinger's decision."

Jimmy poked his fork into three pieces of okra at once. "Will they pray about it too?"

"I don't know," Daddy answered. "But it will be close to a year before we know anything."

"I'll be in high school," Jimmy said.

"You'll be finished with ninth grade," Mama said.

"How do you feel about going to high school?" Daddy asked.

"Okay, I guess."

When Jimmy thought about Cattaloochie County High School, with eight hundred students coming together from the county's three middle schools, his stomach felt queasy. "Ninth grade is a big step," Daddy said.

"Yes, sir."

"Have you thought about any extracurricular activities?"

"What's that?"

"The high school has groups and teams that do things after school."

"I heard about a club that builds model rockets," Mama said. "They also study the stars. You'd be good at painting the rockets. Do you think you would like that?"

"I had something else in mind," Daddy said, putting his napkin beside his plate. "I went by the stadium this afternoon and talked to Coach Nixon. The football team starts practice in a few weeks."

Jimmy put down his fork. Mama's mouth dropped open.

"Lee, you've got to be kidding. There is no way Jimmy should be on a football field."

"I disagree," Daddy replied with a grin. "I think Jimmy is perfectly suited to be on a football field. They have an open spot for a manager, and Coach Nixon is interested in talking to Jimmy about the position."

"A manager?" Jimmy asked excitedly. "Who goes down on the field and rides in the bus with the team and stands behind the coaches and gives the players water and towels?"

"And a lot of other things you'll learn to do."

Jimmy forgot about his food. "When would I start?"

"Two-a-day practices begin in four weeks, but first, you have to talk to Coach Nixon."

"What is he going to ask me?"

"I'm not exactly sure—probably whether you're a hard worker who will obey the rules."

Jimmy stared unseeing across the table, trying to imagine the interview as Daddy continued, "If you want to talk to him, I'll take you tomorrow afternoon."

"Yes, sir!"

To be associated with the Cattaloochie County High School football team would be a thrill beyond words. Jimmy loved Friday night football. He also loved the band. He'd practiced drumming with two sticks on top of a metal trash can in the backyard. Mama told him it sounded great, but it didn't sound right to his ears.

The following day, Jimmy could hardly contain his excitement. Several times he asked Mama how long it would be until Daddy picked him up. The hours dragged by. Finally, Daddy turned into the driveway in front of the house. Jimmy opened the door, ran to the car, and got in.

"Not that hat," Daddy said. "Coach Nixon went to Auburn. Do you have the Cattaloochie cap I bought you last year?"

"Yes, sir."

Jimmy returned the University of Georgia hat to its place and found the cap with a Cattaloochie Captain mascot on it. The short, bearded figure looked like a cross between a Confederate officer and a California gold rush prospector.

"That's better," Daddy said.

GRANDPA HAD ATTENDED PINEY GROVE HIGH, A SMALL, ALL-white school located within the city limits of Piney Grove. By the time Daddy and Mama reached high school age, the city and county schools had been brought together, combining city, county, black, and white. Everyone went to a new school, which made integration easier. Having a successful sports program that exceeded the accomplishments of the older split system helped even more.

The high school, a mile beyond the city limits, was a collection of long, one-story, brown-brick classroom buildings surrounding a taller gymnasium in the middle. The football stadium lay several hundred yards south of the main campus. The athletic offices were beneath the home stands. Signs in front of the athletic department indicated reserved parking spaces for Coach Nixon and his secretary, Mrs. Bradford.

Coach Nixon drove a small green sports car. Daddy parked beside his vehicle. Without any fans present, the stadium felt odd. Jimmy looked at the metal bleachers overhead. He never walked under the bleachers during a game. To do so might result in a shower from a spilled soft drink.

The front door of the athletic office was unlocked. Daddy entered and turned right. At the end of a hallway stood a door with the words "Vance Nixon—Head Coach" written in gold letters. Daddy knocked lightly on the door.

"Come in," answered a nasally voice tinged with a slight lisp.

Coach Nixon's office covered the entire end of the building. In one corner was a large grease board with black and red X's and O's on it. A standard wooden school desk sat in the middle, and in the other corner rested the small bed where Coach Nixon slept every Thursday night during football season.

Daddy and Uncle Bart spoke of Coach Nixon with awe. Sixty years old, Vance Nixon looked more like a badminton instructor than a football coach. Slightly built, the balding football coach weighed half as much as some of the team's offensive linemen, yet he had the force of personality to intimidate a massive player being courted by Southeastern Conference football powerhouses. When angry, Coach Nixon would get on his toes in front of a player and berate him in a torrent of cutting words mixed with saliva. Uncle Bart said no player dared wipe away the spit before the coach turned away.

Coach Nixon stood up from the chair behind his desk as they entered the room.

"Good to see you, Lee," Coach Nixon said.

"You too, Coach. This is—," Daddy began.

"No need to introduce me to Jimmy," the coach interrupted. "I've seen him at the games for years."

Jimmy's eyes widened. He had no idea the coach knew he lived on planet Earth.

"And," Coach Nixon continued, "I know the sound of the horn on his bicycle."

"Did I honk at you?" Jimmy asked.

"Yes. I was at a stoplight the other day, and you very clearly warned the drivers in all directions that you had arrived at the intersection. Are you always careful at stop signs?"

"Yes, sir."

"Do you follow directions?" the coach asked.

Jimmy hesitated. "When someone tells me how to get to a place I've never been before, I don't always understand the right street to turn on. Mama and Daddy help me learn the way before I go by myself. But once I learn the way, I don't get lost."

Coach Nixon smiled. "You have good parents."

"Yes, sir."

"Do you obey teachers and parents?"

"Yes, sir."

"What do you know about the job of manager for the football team?"

Jimmy carefully listed the tasks he'd observed: "Carry extra footballs, give the players water, put tape on players' ankles, clean up the sidelines."

"That's a good start," Coach Nixon said, "but there is a lot more that happens before and after the game."

The coach launched into a lecture about the manager's job. The longer he talked, the more nervous Jimmy became. The manager's job sounded like the most important task on the football team. The coach embellished his description with words far outside the range of Jimmy's vocabulary. Without proper hydration the players ran the risk of heatstroke, even death, he said. The wrong helmet on a player's head could result in a concussion and permanent brain damage. An incorrect jersey number could confuse the quarterback and result in a pass to a tight end instead of a wide receiver.

"Can you handle those responsibilities?" the coach asked.

Jimmy swallowed hard. Daddy spoke. "Once Jimmy learns something, it's in him forever. He's a hard worker and very conscientious."

"Is that true?" Coach Nixon asked Jimmy.

Jimmy wasn't sure about the last word, but he knew Daddy wouldn't lie.

"Yes, sir."

The coach reached across the desk and shook Jimmy's hand.

"Welcome to the Cattaloochie County High School football program. We start practice in three weeks."

Daddy and Coach Nixon talked several more minutes about the team's prospects for the coming season. Jimmy didn't try to follow the conversation. He spent the time looking at everything in the office. The walls were lined with team photos from past years. He wondered which one was Daddy's team.

Jimmy had never seen the coach's whistle up close. It hung from a nail behind the desk. On a shelf beside the grease board was a helmet cracked open down the middle. Jimmy figured it was probably the result of a manager's mistake.

"Thanks, Coach," Daddy said, standing up. "We'll have Jimmy here an hour before practice. Would it help if I stayed the first morning to help get him acclimated?"

"No, I'll put him with Chris Meadows, an experienced manager who will teach him the ropes."

"The boy with the leg problem?" Daddy asked.

"Yes. I think he's a good choice to work with Jimmy. He's overcome a lot of adversity. He has a temper that flares up occasionally, but only when someone puts him down. I like his spunk."

JIMMY WAS QUIET IN THE CAR ON THE RIDE HOME AND STARED out the window. They entered the city limits of Piney Grove.

"Are you okay?" Daddy asked.

"Yes, sir."

"Are you scared that you'll have trouble doing the manager job?"

After a few moments, Jimmy said, "Yes, sir, but it's not like swimming."

"Why not?" Daddy asked.

Jimmy took off his cap and looked at the captain on the front.

"It's like climbing the pole. If I work hard, I can learn how to do it."

They rode in silence the rest of the way to the house.

"Do you believe I will be a good manager?" Jimmy asked as the car rolled to a stop.

Daddy reached out and patted him on the shoulder.

"No doubt about it. You'll be one of the best managers Coach Nixon has ever seen."

JIMMY CLIMBED TO THE TOP OF THE POLE TWO MORE TIMES before football practice started. Both times, Daddy was present, holding on to the safety rope.

Early on a Monday morning, Jimmy sleepily rolled over in bed.

"Wake up!" Daddy called out.

"Where's Mama?" he asked.

"Downstairs fixing breakfast. Today is the first day of football practice. You have to be there an hour early."

Before Daddy finished speaking, Jimmy was sitting up in bed rubbing the sleep from his eyes.

"I'll take a shower and come downstairs," he said.

"No. You'll need a shower after practice, not before. I'm sure working as a manager is hot, sweaty work. The temperature is going to hit ninety-six by noon."

"Yes, sir."

"Do you know the clothes you want to wear?"

Jimmy pointed to a chair near his closet. He and Mama had picked out a shirt and socks the previous night. He had a pair of old running shoes to wear.

"Okay, that's fine," Daddy replied. "And remember, no University of Georgia hats. What college did Coach Nixon attend?"

"Auburn."

"What is their team mascot?"

Daddy had taught Jimmy the mascot of every Southeastern Conference team. Jimmy stood up and stretched. "They can't decide. Sometimes it's an eagle; sometimes it's a tiger."

Daddy smiled. "I would love to hear you say that to Coach Nixon, but don't do it."

"Why not?"

"He's a serious man. From now on, Cattaloochie County High School is the most important team in your life."

"Yes, sir."

JIMMY DRESSED AND RAN INTO THE HALL. HE ADJUSTED THE Cattaloochie cap in the mirror at the head of the stairs.

"I'm not very hungry," he said to Mama when he entered the kitchen.

"That's because you're excited. You need to eat a good breakfast so you won't run out of energy before I pick you up."

Mama put a plate of scrambled eggs, bacon, and two biscuits in front of him. The smell of the food revived Jimmy's appetite. He cut open a biscuit and watched a pat of butter disappear into the hot white bread.

"I'm going to drop you off on my way to work," Daddy said. "Mama will pick you up and take you back for the afternoon practice. Then I'll bring you home after work."

Chewing his food, Jimmy nodded.

"It's going to be hot, so make sure you drink a lot of water," Mama said.

"That's part of my job," Jimmy said. "I'll give the players water."

"And don't forget to drink some yourself," Daddy added. "Grab a cup even if you don't feel thirsty."

"I like hot weather," Jimmy said.

"Not me," Mama said. "If this old house hadn't been modernized, I couldn't live here."

Jimmy finished scooping up his eggs while his parents talked. Daddy was going to have lunch with the Lions Club. Jimmy couldn't remember a Southeastern Conference football team with a lion as a mascot.

"I'm going to work in the flower beds while it's still cool outside," Mama said.

Jimmy paused. "I won't be here to help you."

"That's okay," she replied. "You'll be doing your new manager job."

"Could we do the flower beds tomorrow?" Jimmy asked. "I'd like to be with you. And Grandpa could use some fresh worms."

"No, you have football practice every day for the next two weeks," Daddy answered. "It's like going back to school."

Mama began clearing off the table. "Or a real job."

Jimmy put down his glass of orange juice. "I want to work for the Georgia Power Company."

"Don't worry about planning the rest of your life just yet," Daddy said. "Let's go to the football field."

Jimmy's heart beat faster than normal as they turned onto the access road to the stadium. They weren't the first to arrive. Coach Nixon's little car as well as the vehicles driven by the assistant coaches were already parked on the grass at the edge of the practice field. The men stood in a casual group. Coach Nixon was not in sight. When Jimmy got out of the car and began to walk, his feet left a faint impression on the damp grass.

"The grass is still wet," he said.

"This dew won't last long," Daddy replied.

They approached the assistant coaches. Jimmy recognized a couple of faces but didn't know their names. The men turned toward them as they approached.

"Good morning, Mr. Mitchell," several called out.

One of the familiar faces nodded toward Jimmy with a smile. "And you too, Jimmy."

Jimmy didn't say anything. The men wore identical blue shorts and white T-shirts emblazoned with "Captain Football—Varsity" on the front. Jimmy adjusted his cap and wondered if he'd ever be allowed to wear one of the shirts.

Daddy moved into the midst of the group and began shaking hands and talking. Jimmy stood at the edge and watched. Being at the field was scarier than he'd expected, and the idea that he would be responsible for something related to the football team was almost frightening. Daddy turned to go. Jimmy stepped closer to him and edged back toward the car.

"Are you okay?" Daddy asked.

Jimmy shook his head. "No. I don't know what to do."

"They'll tell you. Until then, stand here and wait. Don't worry."

It would be a lot easier to help Mama weed the flower beds than to stay at the football field. Daddy leaned closer to him and put his arm around his shoulders.

"It's like climbing the pole."

"A little bit at a time."

"That's right. I told the coaches what a hard worker you are. Listen carefully to what you're told and do it."

"Yes, sir. I'll be okay," Jimmy replied with more confidence than he felt.

He watched Daddy's car until it disappeared around a corner. Sighing, Jimmy turned back toward the coaches and moved closer to await instructions. The men continued talking. They didn't seem in a hurry to do anything. Jimmy could see that two of them had packs of chewing tobacco in the back pocket of their shorts. Jimmy had never seen chewing tobacco up close. Grandpa had warned him that chewing tobacco was a nasty habit, a lot worse than chewing bubble gum. Jimmy tilted his head to try to see the picture on the front of the pouch. He stepped closer until he stood directly behind one of the men, an older coach with close-cut gray hair. The pouch portrayed an Indian chief similar to one in a book Jimmy had at home. Suddenly, the coach turned and saw Jimmy staring at his rear end.

"Mitchell!" he yelled.

Jimmy stepped back and turned around to see if his father had returned.

"Your daddy is gone. What are you looking at!" the man demanded.

Jimmy didn't answer. He looked up into a fierce pair of black eyes under bushy eyebrows.

"I'm talking to you, son. Answer me."

"Coach Bolton, remember, he's slow," one of the younger coaches said.

"No, sir," Jimmy responded. "I'm a fast runner."

Coach Bolton looked down at him. "Fast? Show me how fast you can run. Do you see Coach Nixon walking down the hill on the other side of the field behind the goalposts?"

"Yes, sir."

"If I tell you something to say to him, can you remember?"

"Yes, sir."

"Tell him Coach Bolton found the defensive playbook behind the seat of his truck."

"Yes, sir."

"Tell him to repeat it back," the younger coach said. "I'm not sure he understood."

"Don't you remember?" another coach interjected. "This is the boy who testified in the court case that led to Sheriff Brinson's resignation. He has a photographic memory."

"What did I say to you?" Coach Bolton asked Jimmy. "Coach Sellers thinks you have a photographic memory."

"Coach Bolton found the defensive playbook behind the seat of his truck," Jimmy repeated.

"What did I tell you?" said Coach Sellers.

"He's already smarter than half the boys I've got on defense this year," Coach Bolton grunted.

Turning to Jimmy, he said, "Go!"

Jimmy started running across the field. He'd never run on a real football field before. The white lines flew by beneath his feet. He stepped on the numbers and imagined the feeling of a football player with the ball in his arms being chased by the other team. He didn't slow down until he crossed the end-zone line and approached Coach Nixon.

"Nice run, Jimmy," Coach Nixon said. "Did you score?"

Jimmy stood at attention. "Coach Bolton found the defensive playbook behind the seat of his truck."

"That's good," Coach Nixon replied. "I'd hate to make him run wind sprints for losing his playbook."

"What's a wind sprint?" Jimmy asked.

"What you just did, only a little bit shorter distance. You run as fast as you can for thirty or forty yards and do it over and over. It builds up the players' endurance so they can play all the way through the fourth quarter without getting too tired."

"Tell me if you want me to run any wind sprints," Jimmy said.

"You won't if you do your job. Walk with me and tell me again what you think a manager does," the coach said.

Jimmy repeated everything he could remember.

"Today you're going to be the water boy," the coach said. "Do you know where the locker room is located underneath the stadium?"

"Yes, sir."

"One of the other managers will show you. Your job will be to fill up coolers with ice from the machine near the locker room and bring it to the field. There is a water hose on the near sideline that you can use to fill up the coolers. The players will drink from paper cups. If a player throws his cup on the ground instead of putting it in the trash can, I want you to write his number on a sheet of paper and give it to me at the end of practice. Do not pick up any trash yourself. Can you do all that?"

Jimmy hesitated, but he thought he understood.

"Yes, sir."

"Good. There's Chris Meadows. He'll show you where to get the ice."

Jimmy looked across the field and saw a student talking to Coach Bolton. He ran as fast as he could to the coaches.

"Did you tell him?" Coach Bolton asked.

"Yes, sir. And you don't have to run wind sprints."

Several of the coaches laughed. Coach Bolton cut them off with a severe glance.

Jimmy faced the other manager. Chris had red hair and freckles and was strong in his upper body and arms. Jimmy took a deep breath and introduced himself.

"I'm Jimmy Mitchell," he said.

"I'm Chris."

"Coach Nixon told me to get some ice and put it in something," Jimmy began. "But I don't know where it is."

"I'll show you what to do," Chris said. "First, we need to go to the locker room underneath the stadium."

"Do you want to run?" Jimmy asked.

Chris's eyes narrowed.

"Is that supposed to be a joke?"

"No, sir."

Chris stepped closer, put his right fist against Jimmy's chest, and tapped him lightly.

"You may be a ninth grader, but that doesn't give you a free pass to make fun of me. If you want to get along on this football team, you won't ever say anything like that again."

Jimmy's eyes opened wide. "Yes, sir."

In the next instant, Jimmy was flat on his back on the ground with Chris on top of him. The older boy raised his fist to strike Jimmy in the face when a hand reached out and grabbed Chris's arm.

"Cool it, Meadows!" Coach Bolton barked. "What do you think you're doing?"

The coach pulled Chris off Jimmy, who scrambled backward and watched, stunned.

"He smarted off to me, Coach," Chris said. "First he asked me to run across the field, and then he started saying 'yes, sir,' and 'no, sir.' I warned him once and then—"

"Come with me," Coach Bolton said, dragging Chris away from Jimmy.

Jimmy shakily stood up. Coach Sellers came over to him.

"Chris has a problem with one of his legs. He can't run," the coach said.

Jimmy started moving toward Chris.

"I need to tell him I'm sorry."

Coach Sellers reached out and grabbed Jimmy's arm. "Coach Bolton will straighten him out."

Jimmy watched as Coach Bolton talked to Chris, motioned toward Jimmy, then pointed at his own head. In a few moments they returned.

"You boys get to work," Coach Bolton said.

"I'm sorry," Jimmy said.

"Forget it," Chris said.

As they walked, Jimmy could see that Chris had a pronounced limp. Chris didn't speak, and Jimmy kept his mouth shut. They reached the locker room.

"Here is the ice machine," Chris said. "Fill these coolers with ice and carry them to the practice field."

"Yes, sir."

Chris stopped and stared hard at Jimmy for a few seconds before motioning for him to do his work.

The morning practice session passed quickly. The players arrived and sat on the three bottom rows of the bleachers while Coach Nixon gave a short speech. Jimmy couldn't hear what the head coach said, because he was busy filling several orange coolers with ice and carrying them about four hundred feet down a steep hill to the practice field. During one of his trips, Max came over and greeted him.

"How's it going?" Max asked.

Jimmy told him about the near fight with Chris Meadows.

"Wow," Max said. "He's got a reputation for being touchy. I hope everything is straightened out."

"Me too."

Jimmy placed the coolers on a table and filled them with water from a short green hose. There were five coolers in all.

Practice began. Jimmy didn't have time to watch the practice on the field, but what he saw didn't look like a football game. No one threw the football or tackled anyone. The players wore practice jerseys, helmets, and gym shorts. The coaches walked around and yelled at the players who lay on the ground and stretched their legs, did push-ups, ran wind sprints, and hopped through ropes. None of it would help them beat Dake County.

The most difficult part of Jimmy's job turned out to be keeping track of all the players who threw empty paper cups on the field. He was so busy going up and down the hill to refill the coolers with ice that he wasn't present for every water break. Still, he had a long list of numbers, including several repeat offenders, by the end of the morning session.

Sweat poured off the bigger boys when they came to the drink table. Only Max, who had been assigned the number-twelve jersey, paid attention to Jimmy. The other boys ignored him. Max gulped down a cup of water.

"Are you having fun?" Jimmy asked as he slid several cups to the front of the table.

"Practice is bad," Max replied, his face red. "The games are fun. Are you and Chris doing okay?"

"Yes. Where are the footballs? I want Coach Nixon to see you throw the ball."

"The coaches won't get them out until this afternoon," Max replied. "Mornings are mostly for conditioning."

Jimmy was puzzled. "What?"

"We do exercises so that we can get stronger and be in better shape."

"You run wind sprints so you won't get tired in the fourth quarter," Jimmy added.

Max smiled. "That's right. You sound like Coach Nixon."

"Mitchell!" Coach Bolton yelled out. "We need more water at this end of the table."

Max crumpled his cup and dropped in on the ground.

"Don't do that," Jimmy said as he turned away. "Or I'll have to write down your number. Put it in the trash can."

At the end of practice, Coach Nixon called the boys over to the drink table.

"Give me the list," he said to Jimmy.

Jimmy felt the eyes of all the players on him as he handed the sheet of paper to the coach.

Coach Nixon looked down at the list and then pointed to the paper cups that littered the ground. "I expect you young men to leave everything on the field when you practice or play for this team"—he paused—"except trash. No trash playing allowed. No trash talk with players on other teams. And no trash is tossed on the ground for someone else to pick up. Everyone who plays for this team will do his part, every single second from this moment until the end of our final game. Is that clear?"

"Yes, sir!" the players responded.

Coach Nixon continued. "I'll be watching and find out if you mean it. If I don't call your number, you can leave. Those who still want to play football should be back here no later than three o'clock this afternoon. The following players will stay and run ten forty-yard wind sprints to remind them not to throw trash on the ground at the Cattaloochie County High School practice field."

As the coach read off the numbers, a couple of the players glared at Jimmy before they ran back onto the field. Jimmy watched as the boys ran across the field with the coaches yelling at them. Chris interrupted him.

"Clear off the tables. Put the coolers and cups in the locker room. We'll get them back out this afternoon."

Jimmy carried everything up the hill. Chris and the other manager, a boy named Will, ran errands for the coaches. When Jimmy finished, he walked up to Coach Nixon, who was talking with Coach Bolton. Jimmy waited for a pause in their conversation.

"I'll be back at three o'clock," he said. "Mama is going to bring me, and Daddy will pick me up on his way home from work."

Coach Nixon looked at him and stifled a smile.

"Coach Bolton didn't scare you off?" he asked.

"No, sir," Jimmy replied. "I'm not really scared of anything except swimming."

"He and Chris had a little misunderstanding, but everything is fine now," Coach Bolton said.

"We're a team," Coach Nixon said. "No fighting among teammates."

"Yes, sir. I don't like to fight."

Coach Bolton retrieved his pouch of chewing tobacco from his back pocket and pinched a healthy wad. Jimmy's eyes opened big as the coach deposited the leafy load in his right cheek.

"You'll do fine, Mitchell," Coach Bolton said, his voice somewhat muffled. "But don't let me catch you eyeing my tobacco pouch again. I won't share any with you no matter how nice you ask."

"Yes, sir."

— Twenty-seven —

By the end of the first week of football practice, Jimmy had greatly increased his knowledge about the duties of a real-life football manager. He'd carried a large mesh bag of footballs to the practice field, poured lime into the little machine that marked off the field, and learned that Coach Nixon wanted one teaspoon of sugar and two teaspoons of creamer in his coffee. The most interesting job was serving as an assistant to Chris Meadows while the senior manager taped up a player's ankles or wrists. Upon Chris's command, Jimmy would run to the locker room, open the correct drawer in the training-room cabinet, and bring the needed item. Jimmy continued to reply to the manager using "Yes, sir" and No, sir."

They were filling coolers with water when Chris held up his hand.

"Stop," he said. "How old do you think I am?"

Not sure, Jimmy didn't answer.

"Do I look as old as your father?" Chris continued.

That was an easy question.

"No, sir."

"That's my point. You don't talk to someone who is seventeen years old as if he was seventy-one."

"Grandpa is seventy-two," Jimmy said.

"Do you say 'yes, sir' and 'no, sir' to him?"

"Yes, sir."

"That's good, but I want you to stop doing it to me. If it happens one more time, I'm going to pretend I'm one of the coaches and make you run wind sprints until you're so out of breath you won't be able to say anything except 'yes' and 'no.' Do you understand?"

"Yes, sir." Jimmy nodded.

Chris glared at him for a second and then burst out laughing.

"Okay, you called my bluff. Go to the locker room and get the black knee brace I put on top of Ben White's locker. His knee is bothering him. Do you remember his number?"

"No," Jimmy replied.

Each player's locker was the same as his jersey number.

"It's eighty-one," Chris answered. "And you don't have to run."

Toward the end of practice, Chris took Jimmy to the equipment room, where the footballs, extra helmets, spare uniforms, and other items were kept. The room was a long rectangular space divided into three sections by shelves that reached almost to the ceiling. Equipment was organized by size and type. The room was a dumping ground. Chris picked up a scuffed helmet.

"The helmets come in different sizes," he began.

"I know," Jimmy interrupted. "It's like different hat sizes. I have a lot of caps, but unless I wear the right size, it won't stay on my head when I run fast."

"That's right."

Chris turned over a helmet and showed Jimmy the number written on the inside.

"This is the size. Put the helmets in a row on these shelves, beginning with the smaller ones and going to the bigger ones. Then you need to count all the helmets in the room and write the number on a sheet of paper. Can you do that?"

"Yes, sir."

Chris stifled a grin. "Once you're finished, find me so I can check your work. I don't want Coach Nixon to come in here after practice and find that it's been done wrong. I'll be on the practice field."

"I'll be careful," Jimmy promised.

Chris left, and Jimmy sat on the floor. He picked up a helmet and looked inside at the number but wasn't sure if it was big or small. He set it down and turned over another helmet. It had a lower number, but from holding it in his hands he couldn't tell whether it was bigger than the first helmet or not. Looking at a third helmet didn't solve his problem. He sighed in frustration.

He picked up a fourth helmet. When he ran his hand over the top of the helmet, he could feel bumps caused by tiny pieces of plastic flying off as the result of head-to-head contact on the field. From his usual seat with Mama and Daddy in the stands, Jimmy rarely heard the sound of helmets striking each other. He unsnapped the chin strap and put the helmet on his head. The inside of the helmet smelled like the pair of old tennis shoes he wore when he helped Mama in the flower beds. When he shook his head, it rattled around inside the protective headgear.

This gave him an idea.

He took off the helmet and checked the number. He selected another helmet, put it on, and shook his head from side to side. The second helmet was much tighter against his ears. That meant it was smaller. He took off the helmet and looked at the number. He then checked the number of the larger helmet. The relationship between number and size was solved. As a discovery, it didn't rival the Rosetta stone, but for Jimmy it unlocked the key to sorting football helmets.

He was sitting on the floor carefully placing the helmets in rows when he heard several football players enter the front part of the room.

"Close the door," a voice said. "This makes me nervous."

Jimmy heard the door click shut. He picked up another helmet and checked the number. It was one of the smaller ones.

"When will you have the money?" a second voice asked.

"Half before the game. The rest will be delivered by the snake man in the parking lot afterward," a third voice responded.

"Snake man?" the first voice asked.

"A creepy guy with a snake tattoo on his arm who works for the bookie. He's the person I have to talk to. I don't know his real name."

"How do we know this is on the level?" the first voice asked. "Nobody bets that much money on a high school football game."

"You're wrong. The bookie runs pools for guys who bet on more than one game. If they hit, he loses big; if not, he scoops up thousands. You should see his house. It's a mansion. All he needs to do is beat the point spread in a couple of games. That way he can set the odds better than anyone else and sucker people in."

"How do you know all this?" the first voice said.

"He gave Hal a summer job," the third voice spoke.

Jimmy knew Hal Sharpton was the first-string quarterback. His picture appeared many times in the school yearbook, and Jimmy recognized him on the first day of practice.

"Yeah, all I had to do was pick up packages for him in Atlanta. He paid me twice what I made last year sweating all summer for the landscape company. Everything was in cash, no withholding or anything taken out for the government."

Hal spoke, "Pete and I were part of this deal last year."

Hal Sharpton's best friend on and off the field was one of the running backs, Pete Gambrell.

Hal continued. "We were ahead in the Dake County game by five points and had the ball on our eight-yard line. All we had to do was grind out a couple of first downs and we would have won the game. It was a perfect setup. I fumbled the handoff on purpose and let a Dake County player take the ball away from me in the pileup. They scored and won the game. We each collected a thousand dollars."

"What if Dake County wins without our help?"

"We collect anyway, but they don't have a chance," Pete said. "They lost their entire defensive line. The odds against them beating us are going to be through the roof. That's probably why the bookie is willing to pay the extra thousand."

"The three of us can't guarantee a Dake County win," the first voice said.

Jimmy had stopped sorting helmets to listen.

"We don't have to. We can win the game and still collect the cash. Our job will be to make sure the score is closer than anyone expects. The day before the game, we'll find out the spread. If Dake County wins, that's great. According to the snake man, a Cattaloochie loss will mean bonus cash for us."

"But I'd like to make the play-offs," the first voice answered. "To kill ourselves in practice and not have a good season is a waste of a lot of pain."

"For which you'll be well paid if you go along with us," Pete said. "We don't know whether you or Hal is going to be playing quarterback, so both of you have to be in on the deal. I told the snake man our situation, and that's why he agreed to give each of us a thousand dollars. You'll also be on defense, so that might help, but we can't bring in anyone else. It's too risky, and I don't want to split the money. Even if you don't mess up a single play, you'll still get paid, so long as the score ends up on the right side of the spread. The extra cash sure came in handy for me last year, and I don't want to miss out. Senior year is going to involve some expensive partying."

"What about Max Cochran?" the first voice asked. "He must have thrown it fifty yards this afternoon."

"He's a freshman," Hal responded. "He won't even dress out with the varsity."

"And it will just be one game?" the first voice asked.

"Would it matter?" Hal responded. "At a thousand dollars a week, I'm ready to turn pro."

"You know I'm in," the first voice said. "I just need to get used to the idea."

"Good," Hal said. "I'll let him know. There's no backing out."

The boys left, and Jimmy returned to sorting the helmets. The mention of the snake man made him think about Jake Garner. Jimmy didn't know Jake was interested in the football team.

COACH NIXON CANCELED THURSDAY AFTERNOON PRACTICE because all the coaches were attending a coaching clinic in Marietta. Jimmy was eating lunch alone in the kitchen when the phone rang. It was Daddy.

"Do you want to work at the office this afternoon?"

"Yes, sir."

"Good. Let me talk to your mama."

Jimmy called to his mother, who took the phone, listened for a moment, then hung up.

"Do you want to ride your bike to Daddy's office?" she asked.

"Yes, ma'am."

"Are you sure you know the way?"

"Yes, ma'am."

"Do you want me to follow you in the car and make sure you don't get lost?"

"Yes, ma'am."

Mama smiled. "We'll leave in fifteen minutes."

Jimmy went outside, played with Buster, gave him extra water, and put his bike next to Mama's car.

"You lead the way," Mama said as she came down the front steps. "Don't worry about going too fast. I'm not in a hurry."

Jimmy started down the driveway. It was the heat of the day, but the motion of the bike produced a gentle breeze. It was a good thing there weren't any hills between the Mitchell house and the downtown area. Jimmy rolled along at an easy pace with Mama's car always in sight in his rearview mirror. He stopped at every stop sign, honked his horn, and proceeded safely through the intersections. He passed the courthouse and waited patiently for traffic to clear before turning left onto the street where Daddy's office was. He rolled up in triumph. Mama pulled in behind him. Jimmy wiped his sleeve across his forehead and walked back to Mama's car.

"Good job," she said through the open window. "If everyone obeyed the rules of the road as well as you do, there would be fewer accidents. Daddy can follow you home."

"Yes, ma'am."

"Bye. I love you," Mama said.

"I love you," Jimmy replied.

He went inside the office. Kate wasn't at her desk, so he went to see Delores. The secretary was typing on her keyboard.

"Hello, Jimmy," she said brightly. "Your daddy told me you were coming. He's at the courthouse but should be back shortly. Let me show you fresh pictures of my babies."

Delores showed him three photographs in small, clear plastic frames. Otto, Maureen, and Celine were each dressed up in red, white, and blue outfits: Otto had a little blue hat on his head, Maureen was wearing a star-studded vest, and Celine was decked out in a skirt made from multicolored ribbon.

"Aren't these cute?" Delores asked. "It was in celebration of the Fourth of July." Jimmy looked at the pictures and wondered what the cats thought about being dressed up in funny-looking clothes.

"Do you ever dress up Buster?"

"No, ma'am. He only wears his fur."

Delores returned the pictures to their place.

"I'm going to be out of town for several days in a few weeks. You did such a good job with the cats at Christmas that I would like you to help again. Your daddy told me you used the money you earned to buy a used bicycle."

"Yes, ma'am. I rode it all the way from my house today."

"Great, I appreciate you agreeing to help me. It takes a load off my mind when I don't have to worry about my babies."

Jimmy was puzzled, not sure how or when he'd agreed to take care of the cats.

"There is a file to be sorted on the conference room table," she said. "Your daddy may have something else for you to do when he gets back."

Jimmy began sorting the papers. There was an air-conditioning vent over the table, and he cooled off in a couple of minutes. When he finished, he went to Daddy's office, but Daddy wasn't there. Delores was talking on the phone, so Jimmy returned to the conference room. In one corner was a small table where he kept his legal pad and the dictation unit. Jimmy hadn't written anything on the legal pad, but he remained fascinated by the different sound of his voice on the tape recorder. He pressed the record button and began to talk. He played with it for several minutes until Daddy returned.

"I saw your bike outside," Daddy said. "Any problems riding over here?"

"No, sir."

"It will be nice when you can ride to and from the office by yourself. Do you want to put the bike in my car or ride it home after work?"

"I'd like to ride."

"Come with me. I need your help carrying some boxes from my car, and you can tell me about football practice."

Jimmy told about the morning's practice as they made two trips from the car to the office.

"Has Coach Nixon spit on you yet?" Daddy asked.

"No, sir, but it would be worse if Coach Bolton did it."

"Does he still chew Red Man tobacco?"

"I don't know, but there is an Indian on the little bag he carries in his back pocket."

"That's the same brand his father used when he worked for the sheriff's department. You could always tell his car because it had a brown streak down the side."

AFTER FRIDAY AFTERNOON'S FOOTBALL PRACTICE, JIMMY ATE a snack and went directly to bed. He wasn't tired, but he knew from experience that if he didn't force himself to take a nap, he wouldn't have a chance staying awake all night while fishing with Grandpa at Webb's Pond. Jimmy had accompanied Grandpa to the annual carp fishing contest longer than he could remember.

Grandpa had pictures of Jimmy, barely old enough to hold a pole, standing on the bank, hoping to catch a whopper.

Grandpa was the best fisherman in Piney Grove and had several dead fish hanging on the wall in his garage to prove it. Grandma didn't allow any part of a fish inside the house except meat to cook in the frying pan, so one side of the garage became home to a stringer of trophy-size, largemouth bass. Lined up in a neat row, the fish were glued to boards with their mouths open. Jimmy's favorite was chasing a lure positioned by the taxidermist in front of its gaping mouth. Once Grandpa let Jimmy shine a light into the fish's mouth. It was as empty as a cardboard box.

Grandpa used a small boat to fish the lakes of western Georgia and eastern Alabama. He usually went with a friend, either someone who had worked with him at Georgia Power or a buddy from Piney Grove. Many times he'd invited Jimmy to join him, but Jimmy wouldn't go onto the water, and no amount of argument or encouragement could change his mind. He limited his fishing with Grandpa to times when he could sit on a bank with the red clay firmly beneath his chair and the water at a safe distance in front of his feet. Carp fishing suited him best.

No carp swam across the wall of Grandpa's garage. These bottom-feeders weren't pretty to look at or good to eat, so carp lacked appeal to most fishermen. However, the men who fished Webb's Pond believed that convincing a thirty-pounder to suck a hook into its mouth as it vacuumed the bottom of the pond was the ultimate fishing challenge.

Jimmy was peacefully snoozing when Mama came into his room, sat on the bed, and gently shook his shoulder.

"It's six thirty," she said. "Your grandpa will be here in about thirty minutes to pick you up."

Jimmy rolled over and forced his eyes open.

"He's going to let me ride my bike." He yawned. "He'll follow me in the truck like you did the other day when I went to Daddy's office."

It was slightly over four miles from the Mitchell house to Webb's Pond. The roads weren't busy, but bicycle traffic wasn't common. Mama looked at the clock on his nightstand.

"It will be daylight until eight thirty. Are you sure that you'll have enough time to get there before the sun goes down?"

Jimmy sat up on the edge of the bed and stretched his arms in the air.

"Yes, ma'am. Grandpa says it won't be a problem."

"You can do it only if you promise to get in the truck if it gets dark. I don't want you riding a bicycle on a dark road."

"Yes, ma'am."

Mama stood up. "I packed several snacks: vanilla wafers with peanut butter, oatmeal cream pies, and bananas. And I bought something special for Grandpa to eat."

"Beef jerky?" Jimmy asked.

Mama nodded.

Grandma had banned beef jerky following Grandpa's heart attack, but Mama occasionally let Jimmy slip a spicy stick of the seasoned meat to the old man, who ate it with a satisfied grunt.

Jimmy quickly dressed and put his Ready Kilowatt hat on his head. This would be his first time to wear the cap at a fishing event, and the August contest at Webb's was the Bassmaster Classic of local carp fishing.

Downstairs, Daddy was relaxed in a recliner reading a book. When he saw Jimmy, he reached in his pocket and handed him a fifty-dollar bill.

"Here's your entry fee. Give it to Grandpa to keep safe for you."

Mama came into the living room and gave Jimmy a brown lunch sack and small cooler. She'd written his name on the bag just like she did on the days he took his lunch to school.

"Jimmy wants to ride his bike," she said. "Do you think they can get to the pond before dark?"

"Oh, yeah, but don't try to ride home in the morning. You'll be too tired."

"Yes, sir."

Daddy placed his book on the stand beside his chair.

"This might be your year to catch Moby Dick," he said.

"I don't think I could bring him in without help," Jimmy replied.

Moby Dick, a forty-five-pound monster, was the undisputed king of the pond. He'd been caught several times but never during the big tournament. Identified by a large scar that stretched from the corner of his mouth across golden scales covering his back, and a damaged tail fin, he remained a wily adversary. Grandpa had hooked him once and brought him close enough to the bank to make a positive identification before the big fish shook the hook from his mouth and slithered back into the dark depths of the pond. Jimmy had never seen him. A horn sounded.

"There he is," Mama said. "Don't make yourself stay awake if you get too sleepy. It's okay if you take a nap."

"Yes, ma'am."

Jimmy gave Mama a hug and swung open the front door.

Sticking out the back of Grandpa's truck were several very long fishing poles. Jimmy rolled his bike to the truck and handed Grandpa the fifty-dollar bill. Grandpa was wearing his Ready Kilowatt hat too.

"You're official," Grandpa said, slipping the bill into the front pocket of his shirt. "If you win first prize, what would you do with all that money?"

"How much money?"

"If enough people enter, there might be five hundred dollars for first prize, two hundred for second, and a hundred for third. The people who own the pond keep some of the money."

Jimmy sat on his bike. "If it gets dark before we get to the pond, I have to put my bike in the back of the truck."

"And walk the rest of the way?"

"No, sir. I'd ride with you."

"That sounds like a good plan. Do you know the way to the pond?"

"I think so."

Grandpa pointed out the window. "Get on the street in front of your house and ride that way until I tell you to turn."

Jimmy took off on his bike. Grandpa followed close behind. Together they made up a miniature parade. A few cars passed them.

"Turn right at the next stop sign!" Grandpa yelled out the window.

Jimmy slowed to a stop and honked his horn. He turned right, and they left the city limits of Piney Grove. The road was covered with rough asphalt. A dog barked as they passed a farmhouse, but after a hot day in the sun, it didn't give chase. Pine woods began to line the side of the road.

Webb's Pond was located at the end of Webb's Pond Road. Dusk began to creep across the sky as they slowed down and turned left. Grandpa flipped on the headlights of the truck and shone them on a large, hand-painted wooden sign that announced the date and place of the carp tournament. Included on the sign was the name of the previous year's winner and the weight of the fish caught: Dusty Abernathy—28 lbs., 13 oz.

"Stop!" Grandpa called out.

Jimmy pulled to the side of the road and waited. Another truck turned onto the road and passed them.

"Can you ride fast?" Grandpa asked. "It's going to be dark in a few minutes."

"Yes, sir."

"Then go!"

Jimmy took off on the bike. He never rode fast around town because of the stop signs and intersections, but on the flat, open road, he pedaled as furiously as he could. The bicycle tires made a whirring sound on the pavement as he picked up speed. The trees and underbrush beside the road flew by. He went in and out of shadows. With a final burst of speed, he reached the end of the road and a sign posted at the entrance to the pond. He put on his brakes and came to a halt. Breathing heavily, he looked back at Grandpa, who came up beside him.

"You almost outran the truck," Grandpa said through the open window. "I wasn't sure that I could keep up with you."

Jimmy took a few more deep breaths.

"It was like a wind sprint," he said.

"Five wind sprints," Grandpa replied. "Put your bike in the back of the truck. I'll drive you the rest of the way."

After Jimmy loaded his bike, they traveled a short distance down a dirt road and stopped. A man with a flashlight in one hand and a clipboard in the other stood in the middle of the dirt track that led to the water. Grandpa rolled down the window.

"Good evening, Jim," the man said, shining the flashlight into the cab of the truck. "Who's that with you? One of your power-company buddies?"

"He could be. Did you know Jimmy climbed all the way to the top of that pole in my backyard?"

The man stuck his head in the window and let out a low whistle. "That's amazing, Jimmy. Weren't you scared?"

"No, sir," he answered. "I'm not afraid of being up high."

"Well, you've done something I'd never think about trying. Should I put both of you on the list?"

"Yes, Gary," Grandpa said, handing the man Jimmy's money and taking bills from his wallet for his own entry fee. "How many are here?"

"A bunch. Word is out, and I've taken money from folks who live in Carrollton, Griffin, Villa Rica, even Cartersville. If you have a favorite spot, you'd better go straight to it."

"Any estimate on the prize pot?"

"I wouldn't be surprised if it pushes a thousand. We're going to limit the number of fishermen to fifty. It could get crowded at the popular spots."

Grandpa rolled up the window and drove toward a parking area beside a grove of tall pine trees.

"Gary Webb's family owns the pond," he said to Jimmy.

Grandpa stopped beside a shiny green SUV. There weren't any run-down fishing cars. Most of the pickups and SUVs scattered under the trees would have been equally comfortable at a fancy Atlanta shopping mall.

"Grab a couple of poles and the empty bucket," Grandpa said.

The long, sturdy poles looked more suited to surf casting than bank fishing in a seven-acre lake; however, large carp put up such a ferocious fight that they could snap smaller poles. Grandpa compared reeling in a twenty-five-pound carp to lassoing an angry bull and pulling him through a gate not quite wide enough to allow him to pass.

Jimmy dropped his snack bag in a bucket and grabbed two poles. Grandpa filled his arms with two more poles, a small cooler, and a tackle box. On the other side of the pine grove, they entered the open area created by the small lake. In the deepening dusk, lights and lanterns brought by other fishermen wrapped around the pond like giant fireflies. Jimmy could see men crouched down or kneeling beside coolers that held secret bait mixes.

"It's the south end for us," Grandpa said. "We'll find a spot, and then I'll go back to the truck for our lounge chairs. Fishing doesn't start for another half hour. You can guard our cooler."

Jimmy followed Grandpa. Some men called out in greeting as they passed by.

"What are you using tonight, Big Jim?" one man asked.

"Apricot, and if that doesn't work, chocoholic," Grandpa answered as he kept walking.

"I thought you liked strawberry," Jimmy said.

"He knows I'm kidding," Grandpa replied. "In a contest everyone keeps their mix as secret as a witch's brew."

"What's that?" Jimmy asked.

Grandpa grunted. "Don't tell your mama I said that. She wouldn't like it."

As they walked, Grandpa kept shining the flashlight back and forth from the water to the woods.

"There it is," he said. "Over on that tree."

Jimmy followed the direction of the light and saw a short yellow ribbon tied to the end of a small branch.

"I marked this spot a few weeks ago because there is a steep drop-off directly across from that ribbon. It's the deepest place on this end of the pond. Everybody else will crowd around the north end."

Sure enough, Jimmy could see a bunch of lights on the opposite side of the lake.

Grandpa continued, "Our plan is to put out a nice dinner for the big fish that want to avoid a crowded wait at the other end of the pond. There will be no delays at the Mitchell restaurant."

"Yes, sir."

They set up their gear on the bank with the tips of the poles facing the water.

"Sit on the cooler and don't get up until I come back," Grandpa said.

"What did you really put in the cooler?" Jimmy asked. "Is it wild cherry?"

Grandpa put his finger to his lips. "I'll tell you, but only if we're partners."

"What do you mean by partners?"

"We have to agree that if we win a prize, we'll split the money equally. If I catch the biggest fish, I'll give you half the money. If you catch the biggest fish, you'll give me half the money."

"I'll give you all the money," Jimmy answered immediately. "You need it more than I do. Daddy has lots of money and buys me everything I need."

"True," Grandpa said, chuckling, "but that's not the way it works with partners. It's share and share alike. Of course, you'll have to pay back the fifty dollars your daddy gave you."

Jimmy thought a moment. "Okay, but if we win a prize, you keep most of the money and come to church with Grandma on Sunday."

"Who put that idea in your head?"

"I did."

Grandpa took off his cap and ran his fingers through his hair. "I guess it won't kill me to listen to Brother Fitzgerald more than once or twice a year. I'll even put some of the money in the offering plate if that will make you happy."

"Yes, sir."

Grandpa turned to leave.

"Wait," Jimmy said. "What's in the cooler?"

Grandpa lowered his voice. "Some of the best grits a carp ever tasted. And I seasoned them just right with freshwater mussel flavoring."

"I've never heard of that one."

"I ordered it from a place in Canada. I bet no one else is using it. When I was scouting out this end of the pond, I baited up a hook and landed a couple of nice ones in less than an hour. The fish will swim right over the ordinary banana and strawberry flavorings and scoop up our fancy stuff."

Grandpa handed Jimmy the flashlight and left. Jimmy sat in the center of the cooler and shone the light across the water. Darker than the sky overhead, the surface of the water was covered with tiny ripples that made it seem to exhale in long breaths that ran beyond the reach of the light. Jimmy shuddered. He turned the light away from the water. It shone on a man's face covered in a thick gray beard.

Jimmy jumped.

"Sorry, son," the man said, holding his hand before his eyes. "I didn't mean to scare you."

Jimmy lowered the flashlight. The man had a long fishing pole in one hand and a cooler like Grandpa's in the other.

"I've never been to this pond and wondered where they're going to do the weigh-in."

"You'll have to ask my grandpa. He went to get our chairs. He'll be back in a minute."

The man placed his cooler on the ground and extended his hand. Jimmy shook it without standing up.

"I'm Alfred Walker. I drove over from Bartow County, but I fish for carp all over the state."

"I'm Jimmy Mitchell. I live in Piney Grove."

"A local. Do you fish here a lot?"

"Yes, sir. My grandpa has brought me here since I was a little boy. He's the best fisherman in the whole world."

"Is that right? What's in your cooler?"

Jimmy looked down at the white top of the container before answering.

"Bait," he replied.

"Are you willing to share your recipe with a fellow fisherman?"

Jimmy wanted to be respectful but wasn't sure how to respond.

"You'll have to ask Grandpa," he said after a moment's pause. "He's the one who mixed it up. He usually brings plenty."

Mr. Walker smiled. "And I guess you're guarding it until he gets back."

"Yes, sir. We're partners. That means if I win, I give him half the prize money."

"And if he wins, you get half the money?" Walker asked.

"Yes, sir. But I'd give him most of it, because I don't need money. Daddy and Mama buy me everything I need, and I already have a bike and a dog."

"What's your dog's name?"

"Buster."

Mr. Walker stroked his chin. "I'd like to be your partner, but that would be up to your grandpa. I'd hate to drive two hours over here and not even catch a small fish. Can you give me a hint about your bait?"

"What's a hint?"

"A clue, an idea about what it is. If you don't want to tell me it's okay, but we could make it a guessing game."

Jimmy knew about guessing games. It was one of the ways he learned. Daddy let him ask questions, but instead of telling him the answer, he would ask another question that guided Jimmy to the solution. That way the information would stick in Jimmy's mind. He thought for a second then pointed to his arm. Mr. Walker looked puzzled.

"Arm bait?"

Jimmy flexed his bicep like he'd seen the football players do. The other fisherman stared for a second and then smiled.

"Mussel. He's using freshwater mussel."

Jimmy grinned.

Walker picked up his cooler and moved into the shadows. "Thanks, Jimmy," he called as he disappeared from sight.

Grandpa returned.

"Who were you talking to?" he asked.

"A nice man named Mr. Walker. He lives in Bartow County, but he fishes for carp all over the state."

Grandpa opened up the chairs and positioned them firmly on the grass. Beside them he stuck two rod holders in the ground.

"What did he want?" he asked.

"To play a guessing game."

"About what?"

"Our bait recipe."

"Did you tell him?" Grandpa asked sharply.

"No, I made him guess."

Grandpa relaxed. "I bet trying to guess freshwater mussel would be pretty hard."

— Twenty-eight —

Jimmy had watched Grandpa prepare the bait for carp fishing many times. The bait consisted of a large gooey ball of grits seasoned with several teaspoons from the small bottle of fresh mussel attractant. Grandpa wrapped the glob around a hefty sinker positioned behind a large hook, then he attached a second, more complicated bait pattern to a device called a hair rig—a short line that extended in front of the hook. He carefully slid several tasty dough balls on the line and then surrounded the balls with more seasoned grits. In the middle of the two meals rested a naked hook.

Grandpa had taught Jimmy a lot about carp. The slow-moving fish lived to eat, and as they swam along the bottom of a pond or river, they constantly inhaled and exhaled debris in an effort to find something edible. A sharp hook would be quickly discarded unless it rested in the middle of a delectable feast of grits, dough, or specially manufactured ground bait. After it was cast into the water, the grit-based bait disintegrated in a few minutes, creating a meal as beautiful to a carp as a plate of pecan waffles and syrup. With a meal set out in two directions, the carp could be caught coming to dinner or nibbling on dessert. As it scooped up the seasoned grits, the carp would also vacuum up the hook, which could be set with a stiff jerk.

Grandpa elected not to go with a bare hook and carefully positioned a piece of corn cereal on its tip. He then doused the cereal in Texas Pete hot sauce. Jimmy squatted and watched.

"When Moby Dick takes hold of this hook, the hot sauce will make him so mad that he'll put on a run guaranteed to lock the hook in his jaw."

"That's how I want my hook fixed up too."

"Only if you help me."

They worked together and finished as the air horn sounded, signaling the beginning of the tournament. They didn't rush. Carp fishing was a marathon, not a wind sprint. Unlike bass fishing, which involved frequent casts to attract fish with moving targets, carp fishing was all about putting good bait in a good location, where it would stay for a long period of time. Grandpa walked to the edge of the water and carefully cast out to the area where the bottom of the pond sloped downward. He backed away and put his pole in one of the holders driven into the ground.

Jimmy picked up his pole. They walked toward the water together. Jimmy held the pole out in front of him but wouldn't go close to the edge.

"Let me cast from here," he said.

"Did you see where mine landed?" Grandpa asked.

"I think so."

"Cast to the right of it."

They took a few steps to the right. Jimmy held back his pole and let the bait sail across the water. It wasn't a long cast—he didn't want the bait to come off before sinking to the bottom of the pond. It plopped into the water with a splash that seemed loud in the stillness of the night.

"Good job," Grandpa said.

They placed Jimmy's pole in the other holder. Grandpa lit a small propane lantern and positioned it to shine on the tips of the rods. With everything in order, they sat down in the lounge chairs. Grandpa took off his Ready Kilowatt hat and rubbed his head. Jimmy did the same thing. At this point, carp fishing became more of a social event than a sporting contest.

"Fixing up that bait made me hungry," Grandpa said. "Did I see a couple of bananas in your bag of snacks?"

"Yes, sir, but Mama also sent you a treat."

Jimmy reached in the bag and found the beef jerky. He held it out. Grandpa peeled back the wrapper, took a bite, and sighed.

"If I were a fat old carp, I think this would be the bait I couldn't resist."

Jimmy ate a banana and an oatmeal cream pie. He then opened a bottle of spring water. Grandpa poured coffee from a red thermos into a Styrofoam cup. They sat in silence as they ate the food. They caught shadowy glimpses of other fishermen who, like them, were settling into a night of waiting. Jimmy could see the glow of cigarettes and hear the clink of beer bottles being removed from coolers. He could smell Grandpa's coffee.

"Thanks for coming, Jimmy," Grandpa said.

"You're welcome," Jimmy replied.

Grandpa took a couple of sips of coffee. "I'd rather go fishing with you than anyone else in the whole world."

"Why is that, Grandpa?"

"Because I like watching you grow up into a fine young man. I mean, I loved you when you were a little boy, but now you're a special young—" Grandpa stopped.

"That's okay," Jimmy replied. "I know it can mean a good thing to be special when you're the one saying it to me."

"That's right. You've grown up enough that when difficult things happen in your life, you don't let them keep you down. You have a lot of determination, which means you're not a quitter."

"I climbed the pole. All the way to the top."

"Right."

"And I rode my bike from our house to the pond."

"Yes. And you're going to high school and working as a manager for the football team. I believe you are going to surprise a lot of people with what you do in your life. Do you remember what I told you after you climbed the pole?"

"That I have the heart of a champion."

Grandpa smiled. "That's right. What else did I say?"

"That I can do anything I want to do."

"Correct."

Grandpa ate the last bite of beef jerky. He placed his coffee cup on a bare spot on the ground.

"Jimmy, do you ever think about the future?"

"What do you mean?"

"About what you'll do after you graduate from high school."

Jimmy took off his cap and pointed to the skinny figure on the front. "I want to be like you and work for the Georgia Power Company."

"I know we've talked about it, but I can't promise you that it will happen."

"I climbed the pole," Jimmy said.

"Yes, but there are other things you have to do as a lineman. It's a hard job in a lot of ways."

"You can teach me. I won't graduate from high school for"—Jimmy hesitated—"a while. I can learn a lot before that happens."

Jimmy glanced at their fishing poles. The tips of the fiberglass rods were as still as the night air.

"Well, your mama asked me to talk to you about it," Grandpa said. "She doesn't want you to get disappointed if becoming a lineman doesn't work out."

"Don't worry. Mama loves me a lot. But she worries about everything. She'll be proud of me when I become a lineman."

"She's a good wife to your daddy and a good mama to you."

"Yes, sir. I thank God for her after she leaves my room at night. Not every night, because sometimes I go right to sleep, but whenever I'm not too tired, I tell him. He knows."

Grandpa chuckled. "And he knows I tried to talk to you about the future. I hope that satisfies your mama."

They sat quietly. Jimmy stretched and yawned. Every so often, the quiet of the night was broken by the yell of a fisherman who hooked a fish. Jimmy's eyes grew heavy. Grandpa had wedged a lightweight blanket into the lounge chair. As the night cooled, Jimmy opened the blanket. Grandpa spread it over him and tucked it around his arms and under his chin.

"I'm not going to sleep," Jimmy said. "I'm just a little bit cold."

"I know. You don't want to miss the big strike."

The crickets chirped as if it were their last chance for a summer romance. Jimmy, surrounded by the sounds of the night, let his eyes rest for a few minutes. He awoke to a loud grunt from Grandpa. He had one of the poles in his left hand and his thumb on the lever for the bait-runner reel. Jimmy sat up and rubbed his eyes. Grandpa glanced over at him.

"I've got one," Grandpa said through clenched teeth. "And it's worth fighting." Grandpa braced the butt of the rod against his leg.

"He's still taking out line," he said. "I dropped a little drag on him for a few seconds, but he would have snapped it like sewing thread if I'd tried to put on the brakes."

Jimmy joined Grandpa. The tip of the rod inclined at a steady angle toward the water.

"Which pole is it?" Jimmy asked.

"It's mine," Grandpa answered. "Would you like to hold it?"

"Yes, sir."

Grandpa kept his hands on the pole as he passed it to Jimmy. As soon as it was in his grasp, Jimmy could feel the weight of the fish on the other end. Somewhere in the dark water, an angry carp was shaking its head from side to side as it bulled its way in the opposite direction. Grandpa released his grip. Jimmy held on tightly, but the power of the fish made him take two steps toward the water. He planted his feet more solidly on the ground.

"That's it," Grandpa said. "As soon as he slacks off, push down on the drag."

As if on cue, the line went slack. The fish had stopped its run.

"Reel it in!" Grandpa yelled. "It may be coming back this way."

Jimmy furiously cranked the reel, amazed at how much line lay limp.

"He may be gone," Grandpa said disappointedly, "but keep cranking to make sure."

Jimmy made a few more turns on the reel and then almost lost the rod when the line went taut and the fish took off for another run. Grandpa let out a yell.

"That's it, boy! You are onto that fish!"

Jimmy lost his footing and staggered closer to the water.

"Take it, Grandpa!" he said. "I don't want to fall in!"

Grandpa stepped forward and put his hands on the rod above the reel.

"Hold on. Let's walk it back together."

As the line spun out, they retreated up the bank. Only when they were back to the chairs did Grandpa take the rod.

"Good job," Grandpa said. "That's what partners do for each another. If we land this fish and it's a winner, you earned your prize money when you handled that run."

Jimmy didn't realize that he was breathing heavily until he let go of the rod. "Do you think it's Moby Dick?" he asked.

"If not, it's one of his nephews."

Grandpa carefully pressed the lever for the drag. The second run proved much shorter than the first, and Grandpa was able to keep tension on the line even when the fish doubled back toward the bank.

"He's coming back to meet us," Grandpa said. "Fill the bucket with water."

They had brought a large plastic bucket to carry fish to the weighing station. Jimmy picked up the green pail, took a few steps toward the water, and stopped. He looked at the black water and inched forward until about two feet from the edge.

"I don't want to get any closer," he said. "I might fall in."

"Just stay on the bank and scoop up some water! I can't drop him in a dry bucket and carry him to the weighing station."

Jimmy didn't move any closer to the water.

"Jimmy! Go!"

Jimmy pressed his lips tightly together and commanded his feet to march forward. Somewhere between his head and his toes the orders were short-circuited.

"I can't!" he wailed.

"Okay," Grandpa spoke with frustration. "Hold the pole while I do it."

Jimmy retreated. He didn't cry, but he felt embarrassed.

"I'm sorry," he muttered as he took the pole.

"Just hold it where it is."

The tension on the line had greatly decreased. The fish was tired, halfheartedly moving from side to side. Grandpa hurried toward the water. In his haste, he lost his footing and fell, sliding a few feet forward. Jimmy winced. It was his fault that Grandpa had to fill the bucket with water. The old man heaved himself to his feet and dipped the bucket in the water. The pole suddenly jerked forward and flew from Jimmy's hands. It skidded down the bank.

"Grandpa!" Jimmy yelled.

In a move worthy of an eighteen-year-old football player diving for a fumble, Grandpa lunged for the pole as it headed toward the water. His chest landed on the reel with a thud. He grabbed the barrel of the pole. The line zipped through his fingers.

"Ouch!" he called out as he loosened his grip.

Jimmy forgot his fear and ran toward the water. He grabbed the end of the pole with both hands just as Grandpa let go.

"I've got it!" he yelled.

Grandpa rolled onto his back and put his hand to his chest. Jimmy saw him.

"Are you all right?" he asked.

Grandpa eased up to a sitting position. He continued to massage his chest. "I landed on the reel and bruised a rib or something."

Jimmy felt the tension on the line slacken. He began reeling in the fish.

"That's good," Grandpa observed. "After all this fighting, I don't want to lose that fish."

Continuing to turn the reel, Jimmy stood up and walked backward. He saw something flash in the water.

"He's close!" Grandpa said. "Hold it there until I get in position."

Jimmy had seen Grandpa get in the water to land a large fish.

"Are you jumping in?" Jimmy asked.

"Not tonight. Reel it in slow."

Jimmy turned the handle of the reel. The fish now felt like a heavy stone being dragged toward the bank. As the fish entered the shallow water, it began to flop to the surface. In the lantern light, Jimmy could see the burnished gold color that marked a healthy carp. Grandpa grabbed the line and guided the fish into the bucket. He labored up the bank and set the bucket on the ground directly underneath the lantern. Jimmy peered into the water. Exhausted, the fish lay on its side with its gills moving back and forth. Grandpa reached into the bucket and took the hook from the left side of the fish's mouth.

"Did you see how easily the hook came out?" Grandpa asked. "It was at the edge of his mouth, and he'd just about wiggled it loose."

Jimmy reached into the water and pressed his fingers against the close-linked scales that covered the fish's body. It was cold and hard.

"How much does it weigh?" he asked.

"Over twenty pounds for sure," Grandpa replied. "Let's take him to the dam and find out."

Fish were measured and weighed at the east end of the pond. It was a spring-fed reservoir, so there wasn't really a dam, but the high bank on that side of the small lake gave the appearance of an earthen dam.

"What about the other pole?" Jimmy asked. "Should I stay and watch it?"

Grandpa shook his head. "It's four o'clock in the morning, and it hasn't moved in over six hours. We'll chance that it won't budge for five or ten minutes."

Grandpa picked up the bucket, then put it down.

"You carry it," he said. "My left side is bothering me, and I don't want to strain it."

Jimmy picked up the bucket. Filled with water and the large fish, it was heavy, and he had to lean over to keep it steady. Some of the water sloshed out and landed on his shoes. Grandpa walked beside him, shining the flashlight. They passed several fishermen. Some were sleeping in cots, their poles resting in holders with strike alarms. Others were awake, staring out at the water. Jimmy's arm began to ache, but he didn't complain. Grandpa's hurting his ribs was his fault. One man who knew Grandpa spoke to them.

"What do you have, Jim?"

"A lunker that just about killed me. I'll tell you about it later."

They reached the weigh-in station. Gary, the man who greeted them when they arrived, and another man were serving as officials for the tournament. With a sigh of relief, Jimmy placed the bucket on the ground. Gary reached down, grabbed the fish, and put it on a digital scale. Jimmy squinted through his glasses as the numbers went past twenty and stopped at twenty-four pounds, five ounces.

"Whose fish is it?" the other man asked.

"It was caught on Grandpa's pole," Jimmy answered immediately.

After they recorded the weight and time, Grandpa signed a sheet of paper.

"Will you dump him back in the water for me?" Grandpa asked Gary. "I'm sore from a fall, and Jimmy doesn't like to get near the edge."

Gary returned the fish to the bucket and carried it to the edge of the water. He turned the bucket on its side in shallow water. After a moment's hesitation, the carp slipped back into the pond to eat, grow bigger, and perhaps be caught the following year.

"Where does that one put us?" Grandpa asked.

Gary ran his finger down the sheet in front of him and didn't answer. Grandpa and Jimmy stood and waited. Gary finished his pass down the list, and Jimmy saw his hand return to the top of the page.

"Come on, Gary," Grandpa said. "If we don't have this thing locked up, I need to get back to our spot and throw out more bait."

"Calm down, Jim." Gary laughed. "I didn't have to check the list. You're in first place by about two pounds."

"Yes!" Jimmy exclaimed.

"How much longer till you blow the horn?" Grandpa asked Gary.

"Less than three hours."

Grandpa nodded and patted Jimmy on the back. "Let's see if we can lure Moby Dick with a tasty breakfast."

They returned to their fishing spot. Grandpa baited his pole and cast it into the water. Jimmy's pole remained in its holder.

"Church bells are calling me," Grandpa said with a grin. "It looks like I may have to put on my black suit."

"Yes, sir."

With both poles in place, Grandpa settled into his lawn chair.

"All that excitement wore me out," Grandpa said. "I'm going to rest my eyes and dream about what to do with the prize money. Can you stay awake and watch the poles in case Moby Dick decides to dine with us?"

"Yes, sir. I'm not sleepy."

Grandpa pulled his cap over his eyes.

THE CALM BEFORE THE ARRIVAL OF A NEW DAY WAS JIMMY'S favorite part of the night. Everything around him seemed on tiptoe waiting for the sun to burst forth. The ripples that disturbed the water during the night were gone, the surface of the pond still. By this time of the tournament, there were no new stories to tell, and conversation around the lake stopped as the fishermen joined with nature in silent vigil for the morning light. Jimmy checked the tips of the fishing poles. There wasn't the slightest twitch that hinted the presence of fish.

Grandpa was sleeping with his mouth slightly open and his chest rising and falling in peaceful rhythm. In the indistinct light, the familiar wrinkles on his face weren't visible, and his exact age would have been hard for a stranger to guess. To Jimmy, Grandpa was both old and young—a wise patriarch and adventuresome playmate.

Several times, Jimmy saw fishermen walk toward the weigh-in area. He wondered if he and Grandpa would keep first place. Grandma would be excited about Grandpa attending church. Except for Easter Sunday, he hadn't been back since the day Jimmy was saved. Grandpa stirred and sat up in the chair.

"No bites?" he asked sleepily.

"No, sir."

At 7:00 a.m., an air horn sounded, signaling the end of the tournament.

"Reel in your line, and we'll find out if our fish stayed on the leader board," Grandpa said.

Jimmy brought in his line and held it up. The cereal on the hook was gone, but its absence didn't prove a missed strike. Over the course of a night, tiny minnows could pick away at the bait until it fell from the hook. Grandpa cut the rigs from the line and returned everything to its place in his tackle box.

"Leave everything here," he said to Jimmy. "We'll load the truck after the final tally."

None of the fishermen gathering on the dam looked perky after a night in the open air without a shave or a shower. Those who had taken an extra holiday from shaving on the day before the tournament had grown a crop of serious chin stubble. Grandpa rubbed his left cheek. Jimmy could see that it was covered in white whiskers.

When the fishermen had assembled at the dam, Gary stood on a rock and spoke.

"I'm not going to give a speech or tell a joke, because you don't want to hear it. Now if I had a pot of fresh coffee that would be a different story. Then I'd—"

"Who caught the biggest fish?" a voice cried out. "I want my money."

Gary pointed toward the speaker and laughed. "Freddie, that minnow you brought up here would be bait-fish to the winners." He turned to his helper. "Hand me the list. There were some monster carp hauled out of this pond last night."

Gary looked at the sheet with an expression of surprise as if discovering for the first time the names of the winners and the weight of their catch.

"Third place and two hundred dollars goes to Bill Moore. His fish weighed twenty-two pounds, twelve ounces."

Jimmy knew Bill. He sang in the choir at church. There was modest applause. Jimmy, who liked to clap, made the most noise. Moore reached Gary and received his prize money.

Gary, raising his voice to a new level, announced, "Second place and three hundred dollars goes to Jim Mitchell! With help from his grandson, Jimmy, he wrestled in a granddaddy fish that weighed twenty-four pounds, five ounces!"

Grandpa started walking forward and motioned for Jimmy to follow. They wove their way through the crowd as men slapped them on the back and shook

302 • ROBERT WHITLOW

Grandpa's hand. The enthusiastic reaction reminded Jimmy of the congregation after he prayed with Brother Fitzgerald. Gary handed Grandpa some money. Grandpa took off his cap and waved it over his head. Jimmy did the same. Then they returned to the back of the crowd.

Gary cleared his throat. "And the grand prize winner is a Webb's Pond newcomer who cashed in on beginner's luck to land a giant carp weighing twenty-nine pounds, fourteen ounces. Alfred Walker, come up here and claim your thousand-dollar prize! Let's hear it for Alfred!"

All smiles, Walker wove through the crowd. Gary handed Walker a thick stack of bills.

"No need to count it," Gary said. "It's all there."

Walker raised the money to his lips and kissed it.

"What recipe did you use?" a man standing next to Jimmy called out.

Walker turned toward the voice, and his eyes met Jimmy's.

"You know I can't tell," he called out, "but I'll give you a hint."

The winning fisherman flexed his arm and pointed to his muscle.

— Twenty-nine —

Grandpa kept rubbing his chest as they loaded everything into the back of his pickup.

"Second place is pretty good," Grandpa said as he hoisted one of the lounge chairs over the tailgate. "But I'm not as good as your buddy Alfred Walker."

"You're the greatest fisherman in the world," Jimmy replied.

Grandpa positioned the cooler toward the front of the truck bed. He winced in pain as he leaned over the edge.

"I'm so tired and sore, I think I'll let you drive," he joked.

"Could you teach me someday?" Jimmy asked.

Grandpa chuckled. "You'll have to ask your mama about that. Do you want to ride your bike home? There won't be many cars on the road this early on a Saturday morning."

"No, sir."

"Then put your bike in the back and hop in beside it."

Jimmy put his foot on the tailgate.

"Can I ride inside with you?" he asked.

"Of course."

"Buckle up," Grandpa said as he snapped his seat belt in place.

Once the tournament ended, the fishermen didn't waste time departing for home to enjoy a shower and a hot breakfast. Grandpa and Jimmy were among the last to leave the pond. Grandpa wove back and forth through the trees, almost striking a slender pine sapling on Jimmy's side of the vehicle. Jimmy rolled up the window.

"Sorry," Grandpa said. "Keep your arm inside until we reach the highway."

Once on the pavement, Grandpa accelerated. Jimmy's eyes quickly became heavy. His head nodded forward and he wished he could sink into his bed. He leaned against the window glass.

Suddenly, his head jerked sideways as the truck swerved to the center of the road and then onto the shoulder. Jimmy looked up in alarm.

"Watch out!" he yelled.

He glanced at Grandpa. He was asleep with his chest against the steering wheel. Jimmy reached across and shook him.

"Wake up!"

Grandpa didn't wake up. The truck drifted sideways and left the road. Jimmy could hear the sound of gravel beneath the tires. The truck drifted away from the pavement, and the tires dropped into a ditch. The inside of the truck began to tilt sideways. Suddenly, it flipped on its side, and Jimmy's right shoulder slammed against the door. The sound of screeching metal filled the cab as the truck scraped across the gravel and rocks that lined the ditch. The truck kept turning over. Jimmy tried to brace himself, but he was tossed back and forth. For a second he was hanging from his seat belt as the truck rolled onto its top. Jimmy cried out. The truck slowed to a stop as it landed on the tires. It had rolled all the way over.

His heart pounding, Jimmy touched the right side of his head. His hand came away covered with blood. Grandpa, still buckled, lay sideways at an awkward angle on the seat. His eyes were closed. He didn't appear to be bleeding. Jimmy touched Grandpa on the shoulder.

"Grandpa! Wake up!"

Grandpa didn't move. Jimmy shook him harder.

"Grandpa! We had a wreck!"

No response.

Jimmy unbuckled his seat belt, turned sideways, and tried to open the door. It was jammed. He put his feet against it and pushed, but it didn't move. He turned toward Grandpa. Blood ran across Jimmy's eyes, and he wiped it away with the back of his hand. Grandpa's eyes were closed, and his mouth gaped open. Jimmy tried to straighten Grandpa's body, but it was too heavy.

"Grandpa! Can you hear me?"

Jimmy's panic increased. Hot tears flushed from his eyes and mixed with the blood oozing from his head. He pulled up his shirt and wiped his face. He didn't know what to do. In a moment, the tears stopped as quickly as they'd come. He had to think clearly.

"Grandpa," he said in a softer voice.

Jimmy reached out and touched the old man's forehead. It was warm, and Jimmy could feel beads of sweat above Grandpa's eyebrows.

The windshield was cracked. The hood of the truck was smashed in. Jimmy tried to roll down the passenger window, but the handle didn't work. Jimmy looked past Grandpa. The window on the driver's side was partially rolled down, but to get to the window he would have to crawl over Grandpa. Jimmy hesitated. He didn't want to hurt Grandpa, but he had to get out of the truck and go for help.

Blood continued to ooze from his head. He wiped it away with his sleeve. Grabbing the steering wheel, he pulled himself toward the driver's side door and tried to slide his body past Grandpa without hurting him. Jimmy transferred his right hand from the steering wheel to the door handle and pulled himself higher until he rested against Grandpa's leg. He tried to open the door, but it too was jammed shut. He grabbed the knob for the window with his left hand and turned it. It was stiff but moved a few inches before stopping. Jimmy tried to force it, but it didn't budge. Looking up at the window, he realized that he'd turned it the wrong way and closed it. Changing directions, he turned the knob several turns and watched the window slowly come down about two-thirds of the way, then stop. He pushed hard against the knob, but the window wasn't going any lower.

Grabbing the top of the window with a bloody hand, he pulled himself toward the opening. He was able to get his head outside but couldn't manage enough leverage with his feet to force his shoulders through the narrow opening. He tried to find a foothold on the floorboard, but his foot slipped off the brake pedal. He put his feet on the seat and pushed. His shoulders popped through the window, and his body followed. He tumbled onto the rocks and grass beside the road. More blood trickled down his face. The truck was at a slight angle, but he could still see inside. Grandpa remained fallen over onto the seat. He hadn't moved since the truck came to rest and gave no sign that he knew about Jimmy's efforts to escape. Jimmy stuck his face in the window.

"Grandpa! Please move!"

Jimmy was puzzled about why he could crawl from the truck even though bleeding while Grandpa, who didn't have a serious scratch, remained unconscious. Suddenly, Jimmy understood.

Grandpa's heart.

He frantically reached inside the truck and touched Grandpa's chest. He couldn't tell anything. He had to put his ear over Grandpa's heart and listen for the reassuring *thump, thump, thump*. Jimmy climbed up on the running board, but when he tried to put his right leg inside the window, he lost his balance and fell backward, landing hard on his tailbone. He groaned as a sharp pain shot up his spine. He sat still for several seconds before gingerly standing up. He felt slightly dizzy.

A sound in the distance caused him to glance down the road. A car was approaching from the direction of the pond. Items from the back of Grandpa's truck, including Jimmy's bicycle, were strewn alongside the road. Jimmy wiped more blood from his eyes and managed to lift his right arm in the air to wave. His world began to spin, and he blacked out.

WHEN HE WOKE UP, JIMMY WAS LYING ON A STRETCHER BEING lifted into the back of an ambulance. An EMT held his head steady in a neck brace as they slid him in. The doors closed and the ambulance turned onto the road. He heard the sound of a siren as the driver sped down the highway. A man held up a tube and needle. Jimmy tried to speak, but he drifted away before any words formed in his mouth.

He forced his eyes open as he passed through the sliding doors at the emergency room entrance for the Cattaloochie County Hospital. Jimmy felt a slight bump as the stretcher crossed into the building. People were walking everywhere, but someone had taken his glasses and everything looked fuzzy. He had a tube running from a bag on a pole into his left hand. He was rolled into a little room, and two men lifted him onto a bed. He heard a man's voice speak.

"He lost a lot of blood from the gash on his head. It was all over the cab of the truck."

A man came into view directly above him. He was wearing a white coat.

"Let me take a look."

The man removed something from Jimmy's head.

"It's still bleeding. Are his parents here yet?"

"No," a lady's voice responded.

The man in the white coat spoke. "Jimmy, I'm Dr. Pendergrass. I know your father from the country club. Can you understand me?"

"Yes, sir," Jimmy managed.

"You have a cut on your head. I'm going to stitch it up so it can heal. But first, I'm going to give you a shot to numb the skin so it won't hurt. Is that okay with you?"

"Yes, sir."

Jimmy felt pressure on his head.

"Where are my glasses?" he asked in a weak voice. "Did I break them?"

"We'll find them in a minute," the lady's voice answered. "You don't need them right now."

Jimmy stared up toward the ceiling. He could hear the people rattling instruments and washing their hands.

"This is going to sting," Dr. Pendergrass said. "But then it will be numb."

There was another pause.

"Hold him steady," Dr. Pendergrass commanded.

Jimmy felt hands on his head and both arms. Suddenly, streams of liquid fire seared through his scalp. He cried out.

"That's all," Dr. Pendergrass said in a moment. "Shave and prep him."

Jimmy continued to whimper. The doctor leaned over close to his face.

"That's the bad part. We're going to shave the hair away from the cut so I can do a neat job. Once your hair grows back, no one will know you've been in a car wreck."

Mention of the wreck caused images of Grandpa to flood Jimmy's mind.

"Grandpa," he said. "Where's my grandpa?"

"He's here at the hospital too," Dr. Pendergrass answered. "Other doctors are taking care of him."

"I want to see him!" Jimmy said, trying to sit up. "I need to listen to his heart!"

A hand gently pushed him back, and a soothing lady's voice spoke.

"The doctors taking care of him are listening to his heart. You need to lie still so you can be treated. That's what your grandpa would want you to do."

Jimmy knew the woman was right, but he still wanted to see Grandpa. In a few seconds, he could feel someone doing something to his head, but it didn't hurt. He closed his eyes. Dr. Pendergrass returned.

"I'm going to stitch you up. You'll feel pressure but no pain. It's important that you lie still. Can you do that?"

"Yes, sir."

Jimmy knew the doctor was touching his head, but it didn't hurt. He tried not to move. His nose began to itch.

"Can I scratch my nose?" he asked.

"Yes, but don't touch your head," the doctor replied.

Jimmy rubbed the bottom part of his nose until the itch was gone. Dr. Pendergrass continued working. Jimmy could hear snipping sounds.

"That's it," the doctor said, speaking to someone Jimmy couldn't see. "You can finish up."

Dr. Pendergrass came back into Jimmy's line of sight.

"You had a nasty cut on your head, but it's all closed up and will heal fine. I'll be sure to tell your father that you were a good patient."

"Yes, sir."

"His manners are amazing," the lady said. "I wish I could get my kids to be so polite."

The doctor left, and Jimmy closed his eyes. He wasn't sure if he went to sleep, but the next thing he heard was the sound of Mama's voice in the hallway.

"Mama!" he called out weakly.

"I'm here!" she said, rushing into the room.

Her face filled his vision, and he relaxed.

"Thank you for coming," he said, trying to smile.

"Don't be silly," she replied. "We were eating breakfast at a restaurant and didn't find out about the wreck until we returned home. How do you feel?"

"I don't know," Jimmy answered. "Where's Daddy?"

"He and your grandma are with Grandpa."

Jimmy's voice strengthened. He moved his legs toward the edge of the bed.

"I want to see Grandpa!"

Mama took his right hand in hers. "Lie down. You can't. He's in ICU."

"Where?"

"The place they take very sick people. The doctor believes he had another heart attack. That's why the truck ran off the road."

"Will they give him medicine?"

"Yes."

"And he'll get better?"

"We hope so."

Jimmy settled back into the bed. "Good. We won second place in the fishing contest, and he's going to church with us tomorrow."

"That's impossible," Mama replied. "He'll be in the hospital. It will take him a long time to get better."

"But he promised."

"He can't make that decision. The doctors will let us know what he can do."

"Will you tell them about the promise?"

"Yes."

Jimmy's eyes became heavy. "I'm getting sleepy."

"The doctor may have given you something to help you rest. Don't fight it. Relax. I'll be here with you."

Jimmy drifted off again.

HE AWOKE IN A DIFFERENT ROOM. MAMA WAS SITTING IN A chair beside his bed reading a book. He blinked and realized he had a pair of glasses on his face.

"I can see better," he said.

"Good afternoon, sunshine," Mama said, closing her book. "You've been taking a long nap. How do you feel?"

"My head hurts a little bit."

"The doctors want to make sure you don't have what's called a concussion. They believe you're going to be fine but wanted to examine you after you woke up. If you're okay, then we'll go home."

Jimmy touched the bandage covering the cut on his head.

"That's where you have stitches," Mama said.

Jimmy remembered the burning pain of the shots to his head.

"It hurt, and I yelled."

"Don't worry. Dr. Pendergrass told Daddy that you were a good patient."

"Where's Daddy?"

Mama scooted her chair close to the bed and touched Jimmy's cheek. "Grandpa is very sick. Daddy and Grandma are staying near him all the time."

"Grandpa had a heart attack," Jimmy said.

"Yes."

"Is he taking his medicine?"

"Yes, but there are some kinds of sickness that medicine can't help."

Jimmy thought for a moment.

"Did the beef jerky make him have a heart attack?"

"No, it wasn't caused by a stick of beef jerky."

"When can I see him?"

"You need to rest and wait for the doctor."

Jimmy tried to sit up. "I want to see Grandpa!"

"I know, but that can't happen right now. You have to get better yourself."

"I'm okay. Where is he?"

"In another part of the hospital. People can only visit him for a few minutes at a time."

"Why?"

"So the doctors and nurses can do their job."

"Have you seen him?"

"Yes."

"Did he tell you about the fishing contest?"

"No, he was sleeping, just like you."

A doctor came into the room. "The patient is awake!" he announced.

"Yes, and we're having a normal conversation," Mama replied. "Jimmy, this is Dr. Dennard."

Mama moved away from the bed. The doctor shone a light in Jimmy's eyes and asked him some easy questions.

"Can you sit up on the edge of the bed?" he asked.

Jimmy swung his legs off the bed and sat up.

"Does that make you dizzy?"

"No, sir."

"You don't have to call me 'sir.'"

"Don't try to change him," Mama said. "It's deeper in his brain than even a neurologist can go."

Dr. Dennard smiled and asked Jimmy to get out of bed and move around. Jimmy stood up but couldn't go far because of the tube attached to his hand. The doctor spoke to Mama.

"The CT scan of his head didn't reveal a concussion. I don't see any neurological problems, so I'm going to release him. It should take an hour or so to process the paperwork. Let me know if he complains of severe headaches or nausea."

After the doctor left, Jimmy remained seated on the edge of the bed.

"Can I see Grandpa before we go home?" he asked.

"I'm not sure. We'll have to check with his doctors. They have a lot of fancy equipment in his room."

"I won't touch anything."

"I know. Be patient. We'll have to ask permission."

The door opened, and Daddy entered the room. He came over to Jimmy, sat beside him on the bed, and put his arm around his shoulders. His eyes looked sad.

"Hello, son," he said.

Mama spoke. "The neurologist came by. There's no sign of a concussion, so he's going to discharge Jimmy this afternoon."

"I'm glad you're going to be okay," Daddy said, then stopped. His voice sounded shaky as he continued. "You were in a bad wreck. It's a good thing you were wearing your seat belt."

"Yes, sir. Grandpa had his on too. He wouldn't wake up."

Daddy nodded. "I know. Pray for your grandpa. Everybody needs to pray for him."

AN HOUR LATER, JIMMY, DRESSED IN CLEAN CLOTHES, RODE in a wheelchair to the hospital entrance. Since he knew he could walk, the requirement that he ride in the wheelchair didn't make much sense. It was a warm, humid afternoon with dark thunderclouds in the sky. The fishing contest seemed like it happened a long time ago.

"Daddy talked to one of Grandpa's doctors, and you may be able to see him tomorrow," Mama said.

"What about going to church? He promised."

"No, he's too sick."

"I'll pray about that too."

Mama didn't answer.

THE FOLLOWING MORNING, JIMMY GOT UP WITHOUT BEING asked and put on his Sunday clothes. It was promotion Sunday, and Jimmy's age group was slated to move into the class taught by Mr. Robinson. Mama was in the kitchen when he came downstairs.

"Did you call the hospital to see if Grandpa can come to church?" he asked.

"No. Your grandpa is still sleeping. Let me see your head."

While Mama inspected his bandage, Jimmy spoke.

"They need to wake him up so he can get dressed."

"No, Jimmy. Your daddy went to the hospital early this morning. We talked a few minutes ago. Grandpa is still too sick to go anywhere today."

Jimmy's face fell. "I prayed that he'd be better."

Mama gave him a hug.

"He's alive, Jimmy. That's the answer to our prayers."

She released Jimmy from her arms.

"I still want to go to church," he said.

"Does your head hurt?"

"No, ma'am."

Mama looked at the clock. "Okay. I'll get ready and take you."

IT SEEMED ODD DRIVING TO CHURCH WITHOUT DADDY. JIMMY held her hand as they walked toward the educational building.

"I talked to your daddy, and we'll go to the hospital to see Grandpa at two o'clock this afternoon."

"Will he be awake?"

"I don't know."

They entered the educational building.

"Do you know which classroom to go to?" Mama asked.

"Yes, ma'am."

The bandage on Jimmy's head raised more questions in Sunday school than Max's black eye did when he was in the sixth grade. Jimmy tried to smile when Max told him that he would make an awesome pirate, but his heart was heavy with thoughts of Grandpa. Other children tried to pry out details of the wreck and Jimmy's escape from the vehicle.

"Didn't the truck flip all the way over and land right-side up?" Denise asked.

"Yes."

"What was it like when it was rolling—"

Mr. Robinson called the group to order.

"Before I welcome all of you to the class, I want us to pray for Jimmy's grandfather."

Jimmy bowed his head, but instead of praying, he felt tears rush to his eyes. In the light of a new day, the shock of the accident faded, but the depth of feeling he carried for Grandpa could not be silenced. Jimmy sniffled, rubbed his eyes, and, not wanting to be embarrassed, hoped the judge would pray a long prayer. Too soon, the judge said, "Amen." Jimmy kept his right hand over his eyes for a few seconds and then blew his nose on his handkerchief.

Mr. Robinson began the lesson, but Jimmy didn't listen. He couldn't think about anything or anyone except Grandpa. The aching desire to put his head on Grandpa's chest and listen to his heart was more than he could bear. Several times during the fifty-minute class, tears welled up in Jimmy's eyes and rolled down his cheeks. He gave up trying to hide his feelings but managed to sit still as the tears fell from his face into his lap. Jimmy didn't know if Grandpa's heart was okay. His own heart was breaking.

At the end of class, Mr. Robinson asked Denise McMillan to pray. When she finished, the judge looked at Jimmy.

"Jimmy, please stay after class for a minute."

As the other children filed out of the room, Jimmy spoke in a tremulous voice.

"I'm sorry, I tried to listen, but—"

Mr. Robinson interrupted. "That's not why I want to talk to you. I'm very sorry about your grandfather. Is your daddy with him?"

"Yes, sir," Jimmy sniffled. "And Grandpa was supposed to be in church today because we came in second in the fishing contest."

"Fishing contest?"

Jimmy told the judge the terms of his partnership with Grandpa and his prayer that Grandpa might come to the church service and become a Christian. When Jimmy finished, the judge cleared his throat and blew his nose.

"Jimmy, you don't have to be in a church to get saved," he said. "It's something God does inside a person."

"But the reason we have church is so people can get saved."

Mr. Robinson managed a slight smile. "Yes, that's one of the main reasons. But let's look at it another way. What if we took church to your grandpa?"

"How would you do that?"

"I'll ask Brother Fitzgerald to visit him this afternoon. He might be going anyway, but I can make sure it happens."

Jimmy nodded. "Yes, sir. That would be nice. Mama is taking me to the hospital at two o'clock."

The judge nodded. "We'll meet you there."

"You're coming too?"

"Yes. If you can pray, I can help."

Jimmy hesitated. "And could we sing a song?"

"What would you want to sing?"

"Brother Fitzgerald will know."

"All right. Don't worry. Leave everything to me."

Jimmy and Mama sat close together, the lone occupants of the Mitchell family pew. The empty seats on each side emphasized the sense of separation from the other members of the family; however, Jimmy's reserve of tears was completely dry. When Brother Fitzgerald mentioned Grandpa during the pastoral prayer, Jimmy sighed deeply but didn't cry. Mama reached over, took his hand in hers, and squeezed it.

At the end of the service, Jimmy saw Mr. Robinson walk up to Brother Fitzgerald. Mama answered questions from people who asked about Grandpa. Others wanted a closer look at Jimmy's head. In a few minutes, Mr. Robinson parted the crowd.

"Ellen," he said, "Brother Fitzgerald was going to visit Jim tonight, but he's agreed to cancel another meeting and join me at two thirty."

"That's not necessary," Mama began.

"Yes it is," Jimmy blurted. "Grandpa couldn't come to church, so we're taking church to him. I want Grandpa to have church at the hospital so he can get saved. Mr. Robinson told me you don't have to be inside the church to get saved."

"We talked about it after Sunday school," Mr. Robinson added. "And I thought we ought to find a way to honor the spirit of Jimmy's hopes and prayers."

"I understand," Mama said. "Jimmy takes everything literally. His grandpa isn't conscious and may not be able to respond to a visit, but at the least, Lee, his mother, and Jimmy will appreciate it."

— Thirty —

Jimmy and Mama ate lunch at home before going to the hospital. Jimmy picked at his food and looked at the clock. After he helped Mama clear the table, he followed her around the house asking every two or three minutes if it was time to go to the hospital. Finally, Mama sent him outside to make sure Buster had plenty of food and water, but he was back within a minute.

"Come into the living room and sit down," Mama said.

Jimmy followed her. They sat beside each other on the couch.

"Tell me what happened from the time you left Webb's Pond until the ambulance arrived."

Jimmy took a deep breath and did his best. When he mentioned getting into the back of the truck, then changing his mind, Mama shook her head.

"Praise God," she said quietly.

"I remembered what you told me about riding in the back of the truck," Jimmy said. "So I got inside and fastened my seat belt."

"Something good did come out of the hearing with Vera," Mama said quietly.

Not understanding, Jimmy waited.

"Go ahead," Mama said.

Jimmy reached the point when he passed out.

"Everything went black, and I don't remember what happened next."

Mama was silent for a moment.

"Did you see a Watcher?"

"No, ma'am."

"One was there, keeping you from getting into the back of that pickup. You would have been thrown out and killed."

"Yes, ma'am."

Mama leaned over and gave him a hug.

"Do you see the Watchers less than you used to?" she asked when she released him.

"I don't know," Jimmy replied. "What about my bike?"

"I don't know where it is. We'll have to check on it later."

Mama looked at her watch and stood up.

"It's one forty-five. We'll go, but they won't let us in until two o'clock."

"Yes, ma'am," Jimmy replied as he shot toward the front door.

Jimmy was inside the car with his seat belt on before Mama could lock the front door. She backed up the car and turned it around.

"Jimmy, I need to explain what you're going to see when you go into Grandpa's hospital room. He will be lying on the bed asleep, but you won't be able to wake him up."

"I couldn't wake him up after the wreck."

"That's right. He's been sleeping the whole time since he had the heart attack."

"He was tired after we stayed up all night fishing. Sleeping all night helps. I don't feel tired now."

"No, this is a kind of sleep that's caused by the heart attack. His body is asleep because he's sick. He will have a needle in his hand like the one the nurse put in you at the hospital, and he will be hooked up to some machines that check on him when no one is in the room. You can't touch the machines."

"Yes, ma'am. I promise."

"His face is pale, uh, whiter than usual, because his heart is having trouble pumping blood to his body, and there is a tube in his nose giving him extra oxygen to help him breathe. He needs it because he's too weak to breathe very well on his own."

"I won't touch any of the tubes."

"Your daddy will be with you to show you what you can do."

They rode in silence until pulling into the hospital parking lot.

"Will you sing?" Jimmy asked.

"Sing what?" Mama asked in surprise.

"A song, so we can have a church service. Brother Fitzgerald will tell us what to sing. I talked to Mr. Robinson about it."

JIMMY FOLLOWED MAMA TO THE ELEVATOR. THE CATTALOOCHIE County Memorial Hospital had three floors. She pushed the button for the third floor. They stepped into a broad hallway. To the left was the nurses' station for the general patient population, and to the right, a door marked "ICU Waiting Area."

They went into the waiting area. It was a rectangular room with vinyl chairs and couches facing each other. A large clock with a second hand hung on one wall. Small groups of people stood in different parts of the room.

Jimmy saw Grandma, Daddy, and a few people from the church in the corner. When she saw him, Grandma came over to them. She looked sad and her face seemed to have more wrinkles. She gently touched Jimmy's head.

"Are you hurting, dear?" she asked.

"A little bit."

"I'm so thankful you weren't badly hurt. Your grandpa couldn't have stood the thought of it."

"How is he feeling this afternoon?" Jimmy asked, trying to sound grown-up.

"Not very well."

"Can I see him?"

Grandma pointed to the clock. "In a couple of minutes, but you'll have to be careful not to touch anything."

"I've explained the rules to him," Mama said. "And I'll be with him."

Grandma nodded. Her eyes became moist.

"Jimmy, I wish your grandpa could talk to you, but you'll have to use your imagination to fill in the blanks of a conversation. That's what I've been doing."

"What do you mean?" Jimmy asked.

"He's not able to talk, and the doctors aren't sure how much he can hear. But that doesn't mean you can't talk to him. You and I know him well enough to have an idea what he would say to us if he could."

Jimmy thought for a moment.

"I know what he would say if I asked him to bait my hook for me."

"What?" Mama asked.

"No, but I'll show you how to do it," Jimmy answered.

"That's it," Grandma said, glancing up at the clock. "I'm sure Lee will want to go back to see him with you."

At 2:00 p.m., Daddy, Mama, and Jimmy passed through a door at the left end of the waiting room. There were only eight rooms in the ICU area. The doors to the patient areas were open, and in one room Jimmy could see a skinny old woman in a bed. In another room, a man's head was puffy and purple.

"That young man was in a bad car wreck," Daddy said in a low voice. "He came in during the night."

Jimmy followed Daddy into the room and stopped. Grandpa's face had lost its usual color and looked white like it did in the middle of winter. Jimmy stood at the foot of the bed and looked around the room. There were tubes and machines everywhere. Daddy stood close to Grandpa's head and spoke.

"Dad, it's Lee again. Ellen and Jimmy are with me."

Not taking his eyes off Grandpa, Jimmy inched down the side of the bed. When he stood beside Daddy, he looked up.

"Can I listen to his heart?" he asked.

"Okay," Daddy said. "But be careful not to touch any of the tubes."

Daddy pulled away the sheet. Grandpa was wearing a pale green hospital gown. Jimmy lowered his head. Grandpa smelled different today. Jimmy turned his head so his ear would hit the proper spot on Grandpa's chest. He pressed his ear lightly against the gown and closed his eyes. He couldn't hear anything.

Jimmy jerked his head up in alarm.

"I can't hear anything!"

"It's there," Mama said in a soothing voice. "The sound of the machines is making it hard to pick up his heartbeat. Try again."

Jimmy repeated the process, pressing his ear tighter against Grandpa's chest. This time he could hear a faint *thump, thump, thump.*

"Yes," he said softly. "I can hear it."

Daddy put his hand on Jimmy's shoulder. "That's enough."

"No! I want to listen some more."

Daddy removed his hand. Jimmy pressed his ear closer. *Thump, thump, thump.*

The comforting sound brought back memories: the front-porch hello on the day Jimmy proudly showed off the bicycle he bought at the yard sale, a hug at the end of a long hike in the woods when Jimmy wanted to quit but kept going because of Grandpa's encouragement, and a night lying on a blanket under the stars at Webb's Pond when Jimmy fell asleep with his head resting on Grandpa's chest.

Jimmy breathed in unison with Grandpa and let the simple, pure union that had bound them together for as long as he could remember wash over him. Daddy touched his shoulder again.

"Jimmy, we have to go now. We're only allowed to visit for a few minutes every half hour."

Jimmy raised his head.

"Yes, sir."

He could go now. He'd seen his grandpa.

Returning to the waiting room, they found Brother Fitzgerald and Mr. Robinson talking to the church members who had come to visit. All the men shook hands. They had serious looks on their faces, but Jimmy felt at peace. He stood beside Mama and held her hand.

"How is he?" Mr. Robinson asked Daddy.

"About the same."

"What are the doctors telling you?"

"He has extensive damage to the left ventricle. The cardiologist says it's an anterior infarct that involves the scar tissue left four years ago, along with new damage. They started him on beta-blockers and other meds in the ER, but he's lost a lot of heart muscle."

"What's the prognosis?"

Daddy shrugged. "Because he survived the heart attack, there's hope he will slowly improve, but he'll never be able to live at home. There's no way my mother could take care of him by herself. At best, he'll be in a nursing home."

Jimmy stepped closer to the men and pulled Mama with him. Brother Fitzgerald moved over and joined them.

"When can we have church?" Jimmy asked.

"At two thirty," Brother Fitzgerald said.

"Only three people can go in at a time," Daddy said.

"How can we have church for Grandpa with just three people?" Jimmy asked.

"'Where two or three are gathered together in my name, there am I in the midst of them,'" the preacher responded. "That's what the Bible says."

"But I thought it was better to have more people in church," Jimmy said.

"Don't worry about that," Mama said. "This time it's going to be a small congregation."

Jimmy looked at the adults standing before him. He counted them and put his finger on his own chest.

"There are five of us. That's too many."

Brother Fitzgerald turned to Daddy. "I talked to the judge, and he thinks Jimmy and I should go along with either you or Ellen."

Daddy looked at Mama.

"You do it, Lee," she said, "He's your father, and Jimmy is your son."

"Okay," Daddy said, glancing at the clock. "We can go back to see him in about twenty minutes."

"Can we start church now?" Jimmy asked.

"What do you mean?" Daddy asked.

"Brother Fitzgerald can pray, and we can all sing in here."

The preacher looked at Daddy. "This boy is bold, isn't he?"

"There are some things he doesn't fear."

Mr. Robinson turned to Brother Fitzgerald.

"Preacher, call the congregation to order."

What followed was not a typical Sunday afternoon in the ICU waiting area. After Brother Fitzgerald talked to the attendant on duty and checked with the other people in the room, he assembled everyone wanting to participate in a semicircle beneath the clock. Several folks not associated with the Mitchell family joined them.

"Let us pray," Brother Fitzgerald began in a voice that filled the room and caused even those not with the group to bow their heads. He prayed a long prayer, but Jimmy kept his eyes closed to the end.

They sang "Amazing Grace." Jimmy stood beside Mama and enjoyed the clear sound of her voice. The preacher then asked for prayer requests. Family members of the young man who had been in the car wreck told about his situation. The elderly sister of the skinny woman who had suffered a stroke spoke up. More people from other parts of the room joined the group and voiced the burdens of their souls. When they finished, Brother Fitzgerald launched into one of the best prayers Jimmy had ever heard. There were several sniffles around the room as the names and problems of loved ones were mentioned. The preacher finished and glanced up at the clock.

"In a few minutes, I'm going to visit Jim Mitchell, but before I do, I want to talk to all of you about one of the most precious gifts God has given us—time."

Brother Fitzgerald spoke about every person's opportunity to redeem the time allotted to them by almighty God. He didn't yell but talked as if sitting with friends. Jimmy enjoyed it when the preacher hollered on Sunday mornings, but today it seemed right to do it differently. Daddy particularly seemed to be listening.

"Seek the Lord's presence throughout the day," the preacher said. "Let his praise be continually on your lips. And you will find the richness hidden in a life lived with God. Be like King David, who said, 'My times are in thy hands.'"

When he finished, the people quietly moved away. Brother Fitzgerald came up to Daddy, Mama, and Jimmy.

"Jimmy, are you ready?"

"Yes, sir."

DADDY LED THE WAY, FOLLOWED BY BROTHER FITZGERALD and Jimmy. This time Jimmy was prepared for the sight of Grandpa in the bed. He hadn't moved an inch. The three visitors stood at the end of the bed, and Brother Fitzgerald prayed. After he finished, Jimmy spoke.

"Please pray with him the way you did with me when I got saved."

The preacher put his hand on Jimmy's shoulder and looked into his eyes.

"Jimmy, you were able to hear and respond. Your grandfather is unconscious. The best thing to do now is pray that he will get better so I can share the gospel with him at a more opportune time."

"We hope he will wake enough to go to a nursing home," Daddy added.

Jimmy wasn't sure about the meaning of "opportune," but he knew what he wanted.

"No," he insisted. "Pray now."

Brother Fitzgerald looked at Daddy and shrugged.

"It won't hurt anything," the preacher said.

"Will you hold his hand the way you did with me?" Jimmy asked.

"Yes, I will."

Brother Fitzgerald moved to the side of the bed. Jimmy joined him. Daddy remained in the same place. The preacher took Grandpa's limp hand in his, bowed his head, and spoke the words that had come with power to Jimmy when he opened his heart to the Lord Jesus. Jimmy didn't close his eyes but watched Grandpa closely. Grandpa didn't repeat the prayer.

"In the name of Jesus, amen," Brother Fitzgerald finished.

Jimmy put his hand on top of the preacher's hand and repeated, "In the name of Jesus, amen."

As he looked lovingly at Grandpa's face, Jimmy thought he saw slight movement in his eyelids. Jimmy stared harder, and by an act of his will tried to force the old man's eyes completely open. But they didn't budge.

"I'll come back to see him later," Brother Fitzgerald said. "You never know what a person actually hears, but I'd hate to base the hope of salvation on a prayer at a time like this."

"My times are in thy hands," Jimmy said softly.

Both Brother Fitzgerald and Daddy looked at Jimmy in surprise.

"That's what you told us in the waiting room," Jimmy said, turning toward the adults.

As they left the room, Daddy said, "That sort of thing occasionally happens with him. It's not always verbatim, but it's close."

When they returned to the waiting room, Mama gave both Daddy and Jimmy a hug.

"How did it go?" she asked.

"Good," Daddy said. "Brother Fitzgerald did a fine job."

"Most people do. What about you, Jimmy? Are you satisfied?"

"Yes, ma'am. He prayed with Grandpa just like he did with me at the church."

"Did he respond?"

"Not as far as we could see," Daddy said before Jimmy could answer.

"You're right to care so much for him," Mama said to Jimmy. "There's not much we can do but pray. Your grandpa is in God's hands now."

Jimmy smiled. "That's what I think too."

Daddy kissed Mama on the cheek and rubbed Jimmy's hair.

"You're taller than you used to be," he said to Jimmy. "Mama will bring you back to see your grandpa this evening. You did a good thing asking Brother Fitzgerald to come this afternoon."

"When are you coming home?" Mama asked.

"I don't know, but for now I need to be here."

Mama and Jimmy left the hospital.

As they walked across the parking lot, Mama asked, "Who did you see in Grandpa's hospital room?"

"Grandpa," he answered simply.

"That's it?"

"Well, you, Daddy, and Brother Fitzgerald were there."

"I mean, did you see any Watchers?"

"No, ma'am. Do you think any of them stay at the hospital?"

"Oh, yes," Mama said confidently. "I'm sure they're there even if we can't see them."

IT WAS LESS THAN A TEN-MINUTE DRIVE FROM THE HOSPITAL TO the Mitchell home. Jimmy's bicycle was leaning against the front porch. The front wheel was warped, and it bore several new scratches. Attached to it was a note.

I rescued your bike. It needs some work, but I think a new front wheel will get it back in working order. I'm glad you were wearing your seat belt. Allen Askew, Deputy.

"That was nice of Deputy Askew to bring your bike. Daddy can get it fixed next week," Mama said.

Jimmy rolled it around to the backyard. The warped wheel made it wobble. He told Buster about Grandpa, then went upstairs to his bedroom, closed the door, and knelt beside his bed. The verse given to him on the day of his salvation returned.

"Behold, I make all things new," he said. "Please, do that for my grandpa."

He stayed on his knees and repeated the prayer several times. Another face floated across the surface of his mind. It was his daddy.

"And make everything new for Daddy too," he added.

There was a knock on the door. Mama opened it and saw him.

"Are you praying for Grandpa?" she asked.

"Yes, ma'am."

"Jimmy, there's no need to pray anymore. Grandpa is gone."

Jimmy got up and sat on the edge of the bed. Mama came over and put her arm around his shoulders.

"Gone?" he said, staring past Mama.

"Daddy just called. Grandpa's heart stopped beating a few minutes ago. The doctors tried to help but couldn't get it started again."

Jimmy didn't speak as the shocking news hit him.

"Is he in heaven?" he asked after a few seconds.

"We hope so."

Jimmy shook his head in disbelief.

"I won't get to see him anymore."

The sad kind of tears poured out of Jimmy's eyes. He wiped them away with the back of his hand.

"What am I going to do without my grandpa?" he wailed.

Jimmy turned his head, buried his face in Mama's shoulder, and wept. Mama held him. He cried and cried.

"I'm sorry," she said after Jimmy caught his breath and looked up at her. "He was a good man and a wonderful grandpa. We all loved him."

After another minute of tears, Jimmy lifted his head.

"I'll be okay," he said through his sniffles. "I understand."

"There will be other times of sadness," Mama replied.

"Yes, ma'am, but I know I'll see Grandpa again. It will just be a longer time between visits."

THE MITCHELL FAMILY DIDN'T SIT IN THEIR USUAL PEW AT the funeral service. Jimmy followed Mama and Daddy to the front bench on the left side of the sanctuary. Daddy sat beside Grandma, who held a tissue in her hand and wiped her eyes several times during the service. Jimmy didn't cry. Many tears had watered his heartache immediately after Grandpa's death. Now he was more likely to cry at the sight of the field where Grandpa taught him to ride his bicycle.

Brother Fitzgerald welcomed the congregation and prayed. The choir director led a song. Then two men who had known Grandpa for a long time walked up to the pulpit.

The first speaker was a retired lineman from the Georgia Power Company.

"We both started working for the company about the same time. One day we were both on top of a pole bolting on a cross arm. Out of the blue, several hornets attacked and started stinging us. I'm allergic to any kind of bee poison."

The man rubbed his forehead. "I remember getting three stings right across here. I was getting weak and having trouble breathing. Jim was getting popped by the hornets as much as me, but instead of getting off the pole, he came around and brought me down against his chest. He was incredibly strong."

"That's the way he carried me," Jimmy whispered to Daddy.

"He radioed for help, and an ambulance took me to the hospital where I got a shot that saved my life."

The man pointed to a gray-haired woman in the front row.

"Sarah and I got married the next summer," the man said. "We have four children and ten grandchildren. None of them would be here if Jim Mitchell hadn't risked his life to save mine. No better man ever put on a yellow helmet. It was an honor to work with him for almost forty years."

A second man, one of Grandpa's fishing and hunting buddies, told about Grandpa secretly putting a fake deer head with a huge rack of antlers in the woods behind a large tree.

"We were creeping through the underbrush when he stopped and pointed in the distance. We saw the rack on this deer, and Jim said it must have come down out of the Smoky Mountains. We got so excited that we all fired at once. Of course, the buck didn't move, so we fired again. After the third round of shots, Jim started laughing so hard that we stopped and realized we'd been had."

People laughed at the story. Jimmy glanced at Daddy, who was smiling too. After Grandpa's friends talked, Brother Fitzgerald said some nice things about Grandpa but, to Jimmy's surprise, didn't mention praying for him at the hospital. A friend of Grandma's sang a sad song, and Brother Fitzgerald prayed to end the service.

A smaller group of friends and family went to the church cemetery for the burial. The First Baptist Church didn't have a graveyard beside the church, so many years before, the church had purchased land not far from Daddy's office to use as a cemetery. A slow-moving line of cars made the brief journey to the burial site.

Mama held Jimmy's hand as they walked past the grave markers. Jimmy read the names out loud until Mama told him to hush. In front of a freshly dug grave rested a headstone with both Grandpa's and Grandma's names on it. Chiseled beneath the date of Grandpa's birth appeared the date of his death. Jimmy held his breath as the casket was lowered into the ground. He'd seen Grandpa's body during open-casket visitation at the funeral home, but the old man in a black suit lying in the shiny box wasn't the loving companion Jimmy carried in his heart. Jimmy had no desire to touch the dead body or even stare at it very long. He had enough living memories to last a lifetime.

After the casket was lowered and Brother Fitzgerald said another prayer, Grandma shoveled some dirt into the hole. Jimmy watched wide-eyed, shocked that Grandma was going to shovel dirt with her nice clothes on. To his relief, she handed the shovel to Daddy, who did the same thing, then passed the shovel to a dark-suited man Jimmy had seen at the funeral home. The man leaned on the shovel but made no effort to fill in the hole. They left the cemetery with the grave still open.

"Who's going to put dirt in the hole?" Jimmy asked Mama. "Should I offer to help?"

"No, there are men who do that to make money."

"I could do that job," Jimmy said, "if I don't go to work for the Georgia Power Company."

THEY RETURNED TO JIMMY'S HOME. GRANDMA CAME WITH them. On the coffee table in the living room were several copies of a newspaper story about the carp fishing tournament that appeared on the same day as Grandpa's obituary. The fishing story made Grandpa seem more alive than dead. Jimmy's name was also mentioned.

A steady stream of people flowed through the house for the rest of the afternoon. Some of the guests acted as if Grandpa's death wasn't a big deal. They joked and talked about other things. Jimmy stayed close to the people who seemed interested in telling stories about Grandpa. He heard a lot of new information. Nobody asked him to add to a conversation, so Jimmy kept his thoughts about Grandpa to himself.

After everybody left, Daddy took Grandma home. When he returned, he collapsed in a chair in the living room. Mama brought him a cup of coffee fixed the way he liked it. Jimmy followed her.

"I'm beat," Daddy said.

"How was your mother?" Mama asked.

"More tired than I am. She's already in bed."

"We'll invite her over for supper this week," Mama said. "I'm sure some of her friends will do the same."

"Yes, but today was good for her. She enjoyed hearing so many people tell stories. Dad would have liked it a lot too."

"I have a story," Jimmy said. "Do you want to hear it?"

"Sure," Daddy said, taking a sip of coffee. "What is it about?"

"The fishing contest."

"That's right. I never got a chance to ask you about it. Didn't you win second place?"

"Yes, sir. Grandpa and I were partners."

"Start at the beginning," Mama said, folding her hands in her lap. "I want to know everything."

Much had happened since the night at Webb's Pond, but as Jimmy talked, the events came back to him. Talking about Grandpa made him seem alive again. Jimmy reached the part about Alfred Walker guessing the makeup of Grandpa's carp bait recipe.

"I showed Mr. Walker my muscle."

Daddy interrupted. "Did he guess the recipe?"

Jimmy wrinkled his brow. "I'm not sure, but Mr. Walker caught the biggest fish."

Daddy winced and turned to Mama. "It's a good thing Dad never found out about the hint. You know how carp fishermen are about their secrets."

"Keep going," Mama said.

Mama's eyes moistened when he described Grandpa agreeing to go to church if they won a prize. When he reached the part about the fight with the fish, Daddy interrupted.

"Did he have to go into the water to get the rod?"

"No, sir. He fell on it like a football player grabbing a fumble and hurt his side. Do you think that's why he had another heart attack? I've been worried about it."

"No, no. The heart attack was caused by something that had been building up inside his blood vessels for a long time. I'm sure he's happy that fishing was his last activity on earth."

Jimmy sighed. "That makes me feel better. Oh, and we talked about how I could be a lineman for the Georgia Power Company. Grandpa was going to start teaching me."

"Really?" Mama asked in surprise.

"Yes, but now I don't know who will show me what to do."

Daddy looked at Mama and shook his head. Jimmy continued his story. He concluded with the winners of the tournament.

"Everybody clapped and yelled when the man called out Grandpa's name. We walked up front and Grandpa got the money." Jimmy paused. "What happened to the money?"

"Grandpa had it in his pocket," Daddy said. "Grandma has half, and I'm saving your half for you."

"You can keep it," Jimmy said. "And then the man said that Mr. Walker caught the biggest fish. I don't remember what it weighed, but I think we lost by about two pounds. How much is that? I didn't ask Grandpa."

"Not much," Daddy said. "You still caught a whopper of a fish."

"Mr. Walker won one thousand dollars. We put our fishing stuff in the truck, then left the pond."

Jimmy stopped, realizing what came next.

"Do I have to go on?" he asked.

"No," Daddy said. "We only want to hear the happy parts."

— Thirty-one —

Later that night, Jimmy lay on the bed and stared at the ceiling. He remembered Alfred Walker kissing the thousand-dollar first prize. Grandpa didn't fish so he could win money, but because he loved to fish. Jimmy wondered if Hal, Pete, and the other player who wanted to get paid a thousand dollars after the Dake County game loved football or money.

DADDY HAD PLAYED FOOTBALL FOR COACH NIXON AND explained to Jimmy that the first week of high school football practice was devoted to physical conditioning. During the second week, the coaches began to evaluate the players and identify their strengths and weaknesses. Coach Nixon wanted all defensive players, even linemen, to be quick on their feet. An agile player could dodge a block or run around a slower offensive lineman and disrupt the rhythm needed for an offense to move the ball. Coach Nixon and Coach Bolton expected their defensive players to spend most of the game in the opposing team's backfield getting to know the quarterback and running backs on a helmet-to-helmet basis.

On the offensive side of the ball, Coach Nixon had a different point of view. He wasn't committed to either the running or passing game. If two big, fast running backs could be matched with a dominating offensive line, Cattaloochie County would grind down the opposition. If a talented quarterback could throw to a bevy of speedy receivers, the Captains would fill the west Georgia sky with passes. In either case, the opposing defense would be exhausted by the fourth quarter.

DURING IDLE MOMENTS OF THE DAY, JIMMY FREQUENTLY HAD TO remind himself that Grandpa was gone. Over and over, he caught himself starting to say something about Grandpa, then stopped. He'd lost his greatest cheerleader. Mama loved him, but Grandpa believed in his future.

At football practice, Jimmy tried to stay busy and not be sad. Daddy dropped Jimmy off early at the empty practice field.

"The coaches will be here in a minute," Daddy said. "I have to be in federal court in Macon."

"It's okay," Jimmy replied as he closed the door of the car. "I can go to the locker room and wait."

An underground sprinkler system watered the practice field during the night and, when combined with the dew, created a hazy carpet of silver moisture that reached from one end zone to the other. Jimmy took several steps onto the field. When he looked behind, he could see the dark spots left by his shoes.

Grandpa's death made Jimmy wonder about the future. He continued walking across the wet grass. Reaching midfield, he turned around again to see his footprints. He opened his eyes wide in amazement at the crooked path. He thought he'd taken a straight route to the fifty-yard line, but in fact he'd wandered in a zigzag pattern.

"I don't know where I've been until I look back," he said.

The prints reminded him of something Brother Fitzgerald liked to say on Sunday mornings. He said everyone should follow Jesus by staying on the straight and narrow way. Jimmy looked at the unspoiled grass before him and closed his eyes.

"Jesus, I need your help to walk on the straight and narrow way."

He opened his eyes and stepped forward.

"Jimmy Mitchell!" a voice called out.

Jimmy looked up and saw Chris Meadows standing on the hill near the locker room. Over the past weeks, Jimmy's friendship with the head manager had continued to grow. Chris called Jimmy at home after Grandpa's death to tell him that he was sorry.

"Come up here! I need your help!" Chris yelled.

Jimmy ran across the grass without looking back. He was slightly out of breath when he reached the top of the hill.

"What were you doing down there standing in the middle of the field?" Chris asked.

"Thinking and praying."

"Okay, whatever works for you," Chris said. "We need to put together two uniforms. A couple of transfer students are going to be here today, and Coach Nixon left me a note to assemble equipment for them. One is a lineman and the other is a wide receiver. He gave me a list of the sizes they need for each part of their uniforms."

"I know about the helmets," Jimmy said.

"Did you get them all sorted?"

"Yes. I did it the day Hal, Pete, and another player came in. They talked about the Dake County game."

"Dake won't be a problem this year," Chris said. "They barely beat us last year after a stupid fumble at the end of the game. Since then, they lost a bunch of seniors. Your buddy Max Cochran and the junior varsity could give them a good game."

They reached the dented double doors leading to the locker room. Made of metal, the doors were painted in the school colors: one gold and one blue. Chris had a set of keys as big as the ones carried by Mr. Lancaster, the janitor who worked at the First Baptist Church. He unlocked the door. A sour smell lingered in the air of the large room.

"It stinks in here," Chris said. "Open the vents above the lockers while I turn on a couple of floor fans."

Jimmy stood on a stool and pushed open the long, narrow windows over the lockers. The sweet smell of fresh air drifted in.

"You did a good job organizing the helmets!" Chris called out from the equipment room. "We need to get everything to their lockers before practice this morning."

Jimmy returned the stool to its place beside a large grease board used by the coaches to diagram plays. In the equipment room, he found Chris making two piles of uniform items and equipment.

"Coach Nixon will let a player pick his number if it's not already taken. This player wanted eighty-one," Chris said. "Why do you think he would pick that number?"

Jimmy stopped and thought a moment before picking up the pile. "A player whose grandpa is eighty-one years old. If he's wearing jersey number eighty-one, his grandpa will be able to see him on the field and know that his grandson loves him."

Chris shook his head. "The real reason is that he's a wide receiver, but I like yours better."

It took two trips for Jimmy to put everything in locker eighty-one. He hung up the practice jersey and football pants and placed the helmet on a smaller shelf at the top of the locker. Coach Nixon insisted that the players keep their lockers neat. Jimmy could have opened almost any locker in the room and found everything in the correct place. He returned for the second player's equipment.

"According to the uniform, this guy is huge," Chris said.

Jimmy looked at the pile. Shoulder pads, football pants, and helmet. He looked inside the helmet and saw the number. It was the biggest one in the equipment room. Jimmy put it on. It swallowed his head.

"You'd have room for two of your heads in that one," Chris observed. "This guy is going to be number fifty-one. Why would he get that number? It's probably too old for one of his parents and too young for a grandparent."

Jimmy picked up the massive shoulder pads. They hung down to the ground. "That's easy. Mama says that big parents have big children. Maybe this player's father played football and had number fifty-one on his jersey. His son wants the same number."

Chris's mouth dropped open. "Whoever says you're retarded—"

Jimmy stepped back as if he'd been hit in the stomach. He turned and ran from the equipment room. He heard Chris's uneven steps behind him. Jimmy reached the doorknob and yanked the door open. Chris reached him, put his hand against the door, and slammed it shut.

"I want to go outside," Jimmy said, his voice trembling.

"I'm sorry," Chris said, continuing to lean against the door. "That was wrong for me to say. It's not true. You already do a better job than the boy who worked with me last year. You're going to be one of the best managers ever."

Jimmy looked away and held on to the doorknob. Chris put his hand on Jimmy's shoulder.

"Please, come back so we can finish. Don't you think I know what it's like to be different? People have always called me names and made fun of me behind my back."

Keeping his head down, Jimmy released his grip on the door.

"From now on, I promise to be careful what I say," Chris added. "Don't you want to keep being a manager?"

Jimmy glanced sideways. "Yes."

"Why didn't you say 'yes, sir'?"

"Because you're not an adult."

Chris smiled. "Correct. And I bet you're also right about number fifty-one."

JIMMY'S HURT DIDN'T LINGER. BY THE TIME THE COACHES and players began to arrive, his outlook had brightened with the morning sun. He started filling up coolers with ice from the ice machine located near the front door.

"Good morning, Jimmy," Coach Nixon said when he passed by.

"Good morning," Jimmy replied.

Each of the coaches either spoke a greeting or patted him on the back as they entered the room. Chris brought over two more empty orange coolers.

"These are the last two," he said.

"You were right," Jimmy responded. "I'm doing a good job as manager. The coaches like me."

Coach Nixon stepped over to the grease board and blew his whistle. The sound was loud in the full locker room.

"Listen up!" Coach Bolton barked. "Coach Nixon wants your full attention."

The players, some in full uniform, others partially dressed, stopped and turned toward the head coach. Coach Nixon didn't speak until everyone in the room was quiet.

"We have two new players with us this morning," he began. "One is a transfer from Villa Rica. Some of you may remember number eighty-one and the seventy-five-yard touchdown pass he caught when we played them last year. His family has moved to Cattaloochie County, and we expect double that from him when we play Villa Rica in October. This year he's going to be wearing number eighty-one for us. Stand up, David Noonan."

A lean black teenager stood and smiled. The players around him pounded him on the shoulder pads in greeting.

"Our other transfer student isn't as quick on his feet as Noonan, but if he hits you once, you won't forget it. He played last year for San Marino High School in California. He'll be wearing number fifty-one, the same number his father wore when he played professional football. Stand up, Zeke Thomson."

An enormous young man rose to his feet. Only one other player on the team, a senior who played center, matched him in size. Zeke flexed his arms, revealing surprisingly well-defined biceps for a heavy player. One of the Cattaloochie seniors hit Zeke on the shoulder pads. Zeke turned around and reciprocated the blow. The other boy grunted and stumbled backward. Coach Bolton laughed. No one else touched the new player.

"We'll have our first game in two weeks against Dake County. Most teams don't play a big rival the first game of the season, but the opener against Dake County has been on the Cattaloochie schedule since some of your fathers played for the Captains."

Jimmy thought Coach Nixon looked in his direction but couldn't be sure. Coach Nixon's face became even more serious than normal.

"Last year Dake County beat us at the end of the game. Before we go out and start hitting this morning, I want each of you to remember how you felt after that loss."

Coach Nixon paused. Jimmy had been to so many Dake County games that they ran together in his mind. He knew the Dake County football team wore green-and-white uniforms, and the school mascot was a goat. The Dake County cheerleaders brought a live goat with them to the stadium for home games and kept it tethered to a metal stake driven in the ground. When Dake County scored a touchdown, one of the cheerleaders would unhook the goat and run with him in front of the cheering fans. Once, Jimmy spent most of one quarter watching the goat eat pieces of popcorn thrown by fans returning from the concession stand. A nice cheerleader in green and white saw him watching and told him the goat's name was Popcorn. People fed the goat popcorn because they believed it would help their team win. Coach Nixon interrupted Jimmy's daydream.

"Hal Sharpton!" he barked, his voice cracking slightly. "How did you feel after we lost to Dake County last year?"

Jimmy looked at the tall senior quarterback. "It was the worst night of my life since I started playing peewee football."

Coach Nixon lowered his voice. "No more fumbles in front of our own end zone at the end of the game?"

The room became deathly quiet.

Hal looked startled. "No, sir."

Coach Nixon stared hard at the quarterback before shifting his gaze to another player. "Pete Gambrell! What about you? How did you feel after we lost last year?"

The stocky running back shifted his broad shoulders and glanced toward Hal before answering. "I was mad, Coach."

"Mad enough to go hard after a fumble in a pileup?"

"Yes, sir."

"And Brian Brown. Where were you when we lost to Dake County last year?"

Jimmy stood near the second-string quarterback and saw a look of fear come into the young man's eyes. Brown's voice quivered slightly when he answered.

"I was sitting in the stands, Coach. I played in the junior varsity game and didn't dress out for Friday night."

"If you want to be on the field with the varsity this year, then zero mistakes is your goal. Do you understand?"

"Yes, sir."

Coach Nixon slapped his hands together. "Good. Let's go out and have a good practice. You're going to get so tired of hitting each other during the next two weeks that when we go into Dake County's stadium, you'll be ready to unload with both barrels on every green-and-white jersey that comes in your sights."

Jimmy picked up one of the orange water coolers and headed for the door.

"Jimmy!" Chris called out.

Jimmy turned as the other manager limped over to him and pointed to Zeke Thomson's enormous back exiting the room.

"You were right about him," Chris said. "His daddy wore number fifty-one."

BOTH MAMA AND DADDY WERE IN THE CAR WAITING TO PICK up Jimmy following the morning practice. He opened the back door. Mama spoke before he was on the seat.

"How was practice?" she asked.

"More like a real football game. The players wore their uniforms, and they did running plays and passing plays. Max got to be the quarterback, and he threw the ball to a new player, who scored a touchdown. Do you believe Max will get to be the quarterback this year?"

"No," Daddy answered, as he backed up the car. "Coach Nixon never plays ninth graders on varsity."

"Tomorrow I'm going to learn how to hold the poles the men use to show how far the team has to go for a first down."

Jimmy glanced out the window as they passed the drive-in where Grandpa bought him ice-cream cones on summer afternoons. Jimmy loved soft-serve vanilla dipped in melted chocolate. They rode in silence for a few moments.

"Do you think Grandpa will watch the Dake County game?" Jimmy asked.

Daddy looked at Mama, who shook her head.

"If he does," Daddy said, "he'll have the best seat in the stadium."

— Thirty-two —

Before school started, Mama took Jimmy to the high school several times to show him the rooms where his classes would meet. At the end of the first day, he and Max met at their lockers. Jimmy was trying to cram all his books into his new blue backpack.

"Do you have homework in every class?" Max asked.

"No. I don't have any homework. Mrs. Forrest, the special education teacher, helped me with my homework here at school."

"Then leave your books in your locker."

"But Mama likes to see my school books."

Max nodded. "Then take two home tonight and two different ones tomorrow."

Jimmy selected two books for his backpack and slipped it over his shoulders.

"Let's walk to football practice together," Max said.

"Are you ready to play in the Dake County game?" Jimmy asked as they turned into the main hallway.

"I don't think I'll even be wearing a uniform," Max replied. "You're the only person on earth who believes Coach Nixon is going to let me play. My mother may not even come to the game."

"She'd better be there, and Coach Nixon has to let you play so the Captains will win."

Max laughed out loud as they exited the building and began the short hike to the locker room.

"I'm the third-string quarterback behind Hal Sharpton and Brian Brown. They would have to move away or get kicked off the team for me to play."

"But they don't want to beat Dake County," Jimmy replied.

"They'd better, or the coaches will wear them out in practice next week."

They reached the locker room along with a stream of other players. In between running errands for Chris and chasing balls for the field-goal kicker, Jimmy watched Max efficiently run a few plays with the second-team offense.

THE DAKE COUNTY GAME CAME AT THE END OF THE FIRST full week of classes. The entire student body focused on the upcoming football game. Students from each class stayed after school on Wednesday afternoon to work on banners and signs that would line the hallways Thursday. The messages were split between encouragement for the Cattaloochie Captains and threats directed against the Dake County Rams. As a manager, Jimmy didn't have time to participate in art activities, but he spent so much time admiring the banners on the walls that he arrived late for Mrs. Murdock's class. His favorite banner had two panels. In the first, a Captain and a Ram, both with heads down, were running full tilt toward each other. In the second, the Captain stood in triumph over his fallen foe, who lay on his back with his legs up in the air like a dead bug.

Wednesday football practice reached a new level of intensity. It was the last full-contact practice of the week, and the sound of grunts and the smacks of high-speed collisions reached the sidelines. Chris wasn't too friendly, and he wore his own version of a game face. His instructions to Jimmy were short.

"Take a mesh bag of balls and give them to Hal and Brian. They're going to be working with the receivers on plays from the thirty-yard line."

Jimmy dragged the bag behind him. He wasn't sure about the location of the thirty-yard line, but he saw Hal and Brian standing next to each other with receivers split out to either side. Jimmy stood between them holding the bag open so they could easily retrieve them. The two quarterbacks alternated throwing balls. Hal grabbed a ball and tossed it to Brian.

"We have our meeting after practice."

"Where?"

"In the parking lot on the other side of the gym. He'll be in an old white Ford pickup."

Brian threw a pass. He perfectly led the receiver, who caught the ball on a dead run in front of the goalpost a couple of yards into the end zone.

"I still can't get over Coach Nixon's speech," Brian said. "Why did he single us out?"

"Who knows, but it settled everything for me," Hal responded. "If I had any doubt, that took care of it."

It was Hal's turn to toss a pass. He released the ball, but it barely made it to the five-yard line.

"It slipped," he said. "Intercepted."

"Not a very good act," Brian answered. He glanced at Jimmy. "Dump out the rest of the balls. You don't need to hold the bag for us."

"My grandpa used to drive a white pickup," Jimmy offered. "He climbed poles for the Georgia Power Company."

Hal looked at Jimmy as if seeing him for the first time. Brian pointed to his own left temple and shook his head.

"Good for him," Hal said.

"When is the snake man going to give you a thousand dollars?" Jimmy asked.

Both players stopped and turned toward him. A husky tight end running a short pattern turned around to catch a ball that remained in Brian's hands.

"What did you say?" Hal asked.

"The snake man. I've seen part of the snake on his arm but not the head."

"How did you, uh, what are you talking about?" Hal asked.

"You, Pete, and Brian were talking about it in the equipment room. If you don't want to beat Dake County, do you think Coach Nixon would let Max be the quarterback? I know he wants to win."

Brian's voice seemed scared. "Did you talk to Coach Nixon about this?"

Jimmy shook his head. "No."

"Sharpton! Brown!" the offensive coach yelled across the field from the sideline where he stood beside Coach Nixon. "End the tea party and get back to work! Mitchell! We need some water for the offensive line players. Move it! Now!"

Jimmy immediately started running toward the water jug. He didn't want to make Coach Nixon or any of the assistant coaches mad.

"Mitchell!" Hal called out. "See me in the locker room after practice."

The first-team offensive and defensive lines were practicing blocking drills. Jimmy stayed away from the flying bodies. He kept running back and forth to the locker room on errands for the coaches and to fill cups with water. He'd learned where each coach kept his gear, so when Coach Bolton ordered him to bring his red notebook, Jimmy knew exactly where to go and what to do.

Practice ran long, and Jimmy saw Daddy's car parked in the gravel area at the far end of the field. Jimmy followed the coaches and players as they trudged up the hill to the locker room. Jimmy had an empty water cooler in one hand and a bag of footballs draped over his shoulder. Inside the locker room, he reported to Chris for further directions.

"Return the extra gear in that corner to the equipment room," Chris said, gesturing toward the rear of the room. "Do you think you can figure out where everything should go?"

"I can do the helmets," Jimmy replied. "But I'm not sure about the other stuff."

"Look inside the pants for the size. The numbers for the shoulder pads are behind the neck. There isn't much. I'll check on you as soon as I finish everything else."

Jimmy moved the pile into the equipment room. He wanted to work as fast as possible so Daddy wouldn't have to wait for him. Jimmy sorted the pants and shoulder pads and then took the helmets to the rear area of the room. He lined the helmets in a row from smallest to largest. He felt a tap on his back.

"I'm almost done, Chris," he said.

The hand spun him around. It was Hal Sharpton. Behind him stood Brian Brown. Both boys looked very serious.

"You had no business spying on us, you little retard," Hal said.

Jimmy's eyes opened wide.

"I need to go," he said. "My daddy is waiting on me."

Hal put out his arm to block the way. Jimmy could see that the equipment room door was closed. Brian stepped forward.

"You're not leaving this room until you tell us who you've been talking to."

Frightened and confused, Jimmy blurted out, "I don't understand."

"What did you hear?" Brian asked.

"Nothing."

Hal pushed him in the chest. "Don't lie to us. Who did you talk to?"

Jimmy frantically searched for an answer. "Uh, Mrs. Forrest, my teacher," Jimmy blurted.

"What did you tell her?"

"That I would do my homework after supper because we had football practice."

"This is ridiculous," Brian said. "He's an idiot! There's no telling what he's done."

The equipment room door opened, and Chris came in.

"What's going on here?" he asked.

"Nothing, crip," Hal said. "Beat it."

Chris lunged forward and punched Hal in the side of the head. The football player staggered back, and before he could recover, Chris pushed him to the floor and jumped on top of him, raining repeated blows to the head and neck. Jimmy watched in shock. Hal recovered enough to land a hard blow to Chris's mouth, causing the manager's head to jerk back. Brian ran to the door.

"Fight!" he yelled.

In seconds Coach Bolton appeared in the doorway.

THE FOUR BOYS SAT SILENTLY IN COACH NIXON'S OFFICE. The head coach held the phone receiver against his right ear. Daddy stood in the corner of the room behind Jimmy with his hand on his shoulder. Chris, a trickle of blood still seeping from the corner of his mouth, stared straight ahead. Both of Hal's eyes were beginning to swell shut, and he gingerly touched his left cheek. Brian tried to avoid eye contact with the head coach. Images of fists and blood bounced around inside Jimmy's head. He stared at the blood coming from Chris's mouth. Jimmy was breathing fast, and he felt dizzy. Coach Bolton stood beside Coach Nixon's desk.

"As soon as the rest of the parents are here, let me know," Coach Nixon said, hanging up the phone. He turned to the boys assembled in the room. "Everybody except Jimmy and his father go to the locker room with Coach Bolton and wait there."

Hal, Chris, and Brian filed out behind Coach Bolton. As soon as the door closed, Coach Nixon looked at Daddy.

"We couldn't get a straight answer out of him," Coach Nixon said. "He was so upset that nothing made sense."

"Try again," Daddy said. "It might help if I ask the questions."

"Go ahead," Coach Nixon said with a wave of his hand.

"What happened?" Daddy asked.

Jimmy opened his mouth, but all that came out was a stuttering, "Uh, uh, f-f-fight."

The pace of his breathing increased.

"I know that," Daddy said gently. "What caused the fight?"

Coach Nixon interrupted. "Lee, I think he's hyperventilating."

Jimmy's eyes rolled back in his head, and he fell off the chair.

WHEN HE REGAINED CONSCIOUSNESS, JIMMY WAS LYING ON A table in the training room where the players' ankles were taped. The school trainer, Mr. Millsap, stood beside him. Daddy held his right hand. Jimmy tried to sit up.

"Not so fast," Mr. Millsap said. "Rest for a minute."

Jimmy turned his head to the side. No one else was in the room. He closed his eyes. His breathing seemed normal again. He heard a door open and shut. There were voices in the locker room. He opened his eyes.

"I feel better," he said.

"Okay, sit up slowly," Mr. Millsap said.

Jimmy sat up and moved to the edge of the table. "What happened?" he asked.

"You fainted," Daddy replied.

"Like after the wreck?"

"Not nearly so serious. You started breathing too fast and passed out."

"Can you stand up?" Mr. Millsap asked.

"Yes, sir."

Mr. Millsap smiled. "He's better. His manners are back."

Jimmy stood to his feet.

"Dizzy?" Mr. Millsap asked.

"No, sir."

"Let's go home," Daddy said.

MAMA HAD SUPPER ON THE STOVE WHEN THEY WALKED INTO the kitchen.

"Why are you so late?" she asked.

"There was a fight in the locker room," Daddy replied. "And Jimmy saw it."

Mama quickly stepped over to Jimmy and put her hands on the sides of his face. "He looks pale."

"He hyperventilated and passed out," Daddy continued. "He was woozy for a few minutes, but he's fine now."

"What happened?" Mama asked.

"I'm not sure. Coach Nixon promised to call me this evening and let me know what he found out."

"Did anyone hit Jimmy?"

"No."

"What did Jimmy tell you about it?"

"Nothing yet. He was too upset to talk at the school. One of the boys was bleeding from a cut to the mouth, and another had bruises around his eyes. It was a traumatic thing for Jimmy to see. I thought it would be better to let him calm down before asking him any questions."

Mama hugged Jimmy tightly.

"I'm so sorry," she said. "Do you want to go upstairs and lie down?"

Jimmy peeked around Mama's head and looked at the stove.

"No, ma'am. I'm kind of hungry. What's for supper?"

MAMA ANXIOUSLY WATCHED JIMMY EAT THE BAKED CHICKEN. It was covered with tan-colored gravy and so tender that he could easily pull the meat away from the bone with his fork. He dipped each bite in the gravy. Each mouthful made him feel better. Carrots and lima beans occupied the other half of his plate. Mama had baked soft yeast rolls.

"Do you feel better?" Mama asked as he cornered the final bite.

"Yes, ma'am."

The phone rang, and Daddy answered it.

"Yes, Coach," he said. "I can talk. We just finished supper."

Jimmy started to leave the table, but Mama put her hand on her arm and shook her head.

"Stay in case Daddy has a question to ask you."

"May I have another piece of bread?" Jimmy asked.

Mama placed another roll on his plate. Jimmy cut a hole in it and dropped in a pat of butter that melted into the hot bread. He turned the roll on its end and repeated the process.

Daddy was listening, not talking. Finally, he spoke.

"Are the police going to get involved?"

He nodded his head as Coach Nixon responded.

"What do you think Jimmy should do?"

There was another moment of silence.

"I agree. Thanks for calling."

Daddy hung up the phone and returned to the kitchen table.

"They're going to handle punishment of Chris Meadows and Hal Sharpton as an internal matter. It was a serious fight with injuries, but none of the parents wanted to press criminal charges. Both boys are suspended from the team for at least four weeks."

"What about Brian Brown?" Mama asked.

"No punishment. He was in the room but not involved in the fight."

"What does *suspended* mean?" Jimmy asked.

"Hal can't play, and Chris won't be on the sidelines as manager."

"Max can play quarterback," Jimmy said confidently. "He threw a long pass to—"

"What caused the fight?" Mama interrupted.

"Hal made a negative comment about Chris's deformed leg."

"Oh, I hate that kind of thing," Mama said.

"Chris can't run, and it makes him mad when someone makes fun of him," Jimmy explained.

"Mad enough to fracture one of Hal's cheekbones. Chris may lose a tooth, so there was plenty of damage on both sides."

"And Jimmy saw all this?" Mama asked.

"He was there when it started," Daddy said, "but it was just a coincidence."

"Hal and Brian were being mean to me," Jimmy added.

"How?" Daddy asked.

"They wanted to know who I'd told about the snake man."

Mama and Daddy exchanged a look.

"Snake man? Do you think it could be another name for Jake Garner?" Mama asked.

"Maybe," Daddy answered. "But why would Jimmy be talking about Garner? It's been a long time since that trial."

"Jimmy saw him at the courthouse when Garner tried to get you to represent him," Mama responded. "He's always wanted to see the rest of the tattoo on Garner's arm. Isn't that right, dear?"

"Yes, ma'am."

"But why were you talking about him with the other boys?" Daddy asked Jimmy.

"They know him too," Jimmy said. "But they didn't call him Jake Garner. He was just the snake man."

Daddy was silent for a moment. "It could be somebody else."

Mama tossed her head to the side. "How likely is that? You got Garner off, and now he's selling drugs to young people at the high school! I never felt comfortable about that case."

"Don't try to argue constitutional law with me. Protection of Garner's rights is protection for us all." Daddy looked at Jimmy. "Did they say anything about drugs?"

"No, sir, only a book about the Dake County game."

"There's no problem with that as a topic of conversation," Daddy replied, looking at Mama. "The players have to have the playbook memorized from cover to cover."

"Why would Garner be interested in the playbook? Should he be protected now if he's doing something illegal?"

"No."

"Then why don't you report him to the sheriff's department?"

"What do I tell them? That Jimmy thinks Garner has a nickname and has been talking to high school students about the playbook? Probable cause requires more than an unsubstantiated suspicion about an unidentified person."

Daddy turned to Jimmy. "If you hear anything else about this, let me know."

"About what?"

"The snake man."

"Yes, sir."

"But for goodness' sake, don't talk to anyone except us," Mama quickly added. "I don't want anyone to hit you."

"No, ma'am."

— Thirty-three —

With ten minutes left in the fourth quarter and Cattaloochie County comfortably leading Dake County by twenty-one points, Coach Nixon inserted Pete Gambrell into the game as a substitute defensive back. Pete tripped and fell while covering a Dake County wide receiver, and the Rams scored a touchdown. After the kickoff, Brian Brown threw an interception on a screen pass that resulted in another Dake County score. Jimmy watched Coach Bolton throw his clipboard so hard against the ground that it stuck up like a knife.

"Cochran!" Coach Nixon yelled.

Max, who had been allowed to dress out for the game, trotted up with a uniform as clean as when his mother took it from the clothes dryer.

"Do you think you can take a hike from the center and kneel down?" Coach Nixon asked in a spray of saliva.

"Yes, sir."

"Then do it to run out some clock, and we'll see if our defense can win this game."

Jimmy watched proudly as Max ran onto the field. He took the snap from the center and quickly dropped to one knee.

"No, Max, throw it!" Jimmy yelled.

After a repeat of the first play, Jimmy ran over to Coach Nixon, who was surrounded by the assistant coaches. Jimmy weaved his way through.

"Why doesn't Max throw a pass?" he asked.

Not immediately aware of the source of the question, Coach Nixon glanced around.

"He's a good passer," Jimmy said.

"He's doing what I told him to do," the coach replied.

"Get back to the drink table," Coach Bolton added.

Jimmy returned to the table where cups of water waited in neat rows for players who wanted a drink.

With Chris suspended from the team, Jimmy's job duties had increased. He also had to keep a supply of towels ready for the players. Max appeared and grabbed a drink.

"Why didn't you pass the ball to number eighty-one?" Jimmy asked.

"I have to do what Coach Nixon says," Max answered. "If I don't follow instructions, I'll never get another chance to play."

"But you can throw a touchdown pass. I know it!"

"Tell Coach Nixon," Max replied with a smile.

"I tried."

There was a collective groan from the Cattaloochie County fans. Jimmy looked up as a Rams player celebrated a touchdown in the end zone. An offensive lineman came up to Max.

"Come on, Cochran. The coaches want to see you."

The extra point, never a given in high school football, was good. With slightly over two minutes left in the game, the score was tied. Max ran onto the field with the first-team offense. All the players were standing along the sideline, and Jimmy couldn't see what was happening. He looked up into the stands to the place where Mama and Daddy were sitting. Daddy was watching the game, but Mama caught his eye, waved, and put her hands together in prayer. Jimmy put his hands together and waved back.

The crowd roared, and Jimmy saw a pile of players roll into the Cattaloochie sideline. Players had to jump out of the way. At the bottom of the pile, Jimmy saw Max get up and hand the ball to one of the stripe-shirted officials. Jimmy stepped closer. One of the linebackers spoke to another player.

"Cochran has quick feet. I thought he was going to be sacked, but he gained over ten yards."

"We're not going to make it to the end zone by running," the other player responded. "He's going to have to air it out."

Next to the drink table was a green plastic chair used by the trainers when taping the players' ankles and wrists. Jimmy stepped up onto the seat. He could see the field.

Max was behind the center. The ball was snapped, and Max retreated to pass. Everyone was running so fast that Jimmy couldn't take it all in. He focused all his attention on Max, who was looking downfield. Max stepped to the side to avoid a tackle and threw the ball. Jimmy watched as it gracefully arced through the air. A Cattaloochie player caught the ball, and Jimmy let out a cheer. However, the stands behind him were quiet. The referee brought the ball back to the same place.

"He was out of bounds when he caught it," one of the players on the sideline said.

The team ran another play, an incomplete pass. On third down, Max was tackled in the backfield, causing a big celebration by the Dake County players. Coach Nixon signaled for a time-out. Max ran over to the sideline and huddled with the coaches. Jimmy couldn't hear what they were saying or see Max's face. He glanced back at Mama. She made a downward motion with her hands that he didn't understand. The referee blew his whistle, and Max ran onto the field.

The ball was snapped, and Max got ready to pass. A Dake County player jumped up in front of him and then came forward on top of him. Max disappeared from Jimmy's view for a second then reappeared, still on his feet. He started running and went out of bounds beyond the man holding the pole on the sidelines. Jimmy knew getting past the pole was important. Jimmy looked up at the game clock on the scoreboard. It showed thirty seconds remaining. It was first down.

Lined up near the Cattaloochie team was number eighty-one. The ball was snapped, and number eighty-one ran straight down the field. Max took three steps back and threw the ball toward the end zone. Jimmy watched in amazement as the path of the ball and the streaking player came together. The receiver caught the ball and ran into the end zone. Jimmy yelled and jumped off the chair. The linebacker yelled and hugged the player next to him. He then picked Jimmy up and put him down.

The extra-point attempt failed. Cattaloochie County kicked off and tackled the Dake County player who caught the ball. On the next play, a pass was intercepted. Everybody on the Cattaloochie sideline yelled again, but it wasn't very exciting to Jimmy. Max ran back onto the field, and Jimmy hoped for another touchdown. However, Max took the snap and touched his knee to the ground. The horn on top of the scoreboard sounded. The game was over.

Suddenly, the players started wanting drinks. Jimmy scrambled to keep cups on the table. Players dropped empty cups on the ground, but Jimmy was too busy to write down their jersey numbers. As quickly as they'd come, the players left and began walking toward the locker room. Jimmy started gathering up trash.

"Hey, son!" Mama called out. "You're doing a great job!"

Mama and Daddy were on the bottom row of the stands leaning against the railing. Jimmy looked up and waved.

"Yes, he is," Coach Bolton added as he walked past Jimmy and patted him on the back. "It's a good thing we took your advice and let Max Cochran throw the football."

"Yes, sir."

Coach Bolton waved toward Daddy and continued toward the locker room.

"We'll wait for you near the concession stand," Daddy said to Jimmy.

"Yes, sir."

By the time he finished cleaning up, Jimmy was the last person on the sidelines. The fans had moved from the stadium to the parking lot, which was a sea of red taillights. A lot of drivers were honking their car horns. Jimmy could hear victory shouts from students hanging out car windows. When the last piece of paper and scrap of tape had been collected, Jimmy dragged the trash bags to a large trash container behind the visitor stands. He heaved the bags into the container.

Someone turned off the field lights as he began walking toward the Cattaloochie side of the stadium. It was dark as he trudged toward the locker room. More sounds of victory reached his ears when he pulled open the locker room doors. Inside, most of the players were putting on street clothes. Max, a huge smile on his face, was receiving congratulations from everyone who passed by. Jimmy started toward him, but several players cut him off.

"Mitchell!" Coach Bolton called out. "Gather up the game balls and put them in the storage room. When you finish, put all the supplies back in the training closet."

Six weeks before, Jimmy would have been overwhelmed by such an order. Now he didn't give it a second thought. It took three trips to retrieve the balls from various corners of the room and put them in a mesh bin in the storage room. Collecting the training supplies took longer, and by the time he finished, the locker room was almost empty. Coach Bolton came out of his office with a small bag of trash.

"Take this to the trash bin. There's food it in that will smell if I don't get it out of here tonight."

"It's dark, and the lights are off," Jimmy said.

"Your eyes will adjust."

The coach dropped the bag in front of Jimmy and didn't wait for a reply. Jimmy picked it up and retraced his steps down the hill and across the dark field. Most of the cars had left the parking lot, and Jimmy could see the stars. The bag of trash swished against Jimmy's leg as he walked. He reached the opposite side of the field and went behind the stands. The aluminum stands hid the sky, and the space beneath them was dark and shadowy. The trash container loomed as a long black shape before him. The bag was small enough that he could push it through an opening in the side. He turned to go.

"Stop," he heard a voice say.

Jimmy froze.

"I need to count it," the voice continued.

Jimmy moved closer to the container. The voice sounded familiar, but he couldn't tell where it was coming from.

"It's all there. It's your job to split it up."

"I thought there was going to be another five hundred."

"Your money is there. We don't think Sharpton deserves anything."

"That wasn't the deal."

"Do you want to give it back?"

"No."

"There is a lot more where that came from if you're willing to cooperate."

"I'm listening."

Jimmy inched around the container and looked up. Two figures were sitting in the stands directly above him. Their legs blocked his view of the sky. Wanting to avoid whoever it was, he stepped behind the container and walked around the back of the stands to the other end of the field. He crossed the end-zone area. Suddenly, the lights for the stadium came back on. The glare caused him to stop and put his hand against the goalpost.

"Mitchell!" a voice called out.

Jimmy looked but couldn't see anyone.

"Over here!" the voice said.

Jimmy looked toward the Cattaloochie side of the field. Coach Bolton was standing at the top of the stadium waving his arms. Daddy was beside him.

"Come on!" the coach yelled.

Jimmy ran toward them. Daddy walked down the steps and met him on the field.

"Coach Bolton turned on the lights because we were concerned that you'd gotten lost in the dark."

"No, sir."

"Let's go. Everybody has left the stadium, and your mama was worried about you."

Mama gave Jimmy a hug when he appeared. Together with Daddy, they headed toward the parking lot.

"Where were you?" she asked.

"Throwing away trash for Coach Bolton."

"He shouldn't have sent you out in the dark."

In the car, Mama talked nonstop about the game. She'd sat next to Mrs. Cochran and enjoyed her reaction to Max's heroics on the field.

"I think it's wonderful that Max won the game."

"It's a team sport," Daddy said. "He couldn't have done it if Jimmy hadn't given him plenty to drink."

"That's right," Mama agreed. "You're doing a great job as a manager."

"Yes, ma'am."

After he took a shower and put on his pajamas, Jimmy lay in bed and waited for Mama to come into his room and pray with him. She sat on the edge of his bed.

"Mama," he said, "I think the snake man was at the game tonight."

"Why do you say that?"

Jimmy told her what he'd heard in the stands. Mama listened closely, a concerned look on her face.

"Did they know you were listening?" she asked.

"No, ma'am. You told me not to talk to anyone about it, so I walked around the back of the stands to the other end of the field."

Mama stroked his cheek. "That's good. Don't go to sleep yet. I want your daddy to hear this."

Mama left and returned with Daddy.

"Tell him what you told me," Mama said.

Jimmy repeated the conversation.

"Something illegal is happening," Daddy said soberly. "And whoever is doing this has recruited Sharpton, Gambrell, and possibly others."

"What are you going to do?" Mama asked Daddy.

"I'll have a talk with Detective Stephens. He's over all narcotics investigations for the sheriff's department. I wouldn't be surprised if he has a system of informers at the high school who can fill in the blanks."

"Will Hal and Pete get into trouble?" Jimmy asked.

"Maybe, but that's not your problem," Daddy said. "The important thing for you is not to tell anyone about the conversation at the football field. No matter what happens, keep your mouth shut. Can you do that?"

"Yes, sir."

Mama looked at Daddy anxiously.

"I think we should reconsider the private school in Carroll County. Jimmy could let something slip by mistake, and there's no telling what might happen."

"Private school?" Jimmy asked. "What's that?"

"A very nice, small school," Mama answered, resuming her seat on the edge of his bed. "It doesn't have all the problems of a big school like Cattaloochie County High. Your daddy and I have talked about sending you there for a couple of years. I visited, and they have a lot of nice students and teachers. You would be in regular classes and get extra help when you needed it."

"A different school?" Jimmy asked.

"Ellen, let's have this conversation downstairs," Daddy said. "We shouldn't drag Jimmy into it until we've made up our minds."

"What about my job as manager of the football team?" Jimmy asked as understanding of Mama's suggestion dawned. "And Max? And my teachers?"

"You would have new teachers, and we'd help you find activities besides managing the football team," Mama said. "You'd still be able to see Max on the weekends."

"Enough," Daddy said. "Go to sleep. On Monday you're going back to Cattaloochie. Don't worry about a new school."

Mama and Daddy left the room, but Jimmy lay awake.

Worrying.

— Thirty-four —

No one mentioned the private school during the following week. Jimmy started to bring it up at supper but decided that not saying anything might keep it from happening. The thought of leaving the people he'd known since kindergarten upset him.

Football practice settled into a routine. Brian Brown worked with the first-team offense, but Max also got in a few snaps. Friday's game was against Parker High School, a new school on the outskirts of Atlanta.

During football practice, Jimmy didn't have any direct contact with Pete or Brian, and he remembered Daddy's command to keep his mouth shut. Each night, Daddy asked if the subject of the postgame conversation had come up at school, and Jimmy truthfully told him no.

Friday night came, and the Captains easily defeated Parker High. After the Dake County game, most people thought the next game would be much closer. Max dressed out for the game but didn't play. Brian performed well and didn't make any serious mistakes. Pete rushed for over 150 yards. Jimmy did everything asked of him as a manager.

During the ride home from the stadium, Mama said, "Don't forget to feed the cats tomorrow. I did it this afternoon, but you agreed to help Delores, and it's your responsibility."

"Yes, ma'am." Jimmy answered with little enthusiasm in his voice.

"Would you like to ride your bike to her house?" Mama asked.

"Yes, ma'am," he responded more brightly.

Saturday morning dawned with a hint of fall in the air that tickled Jimmy's nose as he went outside to check on Buster. Football practice had cut Jimmy's time with the dog, and Buster jumped around excitedly when Jimmy entered the backyard. Jimmy threw a ball a few times and laughed as Buster overran it and rolled over in a heap.

"I have to take care of Otto, Maureen, and Celine," Jimmy said as he moved toward the gate. "I'll let them rub against me, and when I come home, you can smell my blue jeans as long as you want to."

Mama and Daddy were drinking coffee in the kitchen.

"Sorry I didn't fix breakfast, sunshine," Mama said.

"I ate cereal," Jimmy replied.

"I'll fix meat loaf in the pan for supper," Mama said.

Jimmy grinned. "I bet the cats wish they could eat meat loaf, but I think I'll give them liver dinners."

Daddy reached into his pocket.

"Here's the key to Delores's house. Make sure you don't lose it."

"Yes, sir."

"Do you know how to get there?" Mama asked.

"Yes, ma'am. I ride past Grandpa and Grandma's street—" Jimmy stopped. A wave of sadness suddenly washed over him. "Should I still call it that?"

"Yes," Mama replied quietly. "You can always call it that."

Jimmy sighed. "After I pass their street, then I go through two stop signs. The cats live in a yellow house on the right side of the road."

"Excellent," Daddy said. "Be careful. Lock the door after you finish."

Jimmy's bike, repaired after the wreck, was in good shape. Mama came outside onto the porch to see him off. Jimmy, his Ready Kilowatt cap on his head, honked twice and waved as he turned down the sidewalk.

He wasn't afraid of the familiar streets. Every dip in the sidewalk, each tree along the roadway, every house was a known landmark, but he missed Buster padding alongside him. He passed Ridgeview Drive. He'd not climbed the pole since Grandpa died.

"One," he said when he came to the first stop sign and honked his horn once. He continued another block. A white pickup truck passed him on the road.

"Two," he said when he came to the second stop sign and honked his horn twice.

He rode about fifty yards before reaching the yellow house. He parked his bike in the carport and walked to the front door. Looking in the narrow sidelight window beside the door, he could see the cats milling around in the foyer. He put the key in the lock, turned it, and pushed against the door. It didn't move. He stared at the key. Maybe he should go home and get Mama to help him. Deciding to try again, he put the key back into the lock. Turning it in the opposite direction, he heard a *click,* and the door opened. The mewing cats greeted him.

"Hello, cats," he said. "Would you like a liver dinner?"

The mewing chorus followed him into the kitchen. Delores hadn't kept the dinners organized, and it took a minute to find a large can of liver. He fixed the cats' food, carefully spooning out equal portions for each one. The litter box was dirty, and he took it to the back door. When he opened the door, he thought he heard the sound of the back gate closing. Glancing to the left, he didn't see anything.

By the time he dumped the litter in the garbage can and returned to the kitchen, the cats had finished eating and were ready to go outside. They scampered past him. He put clean litter in the box. It would take several minutes to reorganize the cat's food pantry. He heard a scratching sound at the back door. He turned around, expecting to see Otto, Maureen, or Celine wanting to get back inside.

Instead, he saw Jake Garner.

As soon as their eyes met, Jake threw open the door and rushed into the kitchen. Jimmy threw up his hands in front of him. Jake was wearing white gloves. He grabbed Jimmy's wrists and spun him around.

"Stop!" Jimmy cried out. "Don't hurt me!"

Jake wrapped something sticky around Jimmy's wrists and stuffed a cloth in his mouth. Jimmy forced the cloth out of his mouth with his tongue.

"Help!" he yelled. "Stop!"

Jake stuck the cloth in Jimmy's mouth and held it in place with his hand. Jimmy turned his head to the side and looked down. Staring at him was the head of the snake that coiled around Jake's arm. Its head and mouth were huge, much too large for the snake's body, and long fangs hung from its upper lip. Dark blue drops of venom dripped from the fangs.

More tape came around Jimmy's mouth. Then Jake grabbed Jimmy's glasses and covered his eyes with another cloth. Jake pushed Jimmy through the house. Jimmy tried to yell, but the only sounds that came from his mouth were grunts. He hit his leg against a table, then tripped over a chair and would have fallen if Jake hadn't grabbed him. Jimmy's cap fell off his head, but Jake replaced it.

Jimmy wasn't sure where he was in the house. Jake didn't speak until he pushed Jimmy against a wall and forced him to sit on the floor.

"Stay there!" he commanded in a rough voice.

A door opened, and Jimmy felt the outside air. He heard Jake's footsteps move away, and he tried to stand up. Jake returned, jerked him through the door, and roughly shoved him onto the floorboard of a vehicle. The door closed, but Garner didn't get inside. Jimmy lay still. One of his nostrils was blocked, and it was hard to breathe. He heard the sound of something being put in the back of the vehicle. The door opened, and the motor started.

Jake backed out of the driveway, stopped for a second, and started forward. Jimmy felt every bump in the road, and the side of his head banged against the floorboard. Garner turned on the radio. It was not the sort of music Mama and Daddy listened to. It was so loud that it made it hard for Jimmy to think. Jake stopped several times, turned to the right, and began to pick up speed. He turned off the radio. Jimmy heard a series of beeps as Jake pressed numbers on a cell phone.

"I've got him," Jake said. "After a week going crazy with boredom, it couldn't have been easier. Early this morning, he rode his bike to a house on the south side. Nobody was home. I grabbed him in the kitchen and threw his bike in the back of the truck. I'm already clear of the city limits. He's tied up in the floorboard."

There was silence while Jake listened. Jimmy could faintly hear the other voice on the phone but not enough to understand what was said.

"I think he was taking care of a woman's cats," Jake said. "That's why no one was in the house. I didn't leave any prints, and there won't be any sign of a struggle. The bike gives me a great setup. The only downside about grabbing him in the morning is that I have to keep him hidden all day."

Jake was silent again.

"There will be a call to the sheriff's office sooner rather than later. His parents won't wait around wondering what's going on if he doesn't show up on time. But it won't matter. In five minutes I'll be at the house where we'll be safe and cozy."

A short period of silence followed.

"No. I got the envelope and will pick up the rest at the usual place on my way out of town."

A longer period of silence followed.

"Of course, I'll try to find out what he's told his parents and let you know.

He'll be well acquainted with the hot end of a cigarette before I'm finished with my questions."

Jimmy heard a click as Jake closed the cell phone. The radio came back on. Before the song ended, Jake turned onto a very bumpy road and drove so fast that Jimmy bounced up and down several times. He couldn't figure out why this was happening to him. Then the truck stopped abruptly, and Jimmy hit his head against the floorboard one last time. Jake turned off the motor and left him alone. Jimmy tried to wiggle his hands, but they didn't budge. Pain shot up his arms. His mouth was dry, and he was thirsty. Jake grabbed him by the right arm and dragged him out of the truck. Jimmy fell to his knees.

"Get up," he said.

Jimmy, still blindfolded, struggled to his feet. Jake pushed him forward. Jimmy took a few steps, tripped, and fell face forward. He landed on the right side of his head so hard that he saw stars behind his eyelids. Stunned, he lay on the ground. Jake grabbed him by the back of his shirt, pulled him to his feet, and guided him forward with his hands on Jimmy's shoulders.

"Climb three steps," Jake said.

Jimmy hit something solid with his shoe, then climbed the steps. He crossed a porch and went through the door of a house. Garner turned him around several times, then directed him forward a few steps to the left. A door closed.

"Stand still," Jake commanded.

Jimmy felt Jake's hands at the back of his head. The blindfold came off his eyes. Jake put Jimmy's glasses back on roughly, poking him in the cheek. Jimmy blinked rapidly as his eyes focused. He was in a small bedroom with a bare lightbulb in the ceiling. A mattress without any sheets on it lay on the floor to his right. There was no furniture. A single window had been boarded up on the outside. Jimmy could see slivers of light through the cracks between the boards.

"This is your new home," Jake said. "But just temporarily."

Jimmy started to turn around and face Jake, but a hand quickly hit him in the back of the head.

"Don't move unless I tell you to. If you understand, nod your head." Jimmy nodded.

"I'm the boss around here," Jake said. "You've caused me so much trouble over the past two weeks that I'd like nothing better than to beat you bloody. Do you understand?"

Jimmy wasn't sure what he meant but nodded anyway.

"Sit on the mattress."

Jimmy stumbled over and sat on the mattress. He glanced up at Jake. The snake man's dark hair was cut short, and he'd shaved his beard. He sported three earrings in his right ear. The head of the snake that coiled around his arm bared its fangs.

"Don't look at me!" Jake screamed.

Jimmy's eyes opened wider. Jake lunged toward him.

"Look at the floor!" he yelled.

Jimmy dropped his head and stared at the scuffed wooden floor.

"Watch the floor until I leave the room."

Jimmy kept his head lowered. Out of the corner of his eye, he could see Jake open the door and close it. There followed two distinct clicks. Jimmy looked up. He was alone.

He looked around the room. The walls were painted a tan color. Faded yellow wallpaper peeked out from under peeling paint. The door was wooden and painted dark brown. Jimmy shifted his weight on the mattress. The pain in his arms returned, and his face stung where he'd struck the ground. He tried again to wiggle his hands, but he couldn't. He dropped his head and closed his eyes.

He thought about Mama. Never had his heart ached so much to be with her. He knew what she would do. In an instant, she would release his hands, take the horrible cloth from his mouth, and hug away the pain. Tears came to his eyes and rolled down his cheeks. His chest heaved up and down in rhythm with his sorrow. His nose began to run, but he couldn't turn his head enough to wipe it on his sleeve. He edged back on the mattress until he could lean against the wall. He closed his eyes to block out the room.

He could hear Jake moving through the house. Then there was silence. Jimmy strained to listen. The silence continued. Maybe the snake man had left. Jimmy scooted forward off the mattress and managed to stand up. He walked to the boarded-up window, bent down, and peered through the largest crack. All he could see were the trunks of trees. He was somewhere in the woods. The sun was shining. He wished he could put his lips to the small opening and breathe fresh air.

He heard a click at the door. Turning around, he rushed back to the mattress and sat down. He remembered to stare at the floor as the door opened.

"That's better," Jake said.

Jimmy glanced up. Jake was in the doorway with a cigarette hanging from his lips.

"The floor!" Jake yelled. "Look at the floor!"

Jimmy jerked his head back down.

"Stand up and face the window," Jake ordered.

Jimmy obeyed. Jake came up behind him and exhaled a puff of smoke that wrapped around Jimmy's head.

"Do you like cigarettes?" he asked.

Jimmy shook his head.

"You're going to like them less in a few minutes. Are you ready for me to take off the cloth covering your mouth?"

Jimmy nodded.

"If I do that, you have to promise not to say anything unless I tell you to. Do you understand?"

Jimmy nodded again. He felt Jake's hands at the back of his head. Another wave of smoke came around to his nostrils. He felt the gag loosen, fall from his nose, then from his mouth. Jimmy gasped for breath.

"Is that better?" Jake asked.

"Yes, sir."

Jake hit him sharply in the back of the head. Jimmy stepped forward.

"I didn't tell you to speak!" he screamed.

Jimmy stood still and focused on breathing in as much air as possible. He licked his lips. His mouth was dry.

"Was that gag too tight?"

"Ye—," Jimmy started, then stopped.

Garner hit him again but not as hard.

"That's better. I can ask a question, but that doesn't mean I want an answer."

Jimmy didn't move.

"If I hear a sound I don't like, then the cloth goes over your mouth tighter than I had it before. Do you understand? You can speak."

"Yes, sir," Jimmy answered in a weak voice. Then he flinched in anticipation of a blow.

None came.

"That's the way it's going to work. I like you calling me 'sir.' It's a nice touch."

"Do you need to go to the bathroom?"

Jimmy nodded.

"Okay. I'll show you that I'm not such a bad person."

Jake reached up and tied the blindfold around Jimmy's eyes.

"The bathroom is this way."

Jake led him by the arm from the room and a few steps down a hall. He stopped and adjusted the blindfold just enough for Jimmy to see what lay at his feet.

"Go. I'll be here waiting."

Jimmy stood still.

"What are you waiting for?" Jake asked sharply.

Jimmy didn't answer. Jake laughed.

"How stupid of me," he said. "Your hands are still tied."

He spun Jimmy around. Jimmy felt something cold like metal against his wrists, then heard a ripping sound as the tape was removed. Jimmy grunted in pain but didn't cry out. His hands came free. He rubbed them together.

"Is that better?" Jake asked.

"Yes, sir."

Jake struck him on the side of the face where Jimmy had fallen. It hurt, and Jimmy couldn't help but cry out.

"I didn't tell you to speak!" Jake screamed. "Now get in there before I change my mind! Don't touch the blindfold."

Jimmy went to the bathroom. When he finished, he flushed the toilet and moved to the sink. He felt the faucet knobs for the water.

"That's a good boy," Jake said. "Wash your hands."

Jimmy let the cool water wash over his hands and wrists. He wanted to drink some very badly. He cupped some water in his right hand and raised it to his lips. Before it reached his mouth, Jake knocked his hand away.

"A drink will have to wait," he said. "I have some questions to ask you first."

— Thirty-five —

Jake returned Jimmy to the tiny bedroom.

"Stand still and face the window," he commanded.

Jimmy stood at attention facing the boarded-up window. Jake left the room with the door open. Jimmy glanced over his shoulder. For a split second, he wondered if he should try to run. Trying to escape from Jake Garner would be a lot harder than getting away from Walt. Jimmy kept his feet planted. In a moment, Jake returned and came up close to Jimmy's left ear. More smoke floated up toward the lightbulb.

"I was in the hall waiting to see what you'd do," Jake sneered. "If you had tried to run, I would have broken your jaw."

Jake grabbed Jimmy's hands, jerked them behind his back, and wrapped a few turns of tape around them. The loss of freedom crushed Jimmy. He began to sniffle.

"You don't like that?" Jake asked. "Get used to it."

Jimmy's lower lip quivered. Jake spun him around.

"Now look at me."

Jimmy looked into the face of his tormentor. There were dark circles under Jake's eyes. His short hair stuck out in several directions at once. His nose was creased with a deep scar. Not a tall man, Jake wasn't much larger than Jimmy. He took the cigarette from his mouth and held the glowing end in front of Jimmy's nose. Jimmy tried to hold his breath, but Garner kept the cigarette close until Jimmy had to breathe. He coughed slightly as a wisp of smoke entered his lungs.

"Do you want me to move the cigarette?" Jake asked.

"Yes, sir."

Jake slapped Jimmy with his free hand. Jimmy stepped backward and closed his eyes.

"I didn't tell you to speak!" Jake screamed. "How can anyone be so dumb?"

Jimmy's body shook. He tried to stop, but his shoulders and chest continued to tremble. Garner stared at him for a few seconds, turned, and left the room. He slammed the door and set the locks.

"We'll talk later!" he yelled through the door. "You're going to tell me everything you know!"

Jimmy moved shakily over to the mattress and sat down. His body settled down. He realized that he was breathing hard like the day he passed out in Coach Nixon's office, so he tried to slow down. The shaking stopped, but it took a few moments for his breathing to return to normal. He licked his lips again, but there wasn't much moisture in his mouth. He sighed and closed his eyes. He was suddenly very tired. He leaned over on his left side and pulled his feet onto the mattress. He awoke with a start as the door opened.

"Nap time?" Jake said.

Jake had a bottle of water in his hand and another cigarette in his mouth. Jimmy sat up and looked longingly at the bottle. Jake followed his gaze.

"I thought you didn't like water," Jake said.

Jimmy didn't answer.

"Stand up and come over here," Jake commanded.

Jimmy obeyed.

"Do you want a drink of water?" Jake asked.

Jimmy stood mute.

"Good. You may speak," Jake said.

"Yes, sir."

Garner unscrewed the cap but kept the bottle in his hand.

"You can have a drink if you answer my questions truthfully. Do you remember when you testified in court?"

Jimmy didn't answer.

"And you promised to tell the truth, the whole truth, and nothing but the truth? That's what you're going to have to do if you want a drink of water. Raise your right hand."

Jimmy hesitantly raised his hand.

"I don't have a Bible handy," Jake said, "so we'll have to pretend."

Jake repeated the words of the judicial oath.

"You can answer," he said when he finished.

"Yes, sir."

"Until I tell you otherwise, you can answer all my questions. Do you understand?"

Jimmy was not sure if the question was a trap.

"Answer me!" Garner screamed.

"Yes, sir," Jimmy responded in a trembling voice.

"Who are Hal Sharpton and Pete Gambrell?"

Jimmy took a deep breath. "Hal was the quarterback of the football team, but he got kicked off for fighting—"

"That's enough. And Pete?"

"He's a running back."

"Did you ever hear them say my name?"

"No, sir."

Jake gave him a puzzled look. "Did you ever hear them mention the snake man?"

"Yes, sir."

"Who is the snake man?"

"You are."

"How do you know that?"

"Are you the snake man?" Jimmy asked.

"Don't ask me any questions!" Jake yelled. He raised the bottle of water to his lips and took a long drink. "This is good water, but you're not going to taste it unless you do what I tell you."

"Yes, sir."

"When was the first time you heard Hal and Pete say anything about the snake man?"

"When I was sorting helmets in the equipment room."

"What did you hear?"

Jimmy related the conversation. When he reached the part about Hal's summer job picking up packages in Atlanta for delivery to Piney Grove, Jake swore and took a deep drag on his cigarette. Jimmy stopped talking.

"Go ahead," Jake said, taking another drink from the bottle.

Jimmy continued to the end of the conversation.

"That's all I remember," Jimmy said when he finished.

"What is a bookie?" Garner asked.

"I don't know."

"Did you tell anyone about this conversation?"

"No, sir."

"Liar!" Jake screamed. "Then why did the narcs start asking their little snits questions about Hal, Pete, and me at the high school?"

Jimmy wanted to give an answer but didn't know what to say. Jake stared hard at him.

"Is that the only conversation you overhead about the snake man?"

"No, sir."

Jake nodded. "After the Dake County game. I thought I saw you when the lights came back on at the field. Where were you hiding?"

"I wasn't hiding. I took out some trash and heard Pete talking."

"Who was he talking to?"

"You."

"Are you sure about it?"

"Yes, sir."

"Why?"

"Because now I know how you talk."

"What did you hear?"

Jimmy, aware of Daddy's warning not to tell anyone, hesitated.

Jake stepped forward and raised his voice. "What did you hear?"

Jake glared at him. Holding the bottle of water in front of Jimmy's face, he turned it over and let the precious liquid spill onto the floor.

"Your mistake," he said as he turned to leave the room. "You don't need to answer. I already know."

The door shut; the locks clicked. The intensity of Jimmy's thirst had increased enormously at the sight of the water. He stared at the wet spot on the floor. Getting on his knees, he bent over and touched the dark wood with his tongue. All he tasted was a layer of wet grime. In despair, he turned his face sideways and laid his cheek against the floor. No Watcher appeared to show him the way to a refreshing drink.

Jimmy returned to the mattress but didn't lie down. The initial shock of what had happened to him was over. He was a prisoner. He had no idea how much time had passed since he'd emptied the cats' litter box, but the memory of freedom was already becoming fuzzy.

He heard footsteps in the hallway outside the door, and his shakes returned. The footsteps continued down the hall; the shaking slowed down. When he closed his eyes, images of the snake man played across the back of his eyelids.

He began to pace. He counted five steps across the room and seven from the window to the door. Back and forth he went until he wasn't thinking anymore, just counting. Finally, he stopped in front of the window, bent over, and peeked through the largest crack.

Walking slowly across the narrow view of the outside world were two men wearing camouflage clothing and carrying guns. Seconds after he saw them, they were gone. Jimmy knew what to do.

"Help!" he yelled through the crack. "Help me!"

He kicked on the boards covering the window, but they didn't budge.

"Help!" he yelled again.

The locks on the door clicked in rapid succession, and Jake burst into the room. Jimmy saw him coming and cried out again.

"Help me now!"

Jake knocked him to the floor with a blow to the right side of his head. Jimmy tried to get up, but Jake was on top of him with his hand covering Jimmy's mouth. Jimmy struggled with all his strength but couldn't get free. Garner released his hand for a second, but before Jimmy could scream, Garner jammed a rag into his mouth and, while holding it in place, slapped some tape across Jimmy's face and around his head. Jimmy grunted. There was a loud knocking on the front door.

"Hello! Anybody home?"

Jimmy tried to break free, but Jake flipped him over onto his stomach and wrapped his ankles in tape. Bound hand and foot, Jimmy lay helpless on the floor. Garner got up and left the room. The door closed. Jimmy lay still, hurting in new places.

He prayed that the men would rescue him.

Time passed without sound. Then a single gunshot rang out. Another long period of silence followed. Jimmy shifted on the floor, but no position gave him any relief from the tight bands around his head, hands, and feet. The sides of his head ached from the repeated blows and slaps.

The door to the room opened slowly. Jimmy strained to see the feet of the person or persons about to enter, but no shoes were in sight. He heard a voice.

"They're gone," Jake said into a cell phone. "I had to run them off as trespassers with a shot in the air."

There was silence as Jake listened. Jimmy shut his eyes in despair. He didn't feel like crying.

"Squirrel hunters," Jake said. "Deer season won't be open for several weeks. They were toting shotguns and tried to argue with me that they had permission from the owner to hunt on this land. They may be right, so there's going to have to be a change in our plans. I can't wait until nighttime."

Jake kicked Jimmy in the ribs. A sharp pain shot through his side, and he winced.

"Nah. I don't think they heard him hollering, because they seemed more interested in arguing with me about hunting on the property than anything else."

Jake put his foot directly in front of Jimmy's nose, then pulled it back.

"No, I'm not going to do it here. It's got to look like an accident. Otherwise, this thing will never go away."

Jake closed the cell phone, took out a cigarette, and lit it. He turned Jimmy onto his back with his foot and knelt down beside him.

"Boy," he said. "I would like to introduce your neck to the hot end of this cigarette."

Jake removed the cigarette from his mouth and blew smoke directly into Jimmy's face. He held the orange end of the cigarette close to Jimmy's throat. Jimmy tried to squirm away. Jake withdrew his hand.

"But I can't do that. I don't want to leave any marks on you that don't make sense. Are you still thirsty?"

Jimmy lay still.

"I bet you're very thirsty. But don't worry. In a little while, I promise you'll have all the water you want. You're about to go swimming."

Terror flashed across Jimmy's face.

"I thought that would get a reaction out of you," Jake said. "I hope you like the deep end."

JAKE LEFT THE ROOM, AND SOMETHING IN JIMMY SNAPPED. His stomach was empty, but what little remained forced its way up his throat in a foul tasting bile. Needlelike pain attacked his body in countless directions. He dragged himself to the mattress and rolled over on it. He tried to sit up but collapsed on his side. His fight, his will to live, was gone. All that remained was the wait for death. At least in that, there would be release from torment. Jimmy lay still. Time passed. Jake returned.

"Resting?" he asked.

Jake removed the tape from Jimmy's ankles.

"Let's get going."

Jimmy didn't move. Jake grabbed him by the shirt and forced him up, but Jimmy collapsed back onto the mattress. Jake slapped him across the cheek, but Jimmy didn't respond.

"Checking out on me?" Jake asked. "That will make everything that much easier."

Jake put Jimmy's cap back on, then half carried, half dragged him out of the room. Without a blindfold, Jimmy could see the house. There was a small living room with a single couch. The rest of the room was bare. Jake propped him against the wall by the front door and looked outside.

"No trespassers in sight," he said.

Jake shoved Jimmy across the porch. It was late afternoon. The sun dipped below the treetops of the woods surrounding the small house. The fresh air restored Jimmy, and he took a few steps on his own.

"Feeling better?" Jake asked. "Just don't get too frisky."

Jimmy saw Jake's white pickup parked in the front yard. Jimmy's bicycle was lying on its side in the truck bed. The sight of the bike, a reminder of his normal life, startled him. Jimmy tried to imagine riding the bike along the sidewalk near his house, but the thought broke down before he could follow it. Jake opened the door of the truck and pushed him inside.

"Go back into the dark," Jake said as he pulled a bandana from his pocket and wrapped it around Jimmy's eyes.

Jimmy slid onto the floorboard and leaned his head against the dash. Garner got in and started the engine. He turned the truck around and drove down the bumpy access road. Jimmy, unfeeling, stayed in the black world behind the blindfold. Jake turned on the radio in the middle of a silly song. The singer made a joke and laughed. Jake turned it off.

They reached pavement, turned right, and accelerated.

"Your swimming lesson will be at Webb's Pond," Garner said. "I saw in the paper a few weeks ago that your grandfather won second place in a fishing contest there. It's a shame that he died the next day. The article mentioned that you went fishing with him. Is that right? If that's right, nod your head."

Jimmy nodded.

"Then it would make sense that you'd want to go back there. It's only a few miles from your house. You could ride your bike—kind of a sentimental journey. The only problem is that if you're not careful and ride too close to the edge of the water, the front wheel of your bike could slip in the grass and send you down into the water. Do you remember the deep water near the dam?"

Jimmy didn't respond.

"That's the best place for an accident. Everyone knows you can't swim a lick and could drown in the bathtub. It will be a sad accident. I bet you'll get a bigger write-up in the paper than your grandfather."

Jimmy responded to the mention of Grandpa. To hear his heart go *thump* again and feel his strong arms around him would be heaven.

Scenes with Grandpa began to play in his mind: throwing a baseball, reading a book, climbing the pole, riding his bike. They were the first positive thoughts he'd had since Garner burst into Delores Smythe's kitchen. A flicker of light flamed within Jimmy's heart.

Jimmy put his head down on his knees.

"It's time to say your prayers," Jake said. "We're almost there."

The pavement ended, and they bounced briefly across the grass before stopping. Jake got out and opened the door. He reached in and took off Jimmy's blindfold.

"Get out. No problem with you seeing where you're going from here."

Jimmy got out of the truck and leaned against it.

"Don't touch the door," Jake said sharply. "Step away."

Jimmy took a few shaky steps forward. They were in the place where the vehicles parked for the fishing tournament.

"The presence of my truck won't stand out at all, will it? There are tire marks everywhere."

Jake was wearing white gloves. He lifted Jimmy's bicycle from the back of the truck, reached in again, and retrieved a short rope.

"Let's slip this around your neck. Don't worry. I'm not going to hang you. It's a leash to make sure you don't wander away. You have a nice dog, don't you?"

Jimmy thought about Buster. What would Buster do without him? Jimmy wanted to scream.

Jake wrapped the rope around Jimmy's neck and tied a knot that he could cinch against Jimmy's throat.

"Not too tight. I don't want any rope burns. Those bruises on your face came when you fell down the bank."

Holding the rope with one hand, Jake pushed the bike through the trees with the other. Jimmy walked alongside him. They came out into the open area surrounding the pond. The sun was below the trees now, the water still. A bullfrog at the south end of the pond announced the approach of dusk.

When he saw the water, Jimmy stopped. Jake jerked the rope; Jimmy resisted.

"Don't make me hurt you," Jake warned.

Jimmy shook his head. Jake dropped the bike on the ground, came around, and cinched the rope tighter around Jimmy's neck.

"Come on!" he demanded.

Jimmy was having trouble breathing, but the sight of the water gave him the will to stand firm. He didn't budge. Jake jerked harder, causing Jimmy to lose his footing. He fell forward, knocking over the bike before landing on the ground. Jake swore. His chest heaving, Jimmy lay on the grass. Jake knelt beside him and loosened the rope. Jimmy gulped in air. Jake pulled him up by the arm.

"We'll make two trips."

Leaving the bike, Jake dragged Jimmy forward. When they reached the edge of the dam, Jimmy could see the dark water, and adrenaline coursed through his veins. Instead of trying to resist Jake, he pushed him, causing them both to fall to the ground. Jake lost his grip on the rope. Jimmy rolled to the side and staggered to his feet. He started running away from the water. He made it about twenty feet before Jake tackled him. He pushed Jimmy's face into the grass.

"You are not going to get away from me," Jake said, breathing heavily. "I should have brought some tape for your feet."

Jake wrapped the bandanna around Jimmy's ankles and tied it in a knot.

"This should last long enough for what I need," he said.

He picked Jimmy up in his arms and carried him back to the dam. Jimmy turned his head away from the water. The adrenaline gone, Jimmy went limp. Jake put him down on the grass and checked the bandana around Jimmy's feet.

"I'll be right back."

Jake ran toward the bike. Jimmy raised his head and watched. In a minute, Jake returned, riding the bike to the brink of the dam, about five feet above the water. He placed the front wheel of the bike over the edge of the bank and moved it back and forth a few times. He then pushed the bike down into the water, where it slowly disappeared. Jimmy's bike was gone.

Jake turned his attention to Jimmy. When he leaned over him, Jimmy saw the same evil he'd faced in Walt's eyes, only worse. Jake seemed to look past Jimmy toward something, or someone, else. He flipped Jimmy over onto his stomach and sat on his back. He untied the bandanna from Jimmy's feet. Jimmy tried to kick, but his legs were weak. Jake unwrapped the gag covering Jimmy's mouth.

"Help!" Jimmy yelled.

"Scream all you want. No one will hear you."

"Please help me!" Jimmy repeated, his voice cracking.

Jake slipped one of his arms beneath Jimmy's elbows and pulled them back. Jimmy cried out in pain. Jake held him in this painful position and cut the tape around Jimmy's wrists. Caught in Jake's grip, the release of the tape didn't free Jimmy's hands. Jake dragged Jimmy over the edge of the bank. Jimmy looked down and saw the approaching water. With all the energy left within him, he tried to break free. He kicked his legs, screamed, and tried to jerk his arms free. But Jake's grip was too strong. The dark water came closer and closer. The grass beneath him disappeared.

Jimmy went headfirst into Webb's Pond.

— *Thirty-six* —

Jimmy opened his mouth in a silent scream. He lashed out with his hands but touched nothing. He spun, not sure which way was up. He frantically kicked his legs and came to the surface of the water. He opened his eyes, choked, and gasped for air. He saw Jake, unmoving, standing on the bank. Jimmy went under again. The darkness overtook him. He opened his eyes.

And saw a Watcher.

He could see nothing else in the dark water, yet the Watcher was clear. The Watcher floated without struggle, without panic. He reached out and took Jimmy's right hand. Warmth and security filled Jimmy. Every fear fled from his soul. Water no longer owned his dread.

The touch turned into an invitation. Deep called to deep. Jimmy's spirit echoed *amen*, and a cruel drowning was transformed into a glorious baptism. Jimmy Mitchell entered the realm of unending light.

BEYOND THE FIRST BLAZE OF GLORY, A FAMILIAR FACE WAITED for him. No longer old and wrinkled. Similar yet different. Grandpa, clothed in the splendor of redemption, stood before him. Jimmy gazed in wonder.

The greatest difference lay in the older man's eyes. The clouded sight of earth had become the clear vision of heaven. From the depths of Grandpa's eyes poured forth pure love in a torrent. Jimmy let it wash over him. He felt brand-new.

Grandpa opened his arms and, with a smile that contained the power of a thousand trumpets, beckoned to him. Jimmy moved across the space between them with a grace and nobility that caused Grandpa's eyes to shine even brighter. They came together in an embrace that surpassed their earthly hugs as much as the sun outshines the moon. They held each other, whether for a second or a thousand years made no difference. Time no longer set its cruel parameters on their affection. It was the fellowship of the redeemed—a communion so full, so complete, so absolute, so perfect, that it may be experienced only by those whose hearts have been made ready by the One who is love himself.

Jimmy lowered his head and put his ear against Grandpa's chest. Grandpa stroked his hair. Jimmy raised his head and looked again into Grandpa's face.

"What is it?" he asked.

"The sound of eternal life, a heart that will never fail." Grandpa gestured with his right hand. "And this is the place prepared for you."

Every sense completely and fully alive, Jimmy drank in the beauty and the glory. All the limitations of his earthly life transformed into glorious strength. Wisdom and knowledge beyond the comprehension of the greatest sages belonged to him. Grandpa laughed with unhindered joy.

"I owe much to you," Grandpa said.

"Why?"

Grandpa didn't speak, but Jimmy knew the day in the hospital had opened the doorway to Grandpa's salvation.

"It was my final call," Grandpa answered. "He enabled me to hear more than men knew."

Jimmy saw the hospital room. Brother Fitzgerald praying. Grandpa's bed surrounded by Watchers that even Jimmy hadn't been able to see then. The presence hovering over the older man with new creation power.

"Many are in this place because of their last three minutes," Grandpa continued. "The Father's mercy and grace are great. He desires that none should perish but all come to the knowledge of the truth."

Love for the lost and a longing for them touched Jimmy's heart.

"Jake Garner," Jimmy said softly.

"Yes, even Jake Garner."

LEE MITCHELL CLOSED THE FRONT DOOR BEHIND DETECTIVE Milligan and returned to the living room. Ellen sat on the sofa, her hands wrapped around a wad of tissues, her eyes swollen and red.

"Are you sure you should have mentioned Walt as a possible suspect?" Ellen asked anxiously. "Jake Garner is the one who scares me."

"It's not our job to eliminate anyone from suspicion. Who knows what has been going on in Walt's mind? He's twisted."

The initial worry that Jimmy was simply lost had been replaced by increasing panic as the hours passed and he didn't return. Lee and Ellen conducted an informal search and, when that failed, called the sheriff's department, which launched a full-scale search that included a door-to-door canvass of the neighborhood. Two people interviewed by officers documented Jimmy's bicycle trip to Delores Smythe's house but not his return. According to Detective Milligan, the house itself revealed no clues. Jimmy had fed the cats, cleaned the litter box, and vanished.

"It's a missing-person case, not a criminal investigation, but he promised that they'd talk to Garner, Sharpton, Gambrell, and Brown as soon as possible," Daddy said. "I asked Milligan not to contact Bart until that's done."

Ellen bit her lower lip. "It's getting dark. I can't stand the thought of Jimmy out there alone and scared."

"I'm going out to look again," Lee responded. "Milligan has both phone numbers in case he finds out anything."

"I'm going with you. I can't stand the thought of sitting here doing nothing."

They returned at 3:30 a.m., exhausted, having driven for hours, stopped repeatedly, called Jimmy's name, and waited for any whisper of an answer. Several times they encountered patrol cars also involved in the search. Deputy Askew was so distraught that he didn't try to hide his tears when they talked to him in the parking lot of a convenience store.

"I'll find him," Askew said when he regained his composure. "I will find him."

They fell into bed for a few fitful hours. Once awake, the crushing reality of Jimmy's disappearance filled their world. They sat in the kitchen in silence, drinking coffee. The phone rang. Ellen jumped up, then stopped to let Lee answer. It was Detective Milligan.

"Wait until Ellen can get the other phone," Lee said.

Ellen hurried into the living room, picked up on the other handset, and returned to the kitchen.

"Go ahead," Lee said.

"We don't know where Jimmy is, but we interviewed the boys from the high school. It took a while; however, once one of them talked, the others fell into line. It turns out Garner was giving them money to fix the scores for football games."

"Fix what?" Ellen asked.

"Garner works for a bookie who takes bets on sporting events, including high school football games. He gave the boys money to make mistakes on the field so the score would be closer than everyone thought and enable the bookie to beat the spread. Sharpton worked for the bookie last summer, probably delivering money or drugs from Atlanta. Jimmy overheard them in the locker room talking about what they needed to do in the Dake County game."

"The day of the fight?" Lee asked.

"We're not sure how it all fits together. Did Jimmy ever tell you what he heard in the locker room?"

"No. Just the conversation in the stands when he was at the trash container after the Dake County game."

"The two go together, but the boys claim that they don't know anything about Jimmy's whereabouts. I'm inclined to believe them since they came clean about the other matters."

"What about Garner?" Lee asked.

"We haven't been able to locate him."

"And the bookie?"

"We don't know his name. The boys couldn't identify Garner, except as 'the snake man'; however, the physical description is a one hundred percent match. You and I know Garner. If he or his boss believe Jimmy is a threat—"

Milligan stopped. Ellen looked at Lee with a crestfallen expression.

Lee swallowed. "Garner knows firsthand about Jimmy's memory."

"Let's not jump to conclusions. We'll try to locate Garner, but focus on searching for Jimmy. The radio station started airing a public service announcement at six o'clock this morning. Several officers whose cars he washed have volunteered to work an extra shift today."

"Please tell them thanks," Lee replied, his voice cracking.

"And someone will call you as soon as we know anything."

They hung up the phones. Ellen returned to the kitchen table and put her head in her hands.

"Something horrible has happened," she said flatly. "I can feel it in my heart."

Lee came over and put his hand on her shoulder. "Maybe he spent the night with someone, and now that it's a new day—"

"No," Ellen said, getting up from the chair. "Don't make up stories. I'm going upstairs to his room to pray." When she reached the door, she stopped and turned around. "And if Jake Garner is involved in any way with this, I'm not sure I can forgive you."

Lee looked down at the floor as he listened to Ellen's slow ascent up the stairs. Jimmy's door closed. Grabbing his car keys, Lee left the house.

HE'D LOST TRACK OF THE NUMBER OF TIMES HE RETRACED Jimmy's route to Delores Smythe's house but did it again in the half light of early morning. The sidewalks were deserted, every house at peace. Nothing seemed amiss. If the streets knew the truth, they weren't talking.

Not knowing where to go next, he drove downtown to his office. He went inside and sat for several minutes behind his desk, staring across the room, focusing on nothing. Everything he'd worked to build in his professional life seemed pointless. He wandered into the conference room. On the small table in the corner of the room was Jimmy's legal pad. Lee picked it up and stared at his son's careful attempt to copy his name in the same manner Lee had scrawled it across the top. He opened the drawer of the table and took out the handheld tape recorder. Flipping it on, he listened to the sound of Jimmy's voice expressing his love for his mama.

"Ellen can't handle this," he said softly to himself.

He started to turn it off, but Jimmy continued talking. Puzzled, Lee sat down and listened. When the tape ended, he immediately called Detective Milligan.

"Jimmy remembered details about the first conversation in the locker room," he said.

"How do you know?" Milligan asked.

Lee explained what he heard on the tape.

"That's consistent with what the boys told me," Milligan said.

"Did they know what Jimmy heard and remembered?"

"It's possible. If that's the case, we have to assume Garner knew—" Milligan stopped.

"Find him!" Daddy said.

Milligan was silent for a moment.

"Lee, we're doing all we can. The announcement on the radio is producing calls, and we're sorting them out. One came in from a hunter who may have heard someone yelling for help from an old house in the woods yesterday afternoon."

"Give me details," Lee said quickly.

"I don't have any. I haven't been able to reach the caller. I left him a voice mail. The men on patrol are looking. We'll find him."

Lee hung up the phone. He stared at the legal pad. Where would Jimmy go if he decided not to come directly home from Delores Smythe's house? The thought of Jimmy not following instructions made no sense, but every other option had been eliminated. Lee ticked off in his mind the number of places in and around Piney Grove known to Jimmy. It was a finite universe, and Lee had gone to every one of them the previous day without finding a clue.

Then he remembered Webb's Pond.

In all the swirl of activity following the wreck and his father's death, Lee had forgotten that Jimmy rode his bike to the fishing tournament.

Leaving the office, he drove down Hathaway Street. It was Sunday, and he met individuals and families going to early morning activities at the town's churches. In most of those churches, he knew people would be praying today for Jimmy Mitchell.

At Webb's Road he turned in front of the freshly painted sign announcing Alfred Walker as the most recent winner of the carp fishing contest. He passed the place where his father's truck skidded along the ditch and rolled over. The grass and gravel still showed the marks of the truck's passage. He reached the end of the road and parked under the trees. He got out of the car to the sounds of silence. It was a calm morning.

"Jimmy!" he called out tentatively.

No response.

"Jimmy!" he called out louder.

He listened but heard nothing. Sighing, he put his hand on the car door to leave. But where would he go next? To the office? Home? The pond was a special place to both Jimmy and his father. Ellen could pray in Jimmy's room; Lee decided to take a walk around the small lake and ask for God's help.

He stepped from the trees into the clearing created by the water. The surface of the pond was pocked by tiny circles as fish caught the early morning insects that skated across the water. Lee turned left and walked toward the small end of the pond. He saw a yellow ribbon tied to the end of a tree limb. He reached the far side of the pond, stopped, and looked toward the grove where he'd parked his car.

"God, where is he?" he asked.

It was a simple prayer, a simple request. No answer came.

He continued toward the dam. Reaching it, he stopped and stared into murky water. He looked away from the pond and saw something red in the grass. He walked over to investigate. It was a cap. When he reached it, his heart skipped.

"No," he said as he leaned over to pick it up. "Please, no!"

It was Jimmy's Ready Kilowatt cap.

THE SEARCH TEAM FOUND THE BICYCLE IN A MATTER OF minutes. Lee kept Ellen in the parking area, but when she heard the workers call out that they'd found a bicycle, she broke away and ran toward the dam. When she saw that it was Jimmy's bike, she collapsed on the ground and buried her face in her hands.

Lee and Deputy Askew guided her away from the scene. She tried to protest, but there was no strength in her to resist. They took her toward an ambulance where medics waited.

"They've found the body!" a voice cried out.

Ellen turned toward the dam and tried to break free. Lee and Askew restrained her.

"No, Ellen," Lee pleaded. "Not like this."

"Jimmy!" Ellen wailed. "No!"

She continued to cry out for her son. The body was quickly pulled from the water and wrapped in a white sheet. Medical personnel rushed the body to an ambulance parked near the dam. Lee stood beside his wife in stunned silence. The ambulance drove quickly away from the pond.

"Let them take care of him," Lee managed. "There's nothing we can do now."

ELLEN AND LEE RETURNED HOME. LEE CALLED HIS MOTHER and contacted the funeral home. He hung up the phone. Ellen sat at the kitchen table with her head in her hands. Shock had temporarily dried her tears.

"There's another call that can't wait," she said.

"Who?"

"Vera. She deserves to know before anyone else."

"Are you sure?"

"Yes. Whatever she did in the past won't disqualify her grief. She has the right to share our sorrow."

THE STREAM OF VISITORS TO THE FUNERAL HOME FINALLY began to taper off. Ellen had made a display of photographs and other personal items from Jimmy's room and placed it on a table beside the closed casket. The pictures followed Jimmy's life from beginning to end: coming home from the hospital with Vera and Lee, celebrating Christmas, eating cake in a high chair, riding his Big Wheel, going to school for the first time, fishing with Grandpa, bringing home Buster, riding his bike, climbing the pole, and standing with the football team. Included in the photographs was Vera holding Jimmy in the hospital. Jimmy's Ready Kilowatt cap occupied one corner of the display, and one from the University of Georgia anchored the other. In the middle of the photos was Jimmy's verse in his own handwriting—*Behold, I make all things new.*

Lee looked at Ellen. "I'm beat," he said.

Ellen looked past his shoulder toward the entrance to the room.

"She's here."

Lee turned around. Vera and Lonnie Horton stood beside the guest register. Lee walked over to them. Ellen stayed beside the casket.

"Lee, I'm so very sorry," Vera said.

"Come see," Lee said.

Ellen stepped aside so Vera could see the pictures. When she saw the one that included her, tears began to stream down her cheeks. She turned to Ellen.

"You didn't have to do that," she said when she regained her composure.

"Jimmy kept the picture in his room. He would want it here. He had no ill feelings toward you."

Vera stepped forward and hugged Ellen. "Thank you for loving him when I didn't know how to," she said.

Ellen wiped her eyes with a tissue clutched in her left hand. "Yes, I loved him with my whole heart."

"And that's something no one can take away from you," Vera said. "I wanted to get to know him, but he will always be your son. Please forgive me for the pain I caused—"

"No," Ellen said. "That's not necessary now. We're in this together."

FIRST BAPTIST CHURCH HAD STANDING-ROOM ONLY FOR Jimmy Mitchell's funeral. For the second time in as many months, the Mitchell family occupied the mourners' pew at the front of the church. Vera and her family sat behind them.

Tall, strong, and full of promise for the future, Max Cochran spoke of his friend.

"Jimmy had a funny way of saying things that at first seemed wrong but usually turned out to be right. Over the past few days, I've realized that he had a lot of wisdom. When I finish my education, I hope that I'm as smart about the things that matter as he was."

Max looked down at the pulpit for a second.

"Jimmy was the most unselfish person I've ever known. He would have done anything in the world to help me. The fact that he wanted to help me taught me a lot. When I faced a problem or a situation that seemed too big for me, I often thought about all that he had to overcome. And he did it with a smile on his face."

"I will never forget him," Max said, his voice cracking. Pointing to his heart, he concluded, "Jimmy will always live in here."

Brother Fitzgerald compared Jimmy to Nathanael, in whom Jesus found no guile.

"Jimmy was a pure light with a refreshing view of life. I had the privilege of leading him to salvation, and his simple faith was an inspiration to us all. Piney Grove has suffered a great loss."

They buried Jimmy beside Grandpa.

"THEY WILL BE COMFORTED," JIMMY SAID. "IT IS ONE OF THE promises for those who mourn."

Grandpa stood beside him. "And one day they will join us here, where every tear is wiped away."

The goodness of God swept over them, and their spirits soared in gratitude.

LEE USHERED DETECTIVE MILLIGAN INTO HIS OFFICE AND closed the door.

"What have you found?" Lee asked.

"It wasn't an accident."

Lee closed his eyes and took a deep breath.

"Are you sure?"

"Yes."

"Tell me."

"Someone tried to burn down the house in the woods. Much of it was destroyed, but the bathroom was intact. We found Jimmy's prints all over the sink."

"He took him to the house," Lee said flatly.

"Yes, and kept him there for a while. I'm guessing the hunters snooping around caused him to leave and go to the pond. He intended all along to make it look like an accident. We've issued an arrest warrant for Garner. We'll get him."

"And the bookie?"

"Not yet identified. There are several possibilities. The state authorities are working on it. He may be going underground for a while."

Lee was silent for a second. "Telling Ellen is going to be one of the hardest things I've ever had to do."

Lee and Ellen sat in the living room while he told her about his conversation with Detective Milligan. She sat quietly and didn't interrupt.

"This isn't a surprise," she said when he finished. "I knew Jimmy didn't ride his bike to the pond on his own. It didn't fit with anything I knew about him."

Lee stared down at the floor. "And I don't know how to ask your forgiveness about representing Garner. You warned me that he was trouble, but I was so headstrong and proud of what I did that I was blind to the danger he posed to my family. I know words are hollow but—"

"Stop," she said. "I've had to work through that as well. I've been through every emotion imaginable, but in the end, I can't blame you for what Garner did. It wouldn't be right and would dishonor Jimmy's memory. If he could speak to me now, I know what he would say." Ellen reached out and took his hands in hers. "Lee, I forgive you. We can't be divided. We need to go on together."

Lee looked up with tears glistening in his eyes.

"Thank you," he managed.

JAKE GARNER WAS APPREHENDED AT A USED-CAR LOT IN Dothan, Alabama, when he tried to trade in his pickup. He returned to Piney Grove in handcuffs and leg irons. Steve Laney announced his intention to seek the death penalty, and two lawyers from Carroll County were appointed to represent the snake man. A motion to transfer the case from Cattaloochie County was pending when Garner's lawyers offered to plead guilty in return for life in prison without parole and cooperation in any prosecutions against the bookie who hired him.

"I'll leave it up to you," Laney told Lee and Ellen. "No matter where we try the case, I believe we have a good shot at getting death."

"Take the offer," Lee said.

Ellen nodded. "Yes. Jimmy wouldn't want him to die."

THE DAY GARNER WAS SENTENCED, LEE LEFT THE COURTROOM and went to his mother's house.

"It's done," he told her. "Life without parole."

"How do you feel?"

"Empty. Totally empty."

Lee left the kitchen and went to the backyard. He walked slowly across the grass until he stood at the base of the power pole. He looked up at the white marks that memorialized his son's determination. Jimmy made it to the top of the pole, but Lee knew that wasn't his real accomplishment. Lee had heard the truth many times over the past weeks—Jimmy's success lay not in what he did, but in who he was. Lee rested his hand against the pole and bowed his head.

"God, please fill this empty place. Whatever Jimmy had that I don't, please give it to me. I want to be more like my son." He paused. "I want to be more like your Son."

ELLEN CLOSED THE DOOR TO JIMMY'S ROOM. HIS HATS remained on the shelves, his clothes in the closet, his handwritten promise that God would make all things new reattached to his bulletin board. On days when she felt particularly sad, she would go into the room to seek a reminder of a happier time. She also devoted herself to Buster. Without Jimmy in their lives, woman and dog bonded with each other. Many afternoons Ellen would throw tennis balls across the yard as long as Buster wanted to retrieve them.

ON THE FIRST ANNIVERSARY OF JIMMY'S DEATH, LEE AND Ellen went to the cemetery. It was a hot day, and they waited until late afternoon. No one else was present. They found a fresh bouquet of flowers from Vera Horton lying on top of the tombstone. Ellen put one of Jimmy's caps beside the flowers.

"I still think about him every day, but the ache is easing," she said. "I'm ready to clean out his room. It's the next step."

"What will you do with his things?"

"Give away the clothes, keep a few hats, and box up some of his personal things. I'd like to put his Bible verse in a frame and hang it on the wall in the kitchen."

They stood side by side without speaking, each one traveling the road of personal thoughts. Lee broke the silence. He spoke slowly.

"Ellen, I don't want to rush you, but I've been talking to a social worker who oversees the child foster care program. To care for another child, even on a temporary basis, could be part of our healing."

Ellen faced him.

"No. I mean, uh, I don't think I could do something like that. A child who isn't my own—" She stopped, understanding what she had just said.

Lee took both of her hands in his and looked into her eyes. "I'm not trying to force you to do anything, but there is a five-year-old girl with mental limitations who needs a loving home."

"What kind of limitations?"

"Nothing we couldn't handle. I've reviewed her file. She's a sweet girl who doesn't get bored doing repetitive tasks. She likes to color but only uses green and red. Her favorite picture is a forest of red trees in a sea of green grass. Considering her age, it was amazing how carefully she drew each leaf."

"Why doesn't she use more colors?"

"I'm not sure; she may not have many crayons. Her parents left her with relatives nine months ago and haven't come back to claim her. The social worker tracked down the parents, but they didn't want her and abandoned her to the State. Some of her limitations may be more the result of poor environment than true cognitive deficiencies. Her diet hasn't been good, and no one has given her the attention needed to stimulate mental and social development. She needs love."

Ellen didn't say anything for several seconds.

"Have you met this child?" she asked.

"Yes. She has curly dark hair, blue eyes, and a dimple in her left cheek."

"What's her name?"

"Nichole, but they call her Nikki."

"Nikki," Ellen repeated.

"Is there room in her heart to love another?" Grandpa asked.

"Yes, sir," Jimmy answered. "More than enough."

Acknowledgments

My wife, Kathy, is my greatest source of human inspiration and practical encouragement. Thanks to Allen Arnold, publisher of WestBow Press, who worked with me more as a friend and adviser than as a business partner. Ami McConnell, Traci Depree, and Erin Healy contributed their extraordinary gifts to the editing process. Special thanks to Hal Jenkins for his advice on pole climbing technique.

I also honor the memory of my father, Ancil U. Whitlow, who worked many years for the Georgia Power Company. He would have enjoyed this book.

READ THE ALTERNATE ENDING FOR

Jimmy

AVAILABLE ONLY AT

www.robertwhitlow.com!

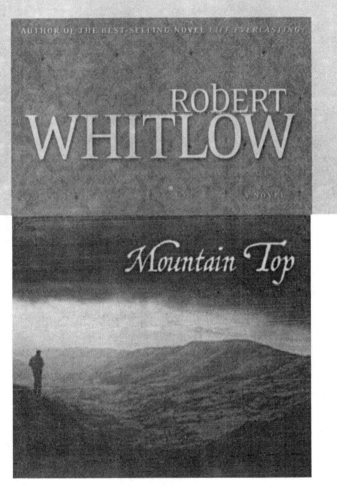

AUTHOR OF THE BEST-SELLING NOVEL *LIFE EVERLASTING*

ROBERT WHITLOW

A NOVEL

Mountain Top

THOMAS NELSON
Since 1798

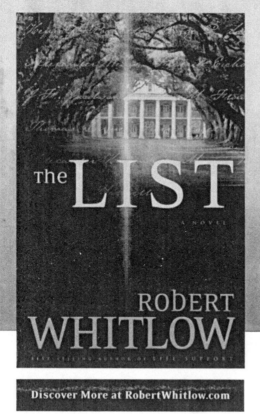

"I have set before you life and death, blessing and cursing:
therefore choose life, that both thou and thy seed may live."
DEUTERONOMY 30:19, KJV

Georgetown, South Carolina, November 30, 1863

THE OLD MAN PUSHED open the front door of the inn against the force of
the coming storm. Slamming the door behind him, the wind's hand
caught his long white beard and whipped it over his shoulder. Leaning
forward, he swayed slightly as he crossed the broad porch and slowly
descended the weathered wooden steps. He wrapped his cloak tightly
around him and pulled his black hat down over his head.

He had feared the group assembled inside would not heed his
words. Five years before the first shot was fired on Fort Sumter he
began warning all who would listen of the coming conflict:

> "Then the Lord said unto me, Out of the north an evil shall break
> forth upon all the inhabitants of the land. . . . And I will utter my
> judgments against them, touching all their wickedness, who have for-
> saken me, and have burned incense unto other gods, and worshiped
> the works of their own hands."

Now, the sound of Lee's army retreating from Gettysburg had
reached their ears. It didn't require a prophet's vision to see into the
future. Judgment was coming. But rather than repenting in the face of

391

wrath, men of power and influence met in Georgetown to save Babylon, not to come out of her.

Because of age and respect he was invited. And he came, not to join them but to warn them. Waiting until their frantic voices stilled, he spoke with all the strength and fervor his spirit could muster. Then, standing in front of a portrait of a stern-faced John C. Calhoun, he delivered a clear, impassioned call: "Lay not up for yourselves treasure upon earth, where moth and rust doth corrupt, and where thieves break through and steal: but lay up for yourselves treasures in heaven, where neither moth nor rust doth corrupt, and where thieves do not break through nor steal: for where your treasure is, there will your heart be also."

Layne and Jacobson had wavered, hesitant to reject completely the words of one they had called sir since first learning to talk. Others sat in silence; a few mocked. He overheard Eicholtz whisper to Johnston that the old man looked more like a scarecrow than a planter. But in the end, LaRochette's smooth speech prevailed. No brands were plucked from the fire—all took the oath; all signed but him.

He had been obedient, but prophetic obedience that fails to accomplish its purpose leaves aching regret for the objects of its mercy. Thus, he felt anger and grief: anger against his enemy, grief for his friends and neighbors. Naturally minded, practical, astute in business, they only saw the need for security and self-preservation. Good churchmen all, yet they were deceived, failing to see the spiritual evil straining for release. "Don't you understand?" Hammond told him. "We must unite and preserve our wealth for the safety and future of our families."

Of course, one knew. He and the old man shared a private moment in the midst of the gathering. LaRochette's eye caught his and flashed the identity and challenge of pure evil. The old man wanted to respond, strip away the pretense of the natural and cross swords in the unseen realm. But there was no call to battle from the Spirit.

"Why don't you let me confront it?" the old man pleaded.

"All things have their appointed time, even the wicked for a day of destruction," came the steady response.

So, upon discharging his trust, he left them to their plans. Holding his hat securely on his head, he stood at the bottom of the steps and looked up at the night sky. The moon and stars flickered on and off as small, dark clouds hurtled across the heavens, clouds without rain but warning of storms to come.

Thinking his task finished, he turned and faced the inn for a final farewell. Light from oil lamps faintly illuminated the windows of the meeting room. Then, as he leaned back against the wind, he felt the seed of another word forming deep within the core of his being, the place where he really lived. Knowing he must wait, he let the word build, push upward, and grow in intensity until its force sent chills through his chest and across his shoulders. Strength to stand against the wind entered his body and brought him to full stature as he stretched out his hands toward the house.

Fueled by a power not found in the oratory of men, he cried out the words of the righteous Judge who spoke with lightning from Sinai:

"I the Lord thy God am a jealous God, visiting the iniquity of the fathers upon the children unto the third and fourth generation of them that hate me; and showing mercy unto thousands of them that love me, and keep my commandments. . . ."

A solitary bolt of lightning split the heavens high overhead.

This is what the Lord says; "A son will be born to my house, and he will expose your evil power and execute My righteous judgments against you."

The wind tore the words out of his mouth and swept them up into the swirling darkness. Inside the house, Jacobson shuddered and turned to Weiss, "What was that?"

"Nothing. Only the wind."

The old man remained motionless until the full power of the Word was released. Knowing it would come to pass, he faced the storm, mounted his horse, and rode off into the darkness.

LaVergne, TN USA
26 April 2010
180557LV00003B/5/P